The Snake Handler's Daughter

The Snake Handler's Daughter

Tales of Sex & Intrigue in Amity, Kentucky

P. A. Lassiter

The New Atlantian Library

THE NEW ATLANTIAN LIBRARY
is an imprint of
ABSOLUTELY AMAZING eBOOKS

Published by Whiz Bang LLC, 926 Truman Avenue, Key West, Florida 33040, USA.

The Snake Handler's Daughter copyright © 2015 by P.A. Lassiter. Electronic compilation/ paperback edition copyright © 2015 by Whiz Bang LLC.

For information contact:
Publisher@AbsolutelyAmazingEbooks.com

ISBN-13: 978-0692446324 (New Atlantian Library, The)
ISBN-10: 069244632X

Contents

The Snake Handler's Daughter

1. Starting Over

Martha Browne tapped her powder puff over the expansive top roll of her belly and added a few taps between the rolls for good measure. She was getting ready for Sunday morning services, the social highlight of her week. Today she put extra care into her preparations, for Trinity Episcopal's new priest was scheduled to preach his first sermon. She'd seen him across the church parking lot several days earlier as he got into his car and drove off. He was striking, pale-haired and trim, in his early forties, she'd guess. Not that much younger than her when you thought about it.

"This time will be different," she told herself as she replaced the Jean Naté box and puff on the black marble of her vanity.

What a relief to purge the memory of Father Zeb! He'd been single too, and she'd liked him quite a bit, but that incident in the cleaning closet...well...things had gotten out of hand. It wasn't her fault he'd had a bad ticker.

"Father Endicott is a much better match," she declared. More robust. Handsomer too.

She turned sideways and hummed a jaunty tune as she appraised her shower-softened flesh in the cheval mirror.

"Not too bad...for sixty-six."

Sure, she was heavy, but all Americans were heavy. That didn't matter. Lots of men preferred a woman with something extra to squeeze. What she didn't altogether like was the way her breasts had settled so low with gravity that they lay flat over the first roll of her voluptuous belly, nipples pointing straight down.

"Never mind. Nothin' a sturdy brassiere can't remedy," she reminded herself.

Beneath Martha's pendulous breasts and that first belly roll swagged another, pocked in the middle by her cavernous bellybutton. The third roll of flesh hung down like an apron, hiding her bald pudendum below.

"I don't know what God was thinkin' when He created that thing. It looks so silly." Not as silly as a man's thingy, but still, awful silly. Fortunately, she rarely saw it anymore.

She plopped on the edge of her bed and let her tummy fall between her knees. Stockings were a problem. She had to hook them with her toes – first one foot then the other – to get them started, then fall back on the bed and lift her legs in the air as she yanked the heavy-weight nylon up her calves and thighs. She completed the maneuver, then rocked back and forth to gain the necessary momentum to catapult herself onto her feet. Breathing heavily, she stretched the stockings up and out, then tucked her belly rolls inside the waistband to keep them from jiggling, because the jiggling made her look fat.

"Thank goodness for Large 'n' Lovely," she muttered. The catalog's pantyhose were generously proportioned for big-boned gals like herself.

After the bottom half was done, the hardest part, Martha wrapped her long-line brassiere around her ribs and attached the hooks. She lifted first one titty, then the

2

other, and settled them into their fabric hammocks before hauling each heavy-duty strap over a shoulder. Once her bazooms were locked in, they stayed propped up for as long as required.

Martha trundled to her walk-in closet and flicked one hanger after another along the dress rail. Not the sunny yellow – she'd worn that last week – not the lime green. *Oh yes.* The turquoise with the orange daisies. That was an eye-catcher.

"Make a joyful *color* unto the Lord," she crowed at her reflection. "Serve the Lord with gladness."

She liked bright colors because they attracted attention without causing complaints. It had gotten back to her that Annie Croot, the nasty old biddy, gossiped about Martha's cleavage at the ladies' quilting circle, saying "Nobody wants to look at granny titties, especially on Sunday!" Not that Martha cared two cents what old "Coot" thought. This dress ought to satisfy her, though, with its modest neckline and ample draping.

Now for the hair. Unfortunately, the skin condition that had rendered Martha bald "down there" also affected the follicles on her head. The few gray hairs that remained lay cobwebbed across her scalp. It wasn't feasible to appear in public anymore without donning one of her fashionable wigs. She didn't care for the stares or the uncensored laughter of boys who pointed at her and made smart remarks.

"They'll lose their hair sooner than they think. *Then* we'll see who's laughing." She chortled as she reached for the curly red wig that reminded her of Little Orphan Annie. The color and style made her feel young. She fussed with her aquamarine clip-on bow, angling it toward her left temple.

"Beautiful," she told her mirror. "Tucked and tidy and ready to go."

Her momma had always said you only get one chance to make a first impression. And Martha needed a success this time. How many more chances would she get?

≈ ≈ ≈

After conducting his second service on Sunday morning, Father Arthur Endicott shook hands with the congregants as they filed from the sanctuary. Trinity Episcopal Church, his newly assigned parish, sat on the corner of Maple Street and Cleveland Avenue in Amity, Kentucky, where the east-west streets were trees and the north-south avenues were presidents. Built from limestone in 1860, the rectangular sanctuary, with its steeply pitched roof and soaring steeple, had been added to for over a century in a series of lesser, connected rectangles jutting horizontally off the back and ending in a large meeting hall.

Arthur followed the last of his parishioners down the long corridor through the rectangles to attend coffee hour, organized weekly by the Episcopal Church Women, or ECW for short. This would be the congregation's first opportunity to meet and speak informally with their new priest.

Probationary priest, he reminded himself.

At the arched entrance to the Fellowship Hall, Arthur paused and touched his palms together, offering silent gratitude for this second chance. Neither Father Daniel's psychological dissection of him nor twelve months of prayer and contemplation had fully resolved the question of why he'd ventured into that notorious Chicago park during prime cruising hours. Arthur suppressed a shiver. He couldn't plead ignorance, and he certainly hadn't been there to share the gospel.

It was past. With God's help, he could put it behind him and get on with the work he was meant to do. He took a steadying breath and stepped across the threshold into the hall.

"What a wonderful sermon, Father!" The shrill voice pierced the ambient conversation and echoed off the cathedral ceiling.

Muffled groans erupted nearby, and Arthur glanced over to see an extraordinary-looking woman clumping across the room toward him. A turquoise garment with orange splotches tented her spherical form from shoulders to knees. A curly, flame-colored wig sat too far forward on her head, ruining the illusion of its being actual hair, while her liver-spotted skin and wrinkled neck belied the intended age range for such a shade.

"That was something, really something!"

The crowd parted for the woman as if she were royalty, though without the reverence generally accorded such.

Arthur smiled and extended his hand. "I'm Arthur Endicott, and you are...?"

"Martha Mae Browne, but everyone calls me Martha, though you know my mother gave me my middle name in honor of Mae West who you'll notice I resemble around the eyes." The aging woman angled her head saucily and peered up at Arthur through indiscernible eyelashes.

Something else was missing too. *A red rubber nose?* The thought rose unbidden, followed by a pang of guilt, and Arthur chastised himself for mentally poking fun at a parishioner, a woman for whom the church was possibly a vital community lifeline. He prepared to offer her a blessing, but she had continued chattering, oblivious.

"...wonder why I wear such bright colors. That's my Mae West side. She always said, 'It's better to be looked over than overlooked.'" The woman cackled, and Arthur smiled uncomfortably.

"It's a pleasure to meet you, Mrs. Browne."

"That's *Miss* Browne, Father, *Miss*. Always a bridesmaid, never a bride, though I'm still hoping!" She patted her wig.

"Martha, dear, have you tried the cranberry bars? They're delicious." Ellie Jones, a woman Arthur recognized from his interview with the Vestry, the church's leadership council, took the gregarious Miss Browne's arm and attempted to pull her toward the kitchen.

"Let go of me," the older woman barked, slapping Ellie's hand before turning back to him. "Father, I'm so happy you're here. We haven't had a decent rector in years."

Miss Browne had spoken too loudly in the suddenly hushed room, and heads swiveled, some bearing shocked, open-mouthed expressions, others barely concealing mirth. Arthur had been assigned to the Amity parish because the church's previous rector, Father Zebediah Wolf, had passed away less than two years prior.

Decent rector.

Arthur cleared his throat and cast about for an appropriate reply. Failing that, he uttered a standard conversation filler, one of several he used when he was otherwise stumped for something to say.

"God bless you, Miss Browne. I hope you'll be one of my regulars on Sunday mornings."

"You can count on it, Father." As Ellie herded Martha toward the refreshment line, Arthur caught the woman's next words over the increasing din. "Did you hear that? Father wants me to be a regular." A few seconds later, he heard her again. "I *said* Father wants me to be a regular."

Someone spoke near his elbow, and Arthur turned to shake the hand extended to him.

≈ ≈ ≈

At the doorway to the hall, Joanne's mother prodded her. "Come on, let's meet the rector."

"I'd rather just go."

"Joanne, you promised to try. Say hello, then we'll leave."

"People are looking at me."

"Honey, you know what the doctor said about that."

"But they *are*."

"Nonsense. The priest is new in town. This is a chance for you to meet someone without having to feel self-conscious."

It was Joanne's first day out of the house, and the church ladies would be whispering behind their hands while pretending not to talk about her. Everybody knew what had happened, though – the self-harming, the hospitalization – and now she had to face them. Thank God for Xanax.

She cringed when she thought of how she'd ended up back home as a thirty-two-year-old woman. Even the biggest slackers from her class had gotten out by age thirty – or most of them, anyway. Her first boyfriend had never graduated from his folks' basement. Probably, he was waiting for them to die so he could move upstairs and continue smoking weed, watching cartoons, and strumming his electric guitar like he had all through school. She'd been an idiot for dating him, but at least he was a worse fuckup than her.

Joanne's mother pulled her across the room toward the priest.

"Hello, Rector. I'm Margaret Bowman, Greta to my friends. This is my daughter, Joanne."

"I'm very pleased to meet you both." The priest held out a hand to Joanne's mother and, when Greta took it, layered his other hand over hers in a heartfelt greeting. He repeated the gesture with Joanne.

"Pleased to meet you, Father," Joanne barely managed to reply, mesmerized as she was by his gaze and by the warmth emanating from him. He fairly *glowed* – it was the only word she could think of to describe the effect. A kind of light, an aura, surrounded his body. As she stood within its radiance, a deep sense of comfort, of relief, washed over her. Her mother nudged her, and Joanne started, suddenly aware she was gaping at the tall, blond-haired priest.

Greta covered for her. "Welcome to Amity, Father. If there's anything we can do to help you settle in, please don't hesitate to ask. Are you moved into the rectory?"

"Unfortunately, the rectory isn't quite ready. I believe Sylvia is organizing a painting party for Saturday. Perhaps you'd both like to come?"

"We'll be there," Greta promised.

"Y-yes," Joanne said, surprising herself.

The women eased away as other parishioners crowded around to talk to the priest.

"That'll get us out of the house," Greta said. "I'll make a casserole."

≈ ≈ ≈

After church, Arthur retreated to his temporary quarters, a loaned cottage, to rest and reflect for a few hours. Several parishioners had invited him to their homes for Sunday dinner, but he'd politely declined. A church community, like any other, could harbor hidden feuds and factions, and as a newcomer, Arthur had no means to discern the motives behind offers of hospitality. A family might want to assert its importance over others in the membership, for example, or a woman may have heard he was single and want to socialize for the wrong reasons. It could be anything, but status- and romance-seeking were common scenarios. Being wary was a disservice to the good people who simply wanted to make him feel welcome, but until he'd learned the lay of the congregational landscape, he'd decided to make himself available primarily at the church where Sylvia Pugh, the capable office administrator, could steer him around hidden hazards.

Arthur was anxious to start his pastorate on the right foot. Doing so was a necessity, in fact, since the diocesan bishop would be monitoring both his work and his personal conduct as part of his probation. Arthur had come within a hair's breadth of being defrocked in Illinois, and a misstep in his new diocese could cost him his career.

It had been his fault entirely, not just the scandal, but the long path that led to it. He'd started dating Scheherazade Simone Fourier in high school, and their relationship continued for so long that, naturally, she'd expected they would marry. On the eve of her twenty-sixth birthday, when Sherry demanded that he step up or step off, he'd been unable to let her go.

"It'll work out," he'd reassured himself as his bride paced down the aisle on her brother's arm. He'd held the marriage – and himself – together for twelve years.

Arthur shook off the memory and made his way to the bedroom closet to remove his Sunday clerics until the evening service. As he unfastened his white collar, his gaze fell upon the private indulgence he'd hung there: a Provocateur calendar with one semi-nude man, photographed exquisitely, for each month. This month featured a leanly muscled dancer bent to one knee with his head bowed and arms outstretched like wings, a supplicating swan.

The church warned priests against behavior that incited lust, but this was a reminder of who he was, something he'd denied for far too long.

2. Signs Following

Martha was furious. Nobody had told *her* about the painting party at the rectory on Saturday. She'd heard someone mention it at coffee hour, and when she went over to ask about it, everybody clammed up.

"I bet the women's group is keeping it from me on purpose. That bitch, Annie Croot! She's always scheming against me." Annie and them were just jealous because Martha had the money to wear nice jewelry, the biggest cubic zirconias on the Home Shopping Channel. People assumed they were diamonds, and she never corrected them.

She punched the gas pedal of her 1975 Johnny Cash Cadillac, creating a dust cloud as it climbed into the Kentucky hills. She'd show old Coot and everyone else. She still had two days to put together an outfit, and she'd be there with bells on. Her Daddy's overalls, appropriate for a painting party theme, could be made feminine and pretty with colorful iron-on flowers.

"What wig goes with overalls?" she wondered aloud.

Martha's stomach clenched tighter the closer she got to Hickory Switch Holler. The Browns owned a fair piece of land there, but the house was a run-down hovel her Daddy's daddy had built in the 1920s. In addition to the main house, several outbuildings lay scattered haphazardly around the property.

Martha drove her Caddy up the packed dirt driveway, maneuvering around ruts that had deepened into culverts. Her bachelor brother, Floyd, sure hadn't done any fixing of the place in the years since Martha had moved to Amity. The Reverend Gideon Brown used to say that his son was a lazy sombitch, and maybe he was right.

As her car approached the collection of shacks constituting the siblings' legacy, Martha honked her horn to alert her brother to her arrival. Course he had no phone out here, but he definitely had a shotgun.

Floyd appeared at the doorway of the washhouse with his tobacco pipe stuck between his teeth. The small, unpainted building with its rusty tin roof had been used for laundry back in the days when they filled the hand-crank washer from an outdoor pump. About twenty years before, Gideon had installed an electric washer-dryer machine on the back porch, and now Martha's elder sibling used the washhouse to dry the tobacco he pilfered from local fields.

"How're ya doin'?" Floyd called.

Martha rotated in the driver's seat, grabbed the bottom of the open window with one hand and the side of the car with the other and hoisted herself to her feet. The sweet scent of tobacco leaves filled her nostrils. "Sure'd be nice to have one o' them seat lifters," she muttered, recalling the contraption she'd seen advertised on late-night TV. When you wanted to stand, you pressed a button, and your seat rose a foot in the air and tilted you out.

"I'm fahn," Martha replied as her brother lumbered toward the car, too late to help her up, of course.

Her hills accent with its flat vowels, hard Rs, and old-timey sentence structure returned spontaneously whenever she drove into the hollers. She'd worked hard to lose it after being repeatedly asked in town whether her people wore shoes and if they had flush toilets. She'd also abandoned the Church of Christ with Signs Following as soon as her Daddy was gone, even though their beliefs derived from Holy Scripture, Mark 16, verses 17-18:

17 And these signs shall follow them that believe;
In my name shall they cast out devils; they shall speak with new tongues;
18 They shall take up serpents; and if they drink any deadly thing, it shall not hurt them;
They shall lay hands on the sick, and they shall recover.

Martha's people were snake handlers from way back, and the Reverend Gideon Brown had been the best in a long line of them. Floyd was pretty good too, but he'd lost most of the use of his left hand after a bad bite twenty-five years before.

"I'm here to git some o' Daddy's clothes," Martha said. "You still got 'em?"

"Shore do. On the back porch where they always is."

"I need me some overalls for paintin' in."

"Plenty o' them there. You go on. I'm strippin' my tobaccer."

Slinging her large handbag over her shoulder, Martha shuffled to the house and heaved herself up the two cinderblock steps onto the rickety porch. The house had never been painted and the roof was rusting through in places, but as the structure deteriorated, it melded more and more into the natural landscape almost like it belonged there, a part of nature.

Two-by-fours propped up the porch roof, and its plank floor continued inside where plywood walls provided the only barrier against winter frost. An oil-drum woodstove hogged most of the floor space in the living room, one end of which housed the television and some beat-up furniture, the other an efficiency kitchen. The cooktop was an early 1970s copper color, and a harvest yellow Frigidaire rumbled in the corner. The house's two bedrooms lay through separate doorways at the back of the main room.

Martha walked through the right-hand bedroom and on to the back porch where she rifled through cardboard boxes until she found what she was looking for, three pairs of striped overalls. Gideon's personal effects hadn't been touched since that summer day fifteen years ago when he took off to shoot badgers and never came home. It had taken the government seven years to declare him legally dead. To think of it! Martha never understood why she'd had to wait so long for her half of the life insurance.

She selected the newest pair of overalls to take with her, then pushed open the rear screen door and made her way across the weedy backyard. She didn't like being in that house any more than she had to, and these days, she didn't have to often. Floyd had taken over both the homestead and the submarine still after their Daddy disappeared. What he thought she lived on, she had no idea. She'd never demanded her share of the property or ongoing profits from the lucrative moonshine business, so her brother probably didn't want to tempt fate by bringing it up.

When she reached the family outhouse, Martha stepped in and sat on the privy lid, closing the creaky door behind her so Floyd would think she was busy and stay away. She had something else to take care of, the more important of the two reasons for her visit. She was well settled in town, and her future looked bright. She no longer feared that would change.

From her bag, Martha withdrew a small pry bar and positioned it between two short boards low on the side wall. After easing them off, she reached into the wall and groped through a curtain of spider webs, wishing she'd grabbed work gloves from her trunk. When her fingers contacted metal, Martha released the breath she hadn't realized she was holding. It was still there. She pulled the flat, square box out of the wall, then replaced the boards by tapping the nails into the same holes. She shook the box gently, then shoved it and the pry bar into her bag.

It was like finding Freedom the day her Daddy showed her his secret stash hole in the outhouse shortly before he disappeared. He'd never liked banks because bankers asked a lot of questions "...that weren't none o' their bidness," Martha mumbled, recalling one of Reverend Brown's favorite sayings.

She was grateful he'd shared his secret with her and not Floyd. Her brother couldn't be trusted with money, as proven by the fact that he never had any. No doubt her Daddy understood that if something were to happen to him, Floyd would fritter away Gideon's fortune – hoarded profits from decades of distilling – and leave his sister with nothing. So Martha had kept the cash and let Floyd keep the house, and when Gideon's life insurance eventually paid out, they split the twenty thousand fifty-fifty. With no funeral costs and no inheritance tax, Floyd thought he'd hit the jackpot.

It had worked out well for Martha, the secret stash giving her enough to live on indefinitely, which was fair. Her Daddy owed her. He owed her a *lot*. She'd never missed him. Not like her momma, whom she still missed after fifty-four years.

Edith had died mucking cages when Martha was a girl, and Martha hadn't entered the snake house since that day, though she'd once loved the rattlers with their silky underbellies and silent power. Since her Daddy's departure, that was something else she'd let Floyd keep – the snakes and everything to do with them, including the Signs Followers.

Martha opened her car door and dropped into the driver's seat, then hauled her legs in after her. She placed her bulging handbag beside her and covered it with her Daddy's overalls before tooting the horn. Floyd stuck his head through the washhouse door and removed the pipe from his mouth.

"You off?"

"Yep, have lots to do."

"See ya then," Floyd said with a wave, not bothering to walk over and say a proper goodbye.

The two of them didn't stand on ceremony. They weren't close and had little in common, though they remained cordial when they met. She'd long since forgiven him his sins against her, and now she had the last of her reparations.

The Cadillac *vroom*'d to life, and Martha carved a circle in the half-dead lawn before rejoining the dirt driveway. She left the holler in a cloud of dust, just as she'd done fifteen years before. That's when she'd taken all but this emergency fund from the outhouse bank, stuffed her belongings in Gideon's car, and moved to Amity. She'd put thirty thousand down on a condo, a fraction of the pot, and never looked back.

Floyd had called her high-falutin' for adding an E to her name, but she didn't care what he thought. Browne was much classier than plain old Brown.

3. Making Right

A rthur started most days with a prayer, not Anglican, not even Christian – pre-Christian, to be precise.

Haec aqua a corpore impuritates, modo simile plumbo mutando ad aurum, elluat. Purga mentem. Purga carnem. Purga animum. Ita vultis, ita siet!

(May this water cast out all impurities from my substance as from lead to gold. Purify my mind; purify my body; purify my heart. As it is wished, so may it be!)

As he prayed aloud, the Latin transporting him to a timeless place, he poured water from the antique pitcher into the washbasin in his borrowed bedroom and ritually cleansed his hands and face. Sometimes he wondered whether he prayed mostly to himself, an entreaty to release his buried shame and self-hate. He smiled wryly at the thought as he dried his face and hands. It was also a worthy endeavor not to take these issues – or himself – too seriously.

As usual, Sylvia beat him to the church, though he arrived promptly at seven-thirty. A dark-haired, petite woman in her forties, Sylvia was the force of nature that kept the church running smoothly in spite of the demands made on her from every direction.

"Good morning, Sylvia."

She turned from the photocopier and offered him a warm smile. "'Morning, Arthur."

"You're here early."

"I try to be in by seven so I have some quiet time before people come in and distract me. That's when I get my best work done." She retrieved a stack of papers from the machine and tamped them into a neat pile.

"Any meetings I need to attend today?"

"No church-related ones. You could join the Overeaters Anonymous group this afternoon if you want to, but you don't look like you need it."

Arthur grinned. "No, food isn't my particular vice." He wondered abruptly whether he ought to divulge his "particular vice" to this woman with whom he would be working closely. Being out was new, and being a priest made it more of a minefield than it was for most. And in Kentucky. Arthur had a pretty good idea how it would play in small-town Kentucky.

"Trinity seems quite involved in the self-help and recovery movement," he remarked, gesturing at the complicated meeting schedule posted above Sylvia's desk.

"You noticed that, huh? You must think we're a sorry bunch of degenerates and addicts and perverts of all sorts here in Amity," Sylvia said.

Arthur laughed. "Not at all. It's a way to minister to people who might not otherwise step into a church."

"It is that. Feel free to attend any meetings you want, and before long, you'll know everyone who aspires to be a mover and shaker around town." Sylvia pulled out her desk chair and sat. "Nobody here is anonymous, though. I think most people try to follow the rules and not talk about each other's private issues around town, but the meetings themselves...well, if you don't belong to at least one recovery group, you miss the best gossip."

"People must get something from the meetings or they wouldn't bother going, I suppose."

"Oh sure, some of the groups – like the mental health and the LGBT-ABC – help each other cope with common problems. Other groups, like the gaming addicts, seem to do more bragging and one-upmanship than any serious recovery."

"LGBT-ABC?"

"The gay and lesbian group." Sylvia pulled a stapler from her top drawer. "I can't keep up with all the letters they've added, Qs and Is and As. My gay nephew just says 'queers,' which is easier to remember, but it's probably not politically correct." Sylvia shrugged, then began separating the papers into piles on her desktop.

What did she know?

Arthur turned and strode to the back of the room where a brass plaque inscribed *The Reverend Dr. Arthur Endicott* hung on a heavy oak door. He turned his key in the lock and entered his private office, determined not to let an offhand remark derail his morning. For the umpteenth time he wondered whether he should have made his sexual orientation clear to the parish's governing board, the Vestry, before accepting the position.

Yes. The answer was yes. He should have, but hadn't, and the omission could come back to haunt him, a fact that made him mildly resentful. Catholic priests didn't have to contend with the issue. Their sexual orientation was considered irrelevant since they took vows of celibacy. Which he had not.

He opened his desk copy of the *Book of Common Prayer* and turned to the morning office, the daily scriptural passage and topic for contemplation. Through the adjoining wall to the sanctuary, he heard the church's antique pipe organ sing to life with the first notes of a Mendelssohn sonata, a surprising, but delightful, backdrop for his spiritual ruminations.

A few minutes later, the heavy exterior door outside the office slammed shut in a gust of wind.

"Yoo hoo! Anybody here? Sylvia?"

"Hello, Martha. How are you?"

"The ECW is trying to keep me away from the painting party at the rectory."

Martha. Arthur scanned his memory. The high-pitched voice sounded familiar.

"Is that right?" Sylvia replied to her. "I'm not sure how the women's group could do that since I'm the one organizing the event."

"Well, Annie Croot kept people from telling me, but I found out anyway. Father asked me to be a *regular* on Sundays. I think he'd want me there."

The woman's comment puzzled Arthur. He considered peeking around his partially open door to see who she was but waited to hear Sylvia's response.

"I'm sure he'd appreciate your help."

"Is he *here?*" The woman's stage whisper came through loud and clear when the pipe organ suddenly went silent.

"I think he's in conference."

Arthur raised his eyebrows at Sylvia's blatant falsehood.

"Well, you tell him I'm coming no matter what Annie Croot says."

"Okay, Martha. Which shift do you want to work?"

"Shift?"

"Yes, people are signing up for four-hour slots, morning or afternoon, so we have enough people for the whole day."

"I'll come for lunch and bring a casserole."

"Then work for the afternoon," Sylvia added, no question implied.

"We'll see how the day goes...." Martha's reply faded.

Arthur stepped to his doorway and saw an auburn-haired woman shuffle out. She wore neon yellow leggings, red flip-flops, and a too-tight pink sweatshirt that was riding up in an unfortunate manner, exposing more backside flesh than one generally expected to see.

Sylvia's phone rang, preempting his questions, and Arthur returned to his desk. The next time the organ quieted, he decided to go meet the organist. Over the years, he'd listened to dozens of church organists and attended numerous recitals, but judging by the Mendelssohn, Stephen Harken – the name from last week's bulletin – might be the best organist Arthur had heard in his forty-three years.

≈ ≈ ≈

Martha wandered into the narthex, the antechamber to the sanctuary. The wall between the two areas contained large windows so coughers or those with crying babies could observe services and listen through speakers without disturbing other worshippers. She peered through the glass and saw the organist seated on the high bench, his body dwarfed by the instrument. His dark hair was raised to an arched point on top and glued into shape with lady's hairspray, or so Martha suspected.

"That nancy boy is always playing something loud and obnoxious," she muttered. "And that big ol' black woman is pumping her arm around as usual."

If the music director liked such loud music, why hadn't she joined the black Baptists or the African Methodist Episcopal Church, where the music was raucous and hallelujah-oriented and the congregation hollered whenever the mood struck them? Actually, it was odd how much the Signs Followers resembled the black churches in their manner of worship but only had white members.

"The blacks are probably too smart to mess around with snakes," Martha said, then snorted at her own audacity. Her Daddy would not have appreciated that joke.

She moseyed through the glass-walled vestibule overlooking the courtyard and on to the short "facilities" hallway to crack the door of the ladies' restroom.

"Pee yuuu!" she exclaimed as the odor of sewer gas accosted her nose. "Highhorse better get off his and do something about this."

The church sexton's name was Charlie Hightower, but in Martha's opinion, he thought too highly of himself for a good Christian. It was her duty to monitor the quality of his church cleaning, especially now that Father Endicott had singled her out as a regular. She shut the door in disgust and shuffled on to check the men's room.

"Anybody in here?" Martha called before poking her auburn bouffant through the doorway.

"Hey! What are you doing?" A bulky, light-haired man in his mid-thirties stood at the sink, his indignant face reflected in the mirror.

Martha removed her head and let the door close. "Come out. I need to get in there." She heard the rustling of paper towels before the door swung open.

"Excuse me," the man barked and tried to pass.

Though nearly a foot shorter than her adversary, Martha stood her ground. "What're you doing here? I've never seen you before. You can't just walk into our church and use the toilet. If you don't leave, I'm calling the police!"

"I'm not doing anything," he replied in a low rumble, "except listening to Stephen practice the organ. Not that it's any of your business."

"Don't you get snippy with me. I'll call Father to straighten this out."

"What is your problem, lady?" The man pushed his broad shoulders past Martha and headed toward the sanctuary.

"So rude," Martha grumbled as she charged into the men's room and sniffed. Not as stinky as the ladies. Still, she'd be giving Highhorse a piece of her mind.

She made her way to the Fellowship Hall, peeking into each Sunday School room along the way to check that nothing was out of order. At the end of the long corridor, she passed through the double doors and continued to the kitchen where she opened the refrigerator and peered inside.

"Darn! No cookies or pie. Pickles, though." Martha reached in and grabbed a Mason jar. Unscrewing the top, she extracted a cucumber pickle with two fingers and poked it into her mouth, puckering at the acidic bite. She withdrew it immediately, shook her head in disgust, and then looked to see if anyone was around.

"Nobody here," she muttered, before shoving the pickle into the jar and replacing it in the fridge. "Better get home, I guess."

She retraced her steps to the narthex where she scanned the sanctuary through the glass. The impertinent man from the bathroom was sitting *in her pew.*

"Sylvia!" she hollered into the cacophony of organ music.

The church office was empty, so Martha took the opportunity to rifle through the papers on the administrator's desk. Finding nothing interesting, she opened the drawer and saw Sylvia's brown leather purse nestled inside. Grabbing a pen and pad, she wrote:

Slyvia,
There's a strange man hanging around and using the church bathroom. He says he's with the organst but somebody should check him out, specially if your leaving your purse in the drawer.
Martha

She placed the important missive squarely in the center of Sylvia's desk blotter, then, noting the priest's closed office door, sighed and lumbered out to her car.

≈ ≈ ≈

Walker was one of the few men Stephen Harken had ever cared to talk to after a night of raunchy sex, and fittingly, the man appreciated organ music (as well as making music with organs, a different thing). Today, in fact, Walker was losing sleep time to listen to him practice. Stephen's boyfriend was a blow-molding technician or, as Stephen routinely quipped, a blowjob technician. One of Walker's talents.

And fucking, of course.

With that errant thought, Stephen's cock twitched, and he missed a chord, mutilating his flowery rendition of the Doxology. His concentration was crap with Walker sitting there in the second row, sexing up the joint.

A peripheral movement caught Stephen's eye, and he glanced up to see the new rector drop to one knee at the back of the center aisle and cross himself. *Whoa!* Father Arthur was a babe! A frickin' Adonis in clerical garb. Probably straight, though, not that Stephen was looking.

Well...no more than usual.

The priest took a seat halfway up the aisle. The man's wavy blond hair, graying slightly at the temples, was sleeked back, giving him a 1920s patrician air, his long, straight nose and refined jaw line enhancing the effect. Stephen felt a sudden urge to jog down the aisle and introduce himself, offer to show the rector around town, buy him a drink, maybe share a get-acquainted grope. Shouldn't the church organist get to know his priest?

Perhaps not in the Biblical sense. Stephen suppressed a giggle and whispered, "Sorry, God. You made me a horndog."

On the last triumphant chord, Stephen mugged at his boyfriend who mimed applause. Walker was one steaming hot hunk of manhood with his chiseled face and bulging muscles, and a wide, toothy smile – infrequent, but glorious – that made you want to turn around and drop trou. Stephen had never been a one-man man, but he'd been trying with Walker for the past year...mostly.

The priest had risen and appeared to be leaving.

"Father, wait!" Stephen dashed down the aisle after him, extending his hand. "I'm Stephen Harken. I was sick last Sunday, but I've wanted to meet you all week."

Their palms connected. "Pleased to meet you, Stephen. Arthur Endicott. I've been enjoying your practice sessions." The priest pulled his hand away. "Where did you study?"

"Juilliard. In New York City."

Father Arthur nodded. "I suspected as much."

Stephen thrilled at the admiration in the priest's voice. People in this hick town rarely thought to ask that question, and if they did, rarely understood the significance of his answer.

"You did? Well," Stephen replied with thick innuendo, "you're not the usual country preacher, are you?"

Walker approached and planted himself next to Stephen, adopting a bouncer's stance, legs braced apart, arms folded across his broad chest.

"Father Endicott, this is Walker Jones, who is neither black nor a professional athlete."

The priest chuckled. "Arthur Endicott. Glad to meet you." He offered Walker his hand. "So, not Walter Jones. Do you get that a lot?"

"No." Walker uncrossed his arms and crushed the priest's knuckles, though the latter didn't flinch.

"Are you a church member?"

"Yes, I come Sundays when I'm not working night shift."

"Where do you work?" the priest inquired.

"GoldStar Plastics."

"Well, I hope to see you Sunday, Walker. It was nice to meet you both."

"See you soon, Father," Stephen chirped.

Babe-a-licious! Definitely his type. The priest bore a resemblance to Walker, in fact, though he was taller, older, and obviously more refined.

Walker stared at the priest's retreating form. Stephen hadn't missed how his boyfriend had gone all prickly meeting him. Walker had requested more than once that he curb his habit of flirting with every good-looking man he encountered. It was a sore point between them.

Stephen shivered with anticipation. He appreciated a little jealousy in a boyfriend. Maybe they'd fight later, then have nasty make-up sex, Stephen's favorite kind. Walker might even take him by force if goaded sufficiently. Stephen enjoyed that from time to time, the thrill of the struggle followed by sweet surrender. His cock stiffened at the thought.

Actually, touching the new rector's hand had had a similar effect. Arthur Endicott set off his gaydar, which didn't mean much, since Stephen was hopeful more often than he was right. He'd not heard anything about the priest having a wife, though.

Slut. So what's new?

≈ ≈ ≈

Arthur had noticed the flirty nonverbal exchange between the two men and decided to leave the sanctuary, not wanting to intrude.

Gay parishioners? A couple? Times were different from when he'd started his career twenty years before. Worlds apart. An Episcopal bishop up north, the Right Reverend Jeremy Roberts, had even divorced his wife and married a man. Arthur could hardly imagine the possibility. But observing these two men – their cozy familiarity, their lack of self-consciousness, even their freedom to quarrel in public – brought up certain feelings.

Back at his desk, Arthur reproached himself. The sexual orientation of his congregants shouldn't matter one whit to their priest. He'd noticed Walker's annoyed expression and aggressive stance, though, after Stephen scurried past him with no acknowledgement. If the two men were a couple, Arthur wouldn't be surprised to find them in his office for counseling in the future. Despite his abject failure in his own marriage, he possessed a keen ability to read others. It was one of the qualities that made him an excellent priest.

4. Request for Change

Martha had nearly finished beautifying her overalls for Saturday's party at the rectory. She'd turned them into hogwashers by cutting off the legs above the knees. Then she added flowers to the bib and pockets to pretty them up.

She scrutinized the eight-foot shelf where her dozen wigs stood like silent soldiers in the war of beauty. If Mrs. Queen-of-the-Universe Sylvia insisted Martha had to work, she couldn't wear her Orphan Annie. It was one of her favorites, and she didn't want it splattered with paint. The Shirley Temple was out too. Her Dorothy Hamill might work. It was a little conservative, so she didn't wear it often. Her long hair drew the most attention, but often just from kids who would point at her and laugh. If her Cher wig got paint on it, maybe that wouldn't be the end of the world.

Martha examined her shoe collection with satisfaction, sixty-eight pairs lined up on special slanted shoe racks. Her doctor had warned her not to wear high heels now she was older and on the heavy side, but she wasn't giving them away. She might lose weight one of these days.

Pulling out her blue orthopedics, the best match for overalls, Martha's fingers brushed the square metal box she'd tucked behind the shoe rack. Five thousand dollars wasn't much given the overall pot, but it had reassured her to know it was there in the outhouse for the past fifteen years in case of emergency. Along with "the insurance."

"I'm insured by Smith & Wesson," Martha muttered. It's what her Daddy used to say when Edith urged him to deposit their money in an insured bank account.

He wasn't kidding either. No one who knew the Reverend Gideon Brown would have dared to steal from him, or cross him in any way, for that matter. Even the G-men from the Infernal Revenue never ventured onto Gideon's land looking for a still because, for one thing, he had the strength of the Almighty at his beck and call. For another, he could harness the might of Smith & Wesson with a squeeze of his well-oiled trigger finger. And lastly, he commanded the Devil – Satan himself – in the form of a dozen diamondbacks in the snake house.

Oh, Martha's Daddy had been a fearsome man!

≈ ≈ ≈

Joanne glanced at the clock in the church office. Ten minutes early. She sat down to wait, shrinking into the voluminous sweater she'd worn to make her feel less conspicuous.

"You liked him, didn't you?" Greta had prodded her over Sunday dinner.

Joanne had stopped constructing the mashed potato mountain on her plate. "There's something about him. He seems like someone you could talk to."

"Do you want to talk to him? I could call for a counseling appointment. It might be good to get a spiritual perspective. And Father Arthur doesn't know anything about your history, so it would be a fresh start."

Joanne's mom had always said that God would never give you more than you could handle. So was it her or God who'd failed the last time she broke down and carved up her left arm? Had He given her too much to take or was she just weak?

The more Joanne thought about such things, the more muddled and hopeless she became. She wasn't at all sure praying could fix her problems, though she was grateful to be regaining the use of her hand, if God had anything to do with that. The outcome hadn't been certain after she'd nearly severed a tendon. Joanne tugged compulsively at the sleeve covering the bandage.

"Hello, Miss Bowman. It's good to see you again. Won't you come in?"

Though she'd met him before, Joanne stifled a gasp at the appearance of the rector with his angular face, broad shoulders, and kind blue eyes, though his good looks weren't what had startled her. It was the light, that glow emanating from him, which she thought she'd imagined the first time they met. Suddenly, Joanne was exceedingly glad her mother had made this appointment. She stood to enter the priest's inner sanctum.

"Father Endicott. Thank you for seeing me."

"Please, have a seat." He gestured toward two comfortable-looking club chairs and a small table, which held a Bible and a box of tissues.

Joanne sat down and gazed at the priest as he moved behind his desk. He propped his elbows on the armrests of his chair and brought his fingers together in the shape of a steeple.

"What can I do for you today?"

Joanne couldn't help staring. His light cast a warm, soothing spell over her, and she leaned as far toward him as she could without falling out of her seat. Her knees stopped shaking, her heart rate slowed, and the ever-present hollowness in her chest ebbed. Was he an angel? She wanted to close her eyes and bask in his presence.

"Are you all right, Joanne?"

"Y-yes, Father," she stammered, then amended, "Well, no, Father. I haven't been all right for some time."

"How can I help?"

"I'm not sure," Joanne replied, slightly embarrassed. He was her mother's priest. Still, she felt better already. "I spent some time in a mental hospital, and now I'm living with my parents while I try to get my life back together. I had a bad breakup and then a worse breakdown." She looked into Arthur's clear eyes and open face. "Not my first," she admitted.

"I see," he said evenly. "Go on."

"Joe and I had been together two years, and then one day he was gone without a warning."

The breakup hadn't been merely devastating; it had been annihilating. No note, no excuse, no explanation whatsoever. Joanne had come home to find their apartment half empty, literally, a jigsaw puzzle with every other piece missing. The sofa was gone, but the two matching chairs remained. Half the dishes and small appliances were missing, along with Joe's clothes, the spare set of sheets, and half the towels. He'd taken one dresser and the desk, but left the bed, taken the lounge chair, but left the nightstands. All very methodical, all very fair.

That was one thing about Joe, he'd always been fair. Always divided the box of Junior Mints into two equal piles on two separate napkins at the movies. Always checked that they spent the same amount on food and bills, but never went half with her on large household purchases, insisting that she buy one, he'd buy the next. Finally, she understood – every moment of their two-year relationship had been about preparing for the day they would split.

Just like that, she'd lost all sense of herself. She couldn't remember what her life was about, what she'd been working toward. Couldn't remember what the point was. Nothing existed except for this great, deep ache inside her. It swallowed her whole.

The priest had said something.

Joanne shook off the memory. "Excuse me, Father?"

"That must have been very difficult for you. How are you coping now?"

"Well, I'm on Prozac and doing a lot better, but it's hard to know where to start. I lost my job when I had the breakdown, and the hospital would only release me to my parents, so I had to give up my apartment. It's humiliating to be back with my mom and dad in my thirties."

"I understand." The priest leaned forward and rested his forearms on the desk.

The soothing sensation intensified, and Joanne closed her eyes.

"I'm frightened all the time," she whispered, then opened her eyes and immediately teared up. She jammed her knuckles into her eye sockets, but the tears flowed around them.

It was impossible to explain how it felt when things got bad, like riding the Gravitron, that carnival ride where you spun around and the floor dropped out from under you. After Joe left, the floor hadn't come back. She'd hovered over a bottomless hole, hanging on by the tips of her fingers, dreading the moment she'd lose her grip. The blackness sucked at her, pulled her toward the unknown. She didn't know what was down there, but it reeked of death.

Psychiatrists called it borderline personality disorder, though that was only her latest diagnosis in a long, jagged line of them. At least the drugs were better than they used to be. She remembered the Thorazine they'd given her in the psych ward long ago when they thought she was schizophrenic. It was so numbing that you could watch a toddler fall under the wheels of a train and wonder what's for lunch.

Joanne gulped air, trying to regain control of her emotions.

"Help yourself to a tissue," the priest said gently and gestured toward the side table.

She pulled one from the box and blew her nose.

"Can you tell me what you're afraid of?"

"It's kind of non-specific, hard to put my finger on, but it feels the worst when I enter a room full of people," she said in a low monotone. "I'm terrified I'll start sobbing or screaming, or do something inappropriate, and everyone will see how crazy I am."

"Then coming to church was a big step for you," he said.

"Yes, that was the first time I've been out since the hospital."

"And how was that for you?" The priest held her gaze, and she sensed he was seeing her. *Really* seeing her. And understanding and accepting too. She felt his glow on her face, on her chest. She clasped her hands in her lap to keep from reaching toward him. Warmth suffused her.

"I'm glad I went. I liked your sermon, and I haven't taken communion for a long time. Maybe I could try building a relationship with God since I have so much trouble with men." Joanne's lips curved up at the corners. *Had she just made a joke?*

The priest smiled back. "Perhaps I can help you with that."

"To be honest, Father, when I met you last Sunday, shaking your hand, I felt something like...hope." Joanne blushed. "I don't know what it is, but today too, meeting with you, I feel better."

"Perhaps God is calling you to find your way back to Him. When one of His children needs help, He's there. You only have to ask."

≈ ≈ ≈

Arthur observed the suffering woman quietly, his chest heavy with empathy. He touched his index fingers to his lips thoughtfully, then spoke.

"You know, Joanne, I believe an emotional crisis is our soul's way of asking us to make a change. Sometimes in the course of our lives, we get off track. Maybe we don't see it and continue in the wrong direction, moving farther away from what we need to be healthy and whole. Our soul calls to us, but if we're not listening, for whatever reason, the strain grows until eventually we break. Then we're forced to stop and pay attention. Perhaps your soul is giving you the opportunity to change your course now, to make different choices for yourself, and thereby, to heal."

Joanne pinched her eyebrows together. "Do you mean this is some kind of punishment for not praying or going to church for such a long time?"

"Oh no, not at all," he said firmly. "Punishment isn't the right word. It could be that your soul is aching to reconnect with God, and you're not paying attention, but it could be something else entirely. Perhaps your work has been unfulfilling or harmful to you in some way, or maybe the relationships you're choosing aren't making your soul sing. Do you understand what I'm saying?"

Joanne's eyes widened, and a light flickered in them.

"Yes, Father," she said softly. "I think I do."

Arthur remained silent to let her reflect on whatever was gelling in her mind. After a few moments, he saw that the heavy shadow she'd brought into his office was lifting. He'd seen it hundreds of times. Giving people permission to imagine something different for themselves allowed them to hear the call of their soul. If they listened, answers would be forthcoming; if they didn't, the warnings would get more extreme.

He should know. He'd failed to heed his soul's call for recognition until his marriage, his ministry, and everything that was important to him crashed down around his ears. The crucial issue would be something different for Joanne, but once she accepted the need for change, the steps to achieve it would become clear.

"Shall we pray together?" he asked.

"Yes," Joanne whispered in reply.

Arthur circled his desk, then lowered his knees to the carpet. Joanne followed suit. Placing his hands on the woman's bowed head, Arthur began to pray.

The instant he touched her, he felt the familiar rush of energy down his arms and the building of heat in his palms. Though it was called different things in different cultures, this transference of healing energy through touch was recognized in every ethos he'd studied. To him, it was simply God's grace making itself known.

5. Work Party

Since finding Martha Browne's warning note earlier in the week, Sylvia had started locking her desk even if she was only going to the restroom. She wasn't concerned about the "strange man" Martha had claimed was lurking in the church, but rather, Martha herself. It was hard to take anything the woman said seriously, so Sylvia ignored her most of the time and humored her when necessary. Martha had returned the following day to report that Charlie Hightower wasn't doing a good job cleaning the church, and why did the ladies' room always stink?

Martha had a point there, but the smell wasn't Charlie's fault. A waste line was leaking a small amount of methane through the concrete, and fixing it meant tearing out the floor and replacing the pipes, possibly to the street. It was an issue of money, planning, and timing. Meanwhile, the ladies either had to put up with the smell or walk to the Fellowship Hall. Sylvia hadn't asked Charlie to close the restroom because she knew from talking to his wife who cleaned it that some of its patrons didn't have the best bladder control.

Friday was hectic as Sylvia made last-minute arrangements for the rectory painting party to ensure that the necessary supplies, volunteers, and food were lined up. Though most of the elderly widows wouldn't miss a church workday, they also wouldn't be much help as labor, so

Sylvia had conscripted her seventeen-year-old twin sons, Rhett and Riley, into service, and they'd enlisted others from the youth group. She'd also hired a skilled local decorator, Darlene Rohrbach, to oversee the painting and had asked her husband Larry to recruit some male volunteers for exterior work and minor repairs. He'd talked his poker buddies into helping.

"Your pals can't drink beer at a church function," Sylvia informed him when he got home from work Friday evening.

"Well, darlin'," he drawled, grinning, "I don't rightly know how I'm gonna prevent it."

Sylvia might be the bossy one in their marriage, but Larry got his way more often than not. The man's charm was lethal. She decided to make stipulations in this case, since arguing would be pointless.

"If they must, then make sure they're discreet, and don't let them hand out beers to the teenagers."

"You got it." He grabbed her around the waist as she stirred goulash at the stove. He yanked her toward him and, despite his heavy, steel-toed work boots, twirled her gracefully through the kitchen before dropping her into a dip.

"Larry, let me up," she complained, rendered helpless by her big bear of a husband, more than a foot taller than her and nearly twice her weight. "I'm trying to cook." She bopped him on the head with the wooden spoon in her hand, leaving a red splotch of sauce in his closely shorn, brown hair.

Larry pulled her upright and planted a big smacker on her lips. "You want it rough, eh?" he joked, squeezing her bottom.

"The boys!" Sylvia hissed, jerking her head toward Rhett and Riley who were blasting zombies from the family room couch. Not that her boys weren't used to their randy father making passes at their mother day and night.

"Don't worry, Mom," Rhett called without taking his eyes from the TV screen. "Riley just found out where babies come from, so you and Dad don't have to tiptoe around anymore."

Riley punched his brother in the ribs. "Shut up, jerkoff!"

Are my boys having sex? The unwelcome thought popped into Sylvia's head. She hadn't heard any girlfriend talk lately, but they weren't particularly forthcoming about the girls they dated, and they never brought them home. Maybe it was time for Larry to initiate the safe sex talk again.

She would make sure to put some condoms in the bathroom, not hidden well, so the boys could "steal" them should they ever need one. She used the birth control patch herself, but Rhett and Riley didn't need to know that.

≈ ≈ ≈

Darlene was in her element, managing the volunteers at the Trinity Episcopal painting party. All the women wanted to work with the new priest, Arthur Endicott, several having whispered that preference to her, so Darlene assigned them to the rectory bedrooms, bathroom, and hallway, and would send Arthur around to roll the ceilings.

Leading the younger set were Sylvia's twin sons who, along with their friends, had taken over the large, L-shaped living and dining areas. The Pugh boys were unusually handsome, dark-haired, and tall – over six feet, Darlene would guess – and, as everyone in town knew, stars of the Amity High School football team. Her ten-year-old son idolized the varsity athletes. The brothers were impossible to differentiate, though she'd noticed one parted his hair on the right and the other on the left. They were stunners in stereovision.

With their height advantage, the twins had tackled the living room ceiling after Darlene showed them how to load a paint roller and angle a pole for leverage.

"Ah'm sorry, but which one're you again?" Darlene asked the hair-parted-on-the-left twin in her soft North Carolina accent.

"I'm Rhett," the boy replied, grinning. "The handsome one."

Darlene took a second to mentally pair the hair parting with the name.

"And I'm the smart one," called Riley from the other end of the room. "Except on weekends, then we switch."

Darlene joined their gleeful laughter. She hadn't had fun in such a long time, and she got a kick out of the way the twins played off each other, predicted one another's movements, and joked around, often finishing each other's sentences. When she glanced up a moment later, she found left-part-Rhett staring at her. When their eyes met, he quickly looked away.

Darlene was accustomed to stares from young and old alike, barely noticed them most of the time. At thirty-three, she still had her pageant looks, and her Barbie-doll figure – both a blessing and a curse – had slimmed down due to stress from Daryl's affair and their subsequent split. She wore her bottle-blond hair past her shoulders, pulled back today in a girlish ponytail to keep it out of the paint.

She headed down the hall to check on the other workers and, when she returned, stopped short in the doorway and suppressed a gasp. The Pugh twins had discarded their T-shirts and were pressing paint poles to the ceiling with chiseled arms, their back and shoulder muscles flexing and rippling as they moved along. After a too-long pause, Darlene snapped her jaw closed and averted her eyes.

How inappropriate! Darlene had been divorced for four months and hadn't had sex for eleven months and thirteen days, but ogling teenagers was a bad sign. She needed to get a life. A sex life.

She scanned the walls and noticed a four-inch stripe across the room that the cutter had missed. She dipped a spare brush in paint and sidestepped a raised pole to reach the area. After covering the bare spot to her satisfaction, she turned to retreat but found a Pugh twin had rolled his pole forward and trapped her in the corner. Startled by his sudden closeness, her wrist juddered, and she splotched paint onto his bare chest.

"I'm so sorry, Riley...I mean Rhett." Flustered, Darlene reached up with the side of her hand to wipe off the paint, but succeeded only in smearing it around. She scrubbed at it some more and the mess got worse.

The teen drew in his breath, and Darlene glanced down, realizing with a shock what she'd just done. His blue jeans strained at the crotch, his youthful erection responding with enthusiasm to her proximity and touch.

"Oh! I'm sorry...really...e-excuse me...."

Tan paint dusted the inverted triangle of hair between the boy's pectoral muscles, which bulged as he tried to maintain upward pressure on the roller in that awkward moment. Darlene's face grew hot, and she ducked under his arms to escape the near embrace she'd forced on him. Her heart hammered as she scurried to the kitchen for a drink of water. Whiskey might have been preferable.

"Jesus, Darlene, what were you thinkin'? He's a teenager," she muttered, staring out the window. *A horny one from the looks of it.* The naughty thought curved her mouth into a secret, embarrassed smile. He might be a teenager, but Rhett Pugh had the look, feel, and smell of a man – a real, live, grownup man.

"Shit, shit, shit." She pounded the heel of her hand on the counter in time to the words.

"I hear there are drinks to be had somewhere."

Darlene spun around to find the priest standing behind her. She nodded, blushing, and led him through the dining room and outside, not daring to look at Rhett, who was rolling paint across the ceiling in double-quick time.

When she and Arthur returned with cans of pop to distribute, Darlene's gaze was drawn again to the sensual tableau in front of her, from dual sets of tanned shoulders to tapered waists to low-slung jeans, swaths of smooth, taut flesh in graceful motion. The closer of the twins had sweat glistening at the nape of his neck below damp tendrils of dark hair.

A moment passed before she realized the priest had spoken to her. "Pardon?"

"I was commenting on the heat," Arthur said. "I wonder if we should turn on the air conditioner."

"The fumes'll get stronger, but it maht be more comfortable," Darlene responded. She lowered her head and hurried down the hall with her armload of pop cans. Had Arthur seen her drooling, acting like a total pervert?

Behind her she heard, "I'm turning on the air. You boys will want to put your shirts on."

Yup. Her face flamed anew.

Around noon, the afternoon crew began to arrive for the potluck picnic. Church ladies huddled around the refrigerator, pulling out casseroles, salads, and desserts parishioners had dropped off in lieu of working. Two long buffet tables sprang up in the backyard and were soon heaped with food.

Darlene heard a commotion and returned to the living room to find an elderly, Weeble-shaped woman squeezing through the front door, a covered dish in her hand. She looked like a party clown, though an unusual one, with her black wig styled into Pocahontas pigtails and her shorty overalls dotted with incongruous, neon-colored daisies. Rolls of fat hung around her knees, and matching rolls flapped on the insides of her arms below the sleeves of her scarlet blouse.

Darlene hurried over. "Can ah help you, ma'am?" She reached for the dish, which the woman readily released. "Are you makin' a delivery?"

"No, I'm not making a delivery. I'm here for the party."

"Ah'm sorry, we're workin' today, though I like your costume. Do you have the right address?"

The woman looked Darlene up and down, then huffed, "Where's Father Arthur? Sylvia said he wanted me to come, so I'm here."

Darlene lowered her eyes in embarrassment. "Oh, pardon me! Ah'm Darlene. What's your name?"

"Martha Browne, and that there is corned beef casserole." Darlene lifted a corner of the aluminum foil to see atomic red blobs and little green dots floating around in white sauce. The dish reminded her of the bits-and-gravy dog food she bought on sale for her Pomeranian. She lowered the foil quickly.

"Come in, Miss Browne. Ah'll take this to the kitchen."

When Martha entered the living room, every jaw in the room went slack. No one spoke, but Darlene saw Rhett and Riley – bare skin now covered – smirk at one another and exit the sliding glass door to the backyard before bursting into laughter.

"Ever'body, this is Miss Browne," Darlene announced to break the awkward silence. A couple of mumbled Hi's floated over as people turned away, suddenly looking busy.

Ellie Jones, an efficient woman in her mid-fifties who'd helped Darlene set up for the day, hustled over. "Hello, Martha. Please join us out back for some potluck."

Martha pinched her nose shut. "It stinks in here. Pee yuu!"

"Well, it is a painting day," Ellie pointed out.

"I s'pose."

As the old woman lumbered across the room and opened the sliding door, Ellie leaned in to whisper in Darlene's ear. "She's less likely to cause trouble if she has a plate of food to focus on."

"I thought she was a hired clown," Darlene whispered back.

Ellie chuckled. "Not on purpose. She can be a handful, though, likes to cause trouble. I usually find it wise to humor her."

The sweet smell of barbecue wafted in. Suddenly hungry, Darlene followed Ellie through a confusion of drop cloths and paint buckets to the backyard. Arthur approached from across the lawn.

"Smells like the food is ready, Rector. Do you need a plate?" Ellie asked.

Ten feet ahead of them, the old woman spun around like a child's top. "Hi, Father! I made it."

Arthur turned toward her. "Oh, hello...um...nice to see you. Thank you for coming," he responded politely.

"Wouldn't miss it!" she exclaimed, her bubble-gum-colored lips stretched into a smile. "I know how much you wanted me here."

A strange look flashed across Arthur's face before his expression smoothed. Darlene would bet cash money that he'd never seen the clown lady before in his life.

≈ ≈ ≈

Having worked up an appetite, Arthur angled toward the buffet table but was prevented from reaching it as parishioners crowded around to greet him and introduce themselves one after another. Halfway through the lunch break, someone shoved an overloaded plate at him, but he barely had a chance to lift a fork to his mouth between the continual handshakes.

When Stephen Harken asked him to take a smoke break, Arthur readily agreed. He wasn't much of a smoker, averaging one cigarette every couple of months, but he was curious about the church organist.

The two retreated to the front porch to "support Kentucky agriculture," as locals liked to say, and with little prelude, Stephen launched into tales of his time in New York City. In a high nasal twang, he told how he'd worked hard in Juilliard's practice studios during the day and even harder at the gay clubs at night, hunting and bedding nameless men.

Arthur remained silent and fixed his gaze across the street. Keeping a poker face when confronted with private confidences was a useful skill in his vocation. People frequently divulged even the most intimate secrets in the presence of a priest, especially when they felt guilty about something, though Stephen didn't strike Arthur as the sort of person who harbored much guilt. His motives seemed to lie elsewhere, a desire to shock, perhaps, or to entice, possibly to corrupt.

"My concert career didn't pan out," Stephen said. "But I was ready to come home anyway." He took a drag from his cigarette and let the smoke leak from his mouth as he continued. "When I turned twenty-five, Thomas dumped me for a twink — a younger twink, I should say — and I hung up my cutaway tails."

Arthur felt restless and uncomfortable in his seat, but a practiced self-discipline kept him still.

"He's a conductor," Stephen went on, "one of those rich, older benefactors who scouts musical talent, pays their way through college. Or...I guess Kevin was an actor, the guy before me." He plucked an invisible piece of lint from his skinny-legged jeans. "I felt honored to be picked. He installed me in his townhouse on Central Park and told my parents it was a scholarship." Stephen cackled, a gritty smoker's laugh. "Thomas didn't care who I screwed as long as I was available when he wanted me."

With Stephen's slim frame and youthful haircut, his dark brown hair shorn on the sides with a lengthier stripe on top, Arthur would have pegged him at twenty-eight or twenty-nine, young to be so accomplished – and so jaded. He seemed almost lighthearted in his chatty frankness, but Arthur sensed his flippant attitude concealed real pain. As a priest and counselor, he couldn't ignore that, but a church work party wasn't the place to address it either.

"You're with Walker now."

"Yes, I met him at church, of all places. I lived in New York for six years, then found the man of my dreams back home in Kentucky."

Arthur detected a note of sarcasm in the description, but couldn't have said why.

"We've been together almost two years," Stephen noted.

"He isn't here today?"

"No, he's at work, but his mom's here."

"His mom?"

"Ellie Jones. You know, the powerhouse of Episcopal Churchwomen, the ECW." More sarcasm, bordering on vitriol. Arthur leaned toward the younger man to counteract his impulse to lean away.

"Oh, Ellie, yes. I hadn't made the connection. She's on the Vestry council as well."

"She and Sylvia pretty much run everything." Stephen snorted, tamped out his cigarette, then rose. "I'm off to practice."

"Not a painter, I take it?"

"Hell, no," Stephen said, then added, "oh, sorry," an idle apology. "I came for lunch. I have to protect my hands."

Arthur suppressed a smile. "Of course." Manual labor wouldn't rank high on Stephen's list of things to do on a Saturday.

During his fifteen minutes with the organist, Arthur – though hyperaware of their common ground – had purposely avoided sharing personal information. It felt inappropriate, priest to parishioner, confessor to penitent, but something also told him he should keep up his guard around Stephen Harken.

Reconciling his sexual orientation with his clerical responsibilities would take time, he knew. Being married made a priest's life easier. Marriage obviated romantic involvement between parishioner and priest, and the load of the office was lighter when two souls stood together to fulfill its obligations.

That comfortable accommodation, however, was no longer an option.

6. Fooling Around

Darlene scanned the sudden glut of teenage girls who'd arrived to work. Over lunch, she'd heard Rhett Pugh trying to convince his brother to stay for the afternoon shift and wondered if it was because of the girls.

Or because of me? She hadn't meant to let that thought in, but there it was, followed quickly by another. *Shame on you for even thinkin' such a thing. He's a kid!*

But to her mind, or maybe to some part of her body she didn't care to identify, Rhett didn't seem like a kid. Remembering the feel of his smooth skin and his response to her touch started a pleasant gripping low in her torso. It was wrong and completely fucked up, but she couldn't help it, could she?

Darlene had noticed another difference between the twins. Left-part Rhett wore red high-top sneakers and right-part Riley wore black ones, which was how she knew the young brunette homing in on the boys had a preference for Rhett, was pressing her nonexistent breasts against his arm as she went on tiptoe to whisper in his ear. The girl reached up and tugged a lock of hair that had flopped across Rhett's forehead, which caused an odd twinge in Darlene's chest.

Enough! Why should she even notice what that teenager and his girlfriend were doing? It was beyond ridiculous. And she had work to do.

She headed down the deserted hallway and stepped around the large fan blowing full blast to help dry the paint. In the master bedroom, the last and largest of the private rooms, she stepped into the walk-in closet to see whether it needed painting. A knock sounded behind her, and she whirled around to find one of the Pugh twins leaning against the doorjamb. Red shoes...Rhett.

"Well...h-hi there," she stammered. *Jesus,* he was handsome.

Rhett lifted the bottom of his T-shirt to wipe the sweat from his face and revealed a set of abdominal muscles like Darlene had only seen in the trashy magazines at Dot's hair salon. She gulped, and her mouth went dry.

He dropped his shirttail and caught her staring at his stomach. He smirked, and Darlene pivoted away, her neck growing hot. She palmed the wall to check if it needed sanding – or maybe just to hold herself up.

"I came to see if you need help," Rhett said in a soft, intimate tone. "Do you want this painted?"

Darlene turned to find the boy's smooth, tanned neck inches from her face, and her reply stuck in her throat. His skin radiated heat and his musky scent swirled in the air between them. She looked into the eyes of this young man with the open face and unguarded emotions, and her conscious will fled. When he dropped his gaze shamelessly to her chest, a cavernous need opened within her, a sudden, desperate desire to be touched. She took his hand and pulled it to her left breast, then wrapped her fingers around his and squeezed.

He froze for an instant. Then he adapted.

He reached for her other breast and began to massage them both, shifting his hands to embrace every part of her unwieldy double-Ds. She moaned softly and arched toward him, pulling him to her with a palm behind his neck. He leaned in willingly, and when his lips were within reach, she raised hers to meet them. He took to kissing like a tadpole to water, and soon he was pushing his tongue forward and tangling it with hers as he kneaded her heavy breasts.

The young man's eagerness and curiosity stirred her in a way she didn't remember feeling with Daryl in their fourteen years together. The contact was heavenly, intoxicating. Fairly drunk on it, she curved her fingers around Rhett's hips and urged him closer until his erection pressed into the front of her jeans. His arousal electrified her, spiking her desire and igniting a fire low in her belly. It had been a long time since she'd had this effect on anyone.

So riveted was she by the squeezing and grinding, the pleasure of the friction, and the boy's naked desire, that Darlene didn't hear footsteps approaching from the hallway until a shocked gasp jolted her to awareness. She jerked away from Rhett and turned to face the wide eyes of Joanne Bowman, a woman she barely knew, before the intruder covered her mouth and fled.

Oh, crap! And who else might have peeked in that Darlene *didn't* notice?

Stunned back to reality by the sudden recognition that what she was doing was not only wrong, but possibly illegal, Darlene rasped, "Ah'm so sorry. Please forgive me."

Hadn't she already said that to him at least once today? What was *wrong* with her?

Joanne tripped on a drop cloth and slammed into the doorframe before escaping from the bedroom. She wouldn't call the police, would she? Darlene instinctively followed her and watched through the kitchen window as Joanne grabbed a pop from a backyard cooler and wandered off alone, no cell phone in sight. Darlene was appalled at herself and a little frightened, but also hugely aroused, a confusing combination.

"Mrs. Rorbie? What do you want us to do? Riley said you're in charge."

She turned to find a posse of girls staring at her. Their collective "look" included various shades of pink, heavy-handed glitter makeup, and skirts so short that Darlene couldn't send any of them up a ladder.

"It's Rohrbach, but you can call me Darlene," she said, then led them into the living room. "Ever'body get a brush, please. Two of you can work here and two in the dining room." It was the obvious defense against her heightened state of arousal, to surround the object of her ridiculous lust with age-appropriate rivals.

Rivals? Darlene grunted in self-disgust.

"Shall we continue where we left off?" Greta Bowman called as she came in through the sliding glass door, followed by Joanne.

"You gonna paint this afternoon?" Darlene replied. "You don't have to." The Bowman women had worked all morning, and Darlene wouldn't mind if they – especially Joanne – left for the day.

"We'll stick around another hour or two." Greta turned to verify this with her daughter, but Joanne just stared at her shoes while tapping a Morse code message on her thigh.

Dire thoughts raced through Darlene's mind, but she tried to appear composed. "All right, why don't you finish cuttin' the bedrooms, then start the hallway. The colors are marked on the walls, tan and ivory."

The sliding door opened, and Arthur came in. Darlene pressed her fingernails into her palms and observed Joanne warily. *Would she rat her out to the priest?* She braced herself for it, but as Arthur approached, Joanne turned toward him, and her entire demeanor changed. An almost lethargic expression settled over her face, and her nervous agitation melted into stillness.

Not sure what to make of it, Darlene preempted any conversation. "How's it going, Arthur? You ready to roll the master bedroom?"

"Yes, if that's what you need," he agreed.

What *did* she need? A stern talking to at least. Maybe an exorcism for her evil thoughts. Did Arthur take confessions? Suddenly, she was glad her church – the Baptist – didn't require it.

Arthur headed down the hallway, nearly bumping shoulders with Rhett who was coming the other way. The youth eyed her shyly before two girls rushed over and dragged him toward the kitchen. Darlene's face heated with shame, but Rhett looked back and curved his lips into a flirty smile.

Her heart stuttered, and her nipples went stiff under her blouse. *Darlene!*

"Where's Father?" a voice shrilled.

Darlene looked up to see the Indian clown lady coming in from outside.

Someone pointed toward the hall, and the woman clumped off in pursuit, wearing a disgruntled expression.

Darlene had rounded up the Rainbow Brite girls and was showing them how to cut paint into the corners when the stumpy woman returned, her face scarlet, eyes narrowed to slits. Her braids swung wildly as she tromped past, hollering, "You better put a stop to what's going on here!" She continued speaking, her voice trailing off as she waddled toward the front door, " ... hussy making a fool of herself ...."

Darlene froze, and her knees began to shake. Had the woman seen something? *What did she know?*

The screen door slammed behind her, and the girls started giggling. Unnerved, Darlene hurried down the hallway and discreetly peeked into the master bedroom. Greta was standing on a ladder in the far corner, painting a tan stripe next to the ivory ceiling. Joanne was doing the same along the baseboard near the door, while Arthur rolled tan paint on the wall over Joanne's head.

"Ever'thing okay in here?"

The priest turned. "Yes, we're making good progress."

"Ladies? Okay?" Darlene pressed, trying to discover what had set off the old woman.

"Just fine, Darlene," Greta responded.

Joanne kept her eyes on her paintbrush and didn't reply.

"Okay, lemme know if you need anythin'."

Neither Greta nor the priest seemed upset, but Joanne could have said something about Darlene's behavior to the clown lady. Or maybe the woman had witnessed it herself.

What a disaster!

Despite her fear of discovery, Darlene scanned for Rhett when she returned to the living room. And there he was, pushing a roller along the far wall while trying to disentangle himself from two girls vining around him. Nearby, a third girl flicked a paintbrush at his brother, who chortled and jumped sideways. An ivory blob of paint landed with a wet splosh on the front of Riley's T-shirt.

"Settle down, you two," Darlene scolded, sounding more irritated than she'd meant to.

They stifled their laughter and turned away from each other. Riley pulled off his shirt, now dripping with paint, wadded it into a ball, and tossed it to a corner. Darlene glanced down to confirm – black shoes. Yes, Riley was flirting with the girl, not Rhett.

Riley reloaded his roller and pushed it up the wall, and that's when Darlene noticed a wine-colored birthmark the size of a quarter under his left armpit, a miniature Australia.

That's how to tell them apart with their clothes off.

She allowed herself a private smirk at the thought, but her amusement was short-lived. Beyond the glass door, she saw the clown lady holding court at the buffet table. *Damn!* She thought the woman had left. Darlene moved swiftly to the gap at the door and strained to hear. The words *shameless* and *disgraceful* came through loud and clear.

Was she talking about her?

≈ ≈ ≈

Sylvia strode around the side of the rectory where she found her husband and his friends eating lunch. Several of the men were drinking from cans hidden in insulating cozies, and she noticed with unease that Frank Crawford was among them. Frank was a drifter with the telltale spider veins and red nose of an alcoholic whom Larry had taken on as his most recent project, giving him work at Pugh's Concrete, their family business. Sylvia loved her husband for his noble desire to help wayward souls, but she didn't always appreciate the hard-time Charlies he brought into their lives. Frank was a silent man with an ominous air. A long, ragged scar ran through his eyebrow and down his cheek, the kind of injury you might get from a makeshift knife in a prison yard. Sylvia shuddered to look at him.

She proceeded through the backyard and into the rectory dining room where she found Riley horsing around with a long-limbed girl in a short skirt.

"Riley, you're here to work," she chided. To the girl, she said, "Aren't you Sharon Youman's daughter?"

The girl giggled. "Yeah, Amber."

The child was what, thirteen? Fourteen? Too young for her son, that was certain. A recipe for disaster. Maybe she'd take up a paintbrush and "supervise."

"Where's Rhett?"

"I'm in here," he called.

Sylvia turned the corner to find one dark-haired nymphet grabbing Rhett's T-shirt and whispering something in his ear, while another flicked water at him with her thumb and forefinger. Unlike his brother, Rhett didn't appear to be enjoying himself and seemed almost relieved at her intrusion. He was the older twin by a few minutes, and the more serious and shy of the two. Riley, boisterous and extroverted, was the one Sylvia generally had to keep an eye on.

"How's it going, Rhett? Girls?" The girls turned toward her and backed away from her son.

"Hi, Mom. It's okay. I'm close to finished in here."

Rhett set the roller in the paint tray and absent-mindedly hiked his jeans up his hips, re-covering the waistband of his underwear. The girls scurried to the kitchen, then peeked through the doorway and giggled into their hands. Rhett glanced over with a sheepish look. Surely he wasn't interested in them. They couldn't be more than ninth graders.

It hardly seemed possible that her sons were old enough to be fighting off girls, though long ago when human life expectancy was thirty-five or forty, the mid-teens would have been prime breeding years. The thought was not comforting.

"Is Darlene here?" Sylvia asked.

"Um, yeah, she's around somewhere," Rhett mumbled.

"I need to talk to her. Guess I'll go look."

Sylvia found Arthur in a back bedroom. "Hey there," she said.

He turned her way and smiled. "Sylvia, hello."

"Have you seen Darlene?"

"Check the front yard," he suggested. "I put some ashtrays on the porch."

≈ ≈ ≈

"Hi, Darlene. What's going on?"

Darlene whirled around to find herself face-to-face with Rhett's mother. She tried for a friendly smile, but a nervous spasm gripped her cheek, and she raised her hand to cover it.

"Sylvia!" Darlene felt a sudden urge to confess but bit her tongue instead.

"Are you all right?" Sylvia said.

"Yeah..."

"Is something wrong? You look upset."

Darlene ground out her cigarette with the toe of her shoe. "Oh...there was a little ruckus. A lady said she seen some hanky-panky goin' on in a bedroom." She was pretty sure she knew what the woman had seen – or been told – so here she was, hiding behind a juniper tree so the old biddy couldn't point a finger at her in front of everybody.

"Did you talk to her? What did she say?" Sylvia inquired.

"No...ah just seen her goin' crazy out back until Mrs. Jones led her off. Ah don't know what she was rattlin' on about." It was only a small lie.

"Crazy, huh? Was she short and fat, about sixty-five, wearing a wig?"

"Yes! Indian braids and, like, a clown costume with overalls." To Darlene's astonishment, Sylvia burst into laughter. "Wh-what?"

"That's Martha Browne for you."

"Yeah, that's her name, Miss Browne." Darlene opened her cigarette case and dug for another Marlboro Light.

"She's always ranting about something," Sylvia said. "Don't worry about her. She left me a note the other day saying there was a strange man creeping around the church."

"Was there?"

"No, not at all. I shouldn't laugh at her," Sylvia said, still chuckling. She tapped her index finger against her temple. "She's a little off. And she doesn't have anything to do but hang around the church and cause trouble. She must have gone home. I didn't see her."

Darlene lit her cigarette and took a long drag, then raised her chin to exhale the smoke upward. She dug her thumb into the tight muscle on the side of her neck.

"Listen," Sylvia said, "can you rescue Rhett from those girls? Maybe split them up to work?"

"Um...which one is Rhett again?" Darlene asked, then cringed. Pretending ignorance might be her first impulse, but that didn't make it right.

"He's working in the living room. Riley's in the dining room. Riley doesn't mind the girls, but maybe he and Amber would get more done if they were separated too."

"Sure, ah can start the girls on the kitchen cabinets. Do you have time to run to the hardware store? Ah'd go myself, but don't want to leave the volunteers on their own."

After Sylvia left, Darlene considered what she'd said about Martha Browne, that she was "off." So if the old lady *had* seen something, nobody – especially Sylvia – would believe her. As long as Joanne didn't tell, everything would be fine. Maybe what she'd done wasn't that bad anyway. It's not like she and Rhett had been *doing* it.

She heard a rustling noise and turned to find the youth himself sidling up to her, chest-to-chest, so close she could smell Coca-Cola and chocolate on his breath. He grasped her cigarette between his thumb and index finger and took a puff, blowing the smoke over her head.

"Rhett...." She raised her palms to push him away despite the powerful draw of his body. He would lean down and kiss her if she didn't stop him. "This ain't a good idea."

"What?" he responded, all innocence. "I came to see if you need help during the week. The painting's not finished, and Father Arthur's supposed to move in next weekend."

"That's right. Ah'm comin' back Tuesday."

"You can't do it all yourself," Rhett declared.

"Well...Arthur will help, ah'm sure."

"I'll help, and Riley too. And we'll bring some others."

Darlene considered for a moment. A group activity should be safe. "Okay, sure. Ah'll be here at nine o'clock. If ever'body comes then, that would help."

"I'll find out how many can make it."

Darlene was touched. "Thank you, Rhett. Ah really appreciate it."

"Sure thing." He reached for her hand and squeezed her fingers. Then he placed the cigarette against her lips while he looked directly into her eyes. He raised one eyebrow, grinned, and then swaggered into the house.

Darlene sighed. *He's nothing like a boy.*

≈ ≈ ≈

There was something about Father Arthur. During the several hours Joanne worked with him, the heaviness that constantly dogged her had lifted. They spoke little and had no physical contact, but she saw the light around him and was drawn to its radiance. The attraction wasn't romantic, more like stepping into a sunbeam or breathing the energizing air near a waterfall. She'd tried to work close to him as much as possible, and the peace she gained by it had lingered for hours afterward.

She hadn't been to church in a long time or known many people she would consider holy, but were other spiritual leaders like Arthur? She considered asking her mother whether she could see the priest's aura, but she didn't want Greta to think she was hallucinating. Once people knew you were capable of that, you could be hard-pressed to convince them you weren't.

Joanne was so buzzed by Father Arthur's magic that she'd been caught off guard by the tryst she stumbled on in the master bedroom. She'd never met the decorator – Darlene – and didn't know anything about her, but Joanne was pretty sure the kid she was making out with was a high school student. He could be eighteen, though. He looked it.

It was none of her business. Who was she to judge anyone's romantic choices? She'd proven herself to be blind, deaf, and particularly dumb when it came to men.

7. A Hand Up

Martha was mad as hell. She'd gone to that painting party, made a new outfit and everything, arrived with her casserole, and found that girl monopolizing Father. Sticking to him like glue, hanging on his every word, throwing herself at him while he worked. Nobody else could get close. Father would be annoyed he didn't get to visit with Martha since he'd asked her to come specially.

"That damn girl," Martha fumed as she drove herself home early, "that Jean Ann. She thinks she can hook him like a catfish just because she's younger. And pretty."

Martha had walked in on the two of them in the back bedroom. Father was standing over the paint tray, and the girl was kneeling beside him, her hand upraised.

Had she touched him? That's what it looked like to Martha, exactly like that. It made her want to vomit. She'd beat it out of that room as fast as she could go.

Martha tried to tell that big-titty girl and the ECW lady what she saw, but nobody did anything. Of course, she hadn't said the actual words – too filthy – but they should have gotten her drift.

The more she thought about it, the more certain she was that the girl had *molested* Father. Martha could see it perfectly in her head. He would have been loading his paint roller when she came over with her paintbrush, all innocent like, kneeled down and touched his privates.

It was shameful...*disgusting*. Father was too good a man to report her, too much of a gentleman to say a word. But Martha had seen it with her own eyes, how he'd backed away, acted like nothing happened. She had a responsibility to protect Father from that girl – from all the girls. It was obvious how many of them wanted him for themselves. A handsome man like that, a *real* man.

Martha clenched her fists. It was awful that Father should be hounded by such no-account floozies, throwing themselves at him and taking advantage at every turn. She had to do something.

What could she do?

≈ ≈ ≈

Arthur dropped into the overstuffed recliner in his borrowed living quarters and massaged his aching left shoulder. The rectory workday had been a success thanks to Sylvia's organizational efforts and Darlene Rohrbach's oversight of the volunteers. He'd met lots of parishioners, including some of the youth, and his soon-to-be home was transforming from tired and dingy to clean and cheerful. Everyone contributed with open hands and open hearts, and the buffet table had sagged under more food than it could hold. The rectory refrigerator remained full of leftovers, which Arthur planned to deliver to the local soup kitchen.

He'd spent much of the morning working with Greta and Joanne Bowman. Greta chatted away while her daughter said little, but Arthur noticed that the darkness Joanne had carried into his office the previous Wednesday was gone. When they had a moment alone, he'd asked her how she was feeling.

"A lot better. Thank you."

"I'm glad to hear that. One day at a time, I always say."

"I want to see you again this week if you don't mind," Joanne said. "I felt so much better when I left your office."

"Yes, let's check in. Call Sylvia and have her put you on my schedule. She'll make sure I don't double book anything."

He would spend time in prayer to prepare for Joanne's next appointment. Easing suffering like hers was the exact purpose of his gift, though that gift had almost gotten him banned from his chosen vocation.

Arthur had spent his entire life both aware of his disturbing faculty and concealing it. He'd had no idea others might acknowledge it, much less have the means to detect it. During his first year at seminary, his spiritual advisor, Father Daniel Lacey, told a stunned Arthur that the House of Bishops had been advised of Arthur's gift, and that he must undergo rigorous evaluation to determine whether he could be ordained.

That was how he learned of the church's long history of charismatic priests beginning with Jesus Christ himself. Father Daniel explained that when individuals with an extrasensory ability, or "charism," presented in modern times, church policy was to discourage them from the priesthood because the temptation for misusing their talents was so strong.

After much scrutiny and extensive counseling, a committee of bishops had deemed Arthur mature and morally steadfast enough to serve as a spiritual healer, and a whole new world opened to him. Who knew the Episcopal Church had protocols for training those like him? Or that the frightening events he'd been subject to his whole life could be controlled and channeled through his hands?

The talent had manifested when Arthur was a child, before he learned the impossibility of such things. Objects in his presence moved without any apparent cause, especially when he was stressed. Once, Arthur's father spanked him for some serious infraction, and when he turned to leave the room, Arthur's favorite Hot Wheels car flew through the air and whacked him on the back of the head. Arthur tried to explain that he hadn't thrown the car, but he was punished anyway. Another time, he'd gone to bed furious at his parents for refusing him some toy he wanted and had awakened to find the foot of his bed banging against the floor. He screamed, but by the time his mother reached him, it had stopped, and he was scolded for creating a commotion. It was years before he recognized the connection between cause and effect.

As those early experiences made clear, the light – as Arthur referred to his gift – wasn't an intrinsically good force, just a force. In seminary, he'd learned to embrace it, to harness and direct it in service of others. He rarely lost control anymore.

Though Arthur himself couldn't see the light, sensitive souls could perceive it. Over the years, self-described psychics, shamans, and seers of every ilk had approached him to marvel at the aura surrounding him. Empathic souls, as well as the weak and needy, could feel the light's energy and were drawn to it. Though he would never compare his meager gifts to those of Jesus, he understood why Christ in His day had attracted crowds wherever He went, whether the people knew who He was or not.

Arthur was gratified to know that Joanne had felt better after their talking and praying and his discreet laying on of hands. He couldn't always tell the effect he had, and few people thought to share with him afterward. Fewer still ever made the precise connection.

As it should be.

He picked up his glass of bourbon, a treat after the long day, and made his way to the desk in the corner of the room. He had a sermon to polish for the morning service.

≈ ≈ ≈

Frank Crawford glanced over his shoulder before approaching the side door that led to the church basement. The handle turned and he stepped inside.

Trinity Episcopal had been unlocked every evening he'd gone there, with one or another twelve-step group convening in the basement. In the last couple of weeks, he'd sat through half-a-dozen meetings, which served the dual functions of keeping him dry and providing a free meal of store-bought cookies and bad coffee. On several occasions, he'd parlayed that access into a place to sleep.

Toward the end of the meeting, whatever it was, Frank would visit the men's room and either wait there or hide in the adjoining janitor's closet until everyone left. Then he'd make his way to a rear storage room and stretch out on a pile of heavy curtains amid a collection of white gowns and wired angel wings. It was a serviceable, if not entirely comfortable, bed, and he had access to a toilet and a sink where he could wash up before sneaking out in the morning.

It was something you could get away with in small-town churches, those havens for lost souls. He surely qualified, though billeting an actual bum might be too literal an interpretation for most churchgoers – if they knew.

Today he'd given back by volunteering with Larry Pugh at the rectory, and the church ladies had fed him well for his efforts: meat, vegetables, even sweets. Frank didn't always have enough money for food for the whole week, and he'd wanted to stash some extra in his pockets, but that would have been crass. He should stop blowing the cash Larry paid him on booze and cigarettes, that's all.

8. Fingers In the Pie

Martha had no opportunity to talk to Father after Sunday services because everyone crowded her out during coffee hour. But she had to tell him what she'd seen. She was his witness.

On Monday, she called the church to find out where Father was staying, but whoever answered the phone wouldn't give her the address when Martha refused to identify herself. It was none of their business who she was. At least she could drive by the rectory and see if Father had moved in. Anyway, she'd left her casserole there when she rushed out on Saturday.

"My dish. I need my dish back."

With that established, she spent an hour making herself pretty, then squeezed behind the wheel of her Johnny Cash Cadillac and hummed a tuneless tune. The rectory wasn't far from her condo, not close enough to walk, but three, maybe four blocks, a two-minute drive.

As her car approached the ranch-style house with the covered front porch, Martha slowed down to do some reconnaissance. She saw no activity, so maybe Father was home alone. She pulled her heavy car up and over the curb. Parallel parking wasn't her thing.

She rang the doorbell but got no answer, so she laid her ear against the door.

"Yoo hoo, Father!" She rapped on the wood. Still no response. "Humph." Martha twisted the doorknob and found it unlocked. "No reason not to go on in." The rectory was part of the church, which belonged to everyone.

The living room looked a mess, much as it had last Saturday. Drop cloths still covered the floor, and the place stank of fresh paint. Martha wandered into the kitchen and saw that the cabinets had no doors. Father couldn't live in the house in this condition.

She opened the refrigerator and found it stuffed full of food, casseroles stacked three high, covered stewpots, cake and pie pans crowding every shelf. She located her dish and eased it from the bottom of the stack. The casserole was untouched. Well, if nobody wanted it, she'd take it home and eat it herself. There was no excuse for wasting food when so many went hungry. Martha well remembered her hungry times after her momma died and Gideon had left her and Floyd to fend for themselves most days.

"What's this?" Martha raised the aluminum foil covering a plate to reveal half a meatloaf. She poked two fingers into the shaped meat and gouged out a large chunk. "Like an A-Rab. Mmm...yum."

She took two more bites, then pulled the plate from the fridge and set it aside. Beneath it, she discovered half a fish pie in a round casserole dish. Though she didn't like fish, she was quite fond of pie. Martha jammed three fingers through the pastry crust and scooped out some vegetables and gravy. A glob dropped to the floor on the way to her mouth, but she ignored it.

"That's what drop cloths are for."

The crust was better than the filling so Martha peeled off a palm's worth of the pastry and gulped it down. With only a little remaining, she dragged her fingers through the stew and picked out the broken bits. Now the dish looked like fish chowder. No one would know the difference.

A bowl with several pieces of fried chicken sat next to it. "This ain't doing nobody no good sitting here." She pulled the foil from the meatloaf and packed the chicken inside, then tucked the packet into her pocket. She spied a pecan pie with only three pieces left.

"Not enough of that to leave," she muttered, glad to see the pie pan was disposable. She wouldn't want to steal.

Two more shelves were crammed with food in sundry containers. Martha turned up her nose at the burgoo, what her brother called "road-kill stew." Her momma used to make it with lima beans, okra, and whatever meat Gid could shoot or trap – opossum, squirrel, even rattlesnake – but poor hill families weren't above cooking real road-kill if it was somewhat fresh.

"No telling what kind of meat's in there," she noted.

Proceeding methodically, Martha uncovered and poked her fingers in dish after dish, skipping only the crudité plates and vegetable salads.

"Corn pudding, one of my favorites. *Ooh*, baked beans." She helped herself to samplings of both and then realized she was full. She hadn't even explored the cakes and pies on the lowest shelf yet. She retrieved the pan of pecan pie and filled the empty half with a selection of desserts. "For later."

Suddenly feeling rushed, Martha replaced the dishes higgledy-piggledy, then slammed the refrigerator door closed. On a whim, she peeked into the freezer and discovered several tubs of ice cream. Unfortunately, her black car was hot on a sunny day, and the dessert would melt fast.

"Never mind."

She stacked the pecan pie on her casserole dish and headed to her car, careful to shut the front door firmly on her way out.

≈ ≈ ≈

Tuesday morning rushed up on Darlene. She'd been busy Monday, taking Zack to the orthodontist, buying groceries, and stowing meals in the freezer so her son had something to eat when she was working.

She invited him to the rectory to paint, but he whined, "Aw, Mom. Do I have to?"

"You might have fun. There'll be other kids – and Rhett and Riley Pugh are coming." Her heart stuttered at the thought.

"That's cool, but my teeth hurt," Zack mumbled.

Darlene believed him since otherwise he'd be thrilled to hang out with the high schoolers.

"Okay, then, ah'm callin' grandma to come over."

The kids showed up at the rectory all at once, Rhett and Riley and their friend Darius, Darius's younger brother Shane, plus Amber and two other girls. Darlene's heart thumped so loudly at seeing Rhett that she was sure everyone in the room could hear it. She'd have welcomed the presence of another adult, but Arthur was busy at the church and Greta might have brought Joanne, whom Darlene couldn't face.

She set the boys to painting the hallway and took the girls outside to paint cabinet doors. She divided her time between the groups and, throughout the morning, managed to ignore Rhett's questioning looks and steamy stares.

Two of the girls left at noon, but Amber stayed, no doubt to spend time with Riley as she clearly had a crush on him. Darius was the football team's quarterback, and he and the Pugh boys joked around and jostled one another like brothers. Today the twins had worn contrasting T-shirts so Darlene knew who was who, though after two days' exposure, she was pretty sure she could tell them apart. Riley's chin was slightly longer, she thought, and Rhett's hair formed more of a cowlick at the crown. Maybe.

Sylvia stopped by late in the afternoon. "If you're done with the kids, I can chauffeur them home," she offered.

"Sure," Darlene replied. "Anyone who doesn't go now will have to wait for me to finish. Y'all put your brushes in the sink before you leave," she called to the group.

The other kids moved noisily toward the door, but Rhett hung back. "I'll help clean up."

"Actually, Darlene, that's a good idea," Sylvia said. "My boys will stay. You shouldn't be here by yourself."

"Uh, Mom," Riley objected, "I was going to Amber's to play vids."

Darlene recognized the change in Sylvia's expression as her friend's hanky-panky alarm going off, and she sucked in her cheeks.

"Is your mother home, Amber?" Sylvia asked.

"Yes, Mrs. Pugh. She got off work at four. She said Riley could stay for supper."

"All right, let's go then. You'll drop Rhett off?" Sylvia said over her shoulder.

"Um...sure." Darlene had hesitated, but it wasn't the dropping off that gave her pause. She wasn't at all sure she should be alone with Rhett, but she couldn't say *that* to his mother. "Leave the front door open," she directed Darius, the last one to leave. "It keeps the air movin'."

"Later, man," Darius called to Rhett.

"Later."

Darlene scanned the walls and ceiling to avoid Rhett's gaze. "Would you please gather the drop cloths and take them to the backyard? Ah'll rinse these brushes, then help you shake 'em out."

"Sure thing."

As they performed their separate tasks, Darlene's thoughts drifted to the drive ahead, being alone with Rhett in the close confines of her car. It was up to her, the adult, to keep her distance and also to make it clear that her earlier behavior had been a mistake and wouldn't be repeated.

She heard him singing as he collected the heavy canvas tarps and lugged them outside. After finishing with the brushes, she found him in the master bedroom dragging a tarp to a pile in the center of the floor. She bent for a corner and, when she straightened, found him standing behind her – *close* behind her.

"Rhett – " She turned to face him, prepared to deliver her speech, but his laser green gaze stopped the words in her throat. He grabbed her around the waist and reeled her in.

Oh no! Darlene started to push him away, but when her hands met the firm curves of his chest, she hesitated for the briefest second. He seized the moment and pulled her closer, then leaned in with the confidence of one who knew his kiss wouldn't be refused.

He's too young! Darlene's conscience screamed, but like last time, her body refused to listen. His heat enveloped her, carrying the scent of soap overlaid with sweat – clean, yet feral – a chemical catalyst that both defined and heightened some half-forgotten need. Her heart raced as Rhett's lips drew near, but at the last instant, she took hold of herself and turned her head to the side.

It didn't deter him. He merely directed his attention to the tender spot at the hinge of her jaw and dragged his lips down her neck. Darlene's head tilted to the side in apparent assent. When his lips reached the crook of her shoulder, he kissed her there, then stretched toward her mouth again, and this time she didn't turn away. He pressed his advantage, thrusting his tongue forward until she gave in and parted her lips to let him dip inside. Rhett's hands slid down to cup her buttocks, and he pulled her to him until she could feel his erection denting her belly.

"Ahh ..." Darlene moaned softly, unable to contain her pleasure at sensations that had been missing from her life for too long.

She let her hands rest on the sexy muscles under his arms, then slide downward to his narrowing waist. Rhett lowered himself to the pile of tarps at their feet and pulled her down on top of him. This young man was no neophyte. His moves were slick and confident. The knowledge didn't lessen Darlene's guilt, but made ignoring it a little easier.

He began to explore her body, squeezing and stroking, while his tongue delved deeper into her mouth. He was so fervent, so sweet. His flesh was so firm. Sprawled awkwardly across the dirty tarpaulins, her mouth as hungry as his, Darlene slipped a hand beneath the youth's T-shirt and smoothed her palm across his pecs, over his nipples.

"*Ungh* ..." he groaned and his movements quickened. He shoved his hands under her shirt, fumbled with the back of her bra and yanked the hooks apart. He palmed her breasts, then pushed her back and rolled onto her. He eased her shirt and bra up, baring her chest.

"Suck ..." she whispered.

He obliged, mouthing and pulling at her sensitive flesh while his hands stroked and massaged. It was unexpectedly liberating to accept this kind of pleasure from a younger man. Darlene felt none of the self-consciousness or inadequacy that she had in high school. Rhett reveled in her body and compensated for his lesser experience with an abundance of enthusiasm. She knew he'd do whatever she asked, though it didn't seem she'd need to ask for much.

She rolled her hips against him, pleasure rippling through her, and he pressed back, rubbing his hard length through her crotch. He grappled with the front of her jeans until they gaped open, then slipped a hand into her panties and probed her liquidy center.

I should stop this... The thought vaporized as quickly as it came. Darlene writhed and moaned, the irresistible sensations obliterating any niggling threads of conscience.

With the excitement of their tryst and the noisy fan rattling in the hallway, neither of them heard the knocking.

≈ ≈ ≈

"Father? Are you here? Father!"

The front door stood wide open, so Martha didn't hesitate to unlatch the screen and enter the rectory. She'd intended to rummage through the refrigerator again, grab that ice cream, but now she had to investigate. Had someone broken in? Maybe a robber! Her Daddy's pistol would have come in handy.

She crept down the hallway, peeking around doorframes. No one there. She sidestepped the big fan and tiptoed to the master bedroom, then stuck her head through the doorway.

"Oh, my Lord!" she shrieked, pressing her hands to her cheeks. "What's going on?" Her shrill cries echoed through the empty rooms.

The couple jerked apart in surprise, and the boy scrambled to his knees, then turned to face her. The girl lay fully exposed, her titties splayed to the sides with her clothes bunched up above them. Her pants were unzipped and light brown pubic hair fluffed out of the opening.

"Oh, my word! Oh, my Lord!" Martha swiveled heavily and lumbered down the hallway in a panic. "Father! Father!"

≈ ≈ ≈

Rhett leaped off her and hurried after the old woman as Darlene struggled to put her clothes in order.

"Ma'am? Ma'am?" Rhett called. "Father Arthur's not here. Ma'am?"

Please don't let her call the church and report this, Darlene prayed. No way would Sylvia not hear about it. *Sylvia!* Rhett was Sylvia's son. She had a son too.

Rhett returned, a little out of breath. "She's gone. I locked the front door."

"That's like closin' the barn door after the cows escape," Darlene grumbled as she buttoned her jeans.

"Or cow, in this case." Rhett snorted a laugh. "Do you know her?"

"Your momma said she's a crazy lady from your church. Ah almost didn't reco'nize her with that Shirley Temple-lookin' hair. She was wearin' black ponytails on Saturday. Ah thought she saw us kissing 'cause she acted the same way, dashin' out of the house hollerin' about shameful goings on."

"Guess we should've locked the door."

"We shouldn't have been *doin'* nothin'," Darlene countered in dismay. "It's my fault. Ah shouldn't have let this happen."

"Don't say that." Rhett moved toward her, arms outstretched.

She backed away and dropped her forehead into her hand. "Dang it."

Rhett ignored her resistance and wrapped his arms around her in a hug. "So she knows my mom, huh?"

Darlene nodded against Rhett's shoulder, disgusted at herself for taking comfort in the arms of the young man she was compromising, but she couldn't help it. He was so *male.* "Sylvia says she's always goin' on about somethin' and nobody pays any attention."

"I hope that's true." Rhett chuckled.

"How can you laugh? This is terrible." She looked into his youthful face. "You're not eighteen, are you." It was more a statement than a question.

"Seventeen. Does it matter?"

"It might to the law."

Rhett smiled, a twinkle in his eyes. "I won't tell if you don't."

Darlene shook her head. "Ah'm sorry, Rhett. Ah don't know what's got into me." She pushed away and bent to pick up a tarp. "Let's get these outside and shook off, then ah'll take you home."

"I'd rather stay here."

She shot him a grim look. "Help," she ordered.

Rhett grabbed the tarps and disappeared down the hall. Darlene patrolled the room for loose trash, then followed. Through the sliding door to the backyard, she observed him lift his fingers to his nose and sniff. Then he reached down to adjust himself inside his obviously strained jeans. When he glanced up and saw her watching, he blushed.

Darlene hurried over and pulled at a tarp, and Rhett helped untangle it from the pile. Together, they flapped it in the air, then repeatedly walked toward each other, matching corners until it was reduced to a two-by-two-foot square. Darlene kept her gaze averted and, each time they drew close, held her breath to avoid inhaling his intoxicating scent. It was dangerous.

They flopped the first tarp into the grass and repeated the procedure nine more times to create two stacks of canvas. Then Rhett picked up the first stack, and they walked around the house.

"So when are we finishing the job?" he asked.

Darlene opened the hatchback of her ancient Subaru. "Ah'll be back Thursday mornin', but it ain't a good idea for you to be here," she told him, her pulse quickening.

"I'll bring Riley. You need some tall help," Rhett declared with an impish smile.

"Ah don' know, Rhett. Let's just lock up and get out of here."

He returned for the second stack of tarps, and Darlene closed up the house, then joined him at the car. They rode through town in silence until she pulled to the curb in front of the Pugh residence.

"See you Thursday, nine o'clock," Rhett announced with a smile.

Darlene scowled at him, and he leaned across the seat and pecked her on the lips.

"Rhett!" she hissed.

He laughed, revealing all his teeth.

Darlene raised a fist, but before she could punch him, he jumped from the car and shut the door. As he loped away, Darlene observed the way his knees and hips moved in a loose, lazy synchronization to propel him across the yard. He scaled the three porch steps in an easy leap and slapped the lintel above his head before crossing to the front door. He turned and lifted his hand in farewell, then disappeared into the house sporting a huge grin.

9. Digging Up Dirt

Arthur arrived at his office a little before eight and was met with Sylvia's report, which cheered him immensely. The painting was nearly finished, and he could move into the rectory on Saturday. Though he would never complain, he'd grown tired of living from a suitcase. He hadn't taken much when he left Elgin a year ago, only what would fit in his car, and with a permanent residence, he could ask Sherry to send his books and other things. Perhaps if he cleared his possessions from the house they'd formerly shared, he could leave behind his ignominious past for good.

Arthur had never stopped loving her, not even during the worst of the accusations and recriminations. He didn't blame her for her bitterness, for he'd begun disappointing her in the husband department soon after they married. He'd foreseen no difficulty in satisfying his wife in his twenties when he was full of testosterone and easily aroused by such a beautiful and loving woman. It was only after the wedding that the enormity of his decision hit him over the head and caused his powers to wane. They both ignored it for a time, but when his meager efforts in the bedroom proved unsuccessful at satisfying her other requirement – children – their relationship soured further.

They hung on through fertility testing and talk of adoption because neither of them took their marriage vows lightly and because everything Arthur had worked for was coming to fruition. He was assistant rector of an important parish, poised to become rector. He'd been married for twelve years and had so much to lose.

It was then that his soul, desperate for recognition, drove him to remove his clerical collar, to escape the bonds of his trumped-up life, and venture into a particular area of a particular park. He'd lost control that night in more ways than one. In a single, life-altering second, a flash lit up the dark, catching him *in flagrante delicto* with his trousers down and a stranger kneeling at his feet. In the next second, a thunderous *Crack!* reverberated through the still night, and Arthur watched in horror as a large oak branch tore from the canopy above him and crashed to the ground, barely missing the fleeing photographer. He couldn't prove he'd caused the destruction, but given his shock and anger, he felt sure he had.

When the picture hit the internet, Arthur was recognized not only for who he was on the inside, but also for the fraud he'd perpetrated on his wife, his congregation, and his church. He'd found himself that night – that great missing piece – but lost everything else.

He headed to his office and settled behind his desk but was immediately interrupted by a syncopated knock at the half-open door. Sylvia normally filtered visitors, either assisting them herself or checking if he was available, but this "shave-and-a-haircut" wasn't Sylvia's knock.

"Hello, Father."

Stephen Harken's face appeared in the doorway, and it registered with Arthur that the organ had gone silent a few minutes before.

"I'm headed to Dunkin' Donuts. Will you join me? It's not far, and they have the best coffee in town."

Arthur chuckled.

"What's funny?"

"I was thinking of the weight-watching group that meets in the basement. Sylvia said their corporate sponsor didn't approve of them renting space next to the doughnut shop, so they moved to the church."

Stephen laughed. "Yeah, that's like holding Gamblers Anonymous meetings at a casino. At least they'd have a good turnout."

Arthur chuckled again. "True, but perhaps it's not the best way to increase attendance."

"Come with me. You let me blather on the other day about New York but didn't mention that you went to God school there yourself."

Arthur raised an eyebrow.

"Sylvia told me," Stephen said. "Anyway, I want to hear about your days in the Big Apple. Come on, take a break."

Normally, Arthur wouldn't have left his office during work hours to drink coffee with a parishioner, but it seemed likely that the young organist was feeling confession remorse. It was a common reaction to making too candid or otherwise ill-considered admissions to a priest.

The two bought coffee and sat at an outdoor table near the sidewalk. Arthur noticed a For Rent sign in the empty storefront window next door.

"You went to the Episcopal seminary in Manhattan, right?" Stephen said. "It's the hardest one, I've heard."

"It had its challenges." Or rather, Arthur had. Like endless personality assessments and character evaluations, and nearly a year's worth of extra training due to his "special circumstances." His charism, in other words.

"In *Chelsea*, right?" Stephen pressed, referring to the neighborhood where the gay liberation movement began. "Back in the day."

"You seem well-informed," Arthur replied, ignoring the implication. He removed the lid from his coffee and blew across it.

"Sylvia, like I said. Plus...gay." Stephen pistoled both index fingers at his torso, an ersatz gangster.

Arthur smiled even as his reticence, both natural and practiced, kicked in. The organist seemed to be fishing, but he was on-duty as priest and confessor and his personal proclivities weren't relevant.

"Chelsea's gotten really commercial, though," Stephen went on, filling the conversational gap as most people did when their counselor remained silent. "The West Village too. Hell's Kitchen is more hip these days, queer-wise." When Arthur didn't respond, Stephen changed direction. "Do you have family?"

"Yes, my father and two siblings, plus nieces and nephews."

"You're not married, then, no kids?"

Arthur let one beat of silence pass, then another. "I was married, but we weren't blessed with children."

Normally, he took the lead in parishioner/priest consultations, even informal ones, and kept the attention focused on the would-be penitent, but Stephen had sidetracked him and led the conversation in an uncomfortable direction. Arthur was determined not to hide, though. He'd suffered too much to tread that worn path again.

"But you're not married now."

Definitely fishing.

"Divorced." Arthur took a draw off the still-too-hot coffee.

Stephen looked poised to ask another question, but then glanced over Arthur's shoulder and exclaimed, "Hey, you caught us! What are you doing here?"

Arthur pivoted and saw Walker Jones approaching. The contrast between Stephen and Walker was striking, the one slim and graceful with a cultivated urban chic appearance, the other big and bulky, but lean like an athlete, wearing faded jeans and a T-shirt that strained across his pecs and around his biceps. At Walker's approach, forgotten memories of Arthur's college wrestling days flashed through his mind.

He stood and offered his hand. "Hello, Walker. Will you join us?"

"Father." Walker shook hands perfunctorily, then sat next to Stephen, wedging in so close that the organist tilted sideways and had to scoot over.

"I thought you were sleeping this morning," Stephen said into Walker's face, only inches away. Tension crackled in the space between them.

Walker stared at Stephen, then broke eye contact and ran his fingers through tousled hair. "I soon will be. Mom's car wouldn't start, so I picked her up. She's got something at the church."

"Your mother is Ellie Jones?" Arthur asked.

"That's right," Walker replied before turning back to Stephen. "What are *you* doing here?"

Stephen shrugged. "Having a coffee break."

"In fact, I need to get back to my office," Arthur said, sensing an imminent quarrel and regretting his unwitting involvement. His presence here was superfluous at best, an irritant at worst, and becoming less than comfortable in any case. "Nice to see you again, Walker. Goodbye, Stephen."

Walker stood, and Arthur could feel the man's gaze on his back as he strode in the direction of the church.

"Bye, Arthur," Stephen called in a high, singsong tone.

≈ ≈ ≈

It pissed Walker off to find his lover being cozy with the priest, especially after Stephen had denied he was interested in him as anything more than a boss. Sharing a private coffee break might be innocent for most people, but Stephen didn't do innocent, wouldn't recognize it if it dropped from the sky wearing wings and a halo. And Walker knew him well enough to recognize when a flirt was more than a flirt. From that first day in the sanctuary, Walker had known Stephen was attracted to Arthur Endicott.

"Why would I flirt with him?" Stephen demurred after the priest left. "I have no idea if he's even gay." He swiveled on the bench, then leaned back onto his hands and stretched out his long legs, a seductive pose – and a not-so-subtle manipulation – which pissed Walker off even more.

"I think you have a pretty good idea," he said darkly.

"He used to be married." Stephen extended his waist to the left, then to the right, sinuous and sexy as a snake.

Walker crossed his arms, refusing to respond. "Lots of people used to be married before they came out."

Stephen abandoned the posturing and sat upright. His eyes went mockingly round. "That's right! Like the bishop with his new boyfriend. It could be a movement, The Fairy Friars. They'll need a banner for the Pride Parade. Wait, no...The Fathers Fairy, you know, like The Brothers Grimm."

Walker clenched his jaw and glared. They'd been down this road before, and he could do without the deflections and phony jokes. Stephen had sworn up and down that he wasn't interested in the trainer from their gym until six weeks ago when Walker came home early from work and discovered the two in bed. *His* bed. He'd joined them – what else could you do? – but an open relationship should mean that everything is out in the open, right? For Stephen to lie and sneak around made no sense. Besides which, it felt shitty and demeaning.

To avoid saying something he shouldn't, Walker turned and left, letting his Dodge RAM speak for him, spitting gravel as it spun away from the curb. One thing he knew for sure – there could be nothing casual about fucking a priest, however unlikely the prospect. He didn't know Father Endicott, but the man was great looking and in his forties, and Stephen had always preferred older men. Unattainability was merely an added lure.

What little Walker knew of Stephen's former New York lover spoke of cosmopolitan tastes and old-money luxury. Allusions had been made to highbrow social circles, over-the-top ritzy parties, and entertainment in box seats. Given that, it was a mystery what Stephen saw in him. Walker was admittedly provincial, had never been west of Colorado or east of Ohio. His knowledge of culture was limited to high church ritual, the art of barbecue, and an incongruous taste for Baroque classics instilled by a musically educated mother.

Stephen was an exotic variant of country, a world-weary artist with a southern accent. He had a quick wit, a sharp tongue, the controlled, lissome grace of a veteran stage performer, and a total lack of inhibition in the bedroom, not to mention a tight, round ass. Walker liked the challenges Stephen presented, though he was never sure what, other than physical gratification and a measure of financial support, Stephen derived from their relationship. Insecurity fostered a jealous streak in him, one he knew his lover encouraged for his own reasons.

≈ ≈ ≈

When Sylvia saw Arthur leave the church with Stephen, warning bells clanged in her head, but then Martha Browne showed up and set off a warning siren that drowned them out. The pesky woman claimed that she'd walked into a bedroom at the rectory and found Sylvia's son canoodling with a half-naked girl.

"It was that big titty girl," Martha accused. "She was on the floor with her private parts hanging out for God and everyone to see!"

Though Martha's accusation was disturbing, Sylvia didn't know whether to believe her. The woman often misinterpreted and exaggerated things to get attention. Still, it was disconcerting when Martha leaned over Sylvia's desk and cried, "That's him right there. That's the boy!"

She pointed to a photo tacked to Sylvia's corkboard of Rhett and Grandpa Bub showing off their catch from a recent fishing excursion.

Sylvia swallowed her shock. "Are you sure that's who you saw?"

"Of course, I'm sure. Right in front of me in Technicolor. I've never been so disgusted."

Rhett didn't have a girlfriend, so if Martha saw anyone, it was probably his brother. Riley had, in fact, been fooling around with a girl on painting day, but Amber was still young and rather flat-chested. And it seemed unlikely the kids would have risked taking off their clothes with people around – *highly* unlikely.

"Okay, Martha," Sylvia said. "I'll certainly speak to him and get to the bottom of it. Oh, hello, Arthur." She hadn't heard the priest return. She must be upset.

"Father! You're a hard man to find." Martha giggled into her hand.

"Good morning...Martha," Arthur said. "Were you looking for me?"

"Oh, yes, Father. I have to talk to you. It's very important."

"Would you like to step into my office?"

Sylvia intervened. "Not now, Arthur. The Vestry meeting is in a few minutes. Martha will have to make an appointment."

"Sylvia's the boss," Arthur said, "but I'll look forward to speaking with you." He glanced at his watch, then headed into his office.

"He looks forward to speaking with me," Martha muttered.

Sylvia ignored her. The woman often talked to herself. "What day and time would you like for your appointment?"

"I don't need an appointment," Martha answered smugly. "I'll see Father at the rectory."

Sylvia lifted her brow at that. Was it Martha who'd been calling repeatedly in fake-sounding voices, asking for the priest's temporary address? The caller wouldn't identify herself, so Sylvia had withheld the information. An uneasy tingle flared at the back of her neck.

Martha moved close and loomed over Sylvia's chair. "You'll do something about that filthy business, right? I'll take it to Father if I have to."

"You have my word. Believe me, I'm as troubled as you are," Sylvia replied.

Whatever the truth was, she and Larry would have a talk with Riley. Even if the kids hadn't exposed themselves to Martha, Sylvia needed to emphasize that Amber was only fourteen and that three years was a big age difference in high school, especially for getting physical.

Martha smoothed a hand over the wig she was wearing, a brown bob, shorter in the back, long out of style. It reminded Sylvia of someone, but she couldn't place who.

"I'm going to Dot's salon. You can report back to me on Sunday." Martha waddled out of the office, trailing an air of self-importance.

Sylvia sighed heavily.

"Ready for the meeting?" Arthur approached her desk.

"Yes. By the way, you left this morning before I could talk to you about agenda item three. I'm proposing to hire Joanne Bowman as our office assistant, quarter-time, for three months. She's a medical secretary, so is overqualified, but she could use a boost to help her through her current struggles, and I could sure use the help. Would you have any objection to that?"

"No, none at all. I painted with her on Sunday and found her quiet, but pleasant and hard-working."

"She has an appointment with you tomorrow. I thought we three could discuss the job then if the Vestry agrees to it."

"That's fine with me," Arthur replied. "Some contact with people would probably benefit Joanne."

Sylvia told her husband about Martha Browne's revelation when he got home from work.

"Riley!" Larry yelled through the door to the basement. "Come up here!"

Riley appeared at the bottom of the stairs, wiping sweat from his face with a crumpled T-shirt.

"What?"

"Up here, please," Sylvia called.

"I get the fifties when I come back," Riley told his brother, then climbed the stairs. "What?"

"Come sit down," Sylvia instructed. Her son joined her at the kitchen table, his expression fixed somewhere between curiosity and apprehension. She could feel Larry hulking behind her. "Maybe you should sit down too," she suggested to her husband. He pulled out a chair, dropped into it, and crossed his arms over his chest.

No use beating around the bush. Sylvia cringed at the dead-on innuendo of that thought, then grimaced that she'd even noticed it. Living with three testosterone-fueled males had ruined her for polite society. Despite her discomfort, she looked Riley straight in the eye and asked the question.

"Are you having sex with Amber?"

"*What?*" Riley leaped from his chair, nearly knocking it over backward before catching it and setting it upright.

Sylvia's tension eased. That looked like honest shock to her, no guilty eyes or loaded silence.

"Sit down," Larry ordered, and Riley did so without taking his wide eyes off Sylvia. "You heard your mother. Are you doin' it with the Youman girl?"

"No! Why would you ask me that? We're not even going out! Did Rhett say – ?"

"Riley," his father interrupted, "you don't have to be going out to be getting it on."

Sylvia threw her husband a look of annoyance.

"I never even kissed her," Riley said with indignation. "We played video games."

Sylvia took the plunge. "Someone in my office this morning said they saw you and Amber making out at the rectory and that...not everyone was fully clothed."

"That's a lie! Ask Rhett. The girls went outside and we stayed in. Then Amber worked with all of us after the other girls left. Anyway, she's just a kid. And not my type," he added sullenly.

My son is old enough to have a type? Sylvia rejected the idea immediately. Riley was just being defensive. "Okay, we believe you." Sylvia raised her palms as a calming gesture.

"Rhett!" Larry yelled. "Come up here."

"What? Are you checking my story?" Riley bristled.

Sylvia noted her son's genuine irritation and realized that what Martha had said was probably untrue. No big surprise there since Martha was prone to exaggeration, if not completely delusional. Still, she had identified the photo on Sylvia's desk.

"Come sit down, Rhett," she said when her other son entered the room.

"What?" He pulled out a chair beside his brother.

Sylvia still marveled at how she and Larry, both of whom she considered average looking, had produced such beautiful children. The high cheekbones, dark brown – almost black – hair, the striking green eyes. She didn't blame the girls for falling all over them.

"Rhett, you're not having sex with Amber Youman, are you?" she said, addressing the possibility she and Larry always had to consider, that someone had mixed up the twins.

"Oh, *hell* no! She's after Riley. And I'm definitely not interested. She's way too young fo – "

"Watch your language," Larry cut in.

"We agree that fourteen is too young for you boys," Sylvia said, "so I'm glad we're on the same page."

"Somebody told Mom they saw us screwin' at the rectory!" Riley exclaimed.

"You're kidding. Who?"

Sylvia saw an odd look cross Rhett's face. Nobody liked being accused, she supposed. She stared at her husband and twitched her head.

Larry cleared his throat. "Your mom wanted me to remind you boys that if you find yourselves getting...involved with a girl, make sure you use a rubber. Do you know how to put one on?"

"Larry! For heaven's sake." Sylvia glared at him, then turned back to her sons. They were both flushing, but also smirking and glancing sideways at each other, holding something back. Those two always got a leg up on their parents, the way they stuck together.

"I'm just sayin', Syl, it's not that easy when you're all excit – in the heat of the moment. They might want to practice." Larry looked at her with his "I know I'm right" face, and she grimaced.

"We're good. We practiced on bananas at school," Riley said. The boys burst into laughter.

Did they really?

"Uh, can I finish my workout now?" Rhett rose and pushed in his chair.

"Me too."

"Yes." Sylvia sighed in relief.

The twins headed toward the basement door.

"Hey," Larry added, "there's some condoms in the bottom drawer of the bathroom. Put a couple in your wallets."

The twins clamored loudly down the stairs, guffawing in stereo.

"Larry!" Sylvia exclaimed, rolling her eyes.

"Oh, yeah," Larry hollered after them in deference to his wife, "and don't have sex!"

Another round of laughter burst up from below. Sylvia rose and mock glared at her husband before dropping her head into his broad chest, her shoulders shaking with stifled mirth.

10. Household Pests

Darlene entered the rectory Thursday morning and took note of what work remained – some touchups in the hall and a few missed places along the baseboards. The kids had painted the cabinet frames on Tuesday, so the doors could be reattached.

Darlene didn't know if Rhett would show up, but it would be better if he didn't. Her mind had returned again and again to memories of his half-lidded gaze under thick, black lashes, his masculine scent, fresh like newly turned earth, and his callused fingers probing her sensitized flesh. It was wrong – *so* wrong – but she was drawn to him.

Shortly before nine o'clock, the doorbell rang and two youths pushed through the door, one tanned and tawny, the other cocoa brown.

"Hey, Darlene," Rhett greeted her. "We came to help. Riley had something else to do."

"Hi, Darlene," Darius said.

"Hi, guys. Thanks for comin'." Only one teenager stood between her and the object of her madness. *Insane!* But a frisson of pleasure tingled up her spine.

"What are we doing?" Rhett asked.

"Come on in, and ah'll show y'all how to hang these doors."

"No painting today?" Darius asked.

"Not much left. You can start in here, and ah'll finish the paint touchups, then come help you."

Darlene had pre-marked the drilling locations for the new hinges and pulls. She gave the boys instructions and set them to it, then went to work in the hall, relieved to be alone.

When she joined them an hour later, they'd managed to hang only two doors and one of them opened in the wrong direction.

"Well, y'all are just goin' to town." The boys were concentrating so hard they didn't notice her mild sarcasm. Darlene watched as Darius dropped the same screw three times trying to position it through the hinge into its starter hole.

"Damn!" he said.

"Hey Dare, give it up, dude, you're hopeless," Rhett jibed.

"This sucks monkey balls!"

"It blows baboon boners." The boys burst into rowdy laughter, and Darlene was distinctly reminded that she was the adult in charge.

"Gentlemen, there's a lady in the house. Shall ah take over, Darius?"

"Yeah, please do." He handed her the screwdriver, then said, "Hey, I gotta go."

"I thought you were staying the morning," Rhett protested.

"No, dude, I told you. I gotta meet Mom at the Piggly Wiggly."

"Douchebag!" Rhett hollered as Darius darted through the living room and exited the house before Darlene could process the altered situation. "Oops, sorry," Rhett said, and flashed a grin.

Did Darius really have to leave, or was that just a charade for her benefit? She decided it didn't particularly matter since the cabinets must be hung. She had no intention of letting anything happen between her and Rhett anyway.

"Drill or screw?" she asked, holding up the cordless drill and a screwdriver.

Rhett crossed his arms and leaned against the counter, giving her a naughty smile.

She narrowed her eyes. "Okay, then. You drill the holes, and ah'll turn the screws." She chuckled at her own joke, then handed him the drill. "Get to it."

Grunts and monosyllabic commands dominated their conversation as the two wrangled the solid wood doors into place on the upper cabinets, Rhett from the floor, Darlene from the countertop.

After working steadily for two hours, Darlene stood back and took stock. Half-a-dozen doors remained lined up against the wall.

"Ah'm hungry and you must be too, a growin' boy like you," she said.

"Starved," Rhett agreed. "Though I'm not a boy." He set down the drill, pivoted, and stalked slowly toward her. Unfortunately, he'd taken her deflection for a challenge.

"Rhett," she warned, putting up a palm, "don't – "

He surged forward, bent over and grabbed her around the thighs, then tossed her over his shoulder like a sack of potatoes.

Cripes, he's strong! "What're you doin'? Put me down!"

"Ah weel!" Rhett teased in a high-pitched mimicry of her accent.

He carried her to the hall and shuffled a tarp into a mound with his feet. Then he crouched down and laid her on her back with her head resting on the tarp.

"Rhett, no! This ain't right!"

"Seems purty right ta me," Rhett drawled. He sprawled beside her, wrapped an arm around her waist, and leaned in to kiss her neck.

Darlene grabbed a handful of Rhett's summer-length hair and pulled his head back, forcing his gaze to meet hers. She should push him away and get up – he wouldn't stop her – but his breath, spicy and dark, heated her neck, and his soft lips betrayed no guile. If he'd smirked just then, or leered, or displayed any hint of hubris, events might have gone differently. But uncertainty and vulnerability lay written on his face, and his eyes conveyed such...hunger. She didn't pause to consider, just grasped his shoulders and pulled him to her.

In a burst of zeal, Rhett sealed her mouth with his and pushed his tongue inside. Darlene buried her fingers in his hair and answered him stroke for stroke, breath for breath. He slipped a leg between hers and nudged impatiently at her hip, his groan dissolving the last of her resistance.

≈ ≈ ≈

Despite the degenerate behavior she'd witnessed at the rectory on her previous visit, Martha couldn't quit thinking about the food just sitting over there in the refrigerator.

"It'll all go to waste." She should go back and retrieve it. Well, unless Father had moved in. Then it wouldn't be right, she supposed. If he *was* there, though, she could tell him she'd seen the awful thing that girl had done, touching him like that.

Martha suddenly recalled the phrase and blurted it out, "Making a pass." That girl had *made a pass* at Father. "A man of God!" She couldn't get away with it.

Unlike the last time Martha visited the rectory, the front door was closed. She pressed the doorbell. No response. She opened the screen and rapped on the door. No answer. When she turned the doorknob, Martha found the door unlocked, so she pushed it open and stuck her head in.

"Father! Father, it's Martha!"

The house looked much as it had two days before, still empty, but the drop cloths had been removed. Martha alerted to the sound of scuffling in the hallway.

"Yoo hoo, Father!" She headed down the hall, shuttling a leftover drop cloth to the side with her foot. "Forgot one," she muttered.

There it was again, a kind of scurrying noise, too heavy for mice. Martha peeked into the first bedroom, the bathroom, then the second bedroom. At the end of the hall, she hesitated, recalling the shock she'd gotten the last time she entered the master bedroom. This time, thankfully, the space was empty. If Father wasn't here, then the scuffling had to be...

"Rats in the attic." She knew about rats. Disgusting creatures. They'd inhabited the Brown homestead like well-fed pets. She'd always hated using the outhouse after dark. Half the time you'd scare up a rat scrambling over the seat or hear it plop into the hole when you opened the door. Her Daddy set live traps around the house and in the outbuildings, and when he caught one, he'd drop it into one or another of the snake cages. Fear of rattlers didn't curb the varmints' breeding habits, though.

Martha clumped her way to the rectory kitchen.

"It's starting to look nice in here," she said to herself. The cabinets sported shiny chrome hardware and a new paint job, though most of the bottom ones had no doors. Martha opened the refrigerator and, to her surprise, found it empty. The scent of vinegar wafted out.

"Where's all the food?" Even the ice cream was gone from the freezer. *Dang!* Maybe somebody had taken the food to Father's current residence, wherever that was. On second thought, that was a good thing.

"Father's too thin," she declared to no one. "He needs a good woman to feed him and look after him." She considered that for a moment. Then, with a new lightness in her step, Martha made her way through the living room and out the door, closing it securely behind her.

≈ ≈ ≈

Ding dong!

Lying prone on the hallway floor, Darlene had had no trouble hearing the doorbell. Startled into movement, she and Rhett scrambled to their knees as the front door creaked on its hinges. A woman called out, and they leaped to their feet, fumbling madly with their clothes.

"Quick! In here," Darlene whispered, grabbing Rhett's hand. She led him through the master bedroom into the closet, then pulled the door closed with a soft click.

"I think it's the same old lady who was here before," Rhett muttered. "Why does she keep coming around?"

Darlene shook her head, disgusted with herself. They huddled together, listening to the woman speak, and grew rigid as her voice neared. They waited breathlessly when she went silent, then relaxed as her footsteps receded.

"Is someone with her? Who's she talking to?" Rhett asked.

"Ah think she's talkin' to herself."

"What's she doing now?"

Darlene cracked the closet door and strained to hear.

"She's in the kitchen, sounds like. That's the fridge openin'."

"Maybe she brought food."

"She acts like she owns the joint, comin' here ever' day," Darlene grumbled.

"She doesn't own the joint...we do," Rhett said as he pushed her against the wall.

Darlene's unbuttoned white blouse gaped open to reveal her beige-colored bra. Rhett twisted the front clasp, and her breasts dropped from their supportive restraints. He gazed at them, seeming mesmerized by the pale orbs with their large pink nipples the color of cotton candy. He bent down and pulled one into his mouth while his fingers experimented with the other. He kneaded, pulled, and sucked, hesitating only when the front door thumped shut.

"She's gone," he mumbled.

"Rhett, stop." Darlene lifted his head, but his hands didn't stop massaging, caressing, tweaking. He laid his lips over hers, then bent his knees and pressed his hard length into the apex of her thighs, sliding up and down. Darlene began to pant, but the contact affected him more. His movements became jerky, his grunts more urgent. He seemed to lose awareness of his hands, which fell still at her breasts, before reawakening to squeeze once or twice, then going still again.

Rhett was a sweet thing, handsome and sexy, and his desire for her a rare, barely remembered thrill. It demanded a response, an acknowledgement at least. Darlene reached between their bodies and cupped his straining erection, squeezed, and then stroked him through the denim.

His tortured moan decided her.

She freed the button and zipper of his fly, then groped inside the dampish cotton of his boxer briefs to wrap her fingers around him, skin on skin. With her other hand, she stretched the elastic at his hips and eased it down. At her touch, he rumbled out a groan, creating a harmonic shiver down her spine that settled restlessly between her legs. Rhett flattened his palms against the wall and dropped his head into the crook of her neck, pressing his lips to her flesh as she massaged him into a fever. Then abruptly, his whole body stiffened, a deep groan rolled up his throat, and Darlene felt warm wetness coat her fingers. He went still, leaning heavily into her.

"*Gawd* ..." he moaned.

A few moments later, he opened his eyes and pushed his weight off her. Then he curled one hand over Darlene's head and kissed her softly, deeply, his neck and face flushed hot above his T-shirt.

"Stay here," she murmured. "I'll be right back."

Rhett released her and leaned a shoulder against the wall. Ten seconds later, she returned carrying a wad of wet paper towels.

"Sorry," he mumbled.

She handed him the towels, and he wiped up, then wrangled his still-swollen penis into his jeans.

"No sorry needed."

Darlene planted a soft peck on his lips and pulled him from the closet. He discarded the paper towels in a half-full garbage bag humped in a corner.

"Ah'm hungry," she said. "How 'bout you?"

"Yeah, but not for food." He wrapped his arms around her waist and tried to pull her to him.

She pushed him away. "We'll get some sammiches, then ah've got to finish this kitchen so Arthur can move in this weekend."

When Darlene turned to leave the room, she felt his hand cradle the curve of her butt. "Rhett!" she chided. But she didn't push it away.

Darlene got home at six and found Zack watching a *Supernatural* rerun.

"You hungry?"

"Yeah, Mom."

"A hamburger okay?"

"Yeah."

After supper, Zack returned to watching TV while Darlene sat at their shared desktop computer. At the search prompt, she typed "statutory rape laws Kentucky," quickly switching to a new window when Zack got up to use the bathroom.

"Close the commode when you're done," she reminded him. "Ah nearly fell in last night."

Darlene found a government website that laid out the laws state by state. She clicked on Kentucky and carefully read the legal definitions for statutory rape, then read them again. Finally satisfied, she closed the search window and sighed with relief. The age of consent in Kentucky was sixteen, unless the older party was in a position of authority over the younger. That didn't apply and Rhett was seventeen, so while she could lose her reputation, her business, her friends, and possibly be run out of town as a pervert, she couldn't be arrested for having sexual contact with Rhett. It wasn't a green light by any means, but at least she wasn't a felon in the eyes of the law.

According to the website, statutory rape laws were surprisingly less stringent in the South than in some northern states. "Guess we're used to child brides down here," she muttered. Due to the age difference between her and Rhett, touching him as she had would constitute sexual assault in Idaho and North Dakota.

"What did you say, Mom?"

"Oh, nothin' honey, just ah'm glad we live in Kentucky."

"I don't know why," Zack said. "It's hillbilly heaven."

Darlene chuckled.

"Redneck rodeo."

Darlene giggled.

"Jesus jamboree."

"Zack!" she scolded, suppressing her laughter. "Where'd you hear that?"

"Dad."

Darlene's heart squeezed for her son. Zack had barely seen his father since the divorce.

11. Moving In

Martha drove to the Piggly Wiggly where she found the big black woman from church working the cash register. Kendra Washington directed the choir, but sometimes she sang solos in a rich contralto full of joy or sorrow, always with a deep reverence for the Lord. Everyone said Trinity Episcopal was lucky to have her as their music director, and Martha would admit she enjoyed hearing the woman sing.

"Hello, Miss Martha." Kendra swiped the groceries over the scanner smoothly and efficiently as she spoke. "How are you?"

"I tell you, aren't we lucky to have our new Father? He's a fine, fine man." Martha opened her pocketbook and extracted her wallet. "I visit the rectory, you know," she boasted.

"I didn't think he was moving in until tomorrow. My kids have been painting over there." Kendra tucked Martha's items into a brown grocery bag. "That'll be thirty-two dollars, fifty-five cents."

"Tomorrow," Martha repeated, then handed Kendra two twenties. "I'm making sure the house is ready for him. And I'm cooking mutton barbecue and sweet potato pie and cornbread. He needs fattening up."

"Well, that's real neighborly of you," Kendra replied. "I'm sure he'll appreciate it. Here's your change and receipt. You have a nice day."

Back at her condo, Martha set to work. She put the mutton in the slow cooker and added the ingredients for her momma's secret sauce: ketchup, molasses, Worcestershire, Tabasco, cider vinegar, spices, and two jiggers of aged Kentucky bourbon, a step up from ordinary moonshine. Ten hours on low would make the meat tender and tasty. Next, she mixed cornbread batter and boiled sweet potatoes for the pie. Two hours later, she'd finished her labor of love.

The next morning, Martha woke before dawn, too excited to sleep. The choir director had said Father was moving in today!

She ate breakfast early, then went to her closet and selected her Tammy Wynette wig to go with her orange, stretch-knit pantsuit. She took extra time with her hair, re-teasing the top and renewing the flip with her fingers, setting everything with hairspray. She rifled through her cosmetics drawer for her favorite eye shadow, sky blue with sparkles, and her Dragon lipstick by Chanel, both of which she generously applied. Then with a brown pencil, she drew arches above her brow bones, something she'd done so often she could manage it in her sleep. When you had no eyebrows, people always noticed there was something wrong about you, ghostlike and creepy, even if they couldn't say why.

Sitting at her desk, Martha took out a sheet of notepaper, considered for a moment, then wrote:

Dear Father,

I'm so happy we are neibors! Here's directions to my house from the rectory.

Go down Lark Street two blocks. Turn left on Cleveland. See the sign FIST GLEN. (It's supposed to say FOREST GLEN, which is a much nicer name, don't you think?) My condo is #9. Visit me anytime. Here's some food to put meat on your bones.

Yours truly,

Martha Mae Browne

At the rectory, Martha hauled herself and her mutton dish up the steps and pressed the doorbell. No answer. When she entered the house, she was surprised to find it empty, just as it had been the day before.

Damn!

She paused to listen for rats, but today they were silent. She'd have to tell Father that d-CON worked good for killing rats, though her Daddy had always said arsenic was the best poison for everything.

Martha opened the refrigerator and set the meat on the top shelf, placing her note in the center of its aluminum foil cover. She made another tiresome journey to her car to retrieve the pie and cornbread, then arranged the dishes on the fridge's second shelf.

The house looked ready for Father to move in. Martha considered waiting for him, but there weren't any chairs to sit on, and she didn't know how to turn on the air conditioner. Maybe she'd come back later.

≈ ≈ ≈

"I hear you're moving today," Stephen said as he poked his head into Arthur's office, uninvited and unannounced, though Arthur didn't especially mind. Getting to know other gay men could help him learn by example – or perhaps counterexample – how to go about living openly.

"Sylvia's taking me to look at the rectory furniture in storage, but we won't haul anything until tomorrow."

"I've seen it. Nice stuff, lots of antiques willed to the church by old farts before they kicked the bucket."

Arthur let a couple of beats pass. "As long as the mattress isn't antique, I'm sure I'll be happy with whatever is available."

A rector's job rarely paid well, but it came with perks like a rent-free home, sometimes furnishings or a vehicle, and the bountiful generosity of parishioners. Single male priests also attracted gifts of food because it was often assumed that a man alone would either eat out every day or starve. Offering home-cooked meals was also a traditional courtship ritual and something to watch out for. The last thing Arthur needed were female parishioners vying for his attention.

"What time is all this work happening tomorrow?" Stephen asked.

"Sylvia scheduled the trucks for nine o'clock."

"Speak of the miniature devil," Stephen said into the outer office. "Sylvia, Arthur needs a new mattress at the rectory, don't you think? Something without a big dip in the middle and stains of unknown origin."

He stepped further into Arthur's office to make room for Sylvia and Ellie in the doorway.

"How do *you* know so much about Father Zeb's mattress?" Sylvia said. "He was old enough to be your grandfather." She raised her eyebrows at Stephen, and Ellie looked away. "You have a point, though. We'll add mattress shopping to our list of things to do today, Arthur."

"Arthur," Ellie said, "I've got members of the ECW lined up to help unpack and arrange your furnishings as they're delivered from storage tomorrow."

A sensation of warmth suffused Arthur's chest. "It sounds like you've planned everything to perfection, all of you. I've never known a priest to be so well provided for. Thank you."

"Well, you arrived with nothing," Ellie replied. "And anyway, it's our pleasure. With your city background, we were surprised you chose our little town for your new parish. We're lucky to have you."

"I'm delighted to be here," Arthur said. It would serve no purpose to clarify that Amity, Kentucky, had been chosen *for* him because it offered few opportunities of the type that had previously led him astray. "Now I'd better work on my sermon so I don't disappoint you on Sunday." Arthur stood to herd the group out of his office.

"I'll drop by the rectory tomorrow," Stephen said.

≈ ≈ ≈

When Sylvia walked into her kitchen after work, she overheard her sons talking in the family room.

"It was you, wasn't it?"

"Mom's home. Shut up!"

The voices became indecipherable when the television volume suddenly spiked.

Ah, my boys. Always keeping secrets. Sylvia sighed.

When Larry came in an hour later, he bent over and bear-hugged his wife in his usual manner, pecked her on the lips, and gave her butt a squeeze for good measure.

"Larry, you smell," Sylvia complained.

"So do you...nice," he replied, dropping his mouth to her neck for a play bite. She whacked him on the back and laughed. In some ways, her husband was still the horny high school boy she'd fallen in love with nearly twenty-five years before, and most of the time, she didn't mind that one bit.

"Do you have men and trucks lined up for tomorrow?" she asked.

"Yep, Dad's bringing the side-panel, and we'll have two pickups and five or six guys." Larry broke off their embrace and stuck his head around the corner. "You two are helping haul furniture tomorrow morning."

Sylvia didn't hear her boys' reply, but assumed it was an assent. They'd been extremely cooperative about assisting at the rectory, volunteering without any parental inducements after that first day. They were growing up, becoming nice young men, which made her glad and sad at the same time.

"I don't want your Dad to hurt his back," she said. "Who's coming besides Bub?"

"Billy Ray, Joe Pike, Dewayne and his boy, one or two others. Oh...and Frank," Larry added as he left the room, no doubt to avoid hearing her response to that.

It was probably un-Christian of her, but Sylvia didn't like Frank Crawford hanging around with his frightening scarred face and shifty eyes. He might be a Gulf War veteran, but she felt sure he was an alcoholic, and possibly a criminal, definitely a homeless drifter. She kept meaning to ask her husband exactly where Frank spent his nights.

≈ ≈ ≈

"Damn it, Riley, leave me alone!"

"That's as good as a yes, my brother." Riley tried to start his second set of decline presses but couldn't manage it for laughing. This was big...so big. He gave up and dropped the dumbbells to the floor. "I assume you got in her pants, since Mom said somebody didn't have their clothes on. Unless you had *your* naked ass in the air."

"Nobody took off any clothes!" Rhett barked.

"So you *did* get in her pants. Does the carpet match the curtains?" Riley was curious about that, but mostly, he was trying to goad his brother into spilling his guts.

Rhett retrieved the abandoned weights. "Get off the bench."

"She's got great tits. Did you grab a couple handfuls? What do you think they are, D-cup? Double-Ds?"

"I wouldn't know."

"Rhett boy bagged a cougar! Or maybe that's *rent* boy. What do you think she'd say to a threesome? Two for the price of one."

"No! Trust me, you and I will not be crossing swords any time soon."

Riley cackled. "Okay, I'll tap in for you then. She'll never know."

"I think she would, since there's a gigantic gap in maturity level between you and me."

"So *you* say."

"I do say. Anyway, she's a good person. Don't talk about her like she's some kind of ho. She's got a kid."

"I don't know how you did it," Riley said in not-entirely-false admiration. "I didn't notice anything going on when I was there."

"You weren't there the whole time, were you?" Rhett hoisted the twenty-five-pound dumbbells to his shoulders and began a slow set of squats.

"You doin' the nasty?"

Rhett rolled his eyes. "Gimme a break!" He trained his eyes on the ceiling, lowered his butt toward the floor, then thrust his body upward.

"Are you?" Riley pushed, staring expectantly.

Rhett finished his reps and set the weights on the floor. He turned away and paced across the room, then came back. "A man can hope," he muttered finally.

"BOO-yah!" Riley raised his palm for a high-five, which his brother ignored. "I hope so too. Must be terrible to keep dragging your virginity around at your age." He snickered.

"You know damn well I'm not a virgin," Rhett retorted.

Riley assumed not but couldn't say for certain, depending on the definition, of course. "You just don't share my vast experience."

Rhett snorted. "Yeah, right."

"Darius gets most of the pussy," Riley admitted. "Black man's advantage."

"Quarterback's advantage, more like."

"Running backs do all right too, especially when they're as handsome as me." Riley flexed his right biceps at the mirrored wall.

"Can't argue with that." Rhett bent down to start his second set of reps.

"So what's the plan?" Riley pressed. "When are you getting down to *bidness*? I bet she knows some good tricks." He stared at his brother, willing him to break.

Rhett finally looked over, a grin spreading slowly across his face. "Yeah, she does."

Success. "Spill! I want deets, man."

"Shhh, they'll hear." Rhett pointed upstairs. "And you better keep your mouth shut about Darlene."

"Or what?"

Rhett hoisted the fifties to his shoulders with a loud grunt. "Or I won't tell you a damn thing."

Riley groaned. "You're killing me, dude!

12. Neighborly

Late the following morning, Sylvia supervised Larry's
volunteers as they unloaded the trucks at the rectory
while Arthur directed them to the appropriate rooms and
the Episcopal Churchwomen unpacked and arranged the
kitchen gear. Within a short time, the hollow spaces began
to fill, and by Saturday evening, the house was habitable, if
not completely organized.

After a long day the crowd went home, leaving Sylvia
with a sense of satisfaction. She waved to Larry and the
twins as they drove off in the truck, then headed inside to
say goodbye to Arthur. She found him settled into a
leather club chair in the living room, staring into space.

"I'm sorry, Arthur, but the gas man didn't show up, so
you won't have hot water or a working stove until
Monday."

"That's all right," he replied, "but come look at this."
He rose and led her to the kitchen where he opened the
refrigerator which, once again, was packed with casseroles,
covered dishes, and disposable aluminum baking pans.
"Ellie and the others brought more food, bless them, so I
don't need to cook. These three dishes, though..." – he
pointed to the barbecue, cornbread, and sweet potato pie –
"...were already here when I arrived this morning. There's
a note." He handed the paper to her.

"Are you sure it wasn't left over from the painting party?"

"No, I took that food to the soup kitchen Monday afternoon. Unfortunately, most of it had to be thrown out because someone had grazed through it with their fingers. I suppose the children got into it."

Sylvia wrinkled her brow. "The kids who were here are old enough to know better. And why would they? The food was laid out for everyone to eat."

Arthur chuckled. "Maybe we have rats."

She had her suspicions. Larry was providing lunch for Frank Crawford when he worked for Pugh's Concrete, but not breakfast or dinner, and Frank would have known about the food left over from painting day. He could have come and helped himself after everyone left.

"This note is from Martha Browne," Sylvia said after reading it. "Did you say she brought this food before we got here today?"

"Yes, I cleaned the refrigerator on Wednesday. She must have dropped it off after that."

So when had Martha seen the kids making out at the rectory? Sylvia wondered. Tuesday or Thursday? Funny...Darlene hadn't mentioned that Martha stopped by when they were working.

"Have you been locking the house?" she asked.

"I don't have a key," Arthur said, "but it wasn't locked when I came on Wednesday. Maybe Darlene has a key."

"I'll look into that. This note from Martha is a little disturbing." Sylvia read it again. "Unless you two have become friends, and I didn't know about it."

"I didn't know about it either," Arthur replied, smiling. "I met her at the church, but we haven't spoken at any length. It was thoughtful of her to bring food."

"Her note is inviting you to her house, with directions even."

"Yes, that's a bit odd."

Sylvia lowered her voice, though she and Arthur were alone. "Between you and me, Arthur, you don't want to encourage Martha. She has a way of misinterpreting people and creating tempests in teapots, if you know what I mean. I'm wondering if she has a crush on you."

"Oh, no," Arthur scoffed gently. "We've barely met. No doubt she's glad the church has a full-time priest."

"You're a kind man, Arthur. I'd advise you to be wary of Martha Browne, though. She can be unpredictable. I know Father Zeb had some trouble with her, though he'd never say exactly what it was. Ellie might know."

"She seems harmless enough, but I appreciate your concern. Her barbecue is good. I can't tell whether it's beef or pork."

"Probably mutton. Barbecued mutton is a Kentucky specialty."

"I quite like it. Her pumpkin pie is good, too, a little unusual."

Sylvia looked into the pan. "That's sweet potato pie, a southern favorite, like collard greens and fried okra."

Arthur grinned. "Oh, of course."

Sylvia started dousing lights as they prepared to leave. "I wish we had a key now the furnishings are in. Lots of locals leave their homes unlocked, but I hate to tempt fate."

"Let's turn the front door deadbolt and leave out the back," Arthur suggested.

As the pair walked around the darkened house, Sylvia spotted a hunched figure, hands in his pockets, approaching the porch.

Frank Crawford? "Hello!" she called aggressively. "Can we help you?"

The man straightened and turned toward them, and the porch light caught the face of Stephen Harken.

"Oh, it's you!" Sylvia said. "What are you doing here?"

Stephen stepped toward them. "I told Arthur I'd pay a visit."

"Hello, Stephen," Arthur said.

"You're too late." Sylvia angled her watch toward the light. "Did you really think we'd be working through the evening?"

Stephen shrugged. "I guess you're leaving then," he said to Arthur.

"Yes, no hot water. And I need to prepare for services tomorrow."

"Where's Walker?" Sylvia asked rather more sharply than she'd intended.

"At home."

Sylvia wrinkled her forehead before looking away. "All right, I'll see you two at church tomorrow."

"Bye, Sylvia, and thank you." Arthur turned to Stephen. "I'll walk you to your car. Mine's parked beyond yours."

≈ ≈ ≈

Stephen nodded silently, eyes downcast. He shoved his hands deeper into his pockets as he and Arthur walked a short way together before the priest headed to his separate vehicle.

"Where've you been?" Walker demanded when he got home. "I made dinner, but it's probably cold now."

"I went to the rectory to help with the move," Stephen half-lied. Walker couldn't get too pissed about that.

"You might have called." He pulled a salad bowl from the fridge and set it on the counter. "Were there a lot of people?"

"Uh...yeah...quite a few," Stephen hedged.

"Did they get everything done?"

"You should've come if you're so curious," Stephen said, turning his face away. He grabbed a plate and shuffled through the silverware drawer as he contrived to change the subject. "What did you do today?"

"I was busy...gym, errands, laundry, groceries. The usual," Walker said.

"Are you coming to church tomorrow?" Stephen took his plate to the dining table and sat down.

"I was planning to. You're playing Pachelbel, right?"

"Yeah, for the offertory. This chicken is tasty," Stephen mumbled around a mouthful of food.

"Thanks, secret ingredient. You won't believe what it is." Walker grinned, the wide-mouthed, sexy one that could make Stephen – or any gay man, probably – do anything Walker wanted, anything at all.

Stephen shivered. "What is it?"

"That powdered ranch dressing you mix with buttermilk? Except you add it to flour and coat the chicken before frying it. Good flavor, right?"

"Surprisingly good. Thanks, babe." Stephen tilted his head up and pursed his lips.

Walker crossed the small space, then bent down and gave him a peck.

"You tryin' to butter me up?" Stephen stuffed another bite into his mouth.

"I *am* buttering you up. After dinner."

"Oh, baby," Stephen purred, his blood rushing southward. "Some *Last Tango in Paris* action. You be Brando. I'll be the French girl."

"As long as you don't shoot me afterward." Walker leaned his hip into the kitchen island he'd built and crossed his arms over his pecs, bulging them against his tight T-shirt.

Damn, he was sexy. Stephen pulled at his left pant leg. "*They Shoot Horses, Don't They?*" he quipped. "Not studs hung like horses."

Walker chuckled. "Doesn't Jane Fonda get shot at the end of that movie?"

"Yeah, but don't worry. Old studs never die – they just get put out to pasture."

"Who're you calling old?" Walker's eyes narrowed, and he jutted his hips forward.

Stephen laughed.

"I promise you, *I* won't be the one passing out after Round One," Walker warned.

"Hey! I 'represent' that remark," Stephen said, "and I don't appreciate you poke-poke-poking me awake either."

"Would you prefer I sucked you awake?" Walker pushed away from the island and glided toward him, a predatory look in his eyes.

"Well...if I had to choose...hmmm...." Stephen stuck his index finger into his cheek and rolled his eyes upward as if pondering the dilemma. His slacks were getting snugger by the second.

"You'd take both." Walker stepped behind his chair and slid a hand down the neck of his Polo shirt.

"Yeah, that's about right," Stephen agreed.

"Hurry up. I'm horny," Walker whispered into his ear.

"Oh, goody!" Stephen shoveled rice into his mouth and mumbled, "I love being a sex object."

Walker growled and pulled him from his chair. "You're done eating, right?"

Dinner, at least.

≈ ≈ ≈

Outside Jimbo's Sports Bar, Frank Crawford clasped his hands behind his back and stretched his chest muscles. Moving furniture wasn't his favorite form of employment, and he hadn't been paid for his efforts either.

Don't be a dick, said a quiet voice in his head. *Nobody owes you anything.* Except the government. The U.S. government owed him something – his life back.

He forced the familiar refrain from his mind. No point in tramping down that dead-end road again. He had other things to worry about.

Working at the rectory had been hot and exhausting, and Frank couldn't remove his shirt to cool off. His back was ugly, and exposing the scars always raised questions he didn't want to answer. Fortunately, Larry brought beer, and the church ladies had fed him well again, which was a bonus. He'd avoided the preacher, or priest, or whatever he was. So-called men of God gave him the creeps.

Now, after a few more drinks, he needed a place to sleep. He wouldn't ask Larry for any more favors, and the trailer the Catholics called a homeless shelter...well, he'd rather sleep outside. The humid air smelled like rain, though, so once again, he decided to crash at the church.

He turned in that direction and lurched forward.

13. Charisma

Sylvia marveled at Joanne's office skills. Her new hire had quickly mastered the online calendar and the word processor, and was now updating the church website. With Joanne taking over the rote functions of the office, Sylvia was free to tackle the tasks that required her special knowledge. So far, she'd had no time to plan the Vestry's annual retreat, for instance, and if she didn't book rooms soon, they'd have nowhere to go.

When Joanne stepped out of the office, Sylvia stood up from her desk. She wanted to confer privately with Arthur about their new assistant.

"Sylvia!"

The familiar shrill tone froze her in her tracks. She drew in a calming breath, turned, then dropped back into her chair.

"Is Father here?"

"Hello, Martha. What can I help you with?"

"I need to speak to Father. In *private.*"

Don't we all. Sylvia frowned. "Didn't I offer to make an appointment for you last week? You said you didn't want one."

"I've been trying to talk to him, but I never get the chance. Everyone crowded around him at church yesterday and Annie Croot made a stink about me stepping on her foot and people kept hollering at me and he's never at the rectory and – "

"Martha," Sylvia cut in, "have you been going into the rectory when nobody is there?"

"What are you talking about? Are you accusing me?" Martha's voice rose alarmingly.

"No, no, calm down. I'm just asking – "

"You can't talk to me like that! I won't ha – "

"Is there something I can help with here?" Arthur asked, stepping into the room.

"Father!" Martha clomped past Sylvia.

"Miss Browne? Would you like to come into my office?"

Sylvia waved her arms frantically behind the woman's back. The last thing Arthur needed was Martha Browne busting in whenever the mood struck her. He caught her eye and shook his head minutely, though, and Sylvia shrugged in resignation. He didn't realize what he was getting himself – and her – into by humoring Martha.

Just then, Joanne returned carrying a stack of loose papers. "Sylvia, where do you keep the pushpins for the bulle – "

"*She's* here? What's *she* doing here? Oh, my word! *Father!*" Martha bellowed.

Sylvia twisted around to see Martha slap her hands over her mouth, then throw them wildly into the air. The woman's horrified expression and beet red face rendered Sylvia speechless. Joanne fled the room.

Arthur stepped forward. "Miss Browne? Are you okay?"

Martha wheeled to face him, her tent-like dress bloating with air. "Oh Father, I *know!* I *seen* it!"

Sylvia hurried toward the disturbed woman, recognizing a Martha emergency in the making.

"I can see you're upset," Sylvia said, adopting her calming voice. "Come to the ladies lounge, and I'll get you some water. We'll have a chat."

Sylvia put a hand on Martha's elbow.

"No! Don't touch me!" Martha yelled, jerking away. "Don't anybody touch me! I have to get out of here!" She whirled toward the exit and charged across the room more quickly than Sylvia would have expected of such a heavy woman.

"Please don't leave when you're upset," Sylvia pleaded. "Can't we talk for a little bit?" Martha was a pain in the neck, but she shouldn't drive in such an agitated state. And Sylvia wanted to know what had set her off to prevent similar episodes in the future.

"No, no, no!" Martha screeched, her hands clamping auburn curls to her head.

Arthur caught up to her at the door. "Miss Browne?"

Martha turned, and Arthur looked into her panicked eyes. Then he extended his palm, and she slowly raised her hand and placed it in his. Sylvia watched in fascination as the stress faded from Martha's face and the agitation visibly drained from her body. Arthur's expression, soft and benevolent, seemed to hold her inert as if she'd turned to clay.

Sylvia took two steps backward, suddenly feeling like a child who'd opened the wrong door in someone else's house.

Thirty seconds ticked by, maybe more, before Arthur broke the silent connection. "God bless you, Miss Browne," he said.

Martha's jaw hung slack for a moment before she shook herself from her apparent stupor. "You can call me Martha, Father," she said quietly.

Arthur patted the hand he held between his and then released it.

"God bless you, Martha," he repeated with a warm smile.

"Thank you, Father." She shuffled out the door and disappeared.

Sylvia gaped at Arthur in astonishment. "What did you *do*? I've never seen Martha react like that. She usually stomps off in a huff, muttering and griping, but when she's that upset, somebody has to chase after her and talk her down."

"Oh, I just said a prayer for her," Arthur replied vaguely, not meeting her eyes.

Sylvia followed him to his office. He sat behind his desk and leaned forward on his elbows, steepling his fingers.

"That was remarkable, Arthur. You really have a soothing effect on her."

The priest looked oddly vacant.

"I'm worried about her behavior," Sylvia went on. "She's been unusually distraught lately. I don't know if she has family I might call, or maybe a doctor. She's never mentioned either."

Arthur just stared into space, so Sylvia kept talking. "There's something else. I hope you won't think I'm a terrible gossip. You're still new here, and you wanted me to warn you when I saw potential problems coming your way."

Arthur rotated his head toward her. "I don't think you're a gossip, Sylvia. I'm counting on you to keep me from going astray."

Sylvia shut the solid oak door behind her.

"Arthur, about Saturday..."

He finally met her gaze. "Yes?"

"...when Stephen Harken came to the rectory in the evening?"

"I remember."

"My instincts tell me that...hmm...I'm not sure how to say this tactfully." Sylvia paused and felt her face warm. "I think Stephen is interested in you."

Arthur's expression didn't register comprehension. "He does seem inquisitive. But friendly."

"Forgive me," she pressed, "but I think he regards you as potentially more than a friend." She waited to see if he would catch on, but his face remained blank, so she said bluntly, "Stephen's gay, Arthur."

"Ah...yes, I know," he said, surprising her. "I've had the pleasure of meeting Walker."

"Oh, okay...good. Yes, they've been together awhile, but Stephen has a reputation for a wandering eye, and when he showed up late on Saturday...well...I'm pretty sure he meant to catch you alone. I don't know what the heck he's thinking, but I wanted you to be aware."

"Stephen and Walker seem well suited," Arthur deflected.

"Yes, but Stephen lived in New York, and according to my nephew, he has a lot more...um...*urban* experience than the local men. I don't want to dwell on that," Sylvia added hurriedly, backing toward the door. "I've said my piece, so I'll just leave it at that."

Arthur looked at her with an open expression and a gentle smile. "Sylvia, I'm also gay."

Sylvia's eyebrows arched. "Oh?" Then the words sank in. "Oh! I'm sorry...I didn't realize."

"No reason you should. I haven't known anyone here long enough to feel comfortable sharing that information." He paused. "Except for you."

"Well...thank you, Arthur, for trusting me with that," Sylvia said. She looked at the floor for a moment before meeting his gaze. "That makes my warning more relevant, though." The next words rushed out of her mouth before she'd thought them through. "Unless you're interested in Stephen?" Her voice squeaked high and she blushed, but Arthur didn't seem to notice.

"Not in that way, no. I'd rather hoped both he and Walker might become friends. Although...." He let the thought trail off.

"You haven't told them you're gay," she guessed.

Arthur shook his head, and Sylvia wondered if his pause had meant something else. She barged ahead anyway. "I think Stephen's operating on that assumption, and to be blunt, I also think he's pursuing you."

Arthur scoffed. "I doubt that. I must have nearly fifteen years on him." He saw her expression, then added, "Well, thanks for sharing your concern, Sylvia. I'll keep it in mind. Oh, and I meant to ask if you and your family would like to come over next Saturday for a barbecue? I want to thank all of you who worked so hard to help me move in."

"That's completely unnecessary, Arthur."

"I'll enjoy it."

"Okay, then," Sylvia agreed. "I'll tentatively say yes for the Pughs."

"Great. I was thinking I'd invite Kendra and her kids, Ellie, Joanne and her folks, Darlene and her son, and Stephen and Walker." Arthur winked at her.

"Ah...good idea!" she said with a grin. "Sounds like fun."

When she returned to her desk, Joanne peeked in from the corridor.

"Is the coast clear?"

"Yes, Martha's gone. Arthur calmed her down, and she left," Sylvia said.

"What's wrong with her? She seems upset with me, but I don't even know her. She acted the same way on painting day." Joanne looked bewildered, but Sylvia could see she was shaken.

"Don't worry about Martha," she replied with a wave of her hand. "She's got problems. It's hard to know what sets her off sometimes, but I'm sure it had nothing to do with you."

"Joanne," Arthur called from his doorway, "I'm having a barbecue on Saturday and would like to invite you and your parents. Shall I call your mother to confirm?"

"I'll have her call you. Will there be a lot of people?" she asked warily.

"You'll know everyone...Sylvia, Ellie, Kendra, Stephen. Sound okay?"

Joanne looked at her feet. "Sure. I think so, anyway."

"Good. Sylvia, do you have Darlene's number?"

"Yes, I'll get it for you."

"That reminds me," Arthur said. "The rectory phone line is connected. Here's the number for the church bulletin."

≈ ≈ ≈

Martha drove home, giddy with excitement. Father had held her hand, and something very special and personal had passed between them. She'd felt better immediately, despite her distress, and even though that nasty girl was lurking around.

"What is she doing there, anyway?" Martha wondered angrily. *Chasing Father? Taking advantage?*

Martha didn't trust her for one second. Sylvia might not realize, but she knew what that girl was capable of. Now she regretted getting so upset because she'd neglected to tell Father that she'd seen that girl assault him – because that's what it was, *assault*. Martha was his witness. There had to be a witness.

She sniffed her palm and detected a trace of scent, soap or maybe cologne.

"I'm not washing it," she declared.

14. Getting Hooked Up

Frank exited Jimbo's tavern and sniffed the evening air. The humidity had been rising all afternoon. After working all day pounding together wooden forms for a concrete pour, Frank decided not to stay out drinking and risk having to sleep in the rain. He hated the shelter, but he hadn't fully bathed or shampooed his ratty, gray ponytail for several days, and at least he could clean up there, wash his clothes, and get a sandwich or some burgoo.

It proved to be the right choice because Frank met an old codger who told him how to get drunk for a fraction of the price of bar drinks. "Tell 'em Twinkle sent you," the hillbilly advised.

The next day after work, Frank checked out the so-called nip joint, walking half a mile from Larry's jobsite to the unassuming address in a scruffy part of town.

"Whaddya want?" a scrawny, hard-bitten woman barked after he knocked on the side door as he'd been instructed to do.

"Twinkle sent me," Frank replied and, after bearing up under the hag's suspicious stare for fifteen seconds, was directed to a room at the back of the house where locals sat playing cards, drinking, and smoking tobacco.

"Whaddya want?" the woman barked again from behind a makeshift bar made from raw plywood.

"Shot of moonshine," Frank replied, not sure what else was available.

"Fifty cents," she announced, filling a double shot glass with clear liquor from a five-gallon jug with a spigot near the bottom.

A fraction of the price of legal whiskey, homemade corn liquor was worth the risk of arrest. The good State of Kentucky did not like losing tax revenue from under-the-table liquor sales, so Alcoholic Beverage Control officers raided nip joints whenever they discovered them. Frank figured the odds of getting caught in a raid at any particular time were low, though.

The hill country artisans knew their moonshine, with secret recipes handed down from one generation to the next, varying in ratios of raw ingredients, flavorings, cooking temperature, timing, and other details of distillation. As he sat on his barstool and drank, Frank heard other patrons order flavored brandies, but he liked the white lightning, and it was the cheapest drunk you could get.

He imbibed until he was pleasantly drunk, then exited the nip joint into the pouring rain. Trying to sleep in a thunderstorm was so unpleasant that he stumbled to the shelter again only to find it full. With nowhere to go and rain saturating the cardboard he held over his head, Frank's feet carried him back to Trinity Episcopal Church.

On this night, an Alcoholics Anonymous meeting had just begun. Though everyone would know he'd been drinking, as long as he wasn't unruly and said the right words – *I lost my way today* – he thought they'd let him stay and eat something, maybe bum a cigarette or two.

Larry had inquired the day before where Frank was sleeping, and Frank told him "at the shelter," made it sound like the greatest thing since Wonder Bread. Larry was going out of his way to help him, and Frank didn't want to cause the man any trouble. He assumed Larry's wife had prompted the good-natured grilling because Larry had looked so uncomfortable asking.

≈ ≈ ≈

On Wednesday morning, Ellie Jones arrived at the church shortly before nine o'clock. As the Vestry member in charge of community outreach, she'd called a meeting to discuss starting a food bank. There'd been layoffs at the plastics factory, and Walker had told her people were struggling to feed their kids on unemployment.

"Hi, Sylvia," Ellie said as she entered the office. "Do you have something to write on? I didn't grab my notebook this morning."

Sylvia located some paper and handed it over. "I'd like to sit in to discuss the schedule for food distribution," she said. "We'll need to work around other groups to some degree."

"Good, I was hoping you'd get involved in your copious free time." Ellie smiled. "I asked Walker to lead the meeting since starting a food bank was his idea, but work interfered. If this project takes off, I'll turn it over to him, though. I'm overcommitted as it is."

"He didn't come to rectory moving day," Sylvia observed.

"He'd just gotten off the night shift, I think. Actually, I can't keep track. The company is handing out pink slips, but the remaining workers are doing double shifts and mandatory overtime. It's crazy, but at least he kept his job."

The two women left the office and started down the long corridor to the Fellowship Hall.

"Stephen showed up," Sylvia remarked.

"At the rectory? I never saw him."

"No, you wouldn't have." Sylvia glanced around before gesturing toward one of the classrooms. "Come in here a minute, would you?"

That sounded slightly ominous. Ellie followed her friend into a room dotted with miniature tables and chairs. Sylvia pushed the door shut, then stared at the ceiling for a moment, her mouth twisting to the side.

"When Arthur and I left the rectory late Saturday evening, we ran into Stephen coming up the sidewalk. Everybody else was long gone." Sylvia paused, then added, "He was not there to work."

Ellie caught her gist immediately. "You think Stephen is chasing our new priest."

"Yes."

"I've noticed it too," Ellie said. "Every time I come to the office, he's in Arthur's doorway chatting."

"I know it's none of my business, but if Stephen's on the prowl again...." Sylvia shifted her weight. "We can't afford to lose Walker. He's one of our best volunteers."

It wasn't an idle concern. Trinity's most talented youth minister had defected to the Lutherans two years before after a highly public breakup with the organist. And Stephen couldn't be fired. His talent drew music lovers from three counties whose open purses helped keep the parish afloat.

"Well," Ellie said regretfully, "my son's a grownup, and I learned long ago not to meddle in my kids' relationships." Then insight came in a flash. "Wait, Arthur's not interested in Stephen, is he?"

"No, no," Sylvia said. "I felt I ought to warn him, though, since he asked me early on to help him steer clear of personal minefields, as he put it. He seemed unaware of Stephen's attentiveness. Of course, he doesn't know him like we do."

Ellie eyed her friend shrewdly. "So Arthur is gay, I take it."

Sylvia exhaled through her teeth and dropped onto a tiny wooden chair, her knees angling upward. "Please don't say I told you. He shared it with me in confidence."

Arthur was also divorced, Ellie knew. A personal memory, a mental dislocation, stole the strength from her legs, and she slumped against the radiator. "That must be a first for Trinity."

Sylvia grinned sheepishly. "Well, I was never too sure about Father Zeb myself."

Ellie chuckled. "True." She paused. "Stephen's not the only one vying for the attention of our handsome priest. Have you noticed? The others are female, though."

"I know," Sylvia agreed, "but he's so modest, he doesn't realize."

"If he's gay, maybe he wouldn't." Through the window, Ellie noticed a spider pulling herself between two mullions, spinning a web, her plump abdomen probably full of eggs.

"He was married, so he's not inexperienced with women, I presume," Sylvia said. "But the way they crowd around him at coffee hour. And the painting party...did you see the fancy food the single women brought? Cutthroat competition." She rolled her eyes. "I warned him to be wary of Martha Browne. Honestly, I think she's head over heels, and she's so unpredictable. She went into the rectory and put food in the refrigerator *before* he moved in. To beat the crowd, I guess."

"Seriously?" Ellie tore her gaze from the industrious arachnid.

"Yes, she left him a strange note."

"I think she has a thing for priests," Ellie said. "She flirted up a storm his first week at coffee hour, then told anyone who'd listen how much he favored her."

Sylvia nodded. "Kendra mentioned that too. Martha said something similar to her at the grocery store. By the way, do you know...did something happen between Martha and Father Zeb? I always got the feeling he was uncomfortable around her, but he wouldn't say a word about it."

Ellie chuckled mirthlessly. "That's what I meant about Martha having a thing for priests. She kept bringing him flowers. Not for the altar or the sanctuary, but bouquets she sneaked into the sacristy where he dressed before services."

Sylvia's eyes widened. "Are you kidding me? That's sacred space. Not to mention private."

"I know. Charlie Hightower said she barged in on Father Zeb half-naked once, and Zeb cursed her out."

Sylvia snorted, then covered her nose and mouth with her hand. "I can't believe I never heard about that."

"It was before your time," Ellie said. "That's when Charlie put automatic locks on the sacristy."

"Well, Arthur should be safe while he's dressing then. From Martha, at least." Sylvia pushed herself to her feet and gave Ellie a sideways glance. "Maybe I shouldn't have said anything to him about Stephen."

"Arthur's not dumb. He'd have figured it out sooner or later."

"Is Walker coming to the barbecue on Saturday?"

"I will encourage him to attend," Ellie said, making a mental note. She was a straight woman in her fifties, granted, but she'd never understood what her son saw in Stephen, whom she regarded as self-centered, superficial, and uncommitted.

Arthur, on the other hand, was none of those things. It wasn't meddling, exactly.

≈ ≈ ≈

Sylvia was pleased with the food bank meeting. Vestry member Dean Worth had taken charge, organizing committees to get things going. Clients would enter through a side door into the basement so they couldn't be viewed from the street. Kentuckians were a proud people, and many would go hungry before letting themselves be paraded as charity cases.

Heading back to the office, Sylvia steeled herself at the sight of Martha Browne standing in front of the bulletin board in the vestibule. The woman appeared to be examining each posted item and writing notes on the back of a church donation card. Sylvia considered hiding in a Sunday School room until the annoying woman left, but that would be juvenile.

"Hello, Martha," she said as she passed. "How are you feeling today?"

"Fine."

"You missed the food bank meeting, if that's what you're here for."

"No, I just stopped by the church," Martha said, then added too casually, "I haven't seen Father today."

All morning, Arthur had stayed in his office with the door closed after receiving word that three parishioners had been admitted to the hospital. He would be phoning the families and making arrangements to visit the patients.

He'd only been in Amity a short time, but Arthur was already sought after for visits to the local hospital and attached nursing home. He was kind, energetic, joyful, and smart. He was a committed Christian, but not in a stodgy way. He could laugh at himself, and Sylvia suspected he hadn't always been a saint. Everyone who met him loved him.

There was something else about him, though. Arthur had a way of making people feel better. Sylvia couldn't explain it, but she'd seen the effect he had on Joanne and Martha, as well as others who came in for pastoral counseling. The transformations were dramatic. Every person who went into Arthur's office distressed came out composed and serene.

"He's working in his office this morning," Sylvia told Martha.

"That's what I thought, and I didn't want to bother him. He's too important to have people barging into his office all the time."

Sylvia stared at Martha for a second before shaking off her surprise. "I agree," she said, and turned to leave.

"I'm waiting to see if he comes out for a break."

Stalking him, in other words. Sylvia stiffened. "Father Arthur has a full schedule of sick and shut-in parishioners to visit today," she snapped. "He's very busy."

"Yes, I know," Martha agreed amicably, unusual for her. She muttered as she shuffled away, "...have his phone number."

"Excuse me?" Sylvia said.

Martha pushed her way out the vestibule exit, and the glass door closed behind her with a thud.

≈ ≈ ≈

Rhett had to see Darlene. He couldn't stop thinking about her, how beautiful and sexy she was, how friendly, and how amazing it had felt when she put her hand on him.

She was nothing like the girls at school. They held back and held back and then made a big deal out of the smallest physical contact. If you just copped a feel, they'd act like you were supposed to be in love with them. Sure, he could get regular sex if he had a girlfriend, but that didn't interest him. His buddies with girlfriends ended up whipped, or they'd fight and break up constantly, and Rhett had too much on his mind to deal with that crap, especially coming into his senior year of football.

Riley and Darius assumed he got laid every time he went out, and he'd been close, but so far, it hadn't been worth the grief trying to convince a girl to go all the way. Last spring, he and Ry had taken Jamie and Haley to the junior prom and afterward drove to Smooch 'n' Cooch Hill.

145

Eventually, he'd gotten Jamie's dress unzipped and felt her up in the front seat, but when he pushed her strapless bra down and tried to kiss her breasts, she'd yanked it back up in a huff. He ended up fingering her beneath her poofy skirt, and she went down on him unasked. He'd never understood what she was thinking that night.

"But I was happy with the outcome," he told Riley later.

"So to speak." They laughed and bumped fists.

The foursome went out another time, and things had gone the same way, with Jamie on top of him in the front seat and Riley and Haley in the back. This time, after Jamie wiggled all over him and he couldn't take it anymore, Rhett unzipped his jeans and pushed them down his hips a ways. Then he lifted her up and lowered her onto his dick. It was shocking how good that felt – hot, slippery, and intense – like her mouth, only better. Jamie had raised up on her knees and let him dip into her a few times, just a couple of inches. He met some resistance there and figured she was still a virgin, but by then he was far from caring about anything except plunging and thrusting.

Cruelly, she chose that moment to change her mind, lifting off and shaking her head no. At least she went down for a consolation BJ. Afterward, he'd pulled her onto his lap and pushed a finger inside her, rubbing where he thought he was supposed to for a long time. She seemed extremely excited, but he didn't know if she came.

Riley tore open a condom wrapper in the back seat, so Rhett knew his brother had gotten laid again. He decided to ask Ry to switch girls the next time since Haley was freer with the pussy. But so far, next time hadn't happened.

He was glad now because his sexual encounters with Darlene were way better. She was a woman and knew what she wanted. The way she moaned when he mouthed her nipples – and even more so when he eased his fingers into her – scorching hot. If they hadn't been interrupted at the rectory, he was almost positive she'd have done the deed.

It was the first time he'd ever felt like pursuing someone. Usually girls came on to him, and he took whatever was offered, but Darlene was different. He wanted her bad. He had to see her again.

15. Reaching Out

What a long day. Arthur had spent the first half of the afternoon at Amity Hospital and the second half at St. Anthony in Lexington. Little Cody Winthrop had suffered multiple bone fractures from falling out of a live oak, while Charlie Mathison, a sixty-seven-year-old farmer, somehow acquired a severe case of whooping cough. Louis Tinkerton, an elderly parishioner, suffered a stroke and had been taken by ambulance to Lexington with paralysis in the right half of his body.

Comforting the sick was an important part of a priest's calling, and Arthur felt blessed to serve as an instrument of God's grace in that regard. In his seventeen years as a priest, he'd witnessed true miracles of healing. More than once, stage four cancer had vanished from a patient's x-rays, spine-damaged patients had stood and walked, and one lifeless patient regained a heartbeat.

Doctors ascribed the miracles to medical science – chemical cocktails, precipitate treatment, the latest research drug – while non-devout patients often attributed a miraculous cure to their vegan diet, directed visualization, or alternative therapies. Such interventions might sustain a recovery, but Arthur knew that only God's light could bridge the infinite span from broken to not broken, from death to life. He channeled the light, coaxed it from its naturally diffuse state, collected it, and directed it as a concentrated beam to where it was needed. The light itself was limitless, but containing and focusing it required both physical and spiritual strength.

On this day he'd summoned the light several times in succession, and the effort had drained him. Folklore surrounding telekinesis pointed to potassium and iron as possible catalysts for the phenomenon, and Arthur had discovered through trial and error that exercising his gift depleted both in his body. Over the next twenty-four hours, he would ingest several times the maximum recommended dosage of both minerals – an amount toxic to most people – to regain his strength.

Five-year-old Cody was an easy case. Since negative thoughts and emotions created barriers to the light, often Arthur's first task was to transmute the patient's emotional state to a quiet serenity, then watch as healing occurred spontaneously. After Arthur had "found" a quarter behind Cody's ear and produced a small teddy bear out of thin air, her fear faded, and the light flowed into her. Cody's parents would discover later that her bones had mended in record time.

Charlie Mathison had needed the most help. He'd developed pneumonia from his bout of whooping cough and struggled to breathe. Arthur's grandfather had once told him that pneumonia was the friend of the old, and as a healer, Arthur understood what he meant. Many people accepted the condition as a means to exit their too-long lives with relative ease. Given that knowledge, Arthur had arrived at Charlie's bedside prepared to help him pass, but found instead a man possessing a powerful will to live. When Arthur laid hands on the farmer's head, the light had flashed into the afflicted man like an invisible bolt of lightning.

Normally, Arthur felt the light collect in his body and build to a tangible force. He would release it then, directing it upward from the base of his spine, down his arms, and through the palms of his hands. In Charlie's case, Arthur had been unable to control the pull created by the man's lust for life, and the transfer of energy had left him drained and dazed. He didn't regret it because, by the time he left, Charlie was breathing freely and had fallen into a deep, restorative sleep. Arthur smiled and gave thanks as he drove on to Lexington.

When the priest reached St. Anthony Hospital, he found more or less what he'd expected. He hadn't met the Tinkertons, but as soon as he touched old Louis's hand, Arthur knew the man didn't have the will to overcome his stroke. Louis was choosing to die, possibly to avoid being a burden on his wife. In such a case, Arthur's duty changed from healing to easing the soul's passage. He'd donned his priest's stole, then laid hands on Louis and offered him the Rite of Extreme Unction, silently welcoming him into God's light. Given permission to die, Louis likely wouldn't survive the night.

As he drove back to Amity, Arthur considered Sylvia's assertion that Stephen Harken harbored a romantic interest in him. Stephen had an intimate manner, and the priest hadn't failed to notice Walker's antagonism when the three of them met. But flirtatiousness wasn't an uncommon trait among stage performers – preachers included – whose success depended upon their ability to seduce an audience. The behavior could be habit as much as anything, or even a desire to exert control over a perceived authority figure.

Arthur felt no romantic attraction toward Stephen, though he was intrigued to meet gay men who lived openly. How had they gotten there? What were their lives like? Surely they suffered for their choices, though perhaps they'd never felt they had a choice, and that was the difference between him and them.

You had no choice either, said a still, small voice in his head. His marriage had been a pretense, wish fulfillment. He'd squeezed himself into ill-fitting shoes and forced himself to play a role until the repressed part of him had rebelled with shocking flair.

A year later, the sting of public humiliation remained sharp, but it hadn't lessened the desire that had brought it about and which still kept him tossing and turning to tortured dreams, waking up sweat-soaked and, occasionally, soiled like a teenager. He hadn't addressed those desires yet, either, he noted with chagrin.

At home, the red light blinked on Arthur's new phone – six messages – a surprise since the line had just been connected. If called to another emergency, he didn't know how he would summon the strength to assist one more soul.

He pressed Play.

Beep. "12:07 PM," said the machine's mechanical voice.

"Hi, Father! It's Martha. I called to say how good it was to see you at the church on Monday. Bye for now." *Click.*

Interesting.

Beep. "12:25 PM."

"Father! It's me! You didn't come home for lunch, I guess. Hi, again. Bye." *Click.*

Hmm....

Beep. "5:01 PM."

"Hello, Father! You're not home from work yet. I hope you had a good day. I'll try you again." *Click.*

Beep. "5:10 PM."

"Hi, Father! Why aren't you home yet?" *Click.*

Arthur scowled.

Beep. "5:25 PM."

"Hi, it's Martha. I waited fifteen minutes this time, but you're still not there. I think I'll call the phone company and ask them to check your line. Don't worry. I don't mind. Hope to see you soon." *Click.*

Beep. "5:45 PM."

"Okay, don't worry about anything, Father. The phone company says your line is working, but if I don't reach you by tomorrow, I'll call them again. I had a very good day today. I decided to bring lilies for the altar on Sunday. I know they're usually meant for Easter or funerals, but I thought you'd like the fragrance near the pulpit. You can get hothouse lilies almost any time, not just in the spring. What are your favorite flowers? Okay, enough chattering for now. Bye bye." *Click.*

Oh, Lord! Should he return the calls or ignore them? Martha hadn't said she required anything and left no phone number, though caller ID would have recorded it. He decided to talk to Sylvia before responding. Perhaps she wasn't as far off the mark about Martha Browne's intent as he'd supposed.

Banishing the unwelcome thought from his mind, he started toward the kitchen to fix himself something to eat. When the phone rang, he cringed, hesitated, then turned around. It might be Sylvia or a parishioner who required pastoral attention.

He reached the door to his den and stopped. Was it cowardice that made him wait for the caller to leave a message?

Beep. "6:02 PM."

"Hi Father, I thought maybe you came home at 6:00 instead of 5:00, but now I'm thinking you don't come home until 6:30. You don't have to call me back. I'll try again. It's Martha." *Click.*

Arthur shook his head in disbelief.

He returned to the kitchen, opened the refrigerator, and gasped in surprise. The top shelf had been cleared and an unfamiliar baking pan placed on one side with a round casserole dish next to it. He raised the foil on the former and saw what appeared to be pork chops covered with large glops of barbecue sauce. The other dish looked like scalloped potatoes. He noticed something odd and removed the glass lid to look more closely. The top layer of sliced potatoes had been cut and carefully arranged to spell "Arthur."

This can't be good. His mouth settled into a grim line. He shut the fridge, and something floated to the floor, a church donation card with a message penciled on the back:

Dear Father,
Your too skinny. I brought some ribsticking food just for you!
LOVE, MARTHA

Arthur groaned. The phone rang.

≈ ≈ ≈

Rhett whistled as he ascended the porch stairs at the address listed for *Interior Decorating by Darlene.* It was a residential street, so Darlene must run her business from home.

He punched the doorbell and waited, his hands jammed into the pockets of his jeans, revealing a stripe of taut abdominal muscles between his hipbones and the designer-labeled elastic several inches lower. A dog yapped hysterically.

The door opened, and behind the screen stood a blond-haired boy with the same heart-shaped face and cerulean eyes as his mother.

"Hi! I'm Rhett Pugh. You must be Zack. Is your mom home?"

The boy gazed at Rhett in surprise, then did a double-take when Riley leaped up the porch stairs behind him.

"I'm Riley. Who are you?"

The boy stared, open-mouthed, then whispered, "Rhett and Riley. Awesome."

"This is Zack," Rhett informed his brother. "Can we come in?"

Zack opened the door and stood aside. "Mom!" he called as the twins entered one after the other.

Darlene appeared at the opposite end of the room wiping her hands on a dishtowel.

"My goodness, Rhett and Riley! What're you two doin' here? Have you had supper?"

Rhett saw her glance at his shoes, then up to his face.

"You got it," he said, grinning, "Rhett."

"We've already eaten," Riley said.

"Come in and sit down. Can ah get you some sweet tea?"

"Yes," the brothers replied in unison.

"Please," Rhett added.

"Hey, you've got an Xbox," Riley exclaimed, stepping toward the television and barely missing the orange puffball sniffing his feet. It yipped and scampered to the corner, diving into a fuzzy purple bed labeled "Princess" in pink rhinestones.

"Yeah, Mom gave it to me for my birthday."

"Rhett, check this out," Riley said, picking up the controller from the coffee table.

"Wanna play?" Zack enthused, digging under some interior design magazines for a second controller.

"Definitely," Riley answered. "What games do you have?"

Rhett wandered over to look at the screen. *Perfect.*

Darlene returned with two glasses, setting one on a coaster for Riley and handing the other to Rhett.

"Thank you," Rhett said, looking into Darlene's face. "You know, maybe I could eat."

"Okay, c'mon. Ah'll rustle you up somethin'."

Rhett followed Darlene to the kitchen and watched her cross the room, her hips swaying rhythmically from side to side. She opened the fridge.

"I'm not really hungry," he admitted.

"Oh?" She tilted her head and gazed at him for a long moment. "Why are you here?"

"I came to see you."

He ambled across the room and caught her scent, like cookies or ice cream. In one quick motion, he snatched her wrist and reeled her in, yanked her close and trapped her in his arms, a move he'd seen his father do countless times with his mother.

"I missed you," he said quietly.

≈ ≈ ≈

Rhett's face was so close Darlene could smell toothpaste on his breath. Her heart fluttered as she unwound his arms from her waist and pushed them away. "My son is here."

"I know. That's why I brought Riley." He took her hands, stepped back, and inspected her from top to bottom.

"He knows...?" Darlene paused in confusion.

"He knew without me telling him. We're twins." Rhett shrugged as if the statement were self-explanatory.

"Did you ask him to keep Zack busy?"

"Nah, but he will."

"How do you know? Can you read his mind?"

He didn't seem to notice her sarcasm. "Kind of. I know what he's thinking and he knows what I'm thinking most of the time."

Darlene glanced toward the door. "This ain't a good idea, Rhett."

"Aren't you glad to see me?" he said, a mock frown pulling down the corners of his mouth.

"'Course ah am." Darlene toed the top of one bare foot with the other. "It's just...it can't go anywhere." She looked up into his glittering green eyes ringed by heavy black lashes like crayon outlines. So beautiful.

"Why not?" Rhett moved forward, crowding her, and she shuffled backward until her hips met the kitchen sink, which halted her retreat.

He stared her down, then with slow, sinuous movements, closed the gap between them and laminated the front of his body to hers. His stout erection dented her belly as he took her face between his hands and leaned in for a kiss. She gasped, and he plunged his tongue inside, his hot, minty breath stealing hers away. Her lips and tongue responded instantly, without permission, though her arms remained at her sides.

Rhett scooped up her hands and pressed them to his chest, which burned like fire under her palms. She tentatively squeezed his muscled flesh, then simply gave in. She explored upward to his neck and shoulders, then downward to his biceps and over his ribs to his waist. From there, her hands crawled under his T-shirt and smoothed across his back.

≈ ≈ ≈

Her touch lit a fire in Rhett, and he reacted instinctively. He dipped his knees and pressed into the junction of her thighs, then straightened his legs slowly, intentionally. The bulge at his crotch sank slightly into her, and he swiped his length upwards, the thin cotton of her leggings providing little barrier to the intimate contact.

Eyes closed, Darlene moaned, and Rhett covered her mouth with his, absorbing the sound. He thrilled to her response, so much more exciting than a schoolgirl's. He cupped her right breast and squeezed gently, then rubbed his thumb across the rigid nipple poking through her T-shirt. He bent his knees again and stroked his erection through her crotch, causing them both to groan as their mouths met.

She leaned away, and Rhett brushed a finger across her full bottom lip. When her lips parted, he pushed his finger between them. Darlene sucked the digit into her mouth, then drew back and sucked it in again. The suggestion sent a shock wave through his groin, and he rocked his hips into her.

Panting, Darlene pulled Rhett's hand from her mouth, pressed it to her stomach beneath her loose shirt, then nudged it behind the waistband of her leggings. Rhett responded, sliding his fingers down inside her panties and into her hot, wet flesh.

"Yes," Darlene whispered, arching into his hand.

Rhett found her opening and, to the sound of her moan, pressed his middle finger inside as far as he could reach. "Rub right there," she panted, digging her fingernails into his arms. He curved his finger and stroked her from the inside.

"There?" he whispered in her ear and received a long, low moan in reply. The sound vibrated in his balls and danced up his almost painfully rigid penis. Beyond excited, Rhett had to concentrate to maintain the motion. He kept at it, transfixed by the sexy expressions that floated across her face. He transferred his free hand from outside her T-shirt to inside, finding her nipple through the thin fabric of her bra and squeezing it. She groaned a deeper tone and pressed into his hand. He barely remembered to breathe.

"Touch my clit," Darlene murmured. Rhett could just make out her words against the electronic noise blaring from the living room, punctuated by cheers and groans from Zack and Riley, whom Darlene seemed to have forgotten.

He knew more or less where the clitoris was located. He pulled his finger from her, feeling a slight suction of resistance, then stroked upward, concentrating on the feel of her flesh. When Darlene squeaked, Rhett swiped his finger across that spot again.

"Right there," Darlene whimpered and eased her thighs further apart.

Rhett felt the hard little knot and stroked it lightly, over and over, then around in a circle. After a while, Darlene's squeaks quickened, then suddenly she went stiff. The earth stopped turning as Rhett held his breath and stroked her once more. With a soft cry, Darlene jerked against him and her muscles began to grip and shake. One more stroke, then one more, and Darlene's knees abruptly gave way. Rhett threw his free arm around her back to support her weight, but managed to stroke once more slowly, watching her face.

With her eyes closed, she sighed, then took his wrist and eased his hand from her clothing. She wrapped her arms around his waist and laid her cheek against his chest. He held her close and rested his chin on top of her head.

As they stood quietly in their embrace, Rhett felt Darlene's breath jump in her chest once, and then again. He leaned back and saw tears running down her face.

"Darlene, what? Did I hurt you?" he whispered in alarm.

She raised her head and looked at him, wet tracks marking her pink-flushed cheeks. "No, darlin', the opposite," she murmured and swiped at her face with the back of her hand. "Kiss me." She stretched up toward him. Confused, but willing, Rhett leaned down and pressed his lips to hers, then softly stroked the long blond ponytail sagging out of its hairband.

"Thank you, Rhett," she whispered. "Thank you so much."

"You're welcome," he replied, automatically polite, though he wasn't entirely sure what she meant. He kissed the top of her head and inhaled the perfume of her hair.

Rhett felt sure Darlene had had an orgasm and wondered if she knew it was the first time he'd witnessed that. It wasn't what he thought it would be. It was much more exciting – a huge thrill – and not so different from his own response when she had stroked him to orgasm. Thinking of which, he now had an erection like concrete. His balls ached, and his cock was trying to jump out of his jeans, but he was happy. Extremely so.

A loud groan and a higher-pitched cheer rose simultaneously from the living room followed by an excited "Yap, yap, yap!" from Princess.

"You suck!" Riley howled.

"Ah, come on, high five!"

"I guess we know who won that game," Rhett observed with a chuckle. "Can I use your bathroom?"

"Sure, darlin', down the hall on the left."

Rhett left the kitchen and turned into the hallway, slipping through the living room before Zack noticed him. He escaped behind the bathroom door, shut and locked it, then whipped open the snap and yanked down the zipper of his jeans. He lowered his pants along with his underwear to free his swollen cock, then spit into his hand and stroked himself. Heavenly, but no doubt temporary, relief came fast.

"Thank gawd," Rhett groaned. Finished, he cleaned up with toilet paper and washed his hands.

So damn *hot*! He marveled at the intimacy Darlene had shared with him. He wanted to do it again – and more – preferably, right now. When Rhett returned to the living room, Riley caught his eye and understanding passed between them.

"Hey, Rhett, you wanna play video soccer? I tromped Riley!" Zack laughed maniacally.

"You know I let you win, punk." Riley wrapped an arm affectionately around Zack's neck and rubbed his knuckles into the kid's scalp. "Noogies for you!"

Zack cackled as Riley held him trapped in the crook of his elbow before releasing him.

"Riley screwed up," Zack taunted, jumping away before he could be grabbed again.

Riley growled and lunged in his direction, and Zack darted down the hall, heehawing all the way. Everybody laughed.

"You done eating?" Riley inquired with a passably innocent expression.

"Yeah."

"We better go then before Mom misses her car."

"Yeah, we don't want her to sic the sheriff on us again."

Darlene looked dumbfounded. "Did she really? Did Sheriff Boudreaux take you in?"

Riley laughed and Rhett joined in. "Nah, just kidding."

"The twins are leaving, Zack," Darlene called in a tone of mild annoyance.

Zack ran into the room, darted behind Riley, and punched him in the butt.

"You turd!" Riley hollered, whipping around to grab Zack and hoist him off the ground. Zack kicked his legs in protest, but not too hard, and laughed like a crazed hyena.

With the horseplay as a distraction, Rhett slipped behind Darlene and kissed her on the back of the neck. She smelled like vanilla and cinnamon, sweet and spicy. He brushed his hand across hers in farewell, then moved to the front door.

"Wait, Rhett," Zack protested. "Don't you wanna play?"

Darlene looked curiously at her son. "How can you tell them apart?"

"Shoes," he replied triumphantly. "Rhett's are red and Riley's are black."

"Good observation, Zack," Rhett said. "Can I play another day? We need to get the car back."

"Tomorrow?"

"You'll have to ask your mom, buddy."

"Can they, Mom? Can they come over tomorrow?"

"We'll see." Darlene fussed with the throw draped over the back of the couch, straightening and smoothing the fabric.

"We'll come back, dude." Riley held up his fist, and Rhett followed suit. Zack knuckle-bumped each in turn.

Once in the car, Riley became Mr. Curious. "You get your whistle waxed?"

Rhett snorted. "No."

"You were in the kitchen long enough. Everything cool?" Riley pressed.

"Yeah." Rhett felt his brother's eyes on him, but he stayed silent for a few moments, staring through the windshield. "You ever make a girl come?"

"Uh, I doubt it." Riley chuckled. "They always act like they might have, but you never know, do you?"

"I do."

"How do you know?"

"They're just like us," Rhett said. "Their legs go all stiff and their pussy seizes up, their muscles jerk a little, and then they go kind of limp."

"You didn't screw her in there, did you?"

"No, hand job. It's easier than I thought." Rhett raised his middle finger from the steering wheel and rotated it in a tiny circle.

"Huh. Cool," Riley acknowledged. "I'm serious, dude. You gotta get me in on the action."

Rhett shrugged dismissively. He could feel his brother's gaze boring through the side of his skull, but Riley remained silent.

That couldn't be good.

16. Trespasses

O n Thursday morning, Ellie stepped into the basement storage room Sylvia had designated for stockpiling groceries and took stock of the assorted junk there. A few minutes later, Walker joined her, and the pipe organ sang to life over their heads.

"How's everything with you?" Ellie asked as she sorted through Christmas decorations – garlands, electric candles, pageant costumes, a jumble of old and worn-out lights.

"Fine. Why?"

"Oh, just wondering."

"Come on, Mom, spit it out," Walker prompted. He retrieved a black garbage bag and began stuffing items Ellie identified as trash into it.

"Are you and..." – she pointed upward with an index finger – "...getting along okay?"

"Pretty much. Why?" Walker's voice betrayed a sudden note of tension. He yanked at an extension cord and a bundle of Christmas lights landed at his feet.

"Sylvia ran into him at the rectory on Saturday evening."

"Yeah, he was helping the priest move."

Ellie straightened and regarded her son. She was jumping into the wrong breach as well as jumping to conclusions, but she and Walker had always been close, and she'd never hesitated to share her thoughts with him.

"I was there all day, and I never saw him."

Walker's mouth became a tight line, and he bent down to pick at the heap of tangled electrical cords. "Dammit," he hissed.

Ellie decided to ignore the curse, despite their presence in the church. "I'm sorry, honey. I thought it was strange is all. It doesn't mean...Sylvia just – "

"Let it go, Mom," he snapped. "Forget it."

Walker wasn't always easy to read, but Ellie could feel the anger rolling off him. She had just pointed out that his boyfriend was lying to him, and knowing Stephen, it was the tip of the iceberg. Okay, so she *was* meddling, but she'd remained oblivious for too many years with Walker's father to watch her son choose the same destructive path. It wasn't in her to keep her mouth shut.

"Look at this." She beckoned Walker over. "Behind these boxes, doesn't this look like a bed?" Faded purple curtains, once a backdrop to the altar, had been arranged into a pallet. "It's indented in the shape of a body, and this bunched up fabric looks like a pillow."

"Yeah, somebody slept here. I wonder who."

"Help me move the curtains," Ellie said. "We'll donate them to Goodwill."

Walker grabbed at the disheveled pile and shook the first drape loose. Something dropped to the floor, and Ellie picked it up.

"What is it?"

"A veteran's medical ID for a 'Franklin Crawford,'" Ellie read. "How do you suppose it got here?"

"The guy probably wandered in off the street. Or maybe he came to an AA or NA meeting. I don't recognize his picture."

"We'll be locking this room from now on." Ellie tucked the card in her pocket.

She and Walker worked for another hour sorting, bagging, and making piles. Several times she attempted conversation, but her son remained silent – brooding, no doubt.

The pipe organ stopped, and a short time later, steps sounded on the stairs.

"How's it going down here? Are you done working, or should I come back later?" Stephen smirked from the doorway.

Ellie saw Walker's face tighten. "Hi, Stephen," she said. "Excuse me, please. I need to talk to Sylvia." She brushed by him on her way out, maintaining a carefully neutral expression.

≈ ≈ ≈

"You lied to me!" Walker accused.

Not this again, Stephen thought with annoyance as he entered the basement bunker. He said, "It's not my fault everybody was gone by the time I got to the rectory."

Walker heaved a ball of fabric at Stephen's head. "You didn't go there to help."

Stephen threw up his arms to block the purple velvet, then ran his fingers through his faux hawk. It had taken ten minutes to sculpt it that morning, effort that was now completely wasted.

"You went to see the priest, and I seriously doubt you had God on your mind. Do you want him? Is that it?"

Walker began popping his knuckles one by one, a habit that drove Stephen mad.

"I told you, I don't even know that he's queer." Stephen slouched against a stack of boxes. The words didn't sound as convincing as he'd intended.

"Well, my mom thinks so, or she wouldn't have brought it up."

Stephen watched as the 225-pound hunk of muscle he called his boyfriend stalked toward him, biceps straining the armholes of his T-shirt. The man's physical presence was not something you could ignore, his sexual allure like a gravitational pull. Walker stopped in front of him, his body so close that his heat warmed Stephen's front. His stomach flipped.

"Damn it, Stephen, I don't want to do this again. Are we finished?" Walker's voice wavered on the last word, and he cleared his throat.

At that moment, Stephen wanted nothing less than he wanted that. He straightened and inched forward, barely resisting the urge to press himself against the solid mass of Walker's torso and beg for a pass. "No, of course not. Anyway, I barely saw him. Sylvia was there, and they were leaving."

"My point is that you lied about it, which means you had something to hide. Just tell me what you want."

Stephen stared into Walker's face, strained with emotion, and watched his boyfriend's frustration rise. How should he know what he wanted? It changed all the time.

Without warning, Walker grabbed the sides of Stephen's head and kissed him hard, held him there in a vice grip, then abruptly shoved him away.

Hot.

Stephen stood motionless for five full seconds, his entire body tingling with arousal. Then he pivoted and left the room. Walker was being all pissy about him spending time with Arthur, but how could he help it? They worked together. Well, sort of. Walker would just have to get over it.

Stephen headed outside and lit a cigarette. He'd never known a man as butch as Walker who didn't screw around. Hell, infidelity was practically the definition of a gay man. No queer couples he knew were entirely monogamous, except the fat, ugly ones who couldn't get anybody else. He wasn't fucking the priest anyway. Maybe a little fantasy now and then. Whatever.

So Arthur is *gay.*

Stephen sucked hard on his Camel Light, pondering that.

≈ ≈ ≈

Sylvia hung up the phone as Arthur emerged from his office. "That was Harold Tinkerton," she said. "Louis passed away. Poor Betty."

"How's she doing?"

"Harold said as well as can be expected which, I take it, is not well at all. They're requesting the funeral for Monday."

Arthur nodded in assent and returned silently to his office.

"Ellie," Sylvia said when her friend came in, "Louis Tinkerton died last night."

"Oh...poor Betty."

"Yes." Sylvia sighed. "How's the project going downstairs?"

"I came up to talk to you about it. Someone's been sleeping in the storage room. We found a makeshift bed and this ID."

Sylvia looked at the medical card and pursed her lips. "I was right about him."

"Why? Who's Franklin Crawford?"

"Frank. He's one of Larry's down-and-outers, working for him the last few weeks. I told Larry to find out where he was sleeping. He doesn't have family around here that I know of."

"It doesn't appear he's done any harm."

"This proves he's a veteran, but still...I trust him about as far as I could throw him." Sylvia snapped the card onto her desktop. "You probably saw him on moving day at the rectory. He's got a scar from his forehead clear down his cheek."

"Oh, I remember him now. He looked like he's had some hard knocks."

"Well, he can't sleep in the church," Sylvia said crossly. "I'll be talking to my husband about this. I hope nothing is missing from storage. Let's go look." She rose to lead the way but stopped when Arthur motioned to her. "Be there in a minute," she said to Ellie.

Sylvia joined Arthur in his office where he unfolded a piece of paper and handed it to her. "Love, Martha," Sylvia read aloud when she reached the end of the note. "She left food in your refrigerator again?"

Arthur nodded. "And ten messages on the answering machine. I wanted to ask your advice before responding."

Sylvia sighed. "I'm sorry to say that Martha is incapable of taking a hint. She'll keep calling until she's told not to. Then she'll probably call some more."

"I thought I'd phone her and explain that I'm available for spiritual consultation at the church, and that the rectory phone is for after-hours emergencies."

"It's a start, but I doubt the problem will end there. I'll call a locksmith today to have the locks changed," Sylvia said. "When you talk to her, you might want to remind her it's a criminal offense to enter a private home without an invitation."

Arthur smiled ruefully.

≈ ≈ ≈

"I promise you, Syl, I asked Frank where he was sleeping, and he told me at the shelter," Larry said later when Sylvia showed him the ID card from the church basement. He grabbed a bottle of Kentucky Ale from the fridge, twisted off the top, and took a long gulp, then wiped his mouth with the back of his hand.

"Well, you need to talk to him again. I don't want him living in the church, and I'm sure the Vestry would agree with me. It's not kosher and, personally, I don't think it's safe. I don't trust him hanging around where kids go to Sunday School and people come to pray and feel comforted. I tell you, he gives me the creeps, Larry." Sylvia shuddered.

"Oh, he's all right. He's been through a lot, fought in the Gulf and all. He works with my crew, and I've had no complaints about him on the job. He drinks, sure, but how many good ol' boys do you know who don't?" He raised his beer bottle toward her and grinned, then took another swig.

"I'm not telling you what to do. Just make it clear he's not welcome at the church unless he's attending a service."

"I'll talk to him, darlin'. With what I'm paying him, he should be able to afford a motel if he doesn't like the shelter."

"Well, here's his VA medical card, which he might need, particularly if he crosses me."

"I'd like to cross you," Larry drawled. He set his beer on the counter, grabbed Sylvia's outstretched arm and yanked her toward him. He clutched her rear end with both hands, trapping her against his body. "Come on, I just showered."

"I need to make supper," she protested. "The boys will be home soon."

"They can wait. Or they can make a sandwich. I got some marital rights need exercisin'."

"Later," Sylvia said firmly as she tried to squirm out of her husband's embrace.

Ignoring her objections, Larry leaned over and gave her a loud, juicy kiss. When she objected again, he gave her another and then another. The man was a charmer. What could she say?

Larry spun her in his arms and directed her toward their bedroom, his hands sneaking around to unbutton her blouse and lower the zipper on her slacks as he shuffled her along. She didn't let him see her smile.

17. The Least of These

"I'm not making accusations here," Larry said to Frank after work the next day, "but my wife found this in a storage room in the church basement."

Frank took the card Larry held out and glanced at it – his VA medical ID. He reached for the decrepit wallet in his back pocket.

"Here's a cheap, but decent, motel on Elm Street," Larry continued, holding out a business card. "They do weekly rentals. Tell Herb I sent you, and he'll give you a deal."

"Bluegrass Inn," Frank read, and with a nod, tucked both cards among the few greenbacks in his wallet. Maybe spending his pay on a room would help him cut down on the booze. At least he could stumble home after a cheap drunk without worrying about rednecks rolling him or cops hauling him to the lockup.

After renting a basic, but comfortable, room at the motel, Frank trekked the quarter mile to his new favorite drinking establishment. On his first visit, he'd dubbed the run-down house "Nutria's Nip Joint" because the hag who served the drinks had a face like one of those giant rats, complete with whiskers. He wasn't complaining – with his condition, sexy cocktail waitresses only led to misery.

Since finding the place, Frank had taken to visiting Nutria's Nip Joint after work to down half-a-dozen shots of moonshine before heading out to scrounge something to eat. But sometimes Nutria herself – whose real name was Ida Roach, he'd learned – would bring him a plate of butter beans with ham bone, or some okra and tomatoes with sausage, or hominy grits with bacon and greens, or sweet peas and new potatoes and a piece of fried catfish. He never had to ask. She just set the food in front of him and wouldn't accept more than a dollar a plate, seeming to know that Frank lived rough and didn't eat regularly.

The first time, he'd looked at her in surprise. "I didn't order this," he said, not prepared to pay for a meal.

She'd gazed sternly at him and pointed a bony finger at the plate, her message clear. After Frank took a bite and nodded his appreciation, she'd shuffled off satisfied.

Ida rarely spoke to her customers, just eyeballed them and waited for their liquor orders. If someone spoke to her, she might grunt or she might ignore him altogether. She wore an old-fashioned cotton housedress and apron like Granny from *The Beverly Hillbillies*. Frank half expected her to set down his plate and announce "Here's yer vittles!" She never did, but "dem vittles" were the best damn food he ate all week.

Frank had assumed Ida's moonshine was made by her litter of sons, the look-alike meatballs who provided security for the joint. So he was surprised to see a grizzled old hillbilly appear behind the bar on this evening. The man wore a pair of overalls with no shirt, and his pendulous man-breasts rested atop the outward curve of his spherical belly.

"Got yer load," he mumbled.

Ida gestured at the hulk guarding the side door to accompany the man out back. Through the doorway behind the bar, Frank observed them lifting plastic jugs of clear, fresh whiskey from the back of an ancient Ford pickup truck. Presumably, the old geezer with the gob of chaw ballooning his lower lip was Ida's distiller. The man was so stereotypically hillbilly that Frank could easily picture him with a shotgun in one hand and a corncob pipe in the other. He'd bet money the man kept both in his run-down truck.

Well, God bless him, whoever he was – he made some mighty fine whiskey.

≈ ≈ ≈

Arthur picked up the church membership directory. No point in putting off the call, which wouldn't get any easier. He'd been a priest for seventeen years, and had had ample opportunities for setting boundaries with parishioners. This intrusion wasn't so different from others, like the time a widow came for counseling a few years before, plopped herself on his lap, and professed her love, or when a seminary student showered him with long personal letters over a period of months, never actually saying what Arthur guessed he'd wanted to say. It was his job to concern himself with the welfare of others, and sometimes those starved for love misinterpreted his spiritual care.

"Hello, Miss Browne?"

"Father! I didn't think you'd *ever* call! Did you find the food I brought? I have lots of recipes you'd like. You're awful skinny and – "

"Excuse me, Miss Browne, but – "

"Call me Martha, Father, us being close and all. We don't have to be formal with each other."

"Miss Browne...Martha...I'm calling because – "

"I got your phone number from the bulletin board, and I was happy to find it because I tried to get your address for a long time and nobody would give it to me. That was before you moved into the rectory because I know where that is, of course, so I was glad when you – "

"Martha," he began, for clearly there would be no conversation if he didn't interrupt her, "the reason I'm calling is, first, to ask if you've had a spiritual crisis of some kind that requires – "

"Oh yes, Father, a crisis, yes! I've wanted to talk to you because I seen what happened – you know, what that girl did to you at the rectory. I know all about these sickos who think they can do whatever dirty, nasty thing they want, and how they take advantage of good, innocent peo – "

"Excuse me, Martha." Arthur was genuinely puzzled. "A girl did something to me?"

"Yes, Father. I didn't want to bring it up because it's embarrassing and all, the way she touched you, but I just-"

"Let me stop you right there. I'm afraid you're operating under a faulty assumption. Nothing improper happened at the rectory that I'm aware of, certainly not to me, as – "

"Oh, yes it did, Father, and it wasn't just that girl, either! The big titty girl – oops! – I didn't mean to say the T word."

The woman giggled, and if Arthur hadn't known better, he'd have guessed her age to be eleven or twelve years.

"That kid too, on Sylvia's desk," she went on, "I seen everything!"

From the woman's excitable but assured delivery, Arthur could believe she'd seen something. That it bore no relationship to reality, he also had no doubt. Nobody had reported trouble at the rectory except for Martha's own trespassing, and the idea that something untoward had happened on Sylvia's desk in Martha's presence was silly. Of course, it didn't mean these concerns weren't very real and disturbing to this woman. Cases like hers required special handling.

"Martha, listen. I don't want you to worry about anything you think you saw at the rectory or – "

"No, I *did* see, Father! I *did* see."

"Okay, then. Now that you've told me, I think it's important for your wellbeing that you let go of your worries. I'm going to pray that God grants you peace, and I want you to take a moment to offer these concerns to Him. Let Him take the burden from you. Can you do that?"

"I'll try, Father. But what that girl did to you was awful!"

"I promise you, Martha, anything that has ever happened to me is already in God's hands."

The line went silent. Arthur waited in silence too until he heard a muted "Okay, Father," then he offered a prayer for the troubled woman.

After hanging up, he considered what had just transpired. He'd failed to address both the trespassing issue and Martha's repetitive phone calls to the rectory. His intuition had been correct, though. She was having a spiritual crisis. Whether her troubles were real or delusional, they were causing great anxiety, and he hoped he'd helped set her mind at ease.

Unfortunately, Martha's distress fell into a category of problems that remained stubbornly resistant to Arthur's form of comfort. It had taken years to develop and learn to control his gift, and as he grew more capable at channeling the light, he also became more impatient with his inability to heal certain kinds of suffering. Unless it arose from an organic cause, like a degenerative disease or a tumor, mental illness had always proved difficult to resolve. Temporary relief was the best he could offer in most cases, a calming energy. He prayed often for the humility to accept his limitations.

On a more practical level, new door locks would prevent Martha from entering the rectory uninvited. If she continued to make excessive phone calls, Arthur would simply request that she stop.

≈ ≈ ≈

Martha knew it. Father had more or less admitted that Joanne groped him and that he'd just prayed instead of doing anything about it. He'd told her to leave things to God, but in her experience, God didn't always punish evildoers, and they ought to be punished. Still, Father had asked her, as his good friend, to let it go, and so she would. She'd be keeping her eye on that girl, though, because her kind always reoffended. They kept lists for people like her.

Martha had taken food to Father's house two days ago, but she had lots of recipes to try on him, and a man needed variety in his menu. She busied herself in her kitchen and by two o'clock had finished baking chicken noodle casserole and bread pudding with Bourbon sauce.

She set the dishes aside to cool and went to dress. Father might not be home, but it never hurt to look pretty.

Martha rolled back on her bed to catch her feet in the waistband of her hot pink leggings and shoved her legs through. Then she rocked until the momentum pitched her forward onto her feet so she could finish the procedure. Pulling her matching pink shirt over her head, she saw it had shrunk in the dryer, for it was riding too high in the front. Unless she hunched her shoulders forward, her bouncy belly flesh was exposed.

"Oh well," she said, brushing it off. "Girls wear shorty T-shirts all the time."

At the rectory, Martha trudged up the sidewalk carrying her baking dishes. She pressed the doorbell, but as usual, no one answered, so she set down the dishes and opened the screen door.

"Father, Father!" She rattled the doorknob, but it was locked. "Well, I *never*." What was the world coming to when a priest had to lock the rectory?

Maybe there'd been robbers in the neighborhood. She rummaged around until she found a stack of newspapers for recycling, then artfully concealed her baking pans underneath it. As she drove away, she prayed that the robbers wouldn't steal the food before Father got home.

18. Scheming

Riley set to work on his new Converse All Stars – red ones – scuffing and soiling them to match Rhett's worn-in high-tops. He sandpapered the toes, ran them through the washer and dryer, then rubbed them with dirt.

On the day of Father Arthur's barbecue, he washed his hair and parted it on the left, same as Rhett's. Wearing opposite parts had always been their little joke, contrived evidence of a burning need to differentiate themselves from one another. It amused them because, of course, each twin knew both himself and his brother perfectly well, so they'd never felt less than unique.

Looking identical, though, had its uses.

≈ ≈ ≈

Rhett tried to act casual at the rectory barbecue, but he found it hard to ignore the way Darlene's hips swayed in her snug jeans as she moved around the yard talking to people – Darius's mom and her girlfriend, Father Arthur, his parents. He had to stop looking at her, though, because someone was bound to notice the pole perpetually tenting his pants.

Darlene headed toward the house, and Rhett waited a discreet sixty seconds before following her. When she emerged from the bathroom, he was waiting.

"Rhett?" Darlene glanced at his shoes.

"Who else would I be?" He smirked and moved toward

her. She backed through the doorway, and he nudged her into the bathroom wall.

"Not here!" Darlene croaked in a whisper. "Somebody will – "

Rhett pressed his lips to hers. Darlene raised her hands as if to push him away, but then didn't.

"I missed you," he murmured in her ear, then breathed in the vanilla scent of her hair.

"Oh, Rhett, this ain't – "

He kissed her again, and she let him, hesitating only a moment before tangling her tongue with his in a thrill of taste and sensation. He grabbed her butt and pressed into her, her soft gasp triggering instinctive movements in his hips. He groaned as his balls tightened against his body.

"...the cook in that household." The woman's voice floated down the hall to the accompaniment of the glass door sliding in its track.

Rhett jumped back.

"We'd better go outside," Darlene whispered. "You first. Ah'll wait a bit, then follow."

Rhett glanced at his crotch. The scare had deflated his dick enough to prevent embarrassment.

"Okay, but I have to see you." He caught her eye before lowering his gaze to the soft cotton that hugged her breasts and allowed her nipples to poke through. *Gawd,* she was hot!

Rhett turned away, impatient and frustrated. He wasn't sure how much longer he could take it. He had to get her naked – soon.

≈ ≈ ≈

"You and your kids are coming to the barbecue, right?" Arthur had confirmed with Kendra Washington the day before when she rang up his groceries at the Piggly Wiggly.

"Wouldn't miss it. Okay if I bring a plus one?" she'd asked.

"Sure, there'll be plenty of food."

Arriving home, Arthur had discovered two covered dishes hidden under a pile of newspapers on his porch and, guessing where they'd come from, had locked his new deadbolt after going inside. Martha Browne had felt free to enter the house on multiple occasions when he wasn't there, so she probably wouldn't hesitate to come in when he was. He'd never been stalked before, and the sensation was distinctly uncomfortable.

From his vantage point at the grill, he scanned the company gathered in his backyard. Everyone had arrived except for Walker Jones.

"Go out for a long one!"

Arthur looked toward the rear of the property where Kendra's guest, a forty-something woman named Geneva Goldman, was throwing a football with Kendra's two boys and one of the Pugh twins. Sylvia had told him that Kendra joined their church after divorcing her husband, a minister in the A.M.E. Zion Church.

Larry Pugh sat at the picnic table talking with Joanne Bowman and her parents, and Ellie Jones and Kendra stood nearby chatting with Sylvia. Stephen Harken was ostensibly helping Arthur with the barbecue, though his wariness of both the gas grill and the cooking utensils made his contribution more conversational than functional.

"So Walker couldn't make it?" Arthur asked.

"He's working overtime but might drop by later." Stephen fiddled with the mass of braided leather and cord bracelets wound around his left wrist.

"Arthur," Ellie called. "Do you want us to bring things from the kitchen?"

"Yes, let's do that. Will you watch the grill for a minute, Stephen?"

A look of alarm crossed the organist's face. "Um...sure, I guess."

Arthur handed Stephen the tongs. "The meat needs to cook with the lid closed for a while, but yell if you see any flames."

"Are you teasing him?" Ellie whispered as she followed Arthur to the house.

Arthur winked at her and smiled. "He seems a bit out of his element."

Ellie chuckled. "Walker's the cook in that household."

The two stepped through the sliding door and headed to the kitchen.

A few moments later, one of the Pugh twins appeared.

"Hello, Rhett. Or is it Riley?" Arthur said.

"Rhett. I was just using the bathroom."

Arthur directed Ellie – who conscripted Rhett, and Darlene when she showed up – to the linens, condiments, and salads, then went outside to check the meat. He found Stephen standing six feet from the grill, arms crossed, looking everywhere but at the cooker, which was venting smoke through its top.

Arthur picked up a hot pad. "How's the chicken doing?"

"Uh...it's still there," Stephen said and bent to flick something from his pointy-toed shoe.

≈ ≈ ≈

Martha's exasperation faded and her anxiety increased by the hour. She'd been calling the rectory since Friday after dropping off her casserole, and by Saturday afternoon, Father still hadn't picked up the phone. She was worried sick.

"Where is he? Did he slip in the bathtub? Is he hurt? Is he *dying?*"

She didn't know how many times she'd phoned, but on the last few calls all she got was an irritating voice that declared, "Mailbox is full," followed by a click.

"If I wanted to send mail, I'd write a letter!" she yelled into the receiver before slamming it down. "What should I do? What should I *do?*"

What she'd wanted to do all day was drive over to the rectory and see Father, but she didn't want to appear too forward. She'd been taught that girls who were too forward got bad reputations and a girl's reputation was all she had. It must be guarded like gold.

At sixty-six, Martha was proud to still be unspoilt, something her Daddy had stressed after her momma died. He'd taken it upon himself to educate her from age twelve about how to stay pure. For her part, she never understood why it was okay for a boy to put his thingy in one place and not another, or why it hurt so much, though her Daddy – and later, Floyd – seemed to like it. According to the Reverend Brown, those were God's edicts from the Bible. Girls had to suffer because Eve ate a bad apple. It didn't make sense really. She didn't even like apples. Also, it always seemed to her that "down there" should be her private business. When she said that, her Daddy told her it was private outside the family, not inside.

"What we do at home stays at home," he'd said, looming over her with his scary face.

Her Daddy had eventually lost interest in educating her, but Floyd took up where Gideon left off and kept at it for years. That didn't seem right. In the first place, she already knew everything, and in the second place, she'd started to think her Daddy had misunderstood what God meant.

Father Arthur was a man of God, but nothing like the Reverend Gideon Brown. Nothing at all.

"I'm going over there right now!" Martha decided. She had to visit the rectory to make sure Father hadn't fallen in the bath. "If not me, then who?"

It took her most of an hour to get ready. The zipper of her favorite party dress wouldn't pull closed in the back, so she left it open and clipped the top edges together with a clothespin. With her Dolly Parton curls covering it at the neck, the dress would look like it was supposed to be open-backed. Showing a little skin was allowed on a Saturday, wasn't it?

After donning her wig, Martha applied green eye shadow and Provocative Pink lipstick. Her Daddy had always said that only whores wore red lipstick and nice girls didn't wear makeup at all, but the longer Gideon had been gone, the more sure she became that he hadn't necessarily been right about everything.

Outside the rectory, Martha began to lever herself from her car, felt a tug, and heard the sound of fabric ripping. Unwilling to restart the difficult maneuver, she continued pulling herself up before turning to survey the damage. The foot-wide lace ruffle at the bottom of her dress had caught on the seat adjustment lever and pulled loose. To avoid bending over, she snatched at her skirt and yanked. The lace tore in half, setting her free.

"My party dress!" she moaned. She could reattach the ruffle, but the tear would be tricky to mend.

She let the fabric drop and saw that a swath of lumpy flesh lay newly exposed at the back of her thighs. It wasn't attractive, but at least the trailing lace resembled a train, which made the dress look more formal. She was determined to ignore her troubles anyway because Father's welfare was at stake.

Since it was an emergency, Martha didn't waste time with the doorbell, just pushed her way through the front door. Thank goodness it wasn't locked.

"Father! Father, are you here? Father, are you okay?" Martha shuffled down the hallway and peeked into the bathroom.

"Hasn't fallen in the tub," she muttered. Few people realized that three-hundred-some Americans died every year when they slipped and hit their heads on bathroom fixtures, seven or eight people per state. How many deaths had Kentucky chalked up for the year?

Martha made her way through the master bedroom and discovered another bathroom, which was also empty. Where was he then? Reversing direction and retracing her steps, she heard laughter and followed the noise to the dining room where she peered through the glass door into the backyard.

"It's a party!"

Martha patted her Dolly wig and glanced down at herself, pleased she'd had the foresight to wear her prettiest dress. She shoved the door aside and trundled down the steps.

There he was, standing at an open barbecue grill. Fragrant steam rose from the meat, and Martha's mouth watered.

"Father!"

The priest looked her way, and clearly, he was excited to see her because his mouth dropped open and his eyes got big.

"I called and called," she hollered toward him. "I was so worried about you!"

She didn't spare a glance for the other people milling around. Father was wearing his clerical collar and a black clerical shirt with the sleeves rolled up to reveal muscled forearms dusted with light brown hair. He was so dignified. So *handsome.*

≈ ≈ ≈

Uh oh.

Watching Martha Browne approach across the grass, Arthur became aware of his mounting distaste for the troublesome woman, followed by an almost knee-jerk impulse to shower her with kindness. She was the sort of wretched soul Christ embraced in his ministry – outcast, unloved, out of step with her community. She was certainly a challenge and no doubt could teach him about patience and acceptance and loving those who are not easy to love.

"Miss Browne?" Arthur closed the grill and moved toward her, an oversized fork in his hand.

"I thought you were hurt! You didn't answer the phone. And it's *Martha,* Father."

Before Arthur could decide how to respond, Sylvia Pugh had darted over, her annoyance evident. "What are you doing here?"

"That's none of your business. I'm here for Father. I thought he was dead in the bathtub. Nobody answered the phone."

"Martha," Sylvia said quietly but firmly, "you are harassing Father Endicott, and it has to stop. You have to stop calling the rectory, and you especially have to stop trespassing. Don't you know it's illegal to enter someone's house without an invitation?"

"You don't know what you're talking about!" Martha snapped. "Father could have been dead, and nobody would know. I had to check on him."

"Miss Browne," Arthur said, "I believe – "

Martha's eyes went wide and wild a second before she screamed. Arthur flinched, then turned to see what had provoked her. Behind him, Joanne Bowman stood gripping the edge of the picnic table. She began to shake visibly.

"Let's go inside," Greta said, grasping her daughter's arm and directing her toward the house.

"What's *she* doing here?" Martha screeched.

"Martha, calm down," Sylvia ordered. "What are you going on about?"

"It's that girl, that bad girl! Father knows."

Ellie Jones stepped over and, along with Sylvia and Arthur, formed a protective wall between Martha and the other dinner guests.

"Are you referring to Joanne Bowman?" Arthur kept his voice low and his arms at his sides. Experience had taught him that the best way to handle a disturbed person was to project an exaggerated sense of calm.

"Yes, that girl ... that *Joanne*."

"Joanne and her parents are my guests," he pointed out.

Sylvia gave Martha a hard look. "You need to leave now. And I insist that you quit dropping by the rectory and bothering Arthur with phone calls."

"But I had to see if he got my chicken noodle casserole," Martha whined.

"Martha," Arthur said solemnly, and she turned to him, "as you can see, I'm perfectly fine, so you have nothing to worry about. And yes, I did find the food. Now let me escort you to your car."

She let him take her elbow, and he guided her around the side of the house while consciously throttling the flow of energy to his hands, a long-established, necessary habit, particularly when he was emotionally aroused. Channeling the light was a sacrament to be administered only when he was spiritually prepared, for it had a destructive side as well as a beneficial one.

"Father, I've been so worried about you and that Joanne. And you're not eating enough. You don't have anyone to look after you."

It was time to be firm with Martha Browne if Arthur had any hope of halting her unwelcome incursions into his private life. It also wasn't kind to let her retain false impressions or indulge in fantasies where he was concerned.

"Martha," he said, measuring his words, "I appreciate your concern. Thank you for that." He waited to make sure she'd received the positive message.

"You're welcome, Father," she responded sweetly, suddenly the bashful schoolgirl.

"Now, to protect our relationship going forward, I must ask you to express your concern a little differently." Arthur caught her eye to be sure she was listening. "First, the rectory phone is intended for after-hours church business rather than social calls, so I would prefer that you use it only for emergencies."

Martha's smile drooped, but Arthur held her gaze and continued. "Second, it would be best if you shared your gift for cooking at church events rather than bring food to the rectory."

Martha's forehead and penciled-on eyebrows scrunched downward, causing the immobile blond hairdo above to lift slightly off her scalp.

"Finally," Arthur concluded, "if you require private counseling, I would ask that you schedule an appointment by calling Sylvia. That's the best way for me to help you with any spiritual difficulties you might be experiencing." He saw the shadow of hurt cross Martha's face before it turned to anger.

"Well, if you don't want to talk to me, then I won't call you anymore or cook for you either. It's easier for me if I don't," she said tartly, her whole face screwed into a scowl.

"As your priest, I'm available to talk with you in my office." Arthur ignored his natural impulse to soften his stance, which could muddy the waters. "If you'd like to stop by the church this week to retrieve your baking dishes, Sylvia can make an appointment for you at that time."

He opened the door of Martha's classic Cadillac and held her elbow while she dropped heavily into the seat, her lips pressed to a thin line.

"I hope I'll see you at services tomorrow," Arthur said sincerely. "Please drive safely."

Martha didn't look at him, but as she pulled away, he noticed two strips of fabric flapping from the bottom of the car door like toilet paper streamers.

He contemplated the situation as he returned to his guests. Parishioners often sought friendship with their priest, but it was important for their welfare that he trod carefully. Martha Browne was expressing needs that could only be met through the healing power of God, and as a conduit, he could facilitate that to a point, but a controlled setting was vital.

Arthur sighed. It wasn't the first time he'd missed having the social buffer of a Mrs. Endicott in his life. But those days were behind him now.

In his absence, Joanne's father had taken charge of the grill. The other guests were filling their plates and finding places to sit.

"That woman is quite the character," John Bowman remarked as he and Arthur sat down in adjacent lawn chairs.

"Martha? Yes. She needs a friend, I think."

"Looks to me like she's chosen you for that honor." John didn't smile, but Arthur detected the amused twinkle in his eye.

He grunted. Despite his personal feelings toward Martha Browne, his calling required him to care for each of God's children to the best of his ability. Even the most difficult had lessons to teach.

19. Skirmishes

Darlene had to get away for a few minutes. The barbecue was stressing her out. She didn't think anyone had seen her and Rhett together in the bathroom, but every time she looked at Sylvia, guilt twisted her stomach. For half a second, she considered how she would feel if she found Sylvia kissing her son, and she shuddered. *Ick!* But it wasn't the same thing. Zack really was a child, and that would be unlawful.

"Shoot!" she exclaimed when her match guttered out.

She stood in the large gap between the juniper tree and the front corner of Arthur's house where she was hidden from both the street and the backyard. She didn't particularly care if others saw her smoke, but she didn't want to explain herself to Zack. Her son had harped at her for weeks to quit, and she *had* quit. She wasn't prepared to tell him that she had *un*-quit – or admit it to herself either.

She struck another match and tried to shield it from the breeze as she lit her cigarette. She was struggling with her third match when masculine hands reached around from behind her and cupped the fragile flame.

Finally! Darlene inhaled deeply and savored the nicotine buzz to her brain for a few seconds. Then she glanced down to see red sneakers bracketing her sandaled feet. She swiveled to find her young beau wearing what rednecks called a shit-eatin' grin.

"Hi."

How he made that one syllable sound so sexy, Darlene had no idea. Blood rushed to her groin, and she swallowed a whimper. She had to forget about what had happened in her kitchen with Rhett and put a stop to this madness before it went any further.

"Hi, your own self."

He lowered his eyes to her chest, and she felt her face flush.

"What?" she demanded.

"I was just admiring your shirt."

She had on a simple knit top, pink, with a modest scoop neckline. "There ain't nothin' special about it."

"It fits real nice," he said, still with that smile.

"You're gonna get us in trouble followin' me around like this."

"Can I have a drag?"

Darlene handed him the cigarette. He inhaled, then began to cough.

"That's all for you!" she said, taking it back.

"I didn't come out here for a cigarette." He waited for Darlene to take another drag before he snatched it away, then dropped it in the dirt, and ground it out with his scuffed red toe.

"Rhett! Ah wasn't finished w – "

He stoppered her mouth with his and pressed his tongue between her lips. This kiss was different, harder and more demanding than before. The intensity of it – its *fury* if she had to put a word to it – caught her off guard, and despite her resolve, she responded. She sank into him, releasing her tension and pent-up emotion in an outpouring of desire. He dove in with unselfconscious zeal, tasted her thoroughly, and danced his tongue around hers. His hands squeezed and caressed her bottom, and she explored his lean, denim-covered butt in return.

They stopped to gasp for air, but their hands kept moving, hers up his sides and over his shoulders into his thick hair, then down to his chest; his up her back, around her ribs, and up to her breasts. He cupped them, one in each hand, as he backed her against the scratchy bricks. She moaned into his kiss, and her fingers dipped behind the waistband of his loose-fitting jeans.

He groaned and shoved his hands under her shirt. He slipped her bra straps off her shoulders and tugged at the cups, lodging the cloth under her breasts like a corset. As his tongue probed her mouth, he rubbed and toyed with her tender nipples until they were taut and sharp.

Darlene could barely breathe. She should *stop this now,* but the pressure on her nipples sent rushes of sensation through her lower belly, causing pleasurable spasms below. Stopping was impossible. She pressed into the hard ridge of his erection to ease her need, then hurriedly unbuttoned and unzipped his jeans. Without thinking, she reached inside to caress him, and he groaned at her touch, thrilling Darlene with the force of his arousal.

"Fuck," he gasped.

After a few breathless moments, her young stud grabbed the hem of her shirt, shoved it up, and unclipped the front clasp of her bra. Her freed breasts dropped into his hands, and he massaged them eagerly, then bent over and sucked a nipple into his mouth, tugging hard.

A loud cry escaped her before she could stifle it. He laid into her then, sensitizing her nipples with his lips and tongue while she stroked him rhythmically with her hand.

Before long, he straightened and let his cheek fall against her hair.

"I'm *coming* ..." he moaned, making no effort to pull away.

Darlene kept stroking, holding her breath in excited anticipation.

He froze, then gasped, and Darlene felt his cock pulse in her hand. She held him until he went still, then swiped her hand over a juniper branch. His arms rested on her shoulders, and his head sagged onto the top of hers.

They remained still for several moments. Then he bent down and kissed her. She pulled up his briefs and felt him harden again.

"I wanna touch you," he whispered in her ear. "I wanna rip off your panties and stick my fingers in your pussy."

Darlene shivered and felt his palm press against her vulva, pushing and rubbing in a rhythmic motion. Cripes! It felt good.

He continued massaging her through her jeans as he rolled and pulled at her left nipple. Tension built between her legs, her breaths shortened, and her heart raced.

"Feel good?" he whispered.

She nodded and inhaled his spicy scent. She couldn't come like this, but she didn't want him to stop. He bent down to suckle her right nipple and then she felt the snap and zipper of her jeans come undone. His fingers slid inside her lacy panties and one finger flicked against her clit.

"Oh!"

He flicked at her again, then began a rhythm of soft swipes until her moans became a series of "oh, oh, ohs," compressing into a single sound. As he kept at it, a tidal wave of pressure built in her groin, coiling inward deeper and tighter. She closed her eyes and dropped her head against the bricks as the exquisite tension built to a peak, teetered for a moment, then released all at once, her muscles clenching and clamping down in blissful sensation.

As the wave retreated, it took Darlene's knees with it, and she faltered but was held by a reassuring arm around her waist. He was so strong, so sexy, so...*yum.*

She caught a gleam of mischief in his eyes, and his lips curled into a smirk. She smirked too as she reached down to zip his jeans, then her own.

"Do up your button," she said as she fastened the clasp on her bra. She pulled down her top and hugged him tight.

"We better get back. People will notice us both missin'."

"Kiss me first," he insisted, then pressed his lips to hers. She enjoyed his taste and feel for a few seconds more before pushing him away.

"Seriously, you go on. Ah'll follow in a couple minutes." Darlene brushed her unsoiled hand across his and flicked her head in the direction of the backyard. He grinned once more, stepped from their hiding spot, and sauntered away, his hips carrying the weight of his jeans low and loose.

She crept from the bushes and made her way to the front door. Thank goodness it was unlocked. She wouldn't have to follow him and raise suspicions. She went to the bathroom to wash her hands and tidy her hair.

As she stepped through the sliding door to rejoin the party, Darlene saw Rhett scoop up the abandoned football and clap Zack on the shoulder before the two of them jogged to the rear of the yard. She watched him demonstrate how to hold the ball for punting, then Rhett's red shoe connected with the pigskin just as Riley, Darius, and Shane crossed the yard to join them.

Now there's husband material. That young man was going to make some girl really happy. Darlene flinched at the thought, then decided on the spot not to consider the future. She had no future with him, but she had the present, and it felt brighter than it had in a long while.

As she turned to join the adults, she heard a shout and caught a startling movement from the corner of her eye. She spun toward the commotion and saw Rhett bending over, holding a palm to his jaw. He jerked upright and charged his brother like a stag in a territorial dispute. Darius dove for him, but missed, and the twins clashed, fists flying. Zack and Shane pulled ineffectually at Rhett's shirt while Darius struggled to get between him and Riley.

Larry Pugh bolted through the yard to intervene, with Sylvia close on his heels. Darlene slapped her hands over her mouth.

Please don't let this have anything to do with me! Why it should, she wasn't sure, but guilt snaked through her gut. It probably happened all the time, though. *Brothers fight, right?*

Larry had the scuffle contained within a couple of minutes. He stood between his sons with a handful of gray T-shirt in each outstretched fist to keep the twins separated, their identical red faces screwed into anger. Darlene saw Sylvia bustling her way.

Uh oh! Darlene shivered in trepidation as her friend – *former friend?* – bore down. Then a throat cleared at her back, and much to her relief, she realized that Sylvia was aiming, not for her, but for the priest standing behind her.

"Arthur, we need to go," Sylvia told him. "Our boys have had a disagreement, and Larry's escorting them to the car. I'm sorry about this. We had a wonderful time and thoroughly enjoyed ourselves. I hope the Martha situation is cleared up."

Darlene busied herself collecting items from the picnic table. As she carried them toward the house, she saw a Pugh twin – Rhett, from his shoes – reappear at the far corner of the yard and discreetly wave goodbye. She smiled at him, then continued inside.

≈ ≈ ≈

The guests were dispersing. Sylvia and her family had gone, and Joanne and her parents left soon after. By the look on Joanne's face, Arthur could tell that Martha Browne's outburst had upset the younger woman.

What had Martha meant by referring to Joanne as a "bad girl" and implying some form of sexual misconduct? As far as he knew, Joanne hadn't ventured far from her parents' home since her stay at the hospital and would have had little opportunity for "badness" to take hold, even if she were the type. Given Martha's behavior toward him and her fixation on Joanne, the aging woman likely suffered from delusions. But though her behavior was distressing, especially to Joanne, it didn't cross the line into threatening or dangerous at a level requiring psychiatric intervention. If he discouraged Martha from dropping by the church when Joanne was working and talked to Joanne about avoiding Martha, perhaps future scenes could be averted. If not, he'd have to take more drastic steps to protect Joanne's fragile psyche.

Darlene came down the back steps toward him. "The cleanup is under control, so ah'm takin' Zack home, Arthur. Thank you for everythin'. The food was wonderful."

"You're welcome. I'm grateful for all your hard work on the rectory, which I'm enjoying immensely," he replied. Darlene wasn't of his flock, but that didn't prevent him from noticing how distracted she'd been all evening or how she'd kept one eye on her son constantly while he played football with the older boys.

Kendra and Geneva were rounding up their crew in preparation to leave. If the two women weren't so obviously unrelated by blood – one African American, the other white with a Jewish surname – Arthur might have thought they were sisters, the way they both took charge of Kendra's kids.

They're a couple! he realized abruptly, and though it shouldn't have made any difference, it pleased him all the same. Maybe one day he'd meet someone special too, possibly even find love. God forgive him, but he could also use an outlet for his sex drive, an ever-present distraction to his work. Acting on that would require more bravery than he'd felt since coming to Amity, and for the moment, it was easier to ignore it. But vigorous exercise – at home to avoid half-naked men in locker rooms – and sublimation into parish work had their limits.

After saying goodbye to the Washington-Goldman clan, Arthur went inside, passing the kitchen where Ellie chatted with someone, and headed down the hall to his private bathroom. Behind him, he heard the front door open, then close.

After washing his hands, he checked his watch. Saturdays were prime workdays for ministers, who had to prepare for Sunday services, but since most people socialized on the weekends, he frequently had to work around scheduled events. He still needed to review his sermon, "Forgiveness as Rebirth," before going to bed.

Already pondering the topic, he exited the bathroom and stopped short to see Stephen Harken slouching against one of the carved bedposts. A pile of jackets had covered the mattress earlier in the evening, but Stephen's black leather was the only one remaining.

Sylvia's warning about Stephen's pursuit of him leapt to mind, and Arthur decided that the best way to defuse it was not to acknowledge it as a possibility.

"Oh, hi Stephen," he said. "You're ready to leave, I see."

Arthur moved to retrieve the leather coat, but Stephen shoved off from the bedpost and blocked his path. "Actually, I've been waiting for everyone else to leave so I could have you to myself."

The brashness of the come-on rendered Arthur momentarily speechless. Stephen pressed forward then, circled his arms around the priest's neck, and crushed their lips together. Arthur froze and, in that suspended fraction of a second, registered a larger presence charging through his bedroom.

"Walker," he gasped, his mind slow to comprehend this turn of events, their cause and effect. He disentangled himself and stepped backward, but Walker thundered toward him like a freight train, all power and momentum.

Walker brushed Stephen aside and lunged, his right arm recoiling, fist clenched.

"No!" Stephen squealed.

Arthur saw the blow coming too late to evade it. He ducked, and Walker's knuckles plowed into his cheekbone instead of his jaw. He heard the crack an instant before he felt the pain. The power of the punch threw him against the wall where he remained, too stunned to escape the angry bull of a man winding up for a second blow.

"Walker Pervis Jones," a female voice commanded, "you stop right there."

Walker reacted instantly, turning away and pulling his punch, which glanced off Arthur's left ear without the force of the first one.

"Pervis?" Stephen squeaked.

Walker stormed from the room, and the front door slammed a few seconds later.

"Pervis?" Stephen repeated with a snort, then bent over in a fit of giggling.

Arthur was vaguely aware of someone else moving through the room. "Go home," the woman said.

But I am home. Oh, wait...

Through his haze, the priest heard, "I'm sorry, Arthur. It's just...." The sentiment, whatever it was, dissolved into gasps and giggles.

Hysteria. He identified Stephen's reaction, despite his own pain and confusion. Unfortunately, slapping the presumptuous twit, though satisfying perhaps, wouldn't be possible.

Arthur slid down the wall to rest on the floor. Had he passed out? The next thing he knew, cool hands peeled his fingers from his brow. He dragged his eyelids open to see Ellie Jones crouching next to him. They were alone.

"I'm a nurse. Let me see."

Arthur recorded her shock before she evened out her expression. It was bad, then. Blood trickled from his palm down his forearm, and he twisted his arm to keep it from dripping on the floor. He pushed himself shakily to his feet.

"First aid supplies?" Ellie said quietly.

"Hall closet."

Arthur stumbled to the bathroom and rinsed off the blood, then pressed a wet washcloth to his eye and returned to the bedroom. He sank to the bed as Ellie reappeared.

"Arthur, I don't know what to say." She sat next to him and dampened a gauze pad with disinfectant. The pungent aroma seared his nostrils and stabbed pain through his eye. "At least let me apologize for my son. Shall I call the police? Do you want to press charges?"

"No," he demurred, "it looks worse than it is." She dabbed at the cut on his brow, and he flinched at the sting.

"It's within your rights to have him arrested for assault."

"It's just a misunderstanding."

Ellie sighed. "I was tidying the kitchen when I heard the front door open. By the time I dried my hands, Walker had headed down the hall, looking for Stephen, I guess. I followed to tell him everyone had gone, but I didn't realize..." – discomfort flashed across her face – "...Stephen was back here with you."

Ellie discarded the bloody gauze, then rifled through the first aid supplies on her lap.

"Nor did I," Arthur said, resisting the urge to explain. How ironic that he was lamenting his lack of a sex life just a few minutes before the incident. Perhaps he'd drawn the unwanted advance, given off the wrong signals.

Thanks, Lord, but no thanks. Stephen's form of profligacy wasn't what he'd had in mind.

Ellie gazed at him curiously before smoothing a butterfly bandage over his eyebrow with a practiced hand. "That should stop the bleeding. Can you see out of your left eye?"

Arthur closed his right one and tried to focus on her through his swollen left lid. "I can see you."

"You might have a concussion. Shall I take you to the hospital?"

"That won't be necessary."

She patted his hand. "Lie down. I'll get some ice."

Arthur started to object, but pain lanced through his eye, so he took her advice. In a few minutes, she returned.

"Here, swallow these." She pressed some tablets into his palm and handed him a glass of water. He did as he was told. "Now hold this to your face."

Arthur took the ice pack and laid it over the tenderest spot.

"You're going to have one heck of a bruise tomorrow. And probably a black eye." She dragged a chair to the bed and sat down. "I'm so disgusted with those boys. I'd like to put them both over my knee, but theoretically, they're adults."

It occurred to Arthur that Ellie was chatting to keep him from dozing off, medical protocol for a blow to the head. He shut his eyes but tried to focus on her words.

"Shall I call Sylvia to find a substitute pastor for tomorrow? We can ask Father Donnelly in Cynthiana or enlist one of the lay ministers. Heaven knows we've had to make do these past couple of years."

Arthur opened his good eye. "Thanks, but no. I don't want to abandon the congregation when I've just arrived."

She studied him for a moment. "How will you explain your injured face?"

Arthur tried for levity. "Bar brawl?"

Ellie raised her eyebrows.

"Angry husband?"

She smiled wryly. "That might be a little too close to the truth."

Arthur sighed and closed his eye. "I'll just decline to explain."

"The gossip mill will be working overtime, you know."

"Par for the course, I'm afraid." He could feel Ellie hovering, so he opened his eye again.

"I'd leave you to rest," she said, "but I'm worried you might have a concussion. Are you sure you shouldn't see a doctor?"

"I'm sure. I ducked, so I don't think my brain banged around too much." Had that even made sense?

"I'll call you in an hour. Honestly, maybe I should stay and keep an eye on you tonight."

"That's very kind, Ellie, but I'll be fine, and I wouldn't want to fuel the rumor mill." Arthur offered a weak smile. "I'll see you tomorrow."

20. Aftermath

Against her better judgment, Ellie left Arthur with an ice pack and a bottle of Tylenol and headed for her car. She considered his comment about feeding rumors. If she stayed overnight at the rectory, someone would see her car parked at Arthur's curb and assume the obvious. Word would spread. Such was the nature of small towns.

What if people did think she was dallying with the priest? Ten years his senior, or thereabouts, she found the idea rather flattering. He was a handsome man, after all, desirable by anyone's standards.

Ellie dropped back to earth with an unladylike snort and jammed her key in the ignition. That's just what she needed, to be smitten with a gay man. Her husband, Geary, had died of undiagnosed AIDS, and Ellie had never recovered her equilibrium enough to marry again. Miraculously HIV-free, she'd turned to raising their two sons to be whom God meant them to be, gay or straight, and never to lie or apologize to anyone about that. As it turned out, she'd gotten one of each, Waylon straight and Walker gay. She loved them both but had always felt closer to Walker, who was so like his father with his too-soft heart wrapped in a shell of toughness and determination. He'd grown up strong and often combative, forced to defend himself for living honestly. Nothing could justify his behavior this evening, though.

She pulled up in front of Walker's house. Stephen's car wasn't there, so she marched to the front door and knocked. Walker opened the door and reluctantly ushered her into his living room.

"What the heck were you thinking?" she demanded.

"I don't know! I don't know!" Walker bellowed as he paced like a caged tiger.

"But you *must* know why you stomped in and punched a priest in the face."

"I screwed up, okay? Happy?" he clipped.

"No, I'm not happy. At the very least, you owe Arthur a huge apology. Do you realize he could have you arrested for assault? His cheek and eye are bruised, and he has a bad cut on his eyebrow."

"Arrgh," Walker groaned and collapsed onto the couch.

Ellie sat across from him and waited for an explanation, but none came. "I don't understand what came over you," she pressed. "Do you have a problem with Arthur?"

Walker exhaled like a steam engine through puckered lips. "I came late," he said to the ceiling, "but Stephen's car was still there, so I went in to find him. I heard him talking, walked down the hall, and when I looked in the bedroom..." – he paused and lowered his eyes to meet hers – "...they were kissing."

Oh. Arthur hadn't mentioned that, but it took her less than a second to realize what had likely happened. "Honey, I don't think – "

"You said Stephen went to the rectory last Saturday night too."

"Yes, but Arthur didn't invite him," Ellie said. "Look, I don't know what you saw, but do you really think our priest is trying to steal your boyfriend? Does that make any sense, knowing Arthur?"

"I don't really know Arthur," Walker retorted.

She said, more gently, "Knowing Stephen, then?" She saw the hurt register on her son's face.

He looked away. "I suppose not."

"Then you have to do the right thing. He's our new rector. And for what it's worth, I think he's a good man."

Walker buried his face in a throw pillow and growled, then tossed it aside. "I guess I made a mistake."

"A big one. I dread seeing Arthur's battered face at church in the morning. I have no idea how he's going to explain it."

Walker dropped his head back against the couch. "Crap, it's my fault." He cracked several knuckles in succession.

"Yes, it is. So fix it if you can." Ellie squeezed her son's shoulder before moving to the front door. "Stephen's here," she said, peeking through the glass. "I'll go."

≈ ≈ ≈

After Ellie left the rectory, Arthur debated what to do. She'd witnessed his injuries, but despite the implications, he preferred not to address the congregation with a black eye and a fist imprint on his cheek. Better one person asking unanswerable questions than dozens doing so. Ellie would think what she would. He trusted her, in any case.

He slid to his knees beside the bed. The movement renewed the stabbing pain in his head, and he fought it for several seconds. Then he clasped his hands and began to pray. He prayed for Walker and Stephen, that they might mend their fences. He prayed for Martha Browne, that her lonely torment might be eased. He prayed for Betty Tinkerton who'd lost her husband of fifty years. Then he prayed that, through God's grace, he might facilitate spiritual renewal and healing for those who sought it on the morrow.

But tonight he must heal himself. Still on his knees, his forearms resting on the mattress, Arthur opened the intangible channel through his solar plexus and concentrated on summoning the light. He allowed it to collect in his body, then directed it through his hands and touched his face. Heat rose in his palms, and the damaged area around his eye began to tingle. He visualized blood vessels mending, swollen tissues shrinking, and trapped blood resorbing into the surrounding flesh. The heat in his hands peaked, then dissipated, and the pain in his face subsided. He offered a prayer of gratitude and rose from his knees.

Prior to his marriage, he'd attempted to heal himself of his "disorder," but his efforts had failed. The light of the Holy Spirit hadn't altered his appreciation of, or cravings for, the male form to any degree that he could detect.

Because there is nothing to heal. His inconvenient sexual preference did not constitute a disease, and it was vanity to think so. No, there was no cure for self-loathing but acceptance, and he was working on that.

He checked his face in the bathroom mirror. The skin around his eye had turned from darkening purple to light gray and the bruise on his cheek had transformed from violet-red to green-gray. Most of the color would be gone by morning, leaving him with nothing to explain except the fatigue that was the cost of his effort. Before retiring, he took a large dose of potassium and swallowed some iron tablets to speed his recovery.

He was so exhausted that he almost didn't hear the phone ring forty-five minutes later. He forced himself to rise and answer it, knowing that if he didn't, Ellie Jones would return out of concern for him.

"Arthur? It's Ellie. I'm checking to make sure you're okay."

"Thank you. Yes, I'm fine."

"Do you have a headache? Any dizziness or blurry vision?"

"No, I'm just tired." Arthur rubbed the back of his neck.

"What day is it?"

"What?"

"Concussion test," Ellie said.

"Oh, Saturday."

"What did you have for breakfast this morning?"

"Toast and coffee."

"Who's the United States Secretary of the Interior?"

Arthur cocked his head. "Um..."

"Just kidding." Ellie chuckled. "Okay, I'll let you go if you're sure you're all right."

"I'm sure. Thanks for your concern, Ellie."

"It's the least I can do since it was my son who...." She stopped, then started again. "I can't tell you how sorry I am. Walker isn't normally a violent person. I don't know what he was thinking." She paused, then said, "Well, that's not true. I can guess."

Arthur could guess too, but as a priest, it was inappropriate for him to comment, even if it made him look guilty. It was up to Stephen to explain his actions to whomever he was bound.

"Well, goodnight then," he said. "Thank you for calling."

"Goodnight. See you at church."

Despite his exhaustion, Arthur lay awake for some time after the call, pondering the situation. If Stephen had feelings for him, he'd have to address them at some point. He thought it more likely, though, that as a natural flirt Stephen was simply testing to see what he could get away with. The organist was good-looking, talented, and charming, and probably used to attracting whatever attention he wanted.

Though some people might be flattered by an advance from a younger suitor, Arthur was annoyed at Stephen's arrogance. Did he think he'd be invited into a priest's bed on the strength of a kiss? Given Arthur's calling and responsibilities, not to mention his moral duty, he wouldn't have considered it even if Stephen weren't already in a relationship. Physical intimacy required, if not romantic love, at least a mutual respect and commitment. Otherwise, it devolved into exploitation, a devaluing of another's humanity for personal gratification.

Arthur sighed and rolled over restlessly. Sylvia had been right, and he should have taken her warnings about both Martha Browne and Stephen Harken more seriously. Today had clearly demonstrated the down side of being gay and unattached – you attracted the attention of both unperceptive women *and* perceptive men.

≈ ≈ ≈

Why was that girl there? Why her and not me?

These thoughts looped continuously through Martha's mind while she pushed the torn lace of her dress under the zigzagging needle of her sewing machine.

She couldn't understand it. That girl...that *Joanne*...had been invited to the party and Martha hadn't. She was such a good friend to Father, looking after him, cooking him meals, and he hadn't even asked her to his party.

"She's after him. I know it," Martha said. She took her foot from the control pedal and snapped up the machine's presser foot to release the fabric. "He probably can't figure how to get rid of her. Her and her dirty mind."

A Jezebel like that could destroy a minister quicker than a rattler strike. She'd seen it in her Daddy's church more than once – a no-account floozy tempting a man of God into fornicating. The righteous were slow to forgive such sins of the flesh, and the fallen would be cast out in spite of emergency prayer meetings and talk of redemption. Father Endicott, a single man, would be the perfect target for this kind of Devil's mischief.

"He must be protected." The words struck Martha as so important and so true that she said them again. "He *must* be protected."

Snick snick. The sewing shears sliced through the last of the dangling threads. Martha flicked them into the trash, then smoothed the repaired ruffle with her fingers.

She was still mad – mad at Sylvia who had been so rude and bossy, at Ellie who had helped gang up on her, and (though she didn't like to admit it) even a little mad at

Father. Being left out of his party stung. It reminded her of her school days when nobody wanted to be her friend, when the other girls made fun of her for being poor and fat and living in the hills. If they could see her now, a member of Trinity Episcopal Church with her Cadillac and her beautiful condo, they'd think twice about how they had treated her.

Martha was a good Christian, though, and after giving Father some time to consider what he'd done, she would forgive him for excluding her. She might even keep him as her best friend, though she hadn't decided for sure.

Father didn't want her to call or drop by the rectory. That's what he'd said. Well then, she'd just have to become more active at the church so they could see each other. She didn't need Sylvia the Witch's permission either. He was the priest, leader of the flock, and when his sheep needed him, he would tend to them. That was his job, though she hoped he would come to see her as more than just his job. Actually, he already had, and that's why she could forgive him for the way he'd treated her.

"To protect our relationship going forward...." That's what he'd said, *our relationship going forward.*

Martha cupped her left elbow where Father had held it as she got into her car. His hand was strong, but soft too, not rough or callused. The memory gave her a warm, buzzy feeling in the pit of her stomach.

Standing at her cheval mirror, she held the newly mended party dress to her shoulders and twirled left and right. No longer perfect, but still beautiful.

It was too late to order flowers for the altar this week. She'd get some for next Sunday, though – some gladiolas in glorious turquoise and salmon and goldenrod – and add a bouquet for the pulpit as an extra surprise for Father. He'd have to wait a week, though, and that would be his punishment for not inviting her to his party. In the meantime, she would dress extra nice for services and greet him as if he hadn't treated her so cruelly. She would be the bigger person and put his painful slight behind her.

That's what you did when you had a relationship.

≈ ≈ ≈

Their dad turned around at the wheel to address him and Rhett, sitting at opposite ends of the back seat.

"What is going on with you two? Do I need to knock your skulls together?"

Most dads probably couldn't seriously threaten their varsity-football-player sons with such a thing. Their dad, though, was a big man who shifted concrete every day and, though more than twenty years their senior, could easily take them on, possibly at the same time – not that he would. Riley recognized the question as mostly rhetorical.

His mom added her two cents. "What were you two thinking to behave like that at Arthur's party? I can't believe how rude and inconsiderate you were! Besides embarrassing your dad and me."

The brothers sat stiffly with their eyes focused on the darkness outside their respective windows. If Riley looked at Rhett, his brother would punch him again, and he'd have to reciprocate, which would be better done out of sight of their parents.

When the car pulled into their driveway, the twins burst out almost before it stopped. Rhett led the way through the kitchen, down the stairs, and across the workout room to their shared bedroom.

"Fucker! What did you do?" Rhett demanded, slamming the door.

"Nothing you didn't do yourself."

"But you pretended to *be* me, didn't you, jackoff! Red shoes, same gray shirt, your hair parted like mine...." Rhett grabbed for Riley's summer-length locks, missed, then pulled an arm back to punch him.

Riley dropped onto his bed and drew in his arms and legs to block his brother's jabs. *Totally* worth it. He tried to hide his smile.

"Fucking asshat! I can't believe you did that," Rhett fumed.

"You'd have done the same thing."

Rhett stalked across the room and punched their dad's old La-Z-Boy recliner. "Tell me what you did with her."

"You know, a little smoochy-smoochy, a little feely-feely."

"Did you get in her shirt?"

Riley grinned and waggled his eyebrows.

His brother stared daggers at him. "In her bra? Her panties?"

"Affirmative and ditto. Amazing tits. Cute bush."

Rhett paced an angry circle around the room. "Did she get in yours?"

"Affirmative."

"Did you get off?"

"Yeah, it was awesome. Got her off too." Riley raised his hand in the air for a high five, but his brother just glared at him. "Don't leave me hangin', dude."

Rhett ignored the gesture and flopped onto his own bed, arms crossed, to glower at the ceiling.

Riley waited the universally recognized amount of time for a twin to "get over it," but his brother didn't speak. He sighed, then sat up and threw his legs over the side of his bed.

"Don't be pissed. I like her." He eyed his brother's mute form and waited a while longer.

"I liked her first," Rhett muttered at last.

"I know. Couldn't help myself." An apology of sorts.

They both went quiet. The bedside clock ticked away seconds that swelled into minutes. Finally, Rhett spoke again, his voice subdued.

"Sweet, right?"

Riley grinned like a crazed chimp. "Totally, bro. Epic."

21. Damage

After his mom left, Walker retreated to the bedroom he and Stephen usually shared and locked the door. He needed a night alone to prevent the fury that he'd misdirected at the priest from reigniting. Stephen didn't try talking to him either, but bedded down in the guest room and left early in the morning.

Walker arrived at church intentionally late, after Stephen would be seated behind the organ for the duration of the service. He would have skipped church entirely except he wanted to see for himself how badly he'd hurt the priest. He was also concerned about the rumors that were certain to crop up, and in spite of his rash behavior, he didn't want to cause the priest trouble or, worst-case scenario, cost him his job. Small southern communities could be hard on outsiders, especially gay men.

Was Arthur gay? It sure had looked that way last night. Walker flushed with renewed anger, though his mom was probably right – whatever had happened between Arthur and Stephen was unlikely to have been the priest's doing.

Walker entered the sanctuary during the opening hymn and slipped into the last pew where he found himself standing next to his mother. She often stationed herself there so she could exit discreetly before the end of the service to prepare for coffee hour.

"Glad you're here," she whispered.

Walker scanned the chancel in search of the priest. There he was, standing in profile at the priest's bench, holding a hymnal. He had no visible injuries on the right side of his face, which made sense since Walker had hit him with a right hook. When the hymn ended and Arthur stepped to the pulpit, Walker scrutinized the priest's face full-on, wishing he'd brought binoculars.

"I don't see any bruises," he said to Ellie as the congregation exchanged hymnals for prayer books.

"Shhh," she chided.

What a relief. Offhand, Walker couldn't remember the last time he'd clocked someone. Was it love that had provoked him after seeing Stephen kissing Arthur? As the congregation stood, sat, and kneeled its way through the service, Walker's gaze alternated between the two of them performing their separate functions, and he considered the question.

He and Stephen had seemed reasonably well-matched in the beginning, two country-bred, church-going men with a shared interest in classical music and classic movies. Walker had built relationships on less. They also shared an undeniable physical chemistry and complementary sexual preferences, with Walker more dominant, a top, and Stephen more seductive and playful, a bottom. Stephen was game for whatever Walker wanted whenever he wanted it. Rarely did he decline an advance. Of course, therein lay the problem.

Walker slipped out of the sanctuary before communion. Stephen arrived home forty minutes later and sauntered into the living room where Walker sat reading the Sunday paper.

"Hi."

Walker didn't look up.

"Are we talking yet?" Stephen asked.

Walker lowered the paper and peered at him. "If you want."

Stephen crossed his arms and jutted out a hip. "I know you're mad, so why don't you just yell at me and get it over with?"

Walker furrowed his brow. The implication that Stephen's slobbering over another man shouldn't upset him ticked him off anew. In the twenty months since they'd moved in together, Stephen had fucked around with his hairdresser, with a horseman from Louisville, and with the trainer from the gym. And those were just the men Walker knew about. He took his time folding the newspaper and laying it on the glass-topped coffee table.

"Are you having an affair with the priest?" he said finally.

"No." Stephen flopped into the lounge chair opposite him.

"You must want to or why would you be kissing him in his bedroom?"

Stephen shrugged. "It was a moment. It just happened."

"Just happened, huh?" Walker snorted. "It's obvious you want him."

Stephen shrugged again.

"Why can't you just admit it?" Walker mindlessly compressed a throw pillow into a palm-sized ball.

"Okay, I admit it. I'm attracted to him."

Had Stephen actually rolled his eyes like a snotty little kid? Anger churned in Walker's gut, and he clenched his jaw to keep it in check. He forced himself to breathe slowly. "Do you have feelings for him?"

"It was one kiss," Stephen said defensively. "No big deal."

My ass! Walker stared into the far corner of the room. Putting the moves on a priest wasn't something a person did casually. Not even Stephen.

"You initiated it, didn't you?" Walker asked, aware of his accusatory tone.

"I suppose." Stephen crossed his legs and examined his fingernails.

"Am I *boring* you?" Walker said dangerously.

"A little." Stephen looked up and smirked.

Walker fought the urge to rip the pillow to shreds. How could you resolve a problem when the other person pretended there *was* no problem? Or worse, laughed it off? He fished for words in the dry well of his frustration. Usually, Stephen jabbered when they fought, talking for both of them until they either reached an agreement or collapsed into bed together. This time, though, he wasn't helping, didn't even seem willing to try, which spoke volumes.

Stephen stood, put a hand on his hip, and tapped his foot impatiently. "Can we just get on with the penalty phase?"

Walker was on his feet before he knew what he was doing. He closed the gap between them in a flash, grabbed his lover, and lifted him into the air.

"Put me down!" Stephen protested, but Walker had already lost it – for the second time in two days.

He hauled his struggling captive to the bedroom and bent him over the mattress, face-down. Digging under his body, Walker unfastened Stephen's dress pants and wrenched them to his knees. Then he ripped open his own fly and released his straining erection. Stephen was reacting rather blithely to this threatening behavior, which ratcheted Walker's anger up another notch.

"You're not going to fuck me without lube, are you?" Stephen whined.

Walker spit into his hand and stroked the crown of his engorged cock. If he'd been able to think at all, he might have wondered why he got so hard when his lover made him angry.

Stephen began to twist and writhe, but Walker trapped his legs against the side of the mattress and shoved him down with a palm to his back.

"Let me get the Astro – "

Walker grabbed a lubed condom from the bedside drawer and rolled it on. Close enough. He jammed his cock into Stephen's ass.

"Dammit, that hurt."

"Now you know how I feel," Walker muttered as he pushed deeper into Stephen's backside, stretching his flesh too fast. Stephen was an anal sex veteran, but that didn't make a forced entry pleasant.

"Fuck," Stephen squawked.

"That's right," Walker rasped, ramming his cock deep, nearly pulling out, then plunging again, pumping aggressively. This was *bad*. Not so much because it was rougher than what Stephen normally liked – it wasn't – more that he wasn't in control of himself.

After a few more strokes, Walker recognized that his intrusion had become enjoyable to Stephen. Though his lover still writhed, his protests had changed to a sexy moaning. Walker swelled with satisfaction, knowing he had some small power over his spoiled – *thrust* – bratty – *thrust* – scheming – *thrust* – boyfriend.

Walker froze in that penultimate moment before the familiar eruption softened the last vestiges of his anger and turned aggression to euphoria. He collapsed over Stephen and wrapped his arms around the slighter man's shoulders, shuddering. Already he was remorseful. How was it that being with someone you cared for could make you like yourself less?

"You could at least give a guy a reach-around," Stephen complained.

Walker rolled to his side, pulling his lover with him, and did exactly that.

"I love you, you know," Stephen whispered as they lay in each other's arms afterward.

"Do you?" But Walker knew that even if that were true, love didn't always conquer all – old saws notwithstanding.

"You're my Pervis."

Stephen snickered, and Walker smacked him on the ass. There was a reason he'd never told Stephen what the P stood for.

≈ ≈ ≈

After the service, Martha hoisted herself from her usual pew – the second one because sitting in the first would be ostentatious – and huffed her way out of the sanctuary and down the long corridor that led to the Fellowship Hall. She wanted to show Father that she had risen above his ungrateful dismissal of her from his party.

Father looked so striking in his emerald green, summer chasuble. She looked her best too in a lime green, form-gripping church dress that showed just the right amount of cleavage for Sunday morning. She smoothed her newly cut-and-styled Cher wig, which Dot had transformed into a Jackie O. bob with a teased crown to give her extra height.

As usual, a large number of people crowded around Father, and they all seemed to be women. Martha had to exert great effort to stand patiently and wait her turn to speak to him.

"Hello, Martha," Father said at last, offering her his hand. "I'm glad you're here this morning."

"Hello, Father. You had a good sermon today, "Forgiveness and Rebirthing." She gripped the priest's hand and pumped vigorously.

"Forgiveness is a powerful spiritual force," he said, pulling his hand away. "God bless you."

He turned to the crippled old lady behind Martha and took her hand. "Good to see you, Mrs. Fitch. How are your joints today?"

Martha had been dismissed. She consoled herself by sniffing her palm where she could almost smell Father's scent, musky and masculine. She locked her hand over her nose as she headed toward the line for coffee and treats.

Behind her, Mrs. Fitch's voice rose high and happy. "I feel like a new woman!"

Martha scowled.

≈ ≈ ≈

Ellie had sat in the last pew, and the pulpit was quite a distance away, to be sure, but she should have seen *some* evidence of Arthur's injuries. She'd thought he might be wearing cover-up makeup, which wouldn't be obvious from that distance, but now he stood only ten feet away greeting parishioners, and she saw no sign of makeup. A slight shadow seemed to darken his left eye, but then he tilted his head and she was no longer sure.

It was utterly bewildering to be seeing things, or rather, not seeing things that had to be there. She'd witnessed the bruises, cleaned up the blood. Her mind was conjuring insane reasons for the gap between her perceptions of last night and the reality of this morning. She wanted to rush over to Arthur and demand an explanation.

"Sylvia!" Ellie called when she saw her friend enter the Fellowship Hall.

Sylvia looked up, and Ellie gestured her over, then grabbed her hand and pulled her to the back of the kitchen. "I have to talk to you."

"What's wrong?"

"After you left the barbecue at the rectory last night? Walker came late and caught Stephen kissing Arthur and punched him in the face." Ellie could hear the stress in her rush of words.

Sylvia's eyes popped wide. "Stephen and Arthur were kissing? You're kidding!" Then she registered the second half of Ellie's statement and said, "Walker punched Stephen? Is he okay?"

"No...I mean, yes. No, I mean Walker punched *Arthur* in the face, hard."

"I didn't see anything wrong with him." Sylvia craned her neck to catch a glimpse of Arthur through the serving cutout in the kitchen wall. "And I can't see Walker hitting anyone, least of all a priest."

"He did, but that's not what's bothering me. Well, it is, but that's not my point." She was barely making sense.

Sylvia tilted her head and pursed her lips. "I don't understand."

Ellie sighed. It wasn't like her to get so rattled. Sylvia would think she was going nuts. "You're not going to believe this, but can you just humor me?"

"Sure, of course."

Ellie steadied herself against the counter. "I stayed to help Arthur. His eyebrow was bleeding, and his cheek was turning black and blue. His eye was swelling shut. He was hurt badly enough that I wanted to find a substitute pastor for today, but he refused." Ellie pulled Sylvia further into the corner out of Arthur's line of sight.

"He seems okay," Sylvia said hesitantly.

"Yes, that's what I'm getting at. Fifteen hours ago, he definitely was *not* okay. He'd obviously been punched in the face."

"Oh." Sylvia gazed into the distance. "And now he looks fine. Like it never happened."

"Exactly. I don't know whether I'm witnessing a miracle or going crazy. Nobody else saw him, so I can't prove how bad it was, but now he's *healed*."

Sylvia turned back to Ellie, then leaned in and said softly, "Listen, I don't think you're crazy." She hesitated.

"I've seen people change – *really* change – between the time they go into his office and the time they come out. Joanne went in for counseling once looking like death and she came out glowing. I don't know how else to put it. She was transformed."

Ellie stared at her friend.

Sylvia went on, "Another day I saw him hold Martha Browne's hand, and in seconds she went from a stampeding water buffalo to a happy cow chewing her cud, as my boys might say. That's not the same as fixing an injury, but there's something special about him." Sylvia's words had sped up, gushing out like she had to finish her speech before somebody pulled her off the stage.

Ellie struggled to grasp her friend's meaning.

"Have you heard of those Cajun 'treaters' who pray over the sick?" Sylvia didn't wait for a response. "I know you've seen hallelujah preachers who bop people in the chest and supposedly cure them of everything from ingrown toenails to cancer. I never believed in that stuff, but – " She stopped abruptly, the metaphorical hook around her neck.

"Are you telling me that Arthur has some kind of...what? Magical power?" Ellie said. "That sounds – "

"Looney, I know. Can you come by the office to talk? My family's waiting, and I can feel them staring holes in the back of my head."

"Yes, I'll be there in the morning."

"Good." Sylvia squeezed Ellie's hand. "We'll ask him. Don't worry. We can't both be crazy."

A piercing screech soared over the crowd noise – the unmistakable sound of everyone's least favorite parishioner. Both women flinched, then looked up simultaneously to where Martha Browne stood in the refreshments line, gaping at the entrance to the Fellowship Hall.

Sylvia rushed out of the kitchen with Ellie on her heels before Martha flew full-tilt out of control.

≈ ≈ ≈

Joanne had been feeling fine, uplifted by Arthur's sermon, so much so that she hadn't given the crazy lady a thought as she stepped into the hall for coffee hour. And that's when the screeching started, sending a chill up Joanne's spine. She looked up to see Martha Browne staring right at her, hollering her head off.

The old woman's repeated verbal attacks, though incoherent and possibly insane, cut Joanne to the marrow. The screaming and ranting bespoke wounds so raw, so elemental, they plucked a harmonic note in Joanne's psyche that continued to vibrate long after the scene ended. Such incidents were exactly why she avoided leaving the house, because she couldn't predict who would cross her path or what devastation they might wreak on her.

Though Arthur had appeared at her side almost instantly, comforting her with a hand to her shoulder, and though Sylvia and Ellie had quickly hustled the screaming Martha out of the room, Joanne couldn't shake the aftereffects of the episode. The fight-or-flight chemicals that flooded her brain soon dissipated, setting in motion a familiar downward spiral.

Now she sat huddled in the corner of her childhood bedroom, lost in a black granite canyon where her thoughts pinged off the sheer walls and echoed back in an endless, shattering rhythm: *You will never escape, you will never be well, you will always feel like you do right now.*

Joanne grasped a three-inch blanket pin in bloodless fingers and jammed it through the epidermis layer of her thigh into the softer dermis beneath. One tiny pressure-release valve, an escape hatch for the pain. She jabbed herself again. A dot of blood oozed from the hole, lined up beside the others in a perfect row, little soldiers shoring up her shattered defenses.

Her mother had first discovered the grid of cut marks on Joanne's forearm when she was twelve. Since then, she'd found new places to pierce her skin so it wouldn't show – the bottoms of her feet, her inner thighs, her lower belly beneath her panty line. Pinholes didn't work as well as razor cuts, but they were less obvious, even to a trained eye.

It was impossible to explain the compulsion to anyone who didn't already understand, and Joanne had long ago given up trying, especially to her mother. Greta loved her unconditionally but with a lack of deep empathy typical of those blessed with sunny dispositions. Her mom's smiling exhortations to "buck up" and "shake it off" only deepened Joanne's loneliness. As did her parents' devotion to, and reliance upon, a God she had never met.

She stabbed herself again, focusing on the welcome sharpness of the sensation. She sucked in a single breath. Again. Then another breath. Even a pinprick, repeatedly applied, could eventually crack granite.

22. Discovery

On Monday morning, Martha donned her Jennifer Aniston wig and one of her pretty summer dresses – tangerine with sunny yellow flowers – and drove to the church. She happened to know that Father worked in his office most mornings, and maybe she would run into him, though that wasn't the reason she was going there.

She'd decided to get more involved with the church, so today she would find Charlie Hightower and point out some of the areas where he could improve his cleaning and maintenance of church property. Her first complaint would be about the ladies' restroom, which had displayed a "Closed" sign the day before. Did Highhorse expect women in their mature years to walk all the way to the Fellowship Hall to powder their noses?

"Dang!" Martha said when she saw Sylvia Pugh's car in the parking lot. That woman thought she was Saint Peter himself, guarding the gate to Father.

Martha shuffled inside and peeked around the office doorjamb. Sylvia and Ellie Jones were staring back at her, so she casually sauntered past.

"Not here to see you two," she muttered under her breath.

She hadn't meant to holler when that girl entered the Fellowship Hall after services. She'd quieted down as soon as the women approached, though she could clearly see that awful Joanne milking the situation to get Father's attention. Father even laid his hand on her shoulder!

Sylvia and Ellie had corralled Martha and hustled her out the nearest exit, barely giving her time to grab a handful of cookies and stuff them in her pocket. Then she'd had to walk all the way around the church to reach her car. So, no, she certainly was *not* there to see them.

In the vestibule, Martha stopped to peruse the bulletin board where Sylvia posted announcements for involved members such as herself. On the table beneath it, a stack of colored pamphlets caught her eye.

"Oh my!" she exclaimed as she reached for one, her face flushing with excitement.

"Meet Our Clergy, Vestry, and Staff" it said across the top, and below that was a waist-up picture of Father dressed in priestly attire, a black clergy shirt and jacket with his white clergyman's collar. A silver cross lay centered on his chest, suspended from a chain around his neck.

"So handsome."

What a fantastic discovery! She could take several of the pamphlets, cut out Father's picture, and hang them around her condo. She opened the tri-folded page. The inside displayed more pictures – the Vestry members, Sylvia, the nancy-boy organist, and the big black woman named Kendra. But another picture stared back at her from the bottom row, shocking her to her shoes: "Joanne Bowman, Office Assistant."

Martha's heart seized and a high staccato shriek escaped before she clapped her hand over her mouth. Sylvia had told her yesterday that it upset Father when she got excitable, and Martha had promised herself to try to do better when he was nearby.

"Oh my God, oh my God, oh my God," she whimpered into her palm.

A hand touched her shoulder. She whirled around and slapped at it, thinking it might be *her*. But it wasn't.

"Martha, what's wrong?" Ellie Jones asked.

Martha pointed at the picture. "*She* works here?"

"Yes, Joanne helps Sylvia in the office."

"But that's not right! She can't work with Father." Martha covered her mouth to stop herself from hollering again.

"I don't see why not," Ellie said. "Joanne is well-qualified."

"*Nooo*," Martha squealed.

≈ ≈ ≈

Arthur sat behind his desk at the church with his feet up, head back, and eyes closed, a position he'd held for at least an hour. Per the guidelines of his clerical probation, he needed to check in with Father Daniel, but he couldn't summon the energy to pick up the phone. Healing himself was like robbing Peter to pay Paul. It drained his vitality, which spoke more to his human limitations in channeling the power of the Holy Spirit than to any lack in the power itself.

He pressed his fingers into the damaged area above his eye and noted the lingering tenderness. He'd repaired the visible wounds to avoid having to explain the who and why to his congregation, but he'd left the underlying injury to resolve in its own time. He needed to preserve his energy for healing those in his spiritual care. Louis

Tinkerton's funeral was scheduled for the afternoon, and funerals were always taxing.

Arthur was reciting the Rite I prayers from his unorthodox position when a distant keening sound caught his attention. He recognized the disturbed and disturbing person to whom it belonged, but he simply couldn't face Martha Browne. He had no resources left for coping with her distress. Then, like an aborted car alarm, the screeching stopped and didn't resume. He offered a few silent words of thanks for the women who'd no doubt taken Martha in hand.

He continued with the Apostles Creed until his attention was diverted by muffled conversation in the main office.

"...be better to wait until tomorrow," Sylvia said.

Ellie's reply was only partially audible. "A case of...think I'm crazy...."

Arthur sighed at his distractibility and gave up on the prayers. No, Ellie wasn't crazy. She'd observed his facial injuries on Saturday night and seen him the following morning with no apparent injuries. She and Sylvia were sure to confront him about the impossible discrepancy.

It wouldn't be the first time. To avoid problems, he never spoke of his healing work and, if pressed on the subject, referred only to God's infinite grace and the power of prayer. People who witnessed Arthur's talent invariably attributed the power to him rather than to its true source, and there was always a danger of attracting followers who mistook him for the Divine or shadowed him with demands to perform "magic."

Since coming to Amity, though, he'd been reconsidering his position. The great upheaval that had brought him here had awakened him to the fundamental dishonesty of his life. He'd masqueraded as a straight, conventional priest for nearly twenty years, which was both limiting and debilitating. If he could bring himself to accept, even embrace, his homosexuality, perhaps he could free up energy to better fulfill his promise and obligations as a healer. He was no Jesus, no Christ, but within the context of a healing ministry, his gift could serve a larger purpose.

When Sylvia and Ellie's curiosity overcame their discomfort and they demanded an explanation for his vanishing facial wounds, he would tell the truth. Then he'd go one step further.

≈ ≈ ≈

"Iss nah i ee kiss ee ak or anysing," Stephen mumbled around his toothbrush.

Walker flicked his dick, flushed, and turned around, then immediately felt the tingle of arousal. Stephen worked at looking pretty, and he was plenty successful at it. He'd just stepped out of the shower, and his shaved torso gleamed with water droplets. His thick, black hair stuck up along the top of his head.

"Huh?" Walker stared at the edge of the towel where it cut low across Stephen's slim hips, revealing a tease of pubic hair.

The two had had hot makeup sex on Sunday afternoon, fucking several times and napping in between. Now it was Monday morning, and Walker had to go to work when he'd rather drag his lover's ass back to bed.

Stephen spit, then rinsed his mouth. "I said, 'It's not like he kissed me back or anything.'"

"The priest?" Walker's fists clenched involuntarily. "Are you done with him?"

Stephen leered at Walker's up-angled cock. "Not if wondering makes you that hard for me."

"Slut." Walker stalked over and snatched away the towel.

Stephen smirked. "Guilty."

Walker snapped the damp terrycloth against Stephen's lean, bare thighs.

"Ow!"

"*My* slut." He tossed the towel at his lover's head and stepped into the shower.

Walker was aware he hadn't been entirely honest about their dustup, that, for instance, in the aftermath of his fury, he'd found the idea of kissing Arthur arousing. The priest was physically attractive – beautiful, really – as well as intelligent, steady, and had a natural magnetism that drew you in. His collar held a certain forbidden appeal too. Episcopal priests didn't take vows of celibacy, but the dog collar set them apart as – if not exactly holy, then at least – more holy than thou.

So Walker hadn't just been jealous when he discovered Stephen in Arthur's bedroom. He'd also been envious. He could imagine grabbing the silk stole the priest wore around his neck and pulling him in... *peeling off his priestly robes, discarding his black shirt and trousers. When the priest had been defrocked, the man beneath revealed, he'd grip his tall, lean body...*

The scenario appealed to Walker's cock, now swollen and taut. He squeezed it in his fist, sliding up and down its length.

I will surely burn in hell.

"Bye, stud." Stephen opened the shower door, then stared at the stiff cock in Walker's hand. "Still horny after all that sex! I'd take care of that, but I'm meeting Kendra to plan music for next month."

"Never mind, I have to get going." Walker bent over for a farewell kiss.

"Save me some!" Stephen called on his way out.

"You know I will."

After work, Walker drove to Rocco's Hardbody Gym to lift weights. Amity was too small for an exclusively gay gym, but most gay men who worked out did so there. Rocco had a wife, but no one ever saw her, and the rumor was that Rocco pinch-hit for the other team. Walker wouldn't know since he didn't mess around with married men, gay or otherwise.

Hoisting dumbbells was easier on the joints, but Walker liked the blunt, dense feel of an iron bar balanced across his body. Plus, when he loaded it up and planted himself under the squat rack or bench press, some other heavily muscled man would invariably step over to spot, and he enjoyed the camaraderie and physical contact. Such interactions frequently led to sexual advances, though Walker didn't act on them when he was in a relationship.

He set the leg press at a warm-up weight of 245 pounds and lowered himself into the seat. *One, two, three...*

Pushing iron quieted the mind, which was one reason he did it, but today, he couldn't stop stewing over his calamitous encounter with Arthur Endicott. Stephen had admitted, more or less, that he'd surprised Arthur with the kiss and that the priest hadn't responded. Jealousy and anger aside, Walker had seriously overreacted. It wasn't like him to lead with his fists, for one thing, and for another, why had he taken out his anger on Arthur when half-a-second's consideration would have told him that Stephen had initiated the encounter?

Walker set the pin to 325 pounds, grabbed the hand grips, and hoisted the stack on his exhale...*two, three, four...*

The answer was obvious. He'd simply blown a gasket, and in his gut, he'd known Arthur was his physical equal, a fair opponent in a fistfight. Walker would never hit Stephen, a slight and mildly effeminate man, whose only real weapon was his tongue. It would be cowardly. Not that that was any excuse for punching a priest.

Walker pinned the weights for his third set. "Oh, shit," he blurted, and several heads turned his way. "Nothing, sorry."

Maybe it hadn't been gut instinct but an overactive sex drive that imagined a powerful body beneath the priest's loose-fitting garments. He hadn't given the man a chance to defend himself, in any case, and according to his mom, he'd hurt Arthur pretty badly. The injuries weren't obvious from the back of the sanctuary, but that didn't mean much.

...eight, nine, ten.

Walker lowered the 400 pounds with a satisfying clang and rose from the leg press. He'd have to swallow his pride, apologize for his inexcusable behavior, and try to make amends. Avoiding the priest would be difficult unless he switched churches, and he wasn't prepared to do that.

Making amends. It held a certain appeal.

≈ ≈ ≈

At her kitchen island, Martha popped some walnuts into her mouth before chopping the rest to add to her brownie mix. She needed to think and nuts were good for the brain.

The situation with Father was so worrying. That Joanne girl must have finagled the church job so she could get at him whenever she wanted. He'd be completely vulnerable with her there right outside his office every day.

Martha stirred a double measure of nuts into the brownie batter, just as her momma used to do. Fifty-four years after Edith's death, Martha still thought about her nearly every day. She was only twelve when she woke up late that Saturday morning without being called. Her Daddy said Momma had gone to visit Grandma three days before, but she was supposed to be back. Usually, she got Martha up and gave her pancakes, or biscuits and gravy, or grits and eggs. But when Martha awoke, she couldn't find her mother. Her Daddy wasn't around either, but he and Floyd went squirrel or opossum hunting on Saturdays, so that was no surprise.

Martha called for Edith and, when she got no reply, went to look for her. Momma wasn't out in the washhouse or down in the root cellar. She hadn't gone to the garden for vegetables or out to forage for greens since her carrying basket remained by the door. It was only after checking every other place she could think of that Martha considered going to the snake house. She wasn't allowed without one of her parents, though she liked to handle the snakes. She and Floyd had been doing it almost since they got big enough not to be mistaken for prey.

The snakes were kept far off, beyond the quarter-acre vegetable garden where they tended to linger if they escaped. The Brown children had been instructed to carry a special forked stick whenever they left the yard, and Martha had learned to trap a stray rattler's head between the forks by the time she was ten or eleven. You didn't kill them except in an emergency because wild rattlesnakes renewed the breeding stock, and the kept ones provided meat when there was nothing else to eat.

Martha fetched a forked stick from the wall of the washhouse and made her way past the garden toward the snake house. Momma could be feeding or separating babies and not have heard Martha call. She approached the old wooden shack and saw that the door was closed.

"Momma!" she called. There was no answer.

She raised the door latch. If it dropped while you were in the snake house, you could pull a string that ran through a hole in the wall to lift and release it, which kept you from accidentally locking yourself in with the snakes.

She pulled the door handle, but the skewed planks were stuck in the frame. She tugged harder with no effect. She pressed her ear against the door, almost sensing the reptiles inside, slithering in their boxes. There was no rattling, which meant the snakes weren't agitated, but

Martha felt a tickle along her scalp, and her stomach tightened. Something wasn't right.

The snake house door had never been so stubborn. She yanked and yanked at it, then finally thought to plant one foot on the wall for leverage. With the extra push, the heavy door suddenly popped open, slammed into her forehead, and knocked her on her butt in the dirt. It hurt bad, but Martha barely noticed the pain in her head because right in front of her, just inside the door, sprawled her momma, her legs like overstuffed sausages inside their harvest-gold, double-knit slacks. Edith's feet flopped through the doorway, and one of her loafers fell to the ground.

What Martha saw next made her scream bloody murder. She crab-walked backward in a panicked scramble to get away. Coiled beside Edith's swollen, Orlon-covered calves was Granddaddy Murphy rising to battle. Gideon's fourteen-pound western diamondback shook fiercely and launched himself just as Martha's legs escaped striking range. The forked stick lay useless where she'd dropped it beside the door, now guarded by the menacing reptile recoiling for another strike. Ten noisy rattles quaked at the nether end of his body.

Momma was dead. There was no need to shake her or listen for a heartbeat or watch for a breath. When Martha finally got her feet under her and leaped up to scurry away, she caught a glimpse of her momma's face. It was purplish-blue, the color of a fist-punching bruise. Edith still gripped her right wrist in her left fist, and the dangling, distorted appendage was barely recognizable as a hand. The snake had struck her there first.

Stench ballooned from the snake house door, worse than the usual odor of reptile dung, worse than a road-kill skunk after a day in the sun. Martha managed a few frantic steps before the vile odor combined with the sight of her mother's poisoned corpse set her stomach heaving. She folded in half and retched, though she had nothing to bring up but bile.

When her stomach calmed, Martha stood and stared, transfixed, at Edith's body, watching her mother's face ripple and roll. It was the hyperactive work of blowfly maggots feeding on the eyes and lips, and inside the nose and mouth. That's what they went for first, seemed like, the soft places.

Granddaddy Murphy, whom Gideon kept for a pet because he was too big and dangerous to take to church, had uncoiled and was gliding toward her. He'd calmed down some but was still guarding his kill. Martha made a wide circle around him to retrieve her stick for the trek back to the house, keeping her eyes on the deadly snake and pinching her nose closed as she moved behind him into the stink cloud.

She bent over to pluck the stick from the ground, and Martha's gaze caught on something sparkly – three shiny pennies lying in the dirt under the threshold of the snake house door. Had Momma kept lucky pennies in her shoe? But why three when she only had two feet? It wasn't worth figuring.

Martha snatched up her forked stick and ran toward the garden in another wide circle around Granddaddy Murphy, knowing better than to try trapping the colossus. Surely she was going nuts for she saw rattlers everywhere, coiled in the okra vines, peeking from behind cornstalks, and slithering around every big clod of dirt. She wished she had two forked sticks or, better yet, the .410 shotgun.

Did she cry? She didn't think so. After her first startled scream, Martha didn't remember hearing any sound but the shaking of rattles and the buzzing of flies.

She couldn't help her mother, couldn't even help herself, because they didn't have a telephone and the nearest one was miles away in town. Some hill folk used citizen-band radios to coordinate 'shine deliveries, speaking in secret code, but her Daddy always said, "I ain't worried 'bout no Revenuers 'cause God is on our side, praise the Lord."

When Gideon and Floyd got home from hunting, they found Martha on the porch in the old cane rocker, staring straight out, rocking back and forth, back and forth, knees pulled in to her chest.

"Where's your ma?" her Daddy asked over and over, but Martha couldn't say. She just rocked and rocked, and left them to figure it out their own selves.

The ringing telephone interrupted Martha's thoughts. Nobody called her. Except for Father Arthur, she didn't have any particular friends in Amity, and the people from her Daddy's – now Floyd's – church mostly didn't keep phones. She hoped it wasn't the police.

"Hello?"

"Martha Brown?" a raspy woman's voice inquired.

"Who's this?"

"Ida Roach. Floyd asked me to call and say he be comin' to town Saturday. Wants to see ya."

"Who are you?"

"Floyd delivers to me."

"Oh. Where's he comin' when?"

"Two, my place."

"Where's that?"

Ida gave the street address of her joint.

"I want to talk to him too," Martha mused aloud.

"Fine."

"Okay, goodbye," Martha said just before the line clicked dead. She scowled at the phone. "So rude!"

23. Revelations

Just as Arthur had expected, Sylvia and Ellie approached him on Tuesday, the third day after he'd healed his facial injuries.

"Can we have a minute?" Sylvia asked from the doorway of his office, Ellie right behind her.

"Certainly, come in. Sit down." Arthur gestured to the chairs across from him, regretting the wariness on Ellie's face.

"You probably know why we're here," Sylvia said.

"I could guess, but why don't you tell me?" Arthur leaned his forearms on the desktop and clasped his hands.

"Well, we've both...Ellie and I...observed certain, uh, anomalies in your, uh...." Sylvia stopped, then took a breath and tried again. "Let's just say if we weren't modern, enlightened, non-hysterical churchwomen, we might have to report you to the bishop..." – she leaned toward him and added in a lower tone – "...for witchcraft." She tried to chuckle, but it sounded stilted and awkward.

"Ah, I wasn't expecting the Spanish Inquisition." *Nobody expects the Spanish Inquisition,* Arthur heard in the pinched nasal tone of a Monty Python character, and he smiled. Then he remembered his own birthplace, a town called Salem, and grew serious. "I'm not a witch, if it makes you feel any better."

"No, of course you aren't!" Sylvia exclaimed too quickly. "I...we weren't implying that."

They were, though, sort of.

"Ellie, what you observed is real," Arthur said, addressing the woman who'd witnessed his transformation. "I won't pretend I don't know what's troubling you."

Her tight expression softened a little.

"My face is still injured beneath the surface. You can't see it, but it's sore." Arthur touched his fingers to his cheekbone. "Walker has an impressive right hook."

Ellie grimaced. "I'm so mad at him I could spit."

"His reaction was understandable, and I don't blame him, but that's not what you wanted to talk about, is it?"

"No," she said, and Sylvia shook her head.

Tension hung thick in the air. Arthur cleared his throat. "This is a little awkward," he began, "but I value your friendship, and I want to be as honest and...straightforward as I can." He offered a smile. "So, first things first. I think you both know that I'm gay."

The women nodded in silent acknowledgement. They probably had questions about that too, given he'd been married for twelve years, but that was another conversation. Arthur took a deep breath and plunged in.

"What you might not know is that God has blessed me with a gift for healing."

Both women stared, their expressions frozen.

"I wasn't the first seminarian to present with the capability, though maybe the first in a generation or two. Our church recognizes certain talents that priest candidates bring to the table, and the theological framework of the seminary allows for their evaluation and training. Healing is one such gift. There are others."

Sylvia's brows knitted. "You're saying you have...what? A supernatural ability? A superpower?" She started to giggle, then caught herself and coughed instead.

"The church calls it a charism, which has a familiar Latin root, the same as charisma. You might say I have charisma." Arthur smiled, but the women didn't respond, so he remained silent and waited.

Eventually Ellie found her tongue. "I haven't heard of this before. What are these...charisms?"

"Charismata is the plural, and they include healing, teaching, influence or leadership, discernment, and a few others. They manifest in different ways at different strengths. Christ embodied them all, as you might expect. Martin Luther King, Jr., was a charismatic teacher and spiritual leader, as was Mahatma Gandhi. Mother Teresa was a great healer. But fortunately, lesser human beings can develop their spiritual gifts as well."

"I don't understand. You can heal injuries? Diseases?" Ellie's eyes bored into him.

"Some, yes." Telling the truth was his part of this exchange; taking it in was up to them.

"But...but...how do you do it?" Ellie pressed, while Sylvia just stared in confusion or disbelief.

"I don't. God does it through me."

Ellie opened her mouth to object, and Arthur held up his palm.

"Hold on. I know what you mean, but the distinction is important. In the church, we regard spiritual abilities as bestowed by God, and we endeavor to use them for His purposes, not our own. Some ordination candidates are rejected because their gifts are deemed too powerful or potentially corrupting in a priest. The New York bishop believed I could learn to control my pride, ego, and other less-than-admirable traits to make my gift useful to the church, and I was let through. He hasn't always been happy with his decision." Arthur smiled wryly. "Before my seminary training, I wasn't a healer. I was more like an unruly Uri Geller."

Sylvia covered her throat with her hand. "The guy who could bend spoons with his mind? He's for real?"

"I believe so, though I've never met him. The talent exists. I haven't tried to bend spoons myself, but I've seen them scoot across a table." As soon as those last words were out of his mouth, Arthur knew he'd said too much.

You shall not tempt the Lord your God, quoth the book of Matthew.

"You can do that? Will you show us?" Sylvia asked, voicing the exact response one should expect after such a display of pride.

Arthur sighed at how little he'd learned over the years. "That would be misusing God's gift, and I've made a vow not to do that. Please forgive me for bringing it up."

Ellie's forehead crinkled in consternation. "I've been a nurse for over twenty-five years, and I've seen some amazing recoveries, but your wounds healed *overnight.* How did you do that?"

Both women were struggling to wrap their minds around his impossible reality, another example of why it was wise to keep his own counsel. Miracles were fine in theory, but witnessing a healing was disorienting and potentially hurtful. Arthur had gone too far to turn back, though.

"It was only a surface healing of the visible tissue," he said. "Normally, I wouldn't call on God's grace for my personal benefit, but it seemed worthwhile not to alarm the congregation."

Sylvia's eyes were wide; her hand still clutched at her throat.

"But Arthur, how does it work?" Ellie pressed. "I still don't understand."

Speaking his truth, that healing was simply an act of faith, would sound like self-righteous censure, so Arthur tried a scientific analogy. "I don't know the answer to that, but I think of my body as something like a particle accelerator."

Sylvia frowned.

"That's a device that collects subatomic particles, neutrons or protons, and shoots them in a concentrated beam. It's used to split atoms, among other things. Likewise, I pull energy from the atmosphere, concentrate it in my body, and then direct it through my hands. I imagine it's like ultraviolet light or microwaves, energy we can't see with our eyes. How it heals – well, that's God's secret. I consider it the power of the Holy Spirit."

Neither Ellie nor Sylvia spoke, and Arthur saw the skepticism on their faces. Convincing them wasn't his aim, though.

"I wanted to talk to you both about this, actually. I feel called to share my gift in a more deliberate way." Sylvia raised her eyebrows, and Arthur answered her implied question. "There's a church in Cincinnati that offers a monthly healing service."

"Do they have someone like you there?" Ellie asked.

"I'm not sure, but the service involves directed prayer and the laying on of hands, which, as you both know, are common practices in our church. Someone with a talent for healing might make it available in that way to avoid attracting the attention of the Spanish inquisitors." Arthur smiled.

Sylvia's hand dropped to her lap, and she exhaled audibly. "It's a lot to take in, Arthur, but *we* asked *you*. Maybe we thought you'd deny it." She picked at a thread from her skirt before looking at him again. "That might have been easier."

"I understand," Arthur said. "But I want to look into offering a regular healing service in Amity, and I'll need your help to organize it." He looked at Ellie. "And I'll need your support to propose it to the Vestry. If you're both willing," he added.

A shroud of silence descended over the room as the women's understanding of their world shifted slightly off center.

≈ ≈ ≈

"Joanne's having a hard time," Sylvia remarked to Arthur the next day.

"Is she still sick?"

"I don't think she's physically sick."

The timing was unfortunate since Sylvia had hoped Joanne could mind the office while she and Arthur and the other church leaders went out of town for the annual Vestry retreat.

Arthur looked thoughtful. "Is she coming in today?"

"Yes, Greta called to say she's on her way, though she'd not doing too well."

"Why don't you have her come see me when she gets here?" Arthur caught Sylvia's eye. "You can join us if she doesn't mind." He crossed the room and retreated to his office.

Arthur was inviting her to witness him in action. He must believe that demonstrating his healing talent had some worthy church purpose since he'd made it clear he didn't do "parlor tricks."

Sylvia hadn't completely digested what he'd shared with her and Ellie. In her heart, she knew he wouldn't lie, but her head was having a hard time accepting his revelation. Jesus performed miracles in the Bible, but those stories were allegorical, not bona fide history, not scientific truth. Healing the blind, curing leprosy, raising Lazarus from the dead with a simple touch? It couldn't be real. *Could it?*

She didn't want to be a doubting Thomas, but how could an educated person not question? She didn't think David Copperfield could make the Statue of Liberty disappear either, though he'd seemed to during a performance in New York. Cody Winthrop's parents did tell her how wonderful Arthur had been with their daughter in the hospital – he'd performed a magic trick, come to think of it – and how quickly her broken leg had mended, but kids were resilient. And Louis Tinkerton had died from his stroke shortly after Arthur visited him at St. Anthony, so he obviously hadn't been healed.

"Hi, Sylvia," Joanne said as she entered the office. She looked disheveled and pale, weariness written on her face.

"Hi, it's good to see you. I'm sorry you've been feeling badly."

"Thanks," Joanne said, her voice flat.

"Father Arthur wants to meet with you. Is it okay if I come in too?"

Joanne nodded.

Arthur came to his office doorway. "Hello, Joanne," he said with a friendly smile. "Come on back."

≈ ≈ ≈

After the session with Arthur, Sylvia invited Joanne to lunch. Despite the ordinariness of the encounter, during which Arthur had placed his hands on Joanne's head and led the three of them in prayer, Joanne's entire demeanor had changed, and Sylvia was dying to talk to her about it.

"When Father Arthur prays over me, I get this tingly sensation, kind of like sex." Joanne blushed. "Sorry, I don't mean like having sex with Father Arthur – that would be weird – I mean it feels good like sex, but clean and shiny, like a golden light moving through my body. I don't know how to explain it, except it's such a high, such a change from the before to the after. It makes me want to dance. The effect is spiritual, I'm sure, the power of prayer and all that, but if I didn't know better, I'd swear Father Arthur has magical powers." Joanne giggled. "That's stupid."

"Maybe not so stupid," Sylvia said, trying to keep her tone casual. "I've noticed how much better you seem to feel after your sessions with him."

"Beats the heck out of electroshock! Anyway, whatever he's got, I wish he'd bottle it. It's like I took a mood elevator, except I don't feel medicated, more like I don't need medicating – I feel *normal*, which for me, feels really good."

The waitress set down two glasses of sweet tea, then pulled out a pad to take their orders. Sylvia chose the barbecued beef sandwich with a side salad, and Joanne selected the Monte Cristo and fries to share.

After the waitress left, Sylvia asked, "What were you saying about a light?"

"Oh, Father Arthur's light...it's more like a glow. Can you see it?"

Sylvia shook her head.

"I'm probably crazy then, but I saw it the first time I met him. I wanted to go stand in it. Just being next to him makes me feel good. It's kind of embarrassing. I think I'm in love with his aura!" She giggled again.

Sylvia laughed along, though her mind reeled. Could Joanne actually *see* the light of the Holy Spirit? The atoms or particles or whatever Arthur claimed to collect and channel through his hands? Why could Joanne see it if she and Ellie couldn't?

"Did Father say something to you about auras or light?"

"Oh, no. He's a priest. I don't imagine he's into New Age stuff like auras and chakras and chi." Joanne snickered. "They'd probably defrock him or something."

Arthur had said he'd been singled out for scrutiny at seminary but then been accepted into the fold as a healer. Why hadn't Sylvia ever heard about this if it was church-sanctioned? Was it a secret? Given the church's long history of witch trials and persecutions over the centuries, maybe it was.

"I'm so glad you're feeling better," she said to change the subject. "The Vestry retreat is coming up, and I wondered if you'd be willing to work in the office on Friday, Saturday, and Monday while we're gone. Mostly you'd be answering the phone, but you'd also need to set up some meeting rooms, and photocopy bulletins for Sunday. There's the internet if you get bored."

"Sure, I can do that, make up for the hours I missed this week."

"Good, that takes care of one thing on my list." Sylvia sipped her tea and regarded this woman who was becoming a friend. "Your mom said you've been struggling this week. Have you been depressed?"

Joanne shrugged. "I have a persistent mental disorder, diagnosed differently over the years – bipolar, borderline personality, depression. Sometimes I'm fine, but then something happens that triggers a relapse, and I fall into a black hole. Drugs help, but they tend to lose their effectiveness over time."

The waitress appeared with their sandwiches and fussed over them for a moment before moving to another table. When the girl was out of earshot, Sylvia said, "I know you were hurting after your boyfriend left, but you've been doing so well. Did something happen recently?"

Joanne picked a crust off her sandwich and pushed it to the edge of her plate. "It's kind of ridiculous."

"Tell me." Sylvia reached across the table to touch her friend's hand.

Joanne sighed and looked up. "You know that weird Martha Browne?"

Sylvia rolled her eyes. "Sadly, I do."

"When I started coming to church, I kept running into her. She has this awful, tangled energy. I've always been sensitive to people's vibrations – if you know what I mean – and hers gives me a terrible feeling of dread. I could tolerate that by itself, but whenever she sees me, she goes completely crazy. You've heard her scream, like she's terrified of me almost, but it's an aggressive thing too, like she might attack me any minute. Maybe I shouldn't be so sensitive, but Sunday was the last straw. It just got to me, and I started falling. I couldn't stop it."

"I can't tell you how sorry I am about Martha." Sylvia squeezed Joanne's hand, then released it. "She'll yell at anybody, but she seems especially reactive to you. Do you have any idea why?"

"None at all." Joanne picked up her fork and stabbed a French fry. "She said something about me being a bad person, but I don't even know her. We've never talked. The only thing I can think of is maybe she's jealous about me working around Father Arthur? But that's crazy." Joanne gave a wry laugh. "There's the pot calling the kettle black."

"Martha has a crush on Arthur. We know that much." Sylvia picked up her sandwich and took a bite.

"Really?" Joanne said, stabbing a few more fries and dipping them in ketchup. "But I don't have any special relationship with him. He's been kind to me, but there's no reason for her or anybody to be jealous of me on his account."

"We both know that, but Martha doesn't seem to."

"Weird. I just wish she didn't affect me so much, but I can't keep her out of my head. She's like a nightmare I can't wake up from."

"Ellie and I think she needs psychiatric help, but we can't do anything unless she's a danger to herself or others. And so far, she's just a nuisance. I'd call her family, but we don't know that she has any."

Joanne took a swig of tea. "I could handle her better if she didn't keep sneaking up on me and screaming like I'm going to hurt her or something. It's almost like she thinks I'm someone else."

"Unfortunately, we're stuck with her for the time being. We can't ban her from the church, but we can try to keep her away from you. And I know Arthur would be happy to pray with you as often as you like."

Joanne smiled gratefully.

≈ ≈ ≈

They were gone, every last one of them. *Impossible!* Joanne leaned forward in the bathtub, spread her knees, and searched for the scabby punctures and cuts. They were three days old, sure, but some evidence of her desperate behavior should remain. Inner thigh skin scarred – she had enough experience to know. But it hadn't. Not only were there no scabs or scars, but no blemishes remained at all. The skin looked perfect, like she'd never taken a blanket pin and then an X-Acto knife to it when the pin didn't bring relief. She was baffled.

She felt so much better, though. When Father Arthur and Sylvia prayed with her, she'd felt the power of the Holy Spirit move through her body and lift her burden. Never in her life had praying to God been so all-encompassing and profound.

Joanne wondered, only half in jest, whether Father Arthur would marry her if she proposed. Living might be worth it if he touched her every day. She didn't feel sexually attracted to him, per se – he seemed too refined for lust – but she'd happily do whatever he wanted in bed if only she could share his powerful connection to God, or even just stand beside him and bathe in his glow now and then.

24. Past in the Present

"I'm tellin' ya, Larry, I wasched it and talked to Yoanne after. She sees hith light, ahways seen it since she met 'im, drawn to hith whatchamacallit...hith aura. Says when he prays w'ther, cloud liffs. Can seet in her face...glows. Says jus' bein' near 'im helps...and I buhlief her."

"You're sounding a little kooky there, hon. Maybe you better have another drink." Larry laughed as Sylvia's upper body slowly tilted sideways on the couch in their family room.

"I dunt think so."

Larry went to the kitchen, then returned to his tipsy wife and pulled her upright before offering her an open packet of saltines. "Here, eat these. They'll absorb some of the alcohol."

"Buh I jus' had one drin," Sylvia slurred. "Big one. Cahm my nerfs."

"One is over your limit, I guess." Larry noticed the pint-sized vodka bottle with three inches of clear liquid remaining in it. He held it up. "Did you drink this?"

"With lem'nade."

"Well, now I see the problem," Larry said and laughed. "This isn't vodka. It's white lightning, *moonshine*, 190 proof. Frank Crawford gave it to me. Didn't you notice the burn?"

"You know I dunt drin. Aaagh, gonna be sick..."

Larry jerked his wife from the couch and rushed her to the kitchen sink. He turned on the cold water as she vomited, holding her up with an arm around her waist and rubbing her back with his palm. Her dark hair clung to her head on a sheen of sweat while her body trembled and heaved.

"Where's Mom?" Rhett asked when the twins got home from wherever they'd been that afternoon.

"She didn't feel good after work, so she went to bed." More like passed out and had to be put to bed, but Larry wouldn't mention that. "So," he said, "are you two looking for summer jobs or coming to work for me?"

"Looking for jobs," the twins mumbled in unison.

"I could use your help during construction season, and you wouldn't have to lift weights to keep in shape."

Grumbling ensued, and Larry hid his grin. He'd learned quite a few parenting lessons from his father. Nothing would motivate his sons to find work like the prospect of shoveling concrete all summer. Larry didn't especially want to boss them on his job sites. They were too good at colluding to avoid work. Timing was one of the primary challenges of concrete, and Larry needed motivated workers to avoid having a truckload harden while he waited for them to prepare the site and spread the mix. Moreover, hand or back injuries, not uncommon in the concrete business, could ruin the boys' chances for football scholarships.

Though Larry liked running his dad's company – with an aging Bub still working alongside him – he didn't necessarily want his sons to follow in his footsteps. He hoped they'd get college degrees and find an easier way to make a living. Hell, they could probably get modeling work if they wanted to. They were every bit as good-looking as those Calvin Klein boys whose images were plastered all over his wife's magazines. Modeling *was* kind of gay, though, and his boys weren't gay.

Not that there's anything wrong with that, Larry added in his head, enlightened twenty-first-century redneck that he was.

He sure didn't want his sons to join the Army or Marines like so many good ol' boys did and end up in some godforsaken 'stan dodging bullets and IEDs. He didn't care how patriotic it was.

Hell, no!

On Monday, Frank Crawford had invited Larry for a beer after work, given him that gift of moonshine in a vodka bottle, and talked a little about his past. He'd seen combat as a gunner in the first Gulf War, the one where computer-guided rockets blew up long-range targets like some surreal video game while Americans watched from their living rooms. Frank had hinted that the facial scars weren't his worst legacy from the war – something had happened to his family jewels, though he hadn't been specific. Messed up his sex life, whatever it was, but Larry didn't want to pry, especially if they were talking amputation.

He shuddered. The idea of his sons – or anyone! – getting their boys blown off gave him the cold sweats. Made him sad too. He didn't even get pissed when Frank failed to show up to work the next day, leaving him a man short.

With Sylvia passed out, Larry drafted the twins for dinner duty and supervised as they browned a pound of hamburger, boiled water for spaghetti, and heated a jar of sauce. He dumped a bag of frozen broccoli into a bowl and stuck it in the microwave.

"Isn't there a vegetable setting somewhere on this thing?"

"Look inside the door, Dad. There's directions," Riley pointed out.

"This broccoli needs something," Rhett said after the three of them sat down to eat.

"Melt some Velveeta on it," Larry suggested.

≈ ≈ ≈

Frank stumbled down the steps outside the nip joint, his hands and feet completely numb after downing a dozen shots of 'shine. He'd missed work. It had been a colossal mistake to tell Larry anything about his service. Talking only disturbed the underground pool of memories that could geyser up and saturate his waking hours at any time. Like today.

How many platoon mates had been wasted because of crap intel that morning? More than he ever wanted to think about.

Fucking desert! You couldn't see...sand blowing everywhere, black smoke hovering from burning oil wells, daylight fading by mid-afternoon. He'd written about the worst day of his life while he was at Walter Reed:

The haji's tanks come out of fucking nowhere! Intel says the zone is all clear, but there they are, T-72's guarding a line all the way to the horizon. Our tanks go nose-to-nose with them, catching heavy fire, when the towelheads blow our tranny, and we're dead in the sand. Squad Four rolls over to evacuate us, but the hajis lob a shell during the transfer, a near miss. Both squads take casualties but continue the evac. Before we get clear, a missile lights up our Bradley. The hajis, we assume, but find out later the hit came from behind – FRIENDLY FIRE! Some REMFs* in an Abrams tank mistook us for enemy combatants and fired a DU sabot. Depleted uranium pierces and ignites everything in its path. Radioactive dust rains down.   [Kuwait, 1991]

[*Rear-Echelon Motherfuckers]

In the two decades since the first Gulf War – "an overwhelming victory with a minimum of American casualties," as history would record it – he'd often wondered whether he was one of the lucky or the unlucky that day. Few were left to talk about it. All he knew was that surviving as he had wasn't all it was cracked up to be. He had a chunk of uranium lodged too close to his spine to be removed, juicing him with radiation every day. His back was webbed with burn scars so thick and tight that his skin ripped if he stretched too far in the wrong direction.

The worst thing by a mile, though, was the visceral reminder of the Gulf – the wind and tattooing sand, the stench of burning oil, the pain and terror – he relived every day. Nobody could give him a diagnosis, much less a cure or even a palliative, for the fierce, goddam burning in his dick whenever he shot his wad. Unofficially, it was called "burning semen syndrome" – officially, it didn't exist – and Frank knew dozens of Gulf veterans had reported the same symptoms. Doctors assumed that, like every other physical ailment left over from the war, it was chemical or radiation poisoning, but nobody knew what to do about it.

Frank had spent weeks in the VA burn unit having skin peeled from his ass and thighs and grafted onto his back. When he finally had enough skin covering to go home, all he could think about was fucking his wife. It had been so long. He hadn't used a rubber because he didn't yet know he should. If he'd whacked off once or twice in the hospital, he never noticed any burning. He'd been on so many painkillers then, though, that he couldn't feel much of anything.

"Fuck!" Frank groaned in bliss the first time he came. Then "FUUUCK!"

"What the hell?" Katie said before shrieking bloody murder alongside him.

It took a couple minutes for the searing pain to subside enough to look for the problem. Frank didn't see anything unusual about his dick, but Katie's pussy was red and inflamed. She'd whined about it for days, and Frank felt terrible. At least he'd been on pain meds.

The doctor gave Katie some Percocet and a topical analgesic to squirt up her snatch, but that's all he could do. He said she'd probably had an allergic reaction to Frank's semen, but neither of them bought that because his jiz burned him too. Besides, Katie never had a problem with it before he enlisted.

Before the war, he corrected. He'd acquired a lot of problems he didn't have before the war.

He never screwed his wife bareback again. Katie kicked him out shortly after that, said he was too messed up and she couldn't cope with him. Fucking had lost its appeal since then too. Nothing like having a red-hot wire shoved up your dick every time you orgasmed. Drinking had become his favorite pastime. What difference did it make if he destroyed his liver? The radiation was bound to get him first.

25. Stalking and Strategizing

After supper, Rhett flopped on his bed and thumbed out a text message.

WHEN CAN I C U?

He pressed Send, then realized Darlene wouldn't know who the message was from.

RHETT, he texted.

The folks had finally caved and bought them phones, red for him, black for Riley.

"Your mom and I assume that as mature almost-seniors, you are responsible enough not to take pictures of your dicks and send them to girls," their dad had pronounced when he surrendered the goods the day before. "They might post them on Facebook, then you'd never get dates." He laughed.

"We take after you, Dad," Riley said, "so that won't be a problem." The brothers high-fived, and Larry chuckled.

"I'm serious, though," he said. "That sexing stuff will come back to haunt you. If you make it to the NFL, Perry Hilton will post the photos, and everyone will check out your dicks on the internet. Like Deever's."

"It's *Perez*," Rhett corrected, "Perez Hilton. And it's sex*ting*, not sex*ing*."

"You know what I mean," Larry said.

Riley snickered. "It's not that Deever's dick is small. He just has big hands."

"And he should've shot it from the bottom," Rhett added. "Makes it look longer." The twins cracked up.

"Just don't do it."

Riley ripped open the package and extracted his new phone. Then he pulled his gym shorts away from his body, aimed the camera into his pants, and started pushing buttons.

"What did I just say?" Larry growled.

"Kidding!" Riley grinned and released the elastic of his shorts. "The phone's not charged, anyway. And I'm wearing underwear."

"Lucky for you," Larry said.

"And for all the girls in his contacts," Rhett added, laughing.

"I better not find compromising pictures of either of you online – ever." Larry gave them his serious father stare.

Rhett glanced at his brother but managed to keep a straight face. "Wait a minute, Dad," he said. "You were looking at Deever's dick online?"

Larry spun away and tromped out of the room, but not before the twins had spied the beet red color rising up his neck.

"Is there something you want to share with us?" Riley called after him, snorting in laughter.

Back downstairs, Rhett's phone chimed. Darlene had answered quickly, a good sign, hopefully. Rhett opened the text.

SATURDAY AFT? ZACK WITH DARYL. WE'LL TALK.

"Yes!" Rhett pumped a fist in the air.

C U THEN, he thumbed back.

Riley sauntered in from the brothers' shared bathroom, naked, one eye scrunched shut as he ground a Q-tip into his ear. "What?"

"Seeing Darlene Saturday," Rhett said. "And *no* you can't come," he added when Riley's cock twitched and started to stiffen.

"Aw, come on. I'll play vids with Zack while you do your thing with Darlene."

"Zack won't be there."

"Even better!" Riley enthused.

"I don't think she'd go for that. Anyway, she wants to talk."

"She likes me," Riley pointed out. "She proved that on Saturday."

"Yeah, if she thinks you're *me*, dickhead!"

Riley's penis stretched outward as if it had been addressed, and Rhett knew what his brother was thinking. "Why don't you do something with that," he grumbled, adjusting his own erection inside his sweatpants.

"I just did," Riley admitted, turning back to the bathroom.

Rhett understood. He had to spank it at least twice a day – usually more – to keep from walking around with a boner all the time. Thinking about Darlene made it worse.

"Part of growing up," their dad had said four or five years before when he caught the twins masturbating.

He'd barged into their main floor bedroom to rouse them for school, and they'd curled simultaneously into roly-poly bugs on their beds, yanking up their covers defensively.

"Try not to go blind. And clean up after yourselves," he'd directed, unfazed. "Your mom's been wondering about the 'toothpaste' stains on your sheets. Socks work." Then he'd walked out of their room and shut the door.

It wasn't long afterward that Larry had framed in two bedrooms downstairs, then removed the separating wall when the twins told him they preferred to share. In the adjoining bathroom, he installed matching sinks and mirrors so the brothers could get ready for school at the same time. He also built a walk-in shower with two showerheads spaced along the wall like a locker room.

"The boys need their space," he'd told their mom when she questioned why he didn't wait until the slow winter season to tackle the project. "And a second master suite adds value to the house." Everyone was happy with the new arrangement.

As for Darlene, Rhett was torn over Riley's request. They'd shared everything always – possessions, friends, even thoughts sometimes – and neither felt wholly at ease when an imbalance existed between them. If only one serving of their favorite cereal remained, they either split it or both ate something else. If Riley drove this time, Rhett drove the next. They didn't have to negotiate; such things were tacitly understood.

But something was changing. Though Rhett had wanted to switch girls a few weeks ago, trade Jamie for Haley, Darlene was different. She was a *woman* – it was fucking massive. Since meeting her, he'd lost interest in high school girls. All he could think about was getting close to her.

The trouble was that Riley was right on his heels, horning his way in, and Rhett had no idea how to keep him out of it. When Riley scammed Darlene at the barbecue, pretending to be him, Rhett had acted instinctively by punching him out. He wasn't sorry either. It was confusing in a way, though, because there'd never been an exclusively *mine* or *yours* where his twin was concerned.

In any case, Rhett wanted his chance with Darlene, and sex with her wasn't a sure thing. She'd hesitated all along because of his age, and if both he and Riley went after her, she might get scared off altogether. One thing was certain, though – now that Riley had gotten a taste of Darlene, he wouldn't back down until he'd had more, and Rhett wasn't at all sure he wanted to share.

≈ ≈ ≈

Darlene had read Rhett's text and agreed to meet him before she could think too much about what she was doing. If she started considering the right and wrong of her behavior, guilt and self-recrimination threatened to overwhelm her.

Still, she wasn't sure she could stop herself even if she wanted to – and heaven knows she didn't want to. She wanted to make love with this eager youth in a man's body, and if that made her a cradle-robbing slut, then, well, she was. It wasn't illegal, though the townspeople might stone her if they knew. All the more reason to keep things under wraps.

Darlene could visit a tavern and find any number of men who'd have sex with her, but that got complicated. After the hookup, the man either chased you more than you wanted, or you wanted him more than he wanted you, and somebody got hurt. With Rhett, she accepted this wasn't a relationship situation and assumed he did too. Their lives were in different places. In a year, he'd be off to college while she stayed in Amity to run her business and raise Zack. In the meantime, couldn't they give each other what they both wanted?

Whatever misgivings she might have, Darlene had done nothing to prevent things from escalating, which meant they *would* escalate. She'd invited a sexually expectant partner to her home where they were guaranteed privacy with her son out of town. It was obvious what would happen, what she would let happen. She felt a sizzle of excitement low in her belly.

≈ ≈ ≈

What the hell am I doing?

For the third time that week, Walker had taken the long way home after going to the gym. Not that there was any long way in Amity, but Adams Avenue cut through a family neighborhood arranged to discourage traffic. You didn't turn off Cleveland and hop over to Adams unless you were visiting someone who lived there.

He *was* visiting someone; the someone just didn't know it. It was asinine, but ever since conjuring his shower fantasy of Father Arthur Endicott, Walker had been rolling by the rectory just after dusk in his Dodge RAM, hoping to catch a glimpse of the man through his uncurtained living room window.

Stalking. That's what it was, plain and simple.

Perhaps this ridiculous obsession wouldn't have started if the priest hadn't done what he did the first time Walker drove there with some vague notion of clearing the air. At six-thirty or seven Monday evening, Arthur had walked into his well-lit living room in gray gym shorts – cut quadriceps bulging, ass round and tight – yanked off his T-shirt and tossed it on a chair. He was as sexy as Walker had imagined, with sculpted pectorals and arms, a slim waist, and dark blond hair splattered across his chest. The hand towel around his neck tickled his chest hair as he tipped back a glass of ice water dripping condensation. Then the half-naked priest casually reached for his crotch and repositioned himself.

Jesus!

Walker hit the brakes. He drew in a sharp breath at the thrill of the taboo, glimpsing the priest out of his chaste clerical garb, secretly watching him undress. He was mesmerized.

Walker's hand drifted to his own crotch as his truck crept past the rectory. He'd been tempted to drive around the block for another look. He'd been even more tempted to drop in with the excuse – which wasn't really an excuse – that he wanted to apologize for his conduct of the previous Saturday. He hadn't done it, though. He didn't trust himself to stand calmly in the priest's doorway, even if the man put on his T-shirt before answering the bell. So Walker had headed home and promised himself he would deal with the situation soon.

Rather than call the priest at the church during business hours or make an appointment with Sylvia to see him, either of which would have been more appropriate, Walker drove past Arthur's house again the following evening. The rectory itself was dark with the only illumination coming from a nearby street lamp and the porch light, which lit automatically at sunset. Nothing to see.

Walker refused to let himself cruise Adams Avenue on Wednesday, but he didn't resist the impulse Thursday evening. It was harmless, surely, to drive down the street and look through the front window of a house. As long as he didn't get out of his truck, it wasn't *stalking* stalking. He just wanted to catch another glimpse.

As his truck rolled past the rectory, still dark, Walker glanced in his rearview mirror and spied a tall, trim man turning the corner – the priest. He wore a black clerical shirt, black jeans, and the full-circle white collar that distinguished Episcopal priests from Catholic.

The fuckable from the unfuckable. The thought, which should have made Walker feel guilty, instead made him smile.

He circled the block without thinking and saw that the rectory was now lit. He killed the truck's headlights and eased his foot from the gas pedal. Through the picture window he had a clear view of Arthur as the priest sat down and pulled off his dog collar, set it on the coffee table, then unbuttoned the top several buttons of his shirt. He picked up a heavy-looking book from the end table beside him and opened it to a bookmarked page.

Was that a Bible? Walker flinched.

What the hell am I doing?

≈ ≈ ≈

Arthur would have to do something about Stephen. The younger man had made a pass at him several days before, and so far, he'd done nothing to address that uncomfortable fact except to avoid Stephen when he came to the church to practice the organ. Now that they'd both had time to reflect on the incident, though, Arthur saw no point in letting the awkwardness drag on.

On Thursday morning, he took his *Book of Common Prayer* to the sanctuary and slid into a rear pew to read the daily office. Half an hour later, Stephen pushed through the double doors and started down the aisle carrying an armload of music books. He stopped when he spied Arthur.

"Hey there, fancy meeting you here," he called in a jokey, overly jovial fashion. "Kendra and I were saying the other day how everyone crowds toward the back of the sanctuary, and I suggested that we take out the last few pews so they'd have to move forward, closer to the front." He cackled. "Or we could put some speakers in the back and turn them up real loud..."

Arthur recognized the patter as nervous cover talk, so he adopted a neutral expression and remained silent to wait it out. Stephen chattered on a while longer, then began easing his way up the aisle.

"...so I better go and start my – "

"Sit with me, Stephen," Arthur directed quietly.

"But if I – "

"Please. We need to talk."

Stephen hesitated, then stretched his lips across his teeth in a too-wide smile and slid into the pew.

The sanctuary's acoustics were superb, and in the interests of privacy, Arthur would have invited Stephen to his office to talk, but this holy space, though cavernous, felt like a womb. The stone walls and wood furnishings had absorbed the prayers and worship of innumerable souls for more than a century, creating a calm, deeply soothing atmosphere. The space was also less intimate than Arthur's office, a benefit in this situation.

"This is about the kiss, isn't it?" Stephen said.

Arthur crossed his legs. "Why don't you tell me what you were thinking?"

Stephen snickered. "You mean it wasn't obvious? I'm rarely accused of being subtle."

"I'd still like to hear."`

The organist batted his eyelashes in a hyperbole of flirting. "We can hardly deny the attraction between us."

"Please," Arthur said, "I think we need to address this in all seriousness."

Stephen's grin faded, and he shifted in his seat. He examined his cuticles, then raised his chin and stared directly into Arthur's eyes. "In all seriousness, I find you attractive – very, actually – and I suppose I was expressing myself in that regard."

Arthur glanced away as blood rose to his face, not a reaction he would have preferred from himself. "Well, that's candid." He paused, then turned back to meet Stephen's eyes. "While I'm flattered, I can't allow that kind of overture from you. It feels disrespectful, and it undermines my responsibilities as your priest."

"You are gay, though, right?"

"I am."

"Woot!" Stephen said, punching air. "I was right. I told Walker you were one of the chosen."

Arthur cleared his throat. "Gay or straight, it makes no difference. Your behavior was inappropriate and unwelcome, and you mustn't repeat it."

"Okay, okay," Stephen conceded. "I had no idea Walker would get so bent out of shape."

"You can consider us both bent out of shape over your actions then. It won't happen again. Agreed?"

"Are you absolutely sure?" Stephen said, smirking.

Arthur leveled his gaze at the organist. "Absolutely sure. Now I'd like to put this episode behind us if we might."

"Oh, all right."

"Thank you, Stephen." Arthur rose. "I won't take up any more of your practice time. I really enjoy listening to you play."

≈ ≈ ≈

Walker's jealousy had been eclipsed by intrigue. According to Stephen, Arthur had put him in his place, said he wasn't interested in Stephen and didn't appreciate being mauled. The priest wouldn't have said it exactly like that, but that was the gist.

What he did say, not unexpectedly, was that he was gay. Why did the confirmation excite Walker? It shouldn't. He and Stephen were together; they were working things out.

After leaving the gym on Friday, Walker again found himself driving by the priest's house like a crazed fan or jilted lover, straining for a glimpse of the man. He considered walking up and ringing the doorbell, but it might have alarmed Arthur to find his erstwhile attacker standing on his porch. No, Walker needed to meet him at the church and apologize first.

A light flicked on in the rectory, and Walker doused his headlights and tapped his brakes before angling his truck into an empty space across the street, not taking time to parallel park. The priest entered his living room, and for the second time that week, Walker wished for a pair of binoculars. He gazed at the demarcating lines across Arthur's hips and thighs where the priest's sport shorts cut across his otherwise unclothed body. The front of Walker's jeans tightened, and he cupped himself through the material.

Arthur crossed the room carrying a small plate of food, and Walker squinted. A sandwich for dinner? After working out? Immediately, he felt the urge to charge into the rectory and cook the man a real meal.

Wait. He could apologize to Arthur for decking him and then, legitimately, ask him to dinner as a way to mend fences. Would he come? What with one host attacking him by kiss and the other by fist, Walker wouldn't blame the priest if he didn't want to venture within a mile of their residence. Still, they were gay shipmates in a sea of rednecks, and as one of the few out couples in the church, didn't he and Stephen have a duty to welcome the priest to their community?

Yes. So he would go to the church, beg Arthur's forgiveness, then invite him for a meal. It was the right thing to do – really, the *only* thing to do. And maybe it would get him past his fixation too.

The priest advanced to the picture window and drew a pair of sheer curtains over the glass. Walker could still distinguish flesh from clothing, but Arthur's form was now blurred as if immersed in murky water.

Damn!

With his peep show ruined, but a plan in mind, Walker backed his truck from the curb and pulled away, anticipation warming his face.

26. Consequences

Ever since brownie-baking day, Martha's thoughts had been consumed with her momma's sad passing, something she'd avoided thinking about all the long decades since it happened. It gave her nightmares and palpitations, always had.

Something had changed, though. Not only was she remembering that awful day, but the memories wouldn't leave her alone. Details she'd long forgotten had sprung into her head during the day, but also at night in her dreams. They wouldn't let her rest.

No way – *no way!* – had Edith let Granddaddy Murphy escape. He was too big and mean and deadly. Only Gideon ever unlocked his cage and usually just to feed him.

So what had happened? Edith must have gone to muck out the straw under the cages or feed some pinkies and fuzzies to the smaller snakes. Granddaddy Murphy couldn't open padlocks, and Gideon kept the only key around his neck, so it had to be him who left the cage open.

Why had the door to the snake house been stuck shut with Edith inside? Her momma should've been able to pull the string and slam the door on Granddaddy Murphy. And if he'd chased her, he'd have gone for the closest strike point, her leg. She never would have reached into his cage, not for any reason, and yet, the first bite – the deadliest one – had been on her hand.

Something else was strange – Edith hadn't been wearing her leather work gloves when Martha found her. She hadn't been prepared to handle the snakes, wasn't dressed for it. She should've had on her heavy boots in case a snake bit her foot. She should have had on gloves. She shouldn't have been wearing her favorite harvest-gold pants. Those were for good, not for mucking the snake house.

These were bad thoughts. Martha struggled to shut them out but kept seeing her Daddy drunk on 'shine, dragging her momma by the hair through the kitchen. He'd been drinking a lot the day before Momma left on her trip. They were fighting about something, knockdown, drag-out. Momma told Martha to go outside, but that didn't help because the fighting kept on all day, even after she went to bed.

Martha tried to push from her mind the newly restored image of her mother's face, blue and red and pus yellow with maggots devouring her eyes. Other things stuck in her mind too – the vicious gleam in Granddaddy Murphy's eyes when she opened the jammed door; the fearful widening of his jaws as he lunged for her; the awful stench of snake manure mixed with death; and three incongruous pennies gleaming in the sunlight beneath the snake house door. Pennies! She'd forgotten about the pennies.

The dead wagon – the county hearse – had come from town and taken Edith away. After all these years, Martha barely remembered the funeral or the days following. At twelve, she took over her momma's duties, the washing, cooking, cleaning...other things, nasty things. It was expected. Every farmhouse required a woman.

Any hope for a life away from the hills faded fast after that. Without her momma to encourage her into the world, and no money to fund it, she lost her get up and go.

And the years had passed.

≈ ≈ ≈

Frank Crawford perched on his usual stool behind the makeshift bar at Ida's, cradling his full stomach with both hands. As a recipient of the woman's austere form of mothering, Frank no longer thought of her as a nutria. She reminded him of a crusty old grandma who refused to spoil her grandchildren by dispensing too much affection.

He'd drunk his Saturday's allotment of 'shine, and Ida had fed him some robust Southern grub – ham hocks, white beans, and greens. Now it was time to move along. A wise man didn't hang around a nip joint all afternoon since you never knew when the Alcoholic Beverage Control officers might storm in and bust the place. The last thing Frank needed was his ass hauled to jail.

With the exception of that one lost day, which Larry had generously shrugged off, he'd been doing well – not drinking overmuch and working regular hours, never late or absent. It was the best he'd done in a long while.

He still had his problems, though. That morning, searing pain in his genitals had awakened him from an otherwise pleasant dream. No matter what he did or didn't do, he couldn't avoid that cruel legacy of his war. He could resist female barflies. He could even forgo jerking off, but the more thoroughly he abstained, the sooner the wet dreams caught up with him. After all, he wasn't so old or damaged that he had no sexual needs. In fact, with his self-imposed restrictions, he probably had more pent-up sexual energy than most men his age. There was just no way to avoid the consequences of an orgasm, intentional or not – the red-hot wire stabbing through his prick. He'd tried pain pills, but they worked too slowly to do much good, and besides, he didn't need another addiction to compound his problems.

Frank supposed there weren't enough sufferers – a few thousand, maybe – for the VA to research a solution. His generation of vets would die off soon enough and neatly eliminate the problem. Perhaps the burning would fade if surgeons dug the radioactive shrapnel out of his back, but paraplegia – the likely outcome of operating so close to the spine – wouldn't be his first choice for relief.

This dismal thought prompted a craving for another drink, but before Frank could catch Ida's eye, a banging at the side door caused everyone in the joint to simultaneously straighten and freeze like disturbed prairie dogs. Regular patrons tapped softly or stomped on the stairs if the meatballs didn't notice their approach through the peephole. Anyone who didn't know the protocol drew Ida herself to the door, and she didn't hesitate to set the meat on them if she didn't like their looks. Unknown visitors could be undercover ABC drumming up evidence for a bust.

The insistent fist pounded the door again, and a shrill voice rang out. "Hello? You in there? Let me in!"

Ida grabbed her shotgun and hurried to chase away the interloper. To Frank's surprise, though, with only a brief delay she opened the door and made way for a woman – nearly as wide as she was tall – to lumber into the joint. The aging creature looked like the entertainment for a children's party in her Carrot Top wig with blue eye shadow troweled up to her cartoon eyebrows and hot pink lipstick smeared around her mouth. The clown effect continued with her getup – a yellow blouse gathered in the middle of her barrel-shaped body and flouncing out like a dancing hippo's tutu, along with yellow leggings, slightly see-through, that highlighted the dents and dips of her enormous pocked thighs. Rhinestones applied with the restraint of Liberace spelled JUICIE across the woman's chest. Tan orthopedic shoes completed the ensemble.

Everyone stared at the bedazzled woman, eyes wide in amazement, and several drunken hoots broke the astonished silence. Was she an entertainer? A prankster? A laugh rose in Frank's throat, but he stifled it when a familiar fat man in overalls lumbered in from the kitchen and hailed the clown lady. On no account would Frank risk upsetting the wizard whose whiskey he regularly imbibed. The man was a genius with a still.

"'Lo there, Martha!"

Though the hillbilly was as tall and hulking as Martha was short and squatty, Frank caught the resemblance in their wide, flat faces, their small, rodent-gray eyes, and their weak chins dangling three or four rolls of fat.

"Floyd!"

"C'mon over here," the big man drawled and tucked a crippled-looking hand inside the bib of his overalls.

The woman named Martha waddled across the room and exited through the open doorway behind the bar.

From his seat at the counter, Frank observed the pair settle at a 1950s-era kitchen table, their large bodies swallowing two aluminum chairs. He decided to stay a while and eavesdrop.

"How've ya been?" Floyd asked.

"Can't complain, I s'pose. How 'bout you?"

"Same."

"You makin' good money off this place?"

"Purty good. I deliver to some joints in Cynthey, but I don't git to Amity much. Thought I'd see how yer doin'."

"Tell you the truth, I got me a problem," Martha confided.

"Zat right?"

"Girl at my church, endangerin' the well-bein' and good name of our Father."

"Our Father?"

"The priest."

"Zat right?"

"Yeah, but never mind. I need me a favor."

"Whazzat?"

"I need me a rattler, a purty big 'un."

"Nah...." Floyd's voice trailed off.

"I wanna set me up one o' them terrary things, you know, like a fish tank. I need a pet."

"You wanna pet snake?" Floyd asked, sounding less surprised than Frank might have expected.

"Daddy had one."

"True, but you don't need no rattler. Jus' git one o' them garden snakes at a store."

"Nah, I want me a rattler. I like the sound of 'em."

"I dunno, Martha. I don't like da idea dat. You ain't handled 'em in a mighty long while."

"It's like guttin' a hog. You never forgit," the woman argued.

"Well...I s'pose I could bring Maybelline. She jus' had a mess o' babies, so she wouldn't surprise ya with a litter." Floyd laughed.

"She big?"

"Purty big. Six-pounder, maybe."

Martha thought for a moment. "That oughta do."

"I'm deliverin' here fer two more weeks. The regular man got collared and has to set up new."

"I'll meet ya here."

"Alrighty."

Without offering any parting words or gestures, the fat lady rose from the groaning chair, trundled through the joint and out the side door, politely held open for her by one of the meatballs.

It was the oddest conversation Frank had ever heard – two hillbillies discussing rattlesnakes like they made good pets. He had no idea what to make of it.

27. Lift Off

Rhett lay on his bed sampling ring tones on his phone while his brother surfed the internet for cool apps.

"You still meeting Darlene tomorrow?" Riley asked.

"Yeah."

"When?"

"Dunno...afternoon."

"How're you getting there?"

"Bike."

Rhett was fully aware of the non-audible subtext of this conversation:

Are you having sex with Darlene tomorrow?

Hope so.

I'm coming with you.

No.

Seriously, it'll be fine.

No.

Riley dropped it, and though Rhett was annoyed about being pressured, he also felt a little bad. His monosyllabic answers sent the clear message that his brother wasn't wanted, and that hadn't happened often – never, really. They were integral to one another, like two strands of twine twisted into rope. The word *I* naturally translated to *we*, the word *mine* to *ours*. Or it always had before.

Rhett's rebuff now sat between them like a big, ugly turd stinking up the room. Riley wasn't one to let things get to him or show it when something did get to him, but he closed his laptop and left. Soon after, a jump rope began slapping rhythmically against the floor of their workout room.

I'm coming anyway.

Riley didn't have to say the words for Rhett to hear them. He scowled and considered that. It wasn't like he could stop him.

Okay, but I better not see you.

And Riley heard that as well.

≈ ≈ ≈

On Saturday Rhett shaved the sparse hair on his upper lip and chin and slapped on Polo for Men, filched from his parents' bathroom. According to his mom, Polo was popular in the early nineties, and though Darlene was nothing like his folks, she was older. The cologne smelled masculine, at least, if a little strong.

Riley watched him from the doorway. "Gonna smell like Dad, huh?"

Rhett ignored him, but made a mental note to ask Darius for the names of some good men's fragrances, since more black guys wore them.

His brother couldn't let it rest. "You better keep her away from Dad after this, 'cause she might go for him instead of you!" He laughed.

"Bite me," Rhett snapped.

"Nah, I'll let Darlene take care of that."

"Shut the fuck up, Ry."

Riley ambled out of the bedroom and up the stairs, and Rhett heard the kitchen door slam shortly thereafter.

When Rhett left the house ten minutes later, his twin was nowhere to be seen.

≈ ≈ ≈

Riley was confused by his brother's defensiveness. It's not like they'd doubled down on a girl all that often, but Rhett had never minded before. They hadn't done the full nasty with the same girl, so that must be the deal. Rhett was going for the gold and asserting his finder's rights in being first with Darlene. Fair enough. Riley would give him space to get laid once or twice, but then all bets were off. He wasn't missing out on the holy grail of sex, a hot older woman. No way.

Riley threw a leg over his mountain bike, pedaled down the driveway and across the street, then jumped the curb, and took off up the sidewalk. He'd have to approach Darlene's house from the back to avoid being seen, but he was pretty sure he'd recognize it when he got there. It was painted blue, he remembered.

Like her eyes. Funny, how he remembered that. Her eyes were cerulean blue, same as the crayon.

He reached Darlene's block in under ten minutes and rode into the alley. It was too bad she didn't know she'd already done him as well as Rhett, or he could just walk in and join them. This time, he'd have to be satisfied with peeking through a window. Rhett would know he was there but probably wouldn't do anything if he kept a low profile.

Darlene's side of the alley was bordered by a dense, eight-foot hedge that blocked access to several backyards, including hers. He grumbled in irritation. How the hell would he get through that?

He circled back and this time noticed that her next-door neighbors had cut a narrow tunnel through the impenetrable shrubbery. Riley jumped off his trusty 24-speed and rolled it into the open slice. A shorter hedge divided this yard from Darlene's. Riley crept along it, trespassing, until he was hidden between the bushes and the neighbor's fishing boat, which gave him cover from both sides while he waited for his brother.

≈ ≈ ≈

After pedaling to Darlene's house, Rhett tramped up her front steps with his mountain bike balanced on his shoulder, then set it behind the porch wall to conceal it from the street. Riley often didn't secure his bike, but Rhett was more cautious since he hated losing things he valued. He was more than ready to lose his virginity, though, and with any luck, today would be the day. He was nervous, but in a good way, like before a football game. This sport wasn't as familiar, but it should come naturally.

Come naturally. Rhett smirked. Whatever else happened, he was pretty sure he would do that, though he hoped to hold out long enough to make it worthwhile for Darlene. *Not much chance of that*, he realized with chagrin. But before he could psyche himself out with worrisome probabilities, Darlene opened the door.

"Hi, Rhett."

"Hi." His gaze dropped involuntarily to the two inches of deep cleavage exposed at the neckline of her blouse.

She chuckled.

Rhett felt a surge of adrenaline, and his nervousness morphed into aroused irritation. Was she baiting him? Did she think he was a kid? *Fuck that!*

He nudged her backward and followed her through the door. Then in an offensive move worthy of a varsity running back, he cupped her chin and pressed his lips over her surprised mouth, sinking his tongue inside. She gasped, and his dick, which had vacillated between semi- and fully erect all day in anticipation of seeing her, stood like a goal post, high and hard. Unable to resist, he grabbed her butt and crushed her pelvis against it.

Of the two brothers, Rhett normally took the role of the "nicer" twin, less pushy, more serious and considerate, and less ready to offend others, especially his elders. But "nice" suddenly seemed extraneous to this negotiation because, for the first time, Rhett grasped the power of his masculinity. Darlene, though technically older than him, was responding as a woman to a *man*. Her eyes had closed, her body had softened to his touch, and as he rolled his hips into her, she began to moan, a low, guttural sound that set his blood on fire.

He'd been right – this sort of urgent seduction came naturally. Rotating Darlene's back to the door, he lifted her to align her crotch with his, and his excitement ratcheted up when she wrapped her legs around his waist. He gripped her rear end and kissed her hard as he hauled her across the room to the white leather couch where he released her to slide down his body until she was seated. Her eyes met and remained on his while she reached for the placket of his low-slung jeans. With a curious mastery, she'd released the four metal buttons and sunk her hand inside his underwear before he could take two breaths. Then he lost all coherent thought as Darlene's smooth palm met the slick head of his dick and slid down its length.

"*Unghh ....*" Rhett instinctively pushed his crotch forward. More wordless sounds escaped him when Darlene sucked him into her mouth.

He couldn't guess how long her lips stroked him or count how many times he thrust, but when her soft hand slid down to cup his balls, it was over. He'd have warned her if speech were possible, but she seemed to know anyway when his body froze in suspended animation before deep spasms gripped him.

"*Jesus gawd,*" he croaked as rapture settled into euphoria.

She released him to lower his jeans and boxer-briefs, then watched as he toed off his shoes and stepped out of his pants. He crossed his arms, buried his elbows in the hem of his "Stolen from Amity High Athletic Department" T-shirt, and whisked it over his head.

Darlene's turquoise eyes wandered up and down, pausing at his abs and the flare of his lats, and without vanity, Rhett recognized that this *woman* was enthralled by his body. She grazed her hands along his belly, up to his pecs and back down to his butt, which she squeezed firmly. Rhett's cock responded to the attention by rising and twitching near her mouth.

"Holy crap on a cracker! You are beautiful." Darlene tugged his wrist, and he dropped to the rug at her feet.

"I want to see you," he said.

What he really wanted was to grip the front of Darlene's blouse and rip it open, but he'd calmed down enough to attempt undoing the little pearl buttons. When his large fingers proved no match for the fiddly things, Darlene took over, unbuttoning her blouse as he impatiently thrust his hands inside from the bottom. His breath caught when she exposed her low-cut pink bra pushing up plump half-moons of ivory flesh. He spied the front clasp and in the light of day had no trouble twisting it open. Her full breasts spilled out, nipples on high alert. He leaned forward to lick the left one, and she gasped, a thrilling reaction that set him suckling in earnest.

Darlene's eyes closed, her head fell back, and she panted from her half-open mouth. When he fumbled with the snap on her shorts, she stood to let him slide them down. He momentarily enjoyed her lacy pink panties before pulling them off too. He tried to swallow, but his mouth had gone dry.

Boldly, he reached out and touched her at her root, swiping his finger through a mysterious maze of soft, wet flesh. He stroked her again, and she moaned, then fell back onto the couch and widened her knees, revealing a central cleft, deep rose in color, its edges fluttering minutely. He wanted nothing more than to plunge his aching cock into the center of it.

"Jus' like that. Keep doin' that," Darlene murmured, her Carolina twang a melody to his ears. "Make me come, Rhett."

He'd never heard his name spoken in such a charged, breathy manner. *Damn!* He didn't want to shoot again before he even got inside her. He swiped his fingers across her several times. She repositioned them slightly, and then he picked up the pace, stroking and rubbing. Gradually, thrillingly, her breath quickened, her moans grew frantic, and like a piece of ripe fruit, she dangled, then dropped.

"Come 'ere, darlin'," Darlene said a few moments later.

Rhett's erection slapped him in the belly as he hoisted himself to the couch and reclined his naked length alongside hers. He ran his hand down Darlene's back to her curvy butt and felt the uncomfortable strain in his cock. Before he could think what to do, her cool palm gently stroked him, and he groaned.

"Did you bring condoms?" she asked. "I have some in the bedr – "

"Right here." He stretched backward to grab his jeans.

Thump! The front edge of the couch cushions compressed and dumped him on the floor. Darlene giggled.

"I meant to do that," Rhett said with a grin. He retrieved his wallet and pulled out one of the three condoms he'd lifted from his dad's stockpile that morning.

"Get up here and let me put that on you."

Rhett scrambled up and handed the packet to Darlene, then positioned himself between her thighs, holding his weight on his hands. With a mind of its own, his cock stretched toward her glistening red center.

"Jus' a minute there, cowboy."

He closed his eyes and inhaled sharply when she grabbed him to roll on the rubber.

"Please ..." he groaned.

"Right here, darlin'." Darlene guided him to her entrance, making everything so easy.

When his flesh touched her spongy, sucking heat, Rhett pushed forward and found a pleasure almost too good to be real. Unlike Jamie, Darlene didn't tease or limit his thrust, but grabbed his ass cheeks and sank him deep into her soft, steamy grip. A choked sound emerged from his throat, and he slung his hips forward and back without thought or intention, the pressure in his balls building relentlessly. Lost in oblivion, he could no more have considered Darlene's pleasure at that moment than leapt to the moon, but she didn't seem to mind.

"That feels so *goood*," she moaned.

The sound urged him on. There was no chance in hell he could stop reaching ... reaching, so he thrust fast and deep, counting down to liftoff. At T-minus-1, he held his breath, then launched into space. He strained forward inside her, reveling in the greatest pleasure of his life.

Then his arms went limp, and though he wanted to kiss her and hold her and – *oh, gawd!* – thank her, he collapsed on his beautiful, sexy lover instead.

≈ ≈ ≈

Damn! Riley rubbed his forehead. From his vantage point outside Darlene's kitchen window, he had a perfect view of the sexy action in the living room. It was way hotter than his dad's secret *Penthouse* stash. Unfortunately, when his brother lowered himself on top of Darlene, he'd gotten so excited he accidentally banged his head on the window frame.

Watching Rhett wasn't as good as being there himself, but it ran a close second since he lived through his brother's skin almost as much as his own. The phenomenon had both a good and a bad side. As offensive backs, Coach Simpson could use the brothers interchangeably to run the ball, block, or catch a pass, but when Rhett sprained his wrist the previous year, Riley couldn't take a handoff reliably for a week. When Riley got the flu, Rhett could barely run the length of the field. It was a twin thing. Riley had long wanted to meet and talk to the Barber twins about stuff like that. Tiki and Ronde had had long, parallel careers as college and pro football players, and Riley hoped he and Rhett might follow in their footsteps. He had big dreams for them both.

Right now, though, he nurtured only one dream – to catch some action with Darlene. Rhett had just gotten laid on her couch, thereby fulfilling Riley's self-imposed condition for jumping into the game, but realistically, Darlene would probably freak out if he just walked in and got naked. He'd have to work up to it somehow since she didn't realize that she'd already messed around with him in the bushes.

Rhett shouldn't mind sharing as long as Darlene had enough *va va voom* for them both, which, admittedly, could be a problem considering how often they both walked around with giant woodies. Still, he'd take what he could get because Darlene was *hot, hot, hot.*

≈ ≈ ≈

"Wake up there, cowboy," Rhett heard through a haze. "Do you always start snorin' the second after you come?"

"Wha ...? Was I snoring? Sorry. I didn't mean to collapse like that."

"That's all right," Darlene said. "You're allowed, except you're crushin' me now."

Rhett quickly transferred his weight to his forearms. "Sorry."

"I was teasin' about you snorin'. But you better pull out, or we'll have a helluva time with that condom. Or maybe not. You don't seem to be gettin' soft." Darlene chuckled.

Through his fog, Rhett realized what she was saying and started to push himself up.

"Grab that rubber," she directed, "or you'll leave it behind."

He knew the protocol, but since he hadn't done it before and his head wasn't all that clear, he'd needed the prompting.

"Bathroom," he mumbled, peeling off the condom as he went.

He gazed into the mirror while he washed his hands. His face was flushed and his hair tousled, but he looked the same despite feeling worlds different. It wasn't like he suddenly understood the mysteries of the universe, but it might be tough to focus on anything for the foreseeable future except getting back inside Darlene.

No wonder Coach didn't want his football players getting laid. He was always telling them to keep it in their pants. ("And if you can't do that," he'd say, "put it in your hand, and if you can't do that, put it in a glove." Some of the guys had turned the advice into rap.) He'd assumed Coach pushed abstinence on moral grounds, but maybe not, because at that moment Rhett couldn't have explained the difference between a dive play and a sweep, or even a plunge and a sneak, to save his life.

He stepped into the hall and almost bumped into Darlene, who was now wearing a tropical print cloth tied in a knot between her breasts. Rhett touched the flowing fabric and a slit opened up the front. He widened it with his hands and stood transfixed, staring at her *Playboy*-worthy form.

"Wow," was all he could say.

"Wow, your own self."

Rhett leaned down to kiss her, and his cock poked her stomach.

"You look like you got another go-round in you," she said with a smile.

Rhett snorted. "At least."

Darlene went into the bathroom and tossed him a towel, which Rhett wrapped around his waist before heading to the kitchen for a glass of water. He stood at the sink and stared out the window as he drank. He couldn't see Riley, but he knew he was there.

"Nice skirt," Darlene said from the doorway.

Rhett pivoted. Looking at her in her flowered wrap and knowing she wore nothing underneath, he suddenly didn't care about his twin's intrusion. His dick, which had started to soften, grew stiff again.

"You could be a model, you *and* your brother, ah'm sure."

Rhett blushed. Not sure what to say, but certain what he wanted, he strode over and encircled her waist. She'd brushed her hair, which now lay in soft waves around her shoulders. He sifted it through his fingers, then brought a handful to his nose to sniff its feminine perfume. Still lacking words, he leaned down and kissed her. She seemed reluctant to heat things up again, but he persisted, and when she finally kissed him back, he tugged the knot at her chest until the fabric sheath dropped to the floor.

He broke the kiss to gaze at her creamy breasts, letting his fingers wander up to brush their sides. Darlene's nipples tightened.

"You're so sexy," he murmured. "I want you again."

Darlene didn't move for a second, just stood there like she was weighing her decision. Then silently, she took his hand and led him to the bedroom.

≈ ≈ ≈

Twenty minutes later, Darlene lay contentedly on her back, trapped beneath a sprawled, dozing Rhett. She hummed softly and stroked his unruly hair. The young man's sincere and unguarded desire had quashed her residual guilt, buried it under an avalanche of other feelings. Though he was almost young enough to be her son, Rhett Pugh made her feel more like a woman than her ex-husband ever had.

Thump.

Darlene started at the sound. A tree branch must have struck the roof. She'd heard a similar noise in the living room, but barely noted it because this handsome young man had been exploring the loneliest and most neglected part of her. He was highly curious, almost like he'd never been between a female's legs before, but that couldn't be, not for the popular football star. No doubt girls were all over him all the time, like glitter on Mariah Carey's boobs.

He was amazing really. He hadn't held out long during intercourse, which didn't surprise her, but he'd needed little or no recovery time, which did surprise her and made the first point moot. Plus, he seemed interested in learning how to please her. It was entirely new to be with someone who didn't operate from a preprogrammed playlist.

She and Daryl had first hooked up in high school, and Darlene remembered how much the boys had varied in maturity level, both physically and mentally. Could she ever hitch herself to a much younger man like Demi had? Not a seventeen-year-old, of course. Darlene wasn't sure marrying someone that age was a good idea, even if having sex with them wasn't illegal.

Them. Why did that pronoun keep running through her mind? She looked at the tranquil face beside her, the thick, dark lashes stretching past high-carved cheekbones and the smooth jaw open slightly in repose. Why? Because two of these Adonises walked the earth, differing only in the presence or absence of a birthmark.

What would it be like to lie sandwiched between them?

Whoa, where had that come from? Rhett's brother, Riley, had been sweet to entertain her son, but he'd shown no interest in getting involved with a thirty-three-year-old woman. It was amazing Rhett had, with any number of teenage girls no doubt at his beck and call.

And high schoolers aren't a corn crop to be harvested, Darlene!

28. Sowing and Reaping

Riley stretched out on the exercise mat on the basement floor. He put his hands behind his neck, took a breath, then curled his long torso up to his knees.

"So you watched the whole thing, huh?" Rhett asked.

"Yeah, though I couldn't see much after you went to the bedroom. The curtain wasn't open very wide."

"Damn, I knew you were there." Rhett shook his head slowly from side to side before settling on the bench for presses.

"I knew ... you knew ... I was there," Riley grunted between crunches.

"So you admit to being a perv."

"You sayin' ... you wouldn't be ... in the same ... situation?"

"No, I would. Just sayin'." They simultaneously rotated their necks and grinned at each other.

Riley resumed his crunches. "So ... she rocked ... your world? *Thirty-five...thirty-six...*"

Rhett rested the twenty-five-pound dumbbells against his chest. "What do you think?" He planted his feet, tightened his lower abs, and pressed the weights into the air above his shoulders.

"She rocked mine ... and I was outside."

"There you go," Rhett replied, continuing his reps.

"So, like, we need a plan. *Forty-four...forty-five...*"

"What do you mean?"

"*Fifty.*" Riley lay back on the mat. "She mention an encore? You didn't disappoint her too bad, did you?"

Rhett lowered the dumbbells to the floor, grabbed a not-recently-washed towel and threw it over Riley's face. Riley wiped the sweat from his forehead, then sniffed the towel.

"Nasty, dude," he said. "So when are you seeing her again?"

Rhett didn't look at him. "Next week. Zack's got church camp."

"You're getting me in, right?"

"I dunno, Ry," his brother hedged. "She might not go for it. She might not even want you to know about her and me."

"Ah," Riley scoffed, "she's gotta know we have no secrets."

Rhett paused. "Yeah, probably."

"What do you say? Can I tap in for you?"

"Hell, no!

"Come on. You know I'd share."

"I'm not giving up my time with her," Rhett declared. "Anyway, she's a person, not a hoagie."

"I dunno. Looked like you were chowing down on her pretty good from what I saw."

Rhett snorted.

"If you don't want to trade off, maybe she'd go for some two-on-one action. You wanna ask her, or should I come finesse it?"

"Shit, Riley. Why bother asking? We both know you'll do whatever you want."

"Yeah, but you don't mind." Riley reclined with his arms over his head and stretched from his fingers to his toes.

After loading sixty-five pounds onto the adjustables, Rhett said, "You gonna spot me, douchebag?"

"Sure, twatface." Riley took a spotter's position behind his brother's head.

"Hell-arious." Rhett inhaled, then heaved the dumbbells upward on his exhalation.

Riley waited until halfway through Rhett's press, then said, "That's right, pussy lips."

"Pussy lips?" Rhett spluttered out a laugh, which constricted his diaphragm and instantly drained the strength from his upper body, as Riley knew it would.

With a Cheshire Cat grin, Riley scooped his palms under Rhett's triceps to prevent the dumbbells from bashing in his brother's skull.

≈ ≈ ≈

After Sunday's church service, Walker joined the procession of congregants passing through the wide doorway of the narthex to greet Father Endicott. He'd have only a moment or two with the priest, but Walker preferred that for their first contact since the bedroom punching incident. He moved forward with trepidation, Stephen at his side. Thankfully, this was the sort of thing his boyfriend did well, provide a verbal buffer in awkward situations. When they reached the front of the line, Stephen opened his mouth to speak, but Arthur addressed him first.

"You did a beautiful job with the Handel piece. It's one of my favorites on the organ." Before Stephen could reply,

Arthur turned to Walker, took his proffered hand between his and said, "Walker, I'm glad to see you."

"You too," Walker mumbled, suddenly speechless at the priest's touch. Arthur's smile seemed genuine, but three seconds later, he reached to the next person in line. Stephen moved on, but Walker felt compelled to seize the moment. "Father, can I see you this week?"

The priest swiveled his head. "Yes, of course. Call Sylvia, and she'll tell you when I'm in the office."

As soon as Arthur offered it, Walker knew an office appointment wasn't what he wanted. He wanted to see Arthur at the rectory after hours – alone. It was ridiculous to feel this pang of disappointment that the priest had automatically responded to him as a parishioner rather than as a man.

What did you expect? You slugged him the last time you met! Walker huffed in irritation at himself. He was lucky Arthur even deigned to shake his hand. The priest had turned the other cheek, metaphorically speaking. *Maybe he'd like to turn* both *cheeks, preferably while naked.* The thought leaped into Walker's head, and he was aware of an uncomfortable tightness in his pants as he walked away.

Despite his distraction, Walker had noticed two significant points during the brief encounter. First, Arthur's face showed no sign of having been walloped a week earlier. He must not have hit him as hard as he'd thought, which was a relief.

Second, Arthur hadn't shaken Stephen's hand in the receiving line. Stephen had kissed the priest in his bedroom but earned no special attention today, while

Walker had sucker punched him and received a two-palmed handshake. *To prevent a repeat?* Okay, maybe that explained it.

Walker escorted Stephen to his car, then cut away when he saw an elderly woman struggling to open her car door around the obstruction of her walker.

"Mrs. Fitch? Let me help you there." Walker hurried over and opened the door, helped her behind the wheel, then placed the folding device in the back seat and shut her door. "You're all set, ma'am."

On the way to his truck, Walker reconsidered inviting Arthur to dinner. It was a dumb idea. After the way he and Stephen had both behaved, if the priest even agreed to come to their place, the event would be painfully awkward.

He needed to see him, though. To apologize. He'd promised his mother.

≈ ≈ ≈

"Try not to hit anybody, 'kay?" Stephen said, smirking, as he left for work the morning of Walker's appointment with Arthur.

"Try not to suck anybody's dick," Walker muttered under his breath.

The couple had been moving forward as if the incident in Arthur's bedroom hadn't happened, but their relationship was subtly different. After an initial intense uptick in their sex life, Walker was losing interest – not in sex, just in having it with Stephen. Trust was an issue.

Stephen hadn't apologized for trying to seduce Arthur or promised not to chase other men who struck his fancy. Was he even capable of monogamy? Of long-term commitment? Whenever Walker brought it up, Stephen would dodge his questions, then distract him with sex. It was a pattern he'd begun to resent. If his boyfriend couldn't come right out and say, "I'm committed to you," then maybe he wasn't.

Walker took extra care preparing for his meeting with the priest. He shaved and dabbed on Rochas Man, a vanilla-and-spice fragrance he liked, though Stephen had bought it for the shape of the bottle ("space-age butt plug," in his words). Walker located his Eddie Borgo gold cross earring and stuck it through his right earlobe.

Hair gel? No...might look like I'm trying too hard. Walker had whacked Jack into submission in the shower to discourage the recent, insistent erections that threatened to reveal his secrets. He also adopted a strategic clothing defense, selecting a long button-down shirt, contoured fit, worn untucked over Levis.

When Walker got to the church, Sylvia wasn't in the office. *Darn!* He'd been counting on her as a social lubricant to ease his way into the meeting with Arthur. He took a deep breath, approached Arthur's office and tapped on the open door.

"Hello, Walker." The priest stood and moved toward him, then gestured at the chairs across from his desk. His eyes were a deep sapphire blue. That was something you couldn't tell from across the street through a window. "Please come in and have a seat," he said.

"Thanks."

Arthur shut the door and then settled himself behind his desk. "What can I do for you today?" he asked as if he had no idea why Walker was there.

"Well ...." Walker leaned over and pulled a loose thread from the hem of his jeans.

Arthur waited.

Walker sat up and cleared his throat. "I want to apologize for hitting you. There was no excuse for it, and I'm just ... sorry ... really sorry. I hope you can forgive me."

Arthur's face revealed nothing but concern. "Of course. I already have."

"Thank you." Walker lowered his eyes, surprised to feel them prickle with emotion. He blinked several times. "Thank you," he repeated softly.

"Do you want to talk about what was going through your mind?"

Walker pushed his right thumb into the knuckles of his left hand and cracked them one after another before he realized he was doing it. "Sorry, bad habit." He dropped both hands to his lap, then transferred them to the chair's armrests. "I was surprised. And angry. When I saw Stephen in your bedroom with everyone else gone ...." He glanced at the half-closed window blinds. "This isn't the first time that's happened," he admitted quietly. "I just ... snapped. But later, I realized he might have surprised you too."

Arthur nodded. "I made my feelings about his behavior clear and asked him not to repeat it."

"He told me." Walker bit his lip. "I'm ashamed that I lost my temper. I guess it's been building up."

"Do you want to talk about that?"

Walker considered it and found that he did. "It's becoming clearer to me that our long-term goals are different. I guess I thought he'd change." Walker smiled ruefully. "And maybe he thought I would. I don't know what to do."

"What do you want to do?"

"Haven't decided. I'm giving it some time."

"That's probably wise." Arthur leaned forward and caught his gaze. "Have you ever hit Stephen when you were angry?" he asked.

Walker's fingers dented the leather armrests. "No, never. I know what you're getting at and why you might think that, but that's not who I am. At all." He flexed his biceps reflexively. "I've had to defend myself – and other people – from gay bashers sometimes...."

His mind flashed through images from that bleak, brutal night ten years before when he'd tried to fight off three bat-wielding rednecks after leaving a gay club. His date had ended up in the hospital, and he'd made bulking up a priority after that.

Walker returned his attention to the priest. "I would never hit anyone who wasn't able to defend himself."

"You must have thought I could defend myself." The corner of Arthur's mouth rose slightly.

Walker's face flushed, but then a realization hit him. "You're a boxer, aren't you?"

Arthur looked surprised by the question. "Boxing is a bit cliché for a priest, but yes. I wrestled in college, then donned boxing gloves after that, mostly for exercise. I still bang away on a speed bag sometimes. How did you know?"

"The way you move. You're light on your feet."

The priest raised his eyebrows.

"I mean..."

Arthur chuckled. "I know what you mean, but if I were truly light on my feet, I could have dodged your right hook."

"I wish you had," Walker mumbled.

"Me too." Arthur smiled, and Walker smirked, an unfamiliar giddiness making his skin tingle. "Tell me, Walker, do you think you've been angry with Stephen for a while?"

"Probably, yeah."

"Would you like to pray about it?"

Frankly, it was a relief to voice his doubts with someone so accepting. Walker hadn't recognized how much his relationship problems were weighing on him. He nodded.

Arthur moved around his desk, then kneeled in front of it, and Walker followed suit, facing him. The priest reached out and grasped Walker's clasped hands between his.

"Dear Lord," Arthur began, "our brother seeks guidance during a time of uncertainty...."

Walker heard nothing more as electricity spiked through his body in an exhilarating rush. His lungs expanded with a surplus of oxygen; his head felt light; and heated blood surged to his erogenous zones like he'd snorted a popper. He was wildly aroused.

29. Feeding the Hungry

Maybelline lay curled in her crate in Martha's bathtub out of sight behind the shower curtain, and mostly out of mind too. Soon she would need live food. Though Martha had asked her brother to bring her a rattler, and though she'd met him a second time at that drinking joint to retrieve it, she didn't have a particular plan for Maybelline. She just knew that a snake was the perfect way to expose evil, especially if that snake had spent time in the House of the Lord.

It all went back to the Garden of Eden when God told Adam and Eve not to eat fruit from the Tree of Knowledge of Good and Evil. A serpent tempted Eve to do it against God's will and thereby revealed her inherent wickedness. That's why snakes were so special, because they had the ability to flush out evildoers. Anyone with evil in his heart was subject to the wrath of God through the fangs of a snake, and that was the plain, gospel truth.

Maybelline wouldn't bite anyone who didn't deserve it, or if she did, they wouldn't die. That was the whole point of taking up serpents. If you died, you must have deserved it.

The only time Martha had reason to doubt the wisdom of the snakes was when her momma was killed. Her Daddy declared that Edith bore secret evil in her heart, but everyone else had said her momma was a saint. For "sticking it out," whatever that meant. One of the deacon's wives had asked Martha if she'd like to come live with their family after Edith's death. Martha said yes, but her Daddy vetoed the idea right quick, said his daughter was needed at home and that was the final word on that subject.

For certain, God's ways were mysterious. Martha had a theory that He was lonely and needed Edith back in Heaven, which made her mad at Him, actually, because she'd missed her momma something awful. Still did, in fact. Her life would be very different if Edith hadn't died. Martha might have had a husband and children – or even grandchildren – by now. It didn't bear thinking about.

She had another, more pressing, problem anyway. Father was leaving town. He'd announced it during Sunday service. Martha didn't know how she'd cope for the three, possibly four, days the weekend after next. What if she needed him?

She'd been trying to comply with his request not to call the rectory except for church business. Important church business came up all the time, though, and she still had trouble getting ahold of Father. If she called the church during the day, either Sylvia or Sylvia's recorded voice answered the phone. Calling the rectory in the evening got her a generic message and a beep. If she talked to the machine, she either got no reply, or Sylvia called her back instead of Father. It was very frustrating.

Right now, for example, she needed to talk to Father about when he was leaving for the Vestry retreat and when he would be back. She knew the days were Friday through Monday, but was he leaving Thursday night or Friday morning? Was he coming back Monday evening or

Tuesday morning? Would he be reachable by telephone if she had a church-related emergency? What women were going on the retreat? She was a *mass* of worries. How could he leave her in the lurch like this? She was being as understanding as she could, but it was hard.

She picked up the telephone and dialed.

"Trinity Episcopal. This is Sylvia. How may I help you?"

Her again. "Who's going on the retreat, and who's looking after the church? Will Father be available by phone?"

"Hi, Martha. You have questions about the Vestry retreat?"

"Who's taking care of parishioners while Father's gone? What if I have an emergency?"

"Joanne Bowman will be staffing the office during regular hours, and Father Donnelly from Cynthiana will be on call and will also lead Sunday services."

Martha grunted her disapproval, but at least Father would be safe while he was out of town since that Joanne girl was staying in Amity.

"Now Martha," Sylvia continued, "if you need something, please come see me before we leave on the retreat because Joanne will have her hands full while I'm gone. Or if it's something that can wait, please call me after I get back. I would appreciate that very much."

"I can't believe you trust *her* to take care of people while you're gone. She can't do anything for me, that's for sure." Martha sniffed and hung up.

It was good news and bad news, but Martha's way forward was clear. She'd have to be patient, though, and wait for the retreat before taking action. One should never tempt the Lord thy God. The Bible was clear on that point.

≈ ≈ ≈

Walker couldn't believe how much Arthur had affected him when they met in his office. He could still feel a subtle buzzing in his body as if his every cell had been infused with a tiny dose of adrenaline. His senses seemed sharper – hearing, smell, taste – and even orgasms felt more explosive and intense. It was all in his mind, of course, but *damn*, he felt good.

He pulled a carton from the back of his truck, hoisted it to his shoulder, and headed across the church lawn. Kendra Washington had organized a food drive at the Piggly Wiggly, and he'd agreed to collect the donations. The food bank was his idea, so the Vestry had voted to put him in charge of the project. He was glad to do it if it kept even one kid from going hungry at the end of a month.

It also gave him an excuse for spending more time at the church. He couldn't stop thinking about the priest, and not as a priest, but as a potential lover, which was exactly what had made him so angry at Stephen. *Hypocrite.*

"Walker, hi."

He turned to find the object of his obsession standing in the doorway of the basement storage room where a chaos of cartons and boxes covered the limited floor space.

"Arthur, h-hello." *I was just thinking about you.*

"Ellie said you were bringing food from the grocery store, and I thought I could help unload it."

"Sure, uh, that would be great." *I'd love you to help unload it.* Walker flushed at the thought and turned away.

"Is your vehicle on the street or in the lot?"

318

"On the street, the black Dodge pickup, and there's still plenty to bring in. If you'd rather unpack, though, I can haul," Walker said, avoiding the word "unload."

"I'll haul," Arthur said, "since you'll know how you want things organized in here."

"Not really." Walker wiped the sweat from his brow with the back of his hand. "This is my first time working on a food bank. You probably know more than I do."

"I don't know much," Arthur said, "but the idea is to group like items together. That makes it easier to move along the shelves and pull things from each category for each bag of groceries. Fruits and vegetables in one area, protein in another, carbohydrates in another."

"Peanut butter and tuna fish together, noodles and potatoes together, and so on?" Walker shuffled some loose cans around on the shelves he and Dean Worth had built the previous weekend.

"Exactly. And baby supplies, like diapers and formula, in a separate area."

Walker nodded. "I can do that."

Arthur carried the rest of the groceries from the truck while Walker began arranging items by category. After the truck was empty, Arthur unboxed items and handed them to Walker to shelve. Walker avoided facing the priest in the close space because images from his ill-considered drive-bys kept cycling through his head.

How crazy he'd been acting, stalking Arthur. And now here he was alone with the man in this small room, all sweaty and fumble-fingered. Walker could feel the priest behind him, the heat of his body like an encroaching presence. He smelled the man's aftershave and the cozy scent of fabric softener on his clothes. Arthur smelled clean like the air in the hills, where the ubiquitous odors of tobacco smoke and car exhaust were too diffuse to detect.

Walker reached for a handoff, and his wrist bumped the priest's hand. A jolt like static electricity shot up Walker's arm, and he jerked away in surprise.

Arthur looked up. "Sorry. Are you okay?"

"Yeah, fine," Walker mumbled. He exhaled deliberately and took the box Arthur extended to him. His dick, which so far had been behaving itself, though just barely, strained uncomfortably against the placket of his jeans. "Taco shells," he said to cover his discomposure.

"Yes." Arthur chuckled. "I'm not sure how practical they are, but kids like tacos."

"Sure," Walker said, keeping his body turned away to hide the bulge in his pants. "Canned beans and government cheese in a taco shell isn't a bad meal."

"I don't think government cheese exists anymore," Arthur remarked.

"No? Gosh, my brother and I practically lived on the stuff after our dad died."

"Oh...you lost your father. I'm sorry. How old were you?"

"It was a long time ago. I was ten. My brother, Waylon, was twelve."

"That's a tough thing for a kid. Was your dad ill?"

"Pneumocystis pneumonia," Walker answered automatically, though he usually left off the "pneumocystis" part.

"AIDS?" The priest's tone registered neither surprise nor judgment, only mild curiosity.

"Most people don't make that connection," Walker said, and began aligning the cans of vegetables in precise soldier rows.

"I've spent some time on AIDS wards."

"Sure, of course."

The priest didn't ask the obvious question, and Walker didn't answer it.

Arthur folded a grocery bag and placed it on a growing stack of them. "So Ellie raised you on her own?"

"Yeah, she worked as a nurse's aide and gave piano lessons on the side while getting her nursing degree."

"She's a great lady, your mom."

"She is," Walker said, "and I take after my dad." He grinned, and Arthur chuckled amicably.

As he'd grown up, Walker came to understand that, like him, Geary Jones had preferred men, though unlike him, he'd pretended otherwise his entire life. In spite of the enormous pain she'd suffered – or maybe because of it – Walker's mom was unreservedly accepting of his sexual orientation. Perhaps she hadn't wanted her son to die of the lethal shame that had killed his father.

The men worked in companionable silence unpacking food and stacking and organizing it on the shelves, though Walker remained acutely aware of the priest's physical presence. Once, Arthur brushed against him in the tight space, and Walker had to grab a shelf support as energy shot through him, making his entire body tingle for several seconds. When Arthur wasn't looking, he jammed his hand behind his waistband to give his dick some breathing space. After that, he took pains to avoid touching the priest as they moved around arranging the goods.

Given his extreme sensitivity to Arthur's presence, Walker wasn't sure how to respond when the priest asked him to lunch.

"My treat," Arthur offered. "I want to thank you for all the effort you've put into this project. It's really important."

"Well...."

"If you have time, Jimbo's Sports Bar makes great sandwiches."

"I know. Um...okay, sure."

Walker maintained a safe distance between himself and Arthur as the two walked the several blocks to Jimbo's and grabbed a table in the popular pub. It was one thing to sport a raging hard-on in his truck outside the priest's house and another thing altogether to sit in a well-lit restaurant while his dick lifted the table off the floor.

≈ ≈ ≈

Arthur was walking a fine line, perhaps, but he'd never been single as a practicing priest and wasn't sure of the rules of engagement. Maybe he should confer with his spiritual advisor, Father Daniel, on the proper forms for socializing, but this spontaneous lunch invitation was fine, surely, a gesture of appreciation, nothing more. And people had to eat.

Arthur enjoyed their lunch, even if Walker had seemed uneasy. No doubt he was still embarrassed by the punching incident, which was partly why Arthur had extended the invitation, to help put that behind them. Over sandwiches the men chatted about sports, music, and local news – avoiding personal topics – then parted ways outside the church when Walker left for his factory shift.

In the short time Arthur had been in Amity, he'd developed great respect for Ellie Jones and was beginning to feel a similar admiration for her son, despite Walker's recent troubled behavior. The man had issues in his primary relationship, which Arthur knew – *oh, how he knew* – could drive one to irrational, if not desperate, action. But Walker's goodness shone brightly in spite of that. He noticed and cared about those less fortunate than himself. He was the primary force behind the church's food bank project, and Sylvia had told him Walker coached sports at the Amity Boys Club, providing an adult male presence lacking in many of the kids' lives. His motivation made sense given what Arthur had learned of Walker's childhood.

Arthur would admit to a spark of attraction for the athletic man, eight or nine years his junior. Physically, they resembled one another in some ways, but Walker carried an edge of danger Arthur knew he didn't possess. Frankly, it was sexually appealing – and *that* was exactly the type of thought that should propel him to the phone for a conference with Father Daniel. It seemed a little silly, though. Walker was an active parishioner with whom he shared some interests, that was all. Back in Illinois, Arthur had lunched one-on-one with parishioners occasionally and nothing improper ever occurred. He'd been married then, true, a boundary generally respected in a church community, but he had no reason to believe his personal ethics had altered with his divorce.

He spent the afternoon looking at budget figures and reviewing the agenda for the upcoming Vestry retreat, the annual event during which church leaders sought spiritual renewal and set priorities for the following year. The retreat would provide the perfect opportunity to present his ideas for the new healing ministry and seek allies in bringing it to fruition.

Walking home after work, Arthur's mind turned again to thoughts of this new era in his life. How did a gay priest reconcile his calling with his personal needs for relationship? And how did he pursue a loving bond within which his sexuality could be expressed? The church officially sanctioned gay marriage, but the membership was deeply divided on the issue, especially for priests. A schism had formed, and up north, Bishop Roberts and his husband had suffered death threats and been reduced to wearing bulletproof vests outside their home. How far was he prepared to go down that road? And yet, how much had denial of his nature already cost him? He prayed about it continually, but so far, no answers had been forthcoming.

Arthur pulled out his cell phone and put in a call to Father Daniel's private line. After six rings, the priest's voice came on the line:

"This is Daniel Lacey. I'm currently on vacation and will be back Tuesday, the 20th. For urgent spiritual care or church-related emergencies, please call...."

Arthur hung up. There was no rush.

Looking back, he wasn't sure how he'd managed to rein in his sexuality for so long. His basic needs had been met at home, which surely helped. Mostly, though, he'd been too invested in his career to allow disruptive thoughts or feelings to destroy what he'd worked so hard for. Perhaps it had always been a matter of time before his true self refused to be silenced. If he'd only listened to the call of his soul, faced the truth with his wife and congregation, he'd never have ended up caught in an intimate act in a public place. Even if he hadn't initiated the encounter, he'd allowed it, and that knowledge still brought a blush of shame to his cheeks. He'd gone to that cruising park knowing, however vaguely, what could happen. Maybe even hoping for it. And he'd blown up his life.

Father Daniel would say that, going forward, Arthur should address his sexuality in a direct, healthy way, which meant dating, preferably out of town. He planned to visit the Cincinnati church and attend the next healing service, and perhaps he could spend some time socializing with the gay membership there. He could go in secular dress, of course. Even priests were allowed time off and some semblance of privacy.

At home, Arthur stepped into his closet, and his glance fell upon the sexy calendar he'd hung there. The current month featured a large, heavily-muscled man – much like Walker, actually – in the act of pulling up his trousers, which he held artfully draped beneath his buttocks. The dark-skinned model was beautiful to behold, but what particularly struck Arthur were the words tattooed across his shoulders, a Biblical reference in bold, medieval script: *King Of Kings*. Extending the theme was a wreath of thorns inked around his bulging right biceps.

In a small way compared to the early Christians, but real, nonetheless, gay men lived under a constant threat of persecution, which living in the shadows perpetuated. Perhaps it was time for all like him to stand up and proclaim the truth of their lives.

For Arthur, at least, it was long overdue.

30. Fun and Games

"Yes, that's right." Sylvia had to yell into the phone to make herself heard over the staccato rhythm of a jackhammer starting up in the men's restroom. "The entire lodge, all three suites."

Sylvia had arranged for the Vestry to spend their annual retreat at Lake Cumberland, a gorgeous Kentucky State Park with cabins and lodges in the woods and abundant recreational opportunities. There seemed to be a problem with the reservation, though, and she was trying not to panic.

"Yes, still here." Sylvia tapped her pencil against a notepad on her desk. "You did? Whew! Okay then, I'll mail the balance today." She hung up and exhaled audibly.

"They found the reservation?" Joanne asked.

"Yes, fortunately. I don't know what we'd have done otherwise with only a week to go."

With that squared away, Sylvia addressed her other project – the church's restroom reconstruction. When laborers dug up the floor in the ladies' room, they found the sewer pipe so corroded that the Vestry decided to replace it clear to the street. Nobody was enjoying the mess or the noise, but the pipes had to be exposed in both restrooms before Charlie Hightower could get bids on the plumbing work.

Assuming the plumbers finished on schedule, Pugh's Concrete would pour new floors while the Vestry members, including Sylvia, were away. The timing wasn't optimal, but Larry was donating the labor, and it was the only free spot in his schedule.

"Are you still fine with taking charge of the office next weekend?" Sylvia asked Joanne. "Larry will be working here, so you won't be alone."

"Yes, I'm planning on it, and I'll be glad to have Larry around. I know he can handle anything bigger than me." Joanne smiled.

"I'll make sure he knows you're here and have him check in with you."

"Thanks, Sylvia. And thanks for whatever you've done to keep Martha Browne from coming around. I haven't seen her for over a week."

Sylvia smiled. "I had a chat with her. She also agreed not to bother you while we're out of town. I told her to talk to me if she needs something and not to call the office while I'm away. I think she'll leave you alone."

"I'm feeling stronger than I was," Joanne said. "If she shows up, I should be fine, and Mom promised to help out if I need her."

"We're off to visit Zack," Rhett announced that evening. "Where are the keys?"

Sylvia had been so impressed by her boys' willingness to spend time with Darlene's more-or-less fatherless child that she'd offered her car for the excursion. Their altruistic behavior seemed part of a new trend. They'd recently responded to a flyer Walker Jones posted on the church bulletin board requesting volunteer softball coaches at the Boys Club. They told her they'd signed up to help several afternoons a week for the rest of the summer.

Sometimes Sylvia felt a little smug about Rhett and Riley. She and Larry had done something right with those boys, and she was proud of them more often than not. They weren't overly cocky and full of themselves like a lot of boys their age. They were cocky enough, granted, but not arrogant, and they took an interest in others.

If Sylvia were being honest, though, she'd have to admit that her sons' good qualities had little to do with their parents. The twins had been resistant to parenting since they were small, deriving most of their comfort and direction from each other. But whether the cause was nature or nurture, they were remarkable boys, and she hoped someday they'd find good mates and make marriages as happy as hers and Larry's.

≈ ≈ ≈

"You're both wearing red tennis shoes," Zack said when he opened the front door.

Rhett glanced at Riley's feet, then glared at his brother. That was no accident. Riley was up to something.

"Hey, Rhett, will you play video soccer with me since I beat Riley last time?" Zack's eyes moved from one twin to the other as if he didn't know where to direct the question. Probably, he didn't.

The twins glanced at each other. "Yeah, I'd like to," Riley answered, thereby freeing Rhett to spend time in the kitchen with Darlene.

Rhett flicked his chin imperceptibly in his brother's direction, a silent thanks.

"Let's go then. How does this work?" Riley asked Zack, though he'd played the game on the twins' previous visit.

Darlene appeared from the hall, fiddling with her ponytail. "Hi! Ah was just finishin' a proposal in my office."

"Hi, Darlene," Rhett said, smiling. Riley nodded a greeting.

"Use this controller," Zack directed Riley.

"Shall ah get some snacks?" Darlene inquired.

"Yeah, Mom."

"I'll help," Rhett offered, following her to the kitchen. As soon as they cleared the view from the living room, Rhett grabbed Darlene's waist from behind and folded himself around her back.

"Hey there," she said softly. "It's good to see you." She swiveled her neck to catch his eye, and Rhett pecked her on the lips. "Ah'll get the snacks." She stepped toward the refrigerator, and Rhett remained plastered to her, clumping along behind. She giggled.

"You boys had supper?" Darlene opened the freezer and retrieved a box of pizza rolls.

"Yeah." Rhett kissed her neck. "We're not too hungry. For food, anyway."

Darlene smiled and set the box on the counter, then pulled the perforated tab to open it. "Ah need a plate," she said and moved to a cabinet, Rhett still attached to her back.

When he tromped with her to the microwave, she giggled again, and he took the opportunity to press his giant boner against her. Darlene shut the oven door and punched buttons while Rhett kissed her neck.

"Hey – " she began, rotating to face him.

Rhett covered her mouth with his, squeezed her butt with both hands, and yanked her tightly against him.

"Mmm," Darlene hummed, "somebody's glad to see me."

"Yeah, I brought you a present. Let me give it to you," Rhett whispered.

"We can't. Not with Zack here."

"I'll come back when he's asleep."

"Ah don't think that's a good idea."

"Sure it is. It's a great idea," Rhett said, encouraged. Anything short of an outright no was as good as a yes under Amity High rules.

"Goal!" Zack screeched in the other room.

"What the f – hell? I mean heck?" Riley hollered.

Ding! Rhett loosened his grip to let Darlene turn and open the microwave.

"Rhett, pull that pitcher of tea out of the fridge, would you please?"

Reluctantly, he separated himself from her, and they carried the snacks and drinks to the living room where Zack was whooping it up with "the other Rhett."

After his folks went to bed that night, Rhett tiptoed past a snoozing Riley and sneaked out of the house. At Darlene's, he tapped his fingertips against the bedroom window where a soft light glowed in the otherwise darkened house.

"Rhett?" she asked warily.

"Yeah, it's me."

The curtains parted, and Darlene's face appeared in the narrow gap. "Back door," she mouthed, pointing over her shoulder.

Rhett crept to the door that led into Darlene's laundry room and waited. When it opened, she motioned "quiet" with a finger to her lips and pulled him into the house, then through the laundry room and kitchen, and down the hall to her bedroom.

Rhett pushed the door shut and turned the lock, then lost no time scraping his T-shirt up his back and over his head. Darlene reached for the front of his jeans, opened them and slipped both the jeans and his underwear down to his ankles. Rhett's swollen cock clung to his belly as he nudged off his shoes, kicked off his pants, and lifted Darlene's oversized sleeping shirt over her head. He slid her panties down and held her hand for balance while she stepped out of them.

When she pulled him to her bed, Rhett stretched his long, naked form over hers, flattening her soft breasts under his weight. Angling his head, he delved into her mouth while the pole between his legs vibrated restlessly between them. He could feel her heat beckoning him, but when he lifted his hips, she seized his probing erection and directed it to the side.

"Condom," she muttered.

"Oh, right." Rhett grunted as he rolled over and stretched for his jeans on the floor.

Once he'd retrieved it, Darlene tore open the wrapper and rolled the latex over him, her touch drawing a soft moan from his throat. He pressed forward impatiently, poking at her mound and inner thighs before Darlene spread her legs and guided him to her entrance. Then he heaved forward and felt her stretch around the tunneling head of his cock.

"Ahhh," he groaned, the sound echoed by Darlene's higher-pitched one.

The sensation was still so thrillingly new and the urge to move so overpowering that Rhett began thrusting immediately. He couldn't think, couldn't decide, couldn't alter the behavior of his body – only give in to it – and in short order, his balls tightened, and a feeling of inevitability gripped the base of his cock.

Darlene grabbed his butt while cum spewed from him in long, glorious bursts. He arched his back, burrowing toward China, and then stilled before dropping heavily onto her. With his face buried in her fragrant hair, he muttered a muffled "sorry," though he wasn't sorry in the least.

He flopped like a soggy noodle for thirty seconds until his head cleared slightly and he realized he might be crushing Darlene. He pushed up onto his forearms.

"You better pull out, darlin'," she murmured.

"I'm still pretty hard."

"We need another condom, though. D'you have one there?"

"Yeah."

Darlene took charge this time, nudging him onto his back and straddling him. She adjusted her position, then slid down over his tenacious erection, closing her eyes in seeming pleasure. Rhett gripped her hips and watched her breasts bounce as she pumped slowly over and over. His jaw fell slack as the mind-boggling sensation built into unbearable tension. He ached to roll her over and stab fast and hard, but he resisted, and shortly thereafter Darlene began to moan. Then abruptly, her muscles squeezed down in a way impossible to resist, and rocketed him into another hellacious orgasm.

This time, Darlene dropped onto his chest and lay there with her eyes closed, her heartbeat gradually slowing along with his. He was drifting off to sleep when her lips coaxed him back with a kiss. His dick leaped inside her.

"You are one fine specimen of a man," she breathed against his mouth.

In Rhett's head, Riley's voice answered in a perfect imitation of Darlene's accent. *Ah shore cain't say the same about choo.* Rhett chuckled.

"What?" Darlene lifted her head to look at him.

"Oh, nothing. I was just thinking what Riley would have said."

"What would he have said?"

Rhett laughed. "That he couldn't say the same thing about you. You're *definitely* not a man." Rhett reached up and palmed Darlene's dangling breasts. For as large as they were, they were surprisingly unfloppy.

"Funny guy, your brother."

"Yeah," Rhett agreed, "he's got a crack for every occasion."

It occurred to him that Riley could be looking through the crack in the curtains at that very moment, but he felt otherwise. No, Riley was nowhere near tonight. It was some kind of concession that made Rhett wonder when his brother would make his next move.

Soon, most likely.

31. Judgment

Martha drove to the church Thursday after dark. The Vestry retreat was scheduled to start Friday, so Joanne would be the only one in the office tomorrow. The test was for her, nobody else. It was God's chance to take care of the problem Martha had pointed out to Him. It had nothing to do with her, really.

She backed her car as close to the church as possible, then went inside for some quick recon. The office door stood open as usual, and Father's door was shut and locked. The setup was perfect. Back outside, Martha opened her trunk and was greeted with an angry shake of Maybelline's rattles. The snake did not appreciate being driven around in the car. Martha hadn't fed her either because Maybelline needed to be alert for Judgment Day.

Martha set the snake crate on the sidewalk, then collected her handbag before tugging open the church's heavy exterior door. She braced it with her weight and pushed Maybelline over the threshold with her foot, letting the door swing closed behind them. The crate swished along the marble tile as Martha scooted it, the noise amplified by a furious Maybelline who was shaking her nether end like nobody's business.

Martha shoved the box through the office doorway, then grasped the shiny doorknob and pulled the door almost closed, leaving just enough room for her arm to fit in the gap. She donned the leather work gloves she'd tucked into her bag, then reached over the crate to unlatch its metal gate and swing it open. Removing her hand swiftly and smoothly, Martha reduced the door gap to a crack to observe Maybelline's reaction to her new habitat. Irate and defensive, the snake slithered from the crate and S-pushed her way across the floor to hide under Sylvia's desk.

"Okay, if that's the way you're gonna be," Martha muttered. She hooked her finger through a breathing hole in the back of the crate and slid it out into the hall. After closing the office door, she hurried to her car, tossed the stinky box in the trunk, and slammed the lid shut.

Maybelline was free to make her judgment, and she'd know what to do. It was out of Martha's hands. In spite of what people believed – that the serpent was evil because he tempted Eve – he'd merely given her the opportunity to reveal her true nature. It wasn't the snake's fault Eve failed the test.

≈ ≈ ≈

On Thursday evening, Walker was cruising slowly past the rectory – now a compulsive habit – when the front door opened and the priest stepped out, catching him in the act. He almost stomped on the accelerator before he realized how crazy that would look. Instead, he rolled down his window and tried to act casual.

"Hi, Walker. What brings you here?" Arthur asked.

"Oh, um...well, I was in the area and thought I'd say 'so long' before you left town," Walker ad-libbed.

"That's thoughtful," the priest replied, seeming to accept the lame excuse. "Do you want to walk to the church with me? I need to collect some things from my office."

"Okay...sure." Walker parked his truck and got out.

Arthur led the way, and Walker fell in beside him, maintaining a wide separation between them. He couldn't think what to say. It wasn't like he could talk about what was on his mind, how good the priest looked half-naked, for example, or how hard his cock got whenever he thought about that.

"How's Stephen?" Arthur asked, breaking the silence – and the mood.

"Fine."

"I heard him practicing Bach this week. I'm sorry I'll miss it on Sunday."

"Uh huh," Walker said stupidly. He didn't feel like discussing his lover and their faltering relationship.

"The Vestry is meeting at Lake Cumberland this weekend," Arthur said. "Have you been there?"

"Yes, it's great. My brother and I used to rent a houseboat and motor around there, swim, fish...drink beer." Walker glanced at the priest, who smiled.

"I'm looking forward to it." Arthur sidestepped toward Walker to avoid a trashcan, and Walker reflexively moved away, taking a few steps into someone's carefully tended bluegrass lawn.

At the church, Arthur held the door and Walker stepped inside, careful not to touch the priest as he passed.

"Sylvia's closed the office," Arthur noted, digging keys from his pocket. "We usually leave it open." He turned the key. "Hmm, guess it wasn't locked."

Arthur crossed the office and continued to his inner sanctum, and Walker sank into Sylvia's chair, rolling backward to stretch his legs. An odd rattling sound vibrated through the air. Was Arthur shaking paper clips back there?

Walker was thoroughly relieved that Arthur hadn't realized what he was doing, driving down Adams Avenue with his headlights off. He felt like he'd been caught peeking through a keyhole when Arthur stepped outside. He should just be a man and say something, admit his attraction. Maybe they'd laugh about it and his fixation would fade.

Arthur returned with a notebook and manila folder. "Shall we walk back?"

"Yeah, let's go." Walker stood and followed the priest. "Should I close this?" He gestured at the office door.

"There's no need to."

They crossed the parking lot in silence before Arthur spoke. "Did you have something you wanted to talk to me about?"

"Oh, um...no...not really." Walker wasn't the most articulate person on the planet, but he couldn't remember when he'd ever been so tongue-tied around anyone. He short-stepped to avoid a sidewalk crack, then adjusted his gait to miss the next one too.

"Can't have you breaking your mother's back," Arthur commented with a chuckle.

"No." Walker's face grew hot. It was an idiotic habit.

The two continued in silence, an uncomfortable one for Walker. Being next to Arthur amped up his adrenalin and short-circuited his brain. But he wanted to say something meaningful, something true.

"I-I'm glad you came to Amity," he finally managed. It was both far more and far less than he'd meant to reveal.

"Me too," the priest said easily. He stretched his arm across Walker's back and clapped him convivially on the opposite shoulder.

Electricity surged through Walker's torso from that point of contact and jolted him into action. He swiveled sideways and gripped Arthur's head – thumbs at his ears, fingers cupping the back of his skull – then leaned in and pressed their lips together fiercely.

For a brief, uncensored moment, the priest responded, and Walker's excitement flared. Arthur staggered backward then, and Walker stuck with him step-for-step, driving him into the shadows and up against the wall of a garage. He bracketed the priest's legs and pressed in close as he tasted him hungrily. Walker felt the thickening ridge of Arthur's erection and rubbed his own against it, intensely aroused, but also warmed to his bones by the unexpected receptivity of this man who'd captured his mind – and possibly his heart.

Arthur's hands rose to Walker's chest, and time slowed in the few seconds before the neutral contact became negative pressure, a pushing away. Walker detached his lips grudgingly. The electrical charge had faded, but a warm buzz remained in his body. He craved more, and also to know what it meant, but could find no words. He searched Arthur's eyes, and Arthur didn't look away. Crickets chirped a chorus in the semi-darkness. Headlights flared as a car approached, then passed.

"I guess you did have something to say to me," Arthur said finally. His expression was calm, but unreadable.

Walker broke eye contact and backed away. "I guess I did."

"Is this what you had in mind when you came by my house tonight?"

Walker's defenses collapsed at Arthur's simple candor. "It's all I've thought about for days...weeks," he murmured.

The priest nodded, at once accepting and absolving. "Shall we walk on?"

They continued in silence, sexual tension electrifying the space between them. When they reached Walker's truck, Arthur remained at the curb with his hands clasped while Walker moved around the vehicle and climbed in. He ducked his head to look at Arthur through the open passenger-side window.

"I'm sorry," he mumbled, feeling more shy than ashamed or embarrassed.

Arthur shook his head as if to negate the apology.

"We both need to pray and reflect. Goodnight, Walker." The priest turned and disappeared into the rectory.

≈ ≈ ≈

Arthur forced himself not to hesitate and not to look back as he went inside and shut the door, wary of what would happen – what he might allow – if Walker followed. It had been so long since he'd experienced pleasurable sensual contact with anyone that when Walker kissed him, desire had overwhelmed him before he could gather his strength to resist. His sense of place, time, and self fell away, and he responded instinctively to the man's confident, demanding touch. The longing that washed over him was so seductive and consuming that it took longer than it should have for him to come to his senses and regain his self-control.

Arthur pulled a bottle and glass from the cupboard and, with a trembling hand, poured himself a "Kentucky martini," straight bourbon strained through ice.

"Shaken *and* stirred," he muttered, and exhaled heavily.

He went to the living room, closed the curtains, and sat to sip his drink. He could still feel Walker's erection pressing insistently against his own. He sucked in a deep, stuttering breath and shuddered at the temptation of it. He'd have liked nothing better than to feel the full force of the man's desire, starting with another whole-body kiss and going from there. In that unsteady moment, it almost seemed worth the consequences to invite Walker to his bed.

He wouldn't, though...couldn't...not for lust alone, and what else could this be on such short acquaintance? Self-restraint was at the heart of his vocational commitment, choosing the right path over the easy one, the enriching over the corrupting. Unchained lust was destructive in ways impossible to foresee. Experience had proven that.

This isn't the same. The thought, like a voice, seemed to come from outside him, and it caught Arthur off guard. Wasn't it? What lay beneath his sudden, overwhelming attraction to this man? Was it merely the result of prolonged self-denial, a pure animal response, or was there something more to it?

He'd been backed against a wall, kissed, and intimately embraced, but where another man might have been outraged, Arthur felt freed. The unexpected kiss in an unguarded moment reprised an earlier scene in his bedroom, but the actors had been shuffled in the interim and that made all the difference. This man, with his factory-callused hands and unplumbed depths, made Arthur feel things he'd forgotten how to feel – attraction, arousing and delicious, and desire, dark and aching.

It wasn't right, though. Walker wasn't free.

When he returned from the Vestry retreat, he'd have to talk to Walker, ask him to visit his office after he decided how to handle the incident – or rather, how to handle himself. *Could* he handle himself? The question loomed large, carrying as it did the weight of his future.

He hadn't actively concealed his sexual orientation in the parish, but he also hadn't publicly declared it. Doing so seemed infinitely complicated, possibly hurtful to unsuspecting parishioners, and, if the parish rejected him or a scandal ensued, catastrophic to his career.

But what of your soul? the voice whispered.

≈ ≈ ≈

Stephen recognized the signs. Walker was less at home and said little when he was there. He ignored blatant come-ons and nudity but took sex in the middle of the night when Stephen was barely awake. Other things. It brought to mind how his New York patron's behavior changed shortly before he told Stephen their multi-year "arrangement" was over. Soon afterward, Stephen found himself on the streets, and his benefactor had found a younger companion.

He was losing his lover, could feel it coming. If he'd known how badly Walker would react to his abortive flirtation with the priest, he might not have pursued it. Sure, he'd been pushing the limits, but Walker had tolerated his peccadillos pretty well in their two years together, and pushing limits was more or less Stephen's *raison d'être*. He liked having his ego (and other parts) stroked by a cadre of admirers. Perhaps it was the performer in him.

He'd thought the Arthur thing would blow over, but Walker clearly hadn't recovered from it. Choosing the priest as his object of interest had been a major miscalculation. He was thinking with his dick, as usual.

Crap! Walker was the best boyfriend he'd ever had, and Stephen cared for him as much as he'd cared for anyone. It was a damn shame.

32. Surprise!

With his wife gone for the weekend, Larry was on his own to rouse and feed the boys before they tackled the church pour. He was billing Trinity Episcopal only for materials on the restroom job, so in addition to hiring Frank Crawford, he'd recruited his father to drive the mixer and his unemployed teenagers as labor.

"Yo! Sons of mine!" Larry hollered from the top of the stairs, having already made two trips to the basement to get them out of bed. Concrete men started work at 7:00 A.M.

"We're up," groggy voices replied in unison.

"Drag your butts up here and eat something. We gotta go in ten minutes."

Groans rose from below, and Larry smiled. Nothing like a day of concrete work to convince your kids that getting a college degree was a worthwhile endeavor. Though playing pro football was the twins' dream, Larry and Sylvia wanted them to expand their options. If the football careers didn't pan out, one or both might want to take over the family business, but they should have the choice not to.

Rhett and Riley shuffled in and slumped onto adjacent bar stools, then forked alternately into the stack of pancakes their dad had prepared.

"There's bacon and eggs too. You're gonna need the fuel." Larry scraped scrambled eggs onto their plates.

Riley got up to retrieve a carton of orange juice from the refrigerator and poured himself a glass.

"Pour me one too," Rhett said, then folded a piece of bacon into his mouth.

At the church, Larry angled his pickup into the parking space beside a pile of gravel where Frank stood waiting for them. When Bub delivered the concrete after lunch, the twins would wheelbarrow it through the vestibule and down the short corridor to the restrooms. But first the gravel had to be hauled in and tamped down and the screed guides attached to the restroom walls.

"Frank and I will put up the guides," Larry said as he turned off the engine. "You boys move the tables and coat racks out of the vestibule, then lay in the plywood sheets to protect the marble floor."

"What if they don't fit?" Rhett asked.

"They don't have to sit flush to the walls, but Frank will rip any plywood that needs it." He fixed his gaze on his sons alternately. "Do not – I repeat, *do not* – mess with the saws. It's hard to carry a football without fingers."

"They'd call us stump backs. We'd be famous," Riley said with a smirk.

Larry scowled.

"Dad, we've had shop," Rhett protested. "We know how to use a saw."

"Just don't. The company's not insured for you. And your mom might sue me – or worse."

By the time Larry had finished arguing with the boys and climbed from the truck, Frank had unloaded the sawhorses and set up a workbench on the sidewalk. The men grabbed their tools and made their way to the ladies' restroom where they positioned the laser level and prepared to snap chalk lines on the walls.

"FUUUCK!!"

The screams erupted from the vestibule in stereo, and a loud crash reverberated through the high-ceilinged space.

My boys! Images of amputated limbs flashed through Larry's mind despite the absence of the saw's whine. He burst from the toilet and charged down the hall braced for blood spatter, but when he reached the vestibule, Larry saw only an upended table and papers scattered across the floor. Rhett and Riley stood with their backs pinned to the right-hand wall of the fifteen-by-fifteen-foot space, their eyes wide and faces bleached of color. A hollow rattling noise raised the hair on his arms.

"Don't move, Dad," Rhett squawked.

Larry stopped short and Frank slammed into him, pushing him forward. Larry caught himself, then went rigid. "Ho-leey shit! How in the hell...?"

Not five feet ahead, a giant rattlesnake coiled menacingly, its upraised head swiveling away from the boys to the men who'd just approached on its right. Its tail shook like a hyperactive maraca.

"You're too close, Larry," Frank said behind him.

Larry slowly shuffled backward into the hallway, and the rattler instantly homed in on the movement by aiming its flat head toward him and lashing its forked tongue. Its coils tightened.

The archway to the narthex lay on the left side of the vestibule and the corridor to the Fellowship Hall opened to the right, but Larry would have to pass the angry reptile to go either way. The exit doors were directly across from him and equally impossible to reach. The men's room had a ventilation window, but it was too narrow for a grown man to crawl through.

"We need a shovel from the truck," Frank said.

"Right, right...a shovel," Larry echoed. Sweat tickled his temples and ran down the back of his neck. He didn't dare lift his hand to wipe it away. In a voice as steady as he could make it, he said, "Boys, I want you out of here. While this thing is focused on me, slide real slow along the wall to the door. Be ready to jump out of its way if it changes direction. I don't know how far rattlers can spring."

"Two-thirds of its length, so three feet or so," Frank informed him matter-of-factly. "It can crawl fast on this smooth surface too, but you should be able to outrun it with a head start."

"Okay, boys, go now," Larry directed, keeping his gaze glued to the reptile. "Not too fast. Don't startle him. When you get outside, bring the shovels to the bathroom window."

With Riley in the lead, the twins slowly sidestepped to the exterior wall, turned the corner, and continued shuffling toward the glass doors. The snake turned its head to follow their progress with beady black eyes.

"Over here, Mr. Snake," Larry intoned to draw the creature's attention.

Riley pushed the bar to release the door latch, then eased the door open. Fresh air streamed in, and the rattlesnake stretched toward it.

"Ack!" Riley yelled and body-slammed the door to dash through.

At the sudden noise and movement, the reptile launched itself at Riley's heels. Rhett leaped back in retreat.

"Riley!" Larry yelled helplessly as the snake lunged.

Riley's quick feet shot him over the threshold just ahead of the snake's fangs. He ran into the courtyard, releasing the door in his wake. The heavy door thumped shut with the snake halfway through.

"Ooh, gross," Rhett groaned. The reptile's innards oozed black, brown, and blue on the white marble, releasing a terrible stench, while its rattles continued to shake. "It's still alive!"

"We have to kill it," Frank said. "I'll take care of it." He hurried through the narthex and past the office to the church's front exit.

Through the glass door, Larry saw Riley creeping back to look at the trapped creature. "Leave it alone!" he shouted. "Frank's coming."

Knowing his boy as he did, Larry could see Riley giving the snake another shot at him just for the sport of it. "Keep your distance, dammit!" he yelled when Riley pretended not to hear and stepped closer. Even a mortally wounded rattlesnake could sink its fangs through flesh and deliver a deadly dose of venom.

Frank appeared around the corner of the church at a run. He grabbed a scoop shovel from the truck bed and rushed over. "Get back, son," he hollered and, to Larry's relief, Riley did.

Inside the vestibule, Larry threw an arm around his other son's neck and pulled him close. Rhett shuddered, and Larry squeezed him once hard. Then they watched as Frank raised the square-headed shovel and sliced off the snake's head in one smooth motion. He waited a few seconds, then opened the glass door and scraped the back half of its body onto the sidewalk.

"What's going on?" Joanne Bowman said from the archway to the narthex.

"Rattlesnake. A big, nasty one!" Rhett told her.

Joanne's face paled. "What? In the church?"

"Yes, it was hiding under the table in the vestibule," Larry said.

She gasped and slapped her hand over her mouth. "What was it doing here? How did it get in?"

"No idea," Larry replied. "But don't worry, it's dead."

They followed Rhett outside to look at the goopy remains of the snake. The vile odor met them at the door, and Joanne pinched her nose shut.

"You okay, Ry?" Larry grabbed his reckless son's shoulder, relief displacing annoyance.

"Yeah, Dad, he missed me."

Rhett cuffed Riley on the arm. "Thanks for leaving me to get bit, fucktard!"

Riley backed away and kicked a divot in the grass. "Sorry, I freaked."

"It's a big one," Frank said. "Six or seven rattles. Do you want them for a souvenir?"

"Hell, yeah," Rhett replied. "Cool."

Frank positioned the edge of the shovel, then sheared off the transparent kernels at the tail end of the snake. He handed the rattles to Rhett. Joanne cringed and turned away.

"Riley, get a garbage bag from the truck," Larry said, "so we can dispose of the thing."

"Larry, would you go to the office with me?" Joanne asked, clearly distressed. "What if there's another one?"

"Breeding mates travel in pairs," Frank said, "but the Western diamondback isn't native to Kentucky, so this one probably escaped from somewhere. I recently heard some hicks talking about their pet rattlers."

Everybody stared at Frank. Larry had never heard the quiet man string that many words together at one time. "How do you know so much about snakes?" he asked.

"Survival skill in New Mexico."

"You're from New Mexico?"

Frank nodded and looked away.

"I'll check the office," Larry said to Joanne and held out his hand for the shovel.

≈ ≈ ≈

Martha had expected Maybelline's decision on Friday, but Saturday morning came and went without a word. Sylvia was gone for the weekend and Martha had promised not to phone the church office, so how was she supposed to know what happened? She waited for as long as she could stand it.

"I'll just go peek in the window," she decided in a flash of inspiration.

She peered down at the lemon yellow sweatshirt she was wearing, one of her favorites. It featured the capital letters MUFF across her chest, surrounded by a red circle with a line going through it. She didn't know what that meant, but the shirt was colorful and had been a great deal for twenty-five cents at a garage sale. A darker color might be a better choice for her current mission, though.

"Oh! I have the *perfect* outfit," she realized.

Half an hour later as she drove down Cleveland Avenue, Martha saw a cement mixer parked near the side entrance to the church. A scattering of sand and scraps of wood lay nearby.

"What's going on?"

She had half a mind to roll down her window and ask what they thought they were doing, making such a mess on church property, but she was also torn. She didn't want Sylvia to find out she'd been at the church after she promised to stay away. Sylvia was such a tattletale she'd probably tell Father, and he might get mad at her.

After Father had escorted her from his party, Martha had decided to teach him a lesson by not talking to him, calling, or visiting the church office for a whole week. If he was mean to her again, she'd have to start his punishment over, which she didn't want to do because it was too hard and painful. After all these years she finally understood what her momma had meant when she said "This hurts me as much as it hurts you" before giving her a spanking. Martha had never believed it before.

Since this was kind of a spy mission and Martha didn't want anyone to see her at the church, she briefly considered parking in the next block. She didn't like to walk, though, so as a compromise she parked three rows from the door and several spaces away from the other car in the lot.

She walked casually toward the church, then peeked over her shoulder before darting across the five feet of "no man's lawn" between the asphalt and the shelter of the foundation plantings. The shrubbery was tall as juniper bushes go but still hid only her lower half, so she'd wisely donned her Daddy's camouflage gear and worn her dark Jackie O. wig. Since she couldn't get arrested for looking in church windows, as far as she knew, she hadn't gone all out and smeared shoe polish on her face.

Martha bushwhacked into the prickly junipers and a gin scent tickled her nose. Some 'shiners used the berries as flavoring, but she didn't care for it herself. She flattened herself to the stone façade and blazed a path to the nearest window, then peeked around the window frame. The blinds were closed.

"Must be Father's office." She struggled past another clingy, smelly bush to the next window only to find more closed blinds. "Shoot!"

A clattering sound came through the window and Martha froze.

"Darn it!" rose a muffled cry, a female voice.

She shoved her way to the next window. If judgment had been meted out, then who was in the office and why wasn't there more commotion? She edged her face into the next square of window glass and saw a woman standing beside Sylvia's desk, her back to Martha.

No! It was *her*, that Joanne, dabbing at something on the front of her blouse. Martha drooped with disappointment. Was it possible that Maybelline had decided in Joanne's favor? Martha didn't see how since she'd been there when the girl touched Father's privates, and now she was hanging around his office all the time. In Martha's experience, bad people stayed bad and usually got worse. Maybe Maybelline was napping and hadn't gotten around to judging yet.

"Damn!"

Martha bashed her way out of the bushes, knocking her wig sideways in the process. Frustrated and vexed, she pawed at her hair, trying to find the front of it as she stomped to her car, muttering bad words the entire way.

33. Trials

"**A** rattlesnake in the church," Rhett mumbled from his bed where he lay sprawled, his muscles sore. Everyone knew concrete was heavy, especially wet concrete – obviously – but until you'd pushed twenty-five loads of it thirty yards in a wheelbarrow, you really had no idea.

"Yeah, that was wild. I wonder what it was doing there, how it got in." Riley clipped off another toenail that flew somewhere wide of the desk-side trashcan he'd positioned below his foot.

"Me too. Scared the bejesus out of me."

"You should've seen your face!" Riley opened his eyes and mouth wide in a bug-eyed imitation.

Rhett snorted. "You looked like you crapped your pants."

Riley positioned the clippers on the next toenail. "I'd rather have my snake in a bush than two snakes in my hand," he mused. "Speaking of which, what's the deal with your girlfriend?"

"What do you mean?"

"When are you supposed to see her again? I want to mark my calendar."

Rhett grabbed a pillow and threw it, knocking the nail clippers from his brother's hand.

"Hey!" Riley protested, then snatched up the pillow and launched it back.

Rhett caught it and tucked it under his head. "She's not my girlfriend."

"You know what I mean. I want a turn."

Rhett nabbed a tennis ball from the nightstand and tossed it above his head, caught it, then tossed it again.

"I'm serious, bro."

Rhett caught the ball and lobbed it up again. He knew what his brother meant. If he didn't let Riley stand in for him in a hookup with Darlene, then his brother would press her for a three-way.

She's mine! he wanted to yell, but saying the words aloud would only underscore the fact that Riley was ignoring them. And how much it mattered.

But his brother knew that too.

"You want to talk about this?" Riley asked in a quieter tone.

Rhett tossed and caught the ball three more times. "I guess not," he said finally, ignoring the twinge in his gut. He pressed the rubber sphere into his chest and stared at the ceiling. "Monday," he said. "Supper. You're invited."

"Why the hell didn't you tell me?"

"Didn't have to. You'd show up anyway."

Rhett thrust upward and free-threw the ball into Riley's trashcan, a perfect, no-rim shot.

"True," Riley admitted with a grin, plucking the ball out of the air on its bounce.

≈ ≈ ≈

Martha went to church on Sunday as usual, though Father Donnelly could in no way be compared to Father

Arthur. For one thing, he wasn't handsome. Father Donnelly was a redhead with freckles. Whoever heard of a priest with freckles? How could you take him seriously? Plus, he was older than Father Arthur by at least a decade and was losing his hair. He was an okay priest, she supposed, but not someone you could get close with.

Though Father Arthur was away, Martha couldn't skip church because she needed to know what happened with Maybelline. She arrived fifteen minutes early for the second service and loitered in the narthex, but she heard nothing about her snake. Not one word. When the invocation began, she stomped her foot in frustration, then shuffled up the center aisle to her usual seat. She plopped down heavily, glad at least to have the row to herself. Sometimes new people filed into the second pew and she had to flash them dirty looks until they got the message that they were in the wrong place.

The service dragged on, boring and tedious without Father's glorious voice to listen to and his handsome face to gaze at. He often looked right at her when he spoke, and that's how she knew she was special to him in the same way he was special to her.

She'd called the rectory on both Friday and Saturday because how could Father mind if he wasn't there? It was only fair that she should get to hear his new voice greeting on the answering machine if he left for a whole weekend. It had been infuriating, though, because the machine wouldn't let her finish her message. She'd be right in the middle of telling Father about her day, and it would go *Beep* and hang up. She'd had to call back several times to continue each conversation. It was even worse when she'd called before church because a nasal-voiced lady had said, "Mailbox is full," and hung up. Martha didn't hear Father's voice and couldn't leave a message either. So rude!

As soon as the service ended, Martha clambered up to escape the sanctuary. The nancy-boy organist was playing so loud and the song had so many notes that it tweaked her nerves. That rock-and-roll noise wasn't appropriate in a church. Didn't he know that? Mr. J. S. Bach could stay in the 1960s where he belonged with his music that made you hallucinate. Though she was stuck in the holler during those years, she'd heard all about it from her brother. People smoked "wacky tobaccey" and had intimate relations with everyone in sight.

"I'm telling Father when he gets back. We don't need that revelationary stuff in our church!" Martha griped, holding her hands over her ears.

She joined the exodus to the Fellowship Hall for coffee hour, glad to see Charlie Hightower was finally doing something about the ladies' room. A sign blocking the hallway said "KEEP OUT. WET CONCRETE."

"About time," Martha said when she passed. A layer of wood sat atop the floor of the roped-off hallway creating a lip along the edge. "Somebody could fall!" she exclaimed. An elderly couple looked at her, obviously in agreement. "Everything goes to hell when Father's not here," she told them. They turned away quickly.

No sign of the girl. At least that was something.

"Oh, there she is," Martha grumbled when Joanne entered the Fellowship Hall ten minutes later. "Damn, damn, damn!"

People turned and stared, and Martha had to suppress the urge to stick out her tongue at them. She patted her Farrah Fawcett wig and glanced down. *Oh.* Her apricot shift had wedged between two rolls of her belly, making the hemline rise high up her thighs in the front. Her Large 'n' Lovely undergarments weren't doing their job today. She pulled the fabric free and straightened her dress.

"What is Maybelline thinking?" she wondered aloud.

The office was open, so the snake could be hiding anywhere by now, ready to cast judgment on anyone, not that that was her problem. The snake wouldn't bite her. She was about as pure and holy as a soul could be. She honored her parents, didn't prevaricate, only rarely took the Lord's name in vain. She'd never fornicated as so many girls did nowadays and had even retained her maidenhood – just like the Virgin Mary when you thought about it.

She hate-hate-*hated* that Joanne was standing in the refreshments line, pretty as you please. She simply must know what had happened.

Martha sneaked over and nudged her way into the line a few people behind the girl, then perked up her ears.

"It was unbelievable. It's still creeping me out," Joanne said to the woman beside her.

What was? What?

"Of course it is," the woman replied. "I'm a little nervous myself."

"You should have seen it, Mom. It was huge! And the smell...I almost threw up."

"Shhh, people are eating here," the mom said.

The two selected some cookies and moved off.

"Damn!" Martha blurted again.

A high-spirited ruckus broke out, and she looked over to see a group of boys – two white, two black – horsing around. She turned away.

Wait a minute. Those white boys looked familiar, and they were worked up about something. She strained to hear.

"You're kidding me! A snake?" the older black boy said.

"A rattlesnake," answered a white one.

"He almost bit me!"

"Yeah, Ry dashed, and the snake dove for him. I held my ground like a man."

"They're talking about Maybelline!" Martha abandoned the food counter and clomped toward the boys, who started scuffling and laughing.

"What happened? What happened?" Martha said under her breath. Then she saw for herself as one of the boys pulled something from his pocket and held it up for the others to see. He shook his fingers, and she heard the unmistakable *clickity click* of a rattlesnake's tail.

"Maybelline!" Martha slapped her hands to her cheeks. "They killed Maybelline!"

≈ ≈ ≈

"What a crazy old bat," Riley remarked after his dad stepped in and guided the shrieking fat lady out of the church.

She'd waddled toward them – him and Rhett, Darius and Shane – waving her arms and bellowing. They'd tried to be polite, but she raised her fists and he'd had to grab her wrists to stop her from hitting him.

"Who was that?" Darius asked.

"No idea," Rhett said, "but she was ranting about makeup, I think."

"The BJ lips, right?" Riley said with a sideways grin at his twin. They'd seen this freakin' hot commercial where a woman's poochy pink lips filled the screen while a sexy voice whispered "...with honey nectar..." like they were advertising a blow job.

Maybelline lipstick...just the shade to decorate your cock!

"Seemed like she was grabbing for your rattles, dude!" Shane said, interrupting Riley's fantasy.

"Yeah," he replied, "maybe she's scared of snakes."

≈ ≈ ≈

Martha was mad as hell. Those damn kids had killed Maybelline! When she saw her snake's rattles in that boy's hand, she'd charged over and tried to take them back. They were hers!

She wasn't sure what happened after that, but she found herself outside before she could protest. The big man who escorted her to her car had asked what she was upset about, but by then she'd pulled herself together enough to realize she shouldn't answer. If they knew Maybelline belonged to her, they might blame her for whatever had happened. Unfortunately, it also meant Martha couldn't ask what *had* happened and why those horrid boys had killed her snake. She'd bet beavers to buzzards that Joanne had put them up to it, though, to avoid God's judgment. How dare she defy Him?

There was only one thing left to do. Martha had to confront the girl and expose her evil ways, make everyone see her for what she was. Time was running short. Father would be home in one day, and there was no way – *no darn way* – she would let things continue as they were. Father must be protected.

Unlike the prophet Daniel, though, Martha couldn't walk into the lion's den and not get eaten, couldn't throw herself into the fire without getting burned. And so she sat at her kitchen table, peering one-eyed into the barrel of her Daddy's Smith & Wesson revolver, which was showing a little exterior rust. She dipped a bore brush in solvent and twisted it through the barrel in both directions, then repeated the procedure for each of its five cylinders. No corrosion, which was good. She rubbed it down with gun oil and fine steel wool. When you grew up in a family that fed itself by hunting, you knew how to clean a gun.

Martha didn't overthink the implications of carrying. She wouldn't have to use the weapon. Once she made it clear to Joanne that she knew *everything* and demanded she go away and leave Father alone, the girl wouldn't resist. Her kind were like cockroaches that scattered the instant you turned on the light. As far as Martha was concerned, that girl could scurry away and hide in somebody else's kitchen.

34. Fade to Black

Joanne pressed CTRL-S to save her resume. She loved working with Sylvia, but she needed to make some real money to move out of her folks' place and get on with her life. Counseling with Father Arthur had boosted her confidence, and she was ready to consider full-time employment.

The debilitating presence of Martha Browne had been the only negative to the church job. The woman seemed obsessed with her. Joanne shuddered. Between the rattlesnake incident and worrying that the old lady would show up and harass her, she was eagerly awaiting Sylvia and Arthur's return to the office.

Bored with the *Lexington Tribune* want ads, Joanne scanned through the personals. Nothing interesting. Out of curiosity, she returned to the keyboard and pulled up MatchMe.com, then entered a search for men in her age range countywide. *Whoa!* Several hundred hits. She perused the mini-bios for farmers, salesmen, a teacher, a pharmacist (the latter seeming particularly appropriate). What might an ad for herself look like?

Former locked-ward resident w/ fear of outdoors seeks prince to cohabit in parents' basement. Hobbies: Dingdongs, razor blades, online dating.

Yeah, she was a real prize. Still, it might be worth a try. Maybe someone nice would take pity on her. This one looked promising:

> *Christian man, 36, wants companion for candlelit dinners, walks in park, cruising on lake. Enjoys dogs, C&W, line dancing.*

She didn't know a thing about line dancing and wasn't a big fan of country music, but the guy was cute. Another possibility:

> *34-yo rancher seeks woman, 30-40, for date nights, laughs, romance. Likes horses, Harleys, hot mamas...*

She didn't qualify as hot, especially, but she liked horses and laughs would be nice for a change.

> *33yo swm looking for swf 25-35 for city lights, wild nights. Into tats, body mods, metal...*

Joanne was so engrossed in this smorgasbord of possibilities that she failed to hear the exterior church door swing open. It wasn't until a metal trashcan clanked into the copy machine behind her that she realized someone had entered the office. Her body jerked involuntarily, and she let out a squeak of surprise. She'd just begun to swivel her chair when a loud noise blasted her ears; she felt a harsh burn in her nose; and the world went black.

≈ ≈ ≈

Frank Crawford hit the new concrete floor before his mind registered the sound, the vestigial response surfacing like a shark from beneath the waterline. His vision tunneled down to a gleam of chrome under the men's room sink. His limbs shook uncontrollably, and he compressed his body into the least amount of space a living human could inhabit, then left it altogether and floated toward the ceiling.

Time passed, he didn't know how much, before the panic that had short-circuited his brain receded and Frank recognized he was not in danger. He slowly returned to his body, which had curled inward, one arm protecting his head, the other his torso. He shook his head and rolled sluggishly to his hands and knees, then forced himself to his feet. The sharp report, which had sounded too much like a proximate gunshot, had thrust him back into the sands of Kuwait as if he hadn't been stateside for twenty-odd years.

"God, will it never end?" he moaned into empty space.

Embrace the suck. The words came to him in Sergeant White's piercing tenor – his platoon's mantra for surviving the Persian Desert.

He should investigate the noise, though it was probably an engine backfire or kids lighting a firecracker. Possibly some good ol' boy had fired a gun into the air. Every bozo and halfwit lunatic in Kentucky owned firearms.

He exited the bathroom and made his way to the glass doors in the vestibule, pushed through them and walked toward the street, looking for the source of the sound. There were no children running away, no ancient Chevys blowing smoke from rusty exhaust pipes, and no gun-wielding rednecks in pickup trucks, though with the delay caused by his little episode, he might have missed them.

Frank traversed the church's perimeter, scanning the grounds and the street, his nerves on hair-trigger alert. If someone had touched him at that moment, he'd have gone for the throat, the combat reflexes were so well burned into his brain's synapses. His tendency to strike first, think second, explained why he hadn't settled anywhere after returning to the States. He'd seriously injured more than one street tough who'd tried to roll a homeless drunk. Frank was proficient with a knife and still kept one in his boot, though he was off the streets at the moment.

After circling the church and finding no cause for alarm, Frank reentered the front of the building and strode past the closed office door, unmindful of the electronic beeping noise coming from behind it. That the blast might have originated *inside* the church didn't occur to him, so he returned to his task of pulling screed guides from the men's room walls.

≈ ≈ ≈

Martha hadn't stopped fretting all day. After the thing – the incident – happened, she'd gone driving, and in the isolation of her car, talked to Jesus.

"Dear Lord, something bad happened. It wasn't my fault. I was doing the right thing, following Your will. She didn't belong at our church. You know, like Eve in the Garden of Eden. It was the same, really."

If that girl had kept on like she was, always at the church office, spending private time with Father, following him around – going to his house for parties! – everyone would gossip. They might think he was messing around with her. His reputation was at stake. His *reputation.* What if he lost his position because that...that *Jezebel*...couldn't keep her hands off him?

Father had denied anything happened, but Martha had eyes. Okay...so maybe, just *maybe*, Father didn't exactly mind what the girl did to him – all the more reason to protect him from temptation! God would certainly understand that.

At home, Martha pulled down her shades so nobody could see into her condo while she paced her living room. It wasn't like she'd meant to shoot the gun. It just *happened.* Anyway, she saw the screen that girl was looking at. Filled with pictures of men.

"Like ... like ... pornography!" Martha whispered in horror when the word popped into her head. "On the church computer!" It was revolting.

True, Martha had never actually seen pornography. She knew Floyd kept dirty magazines under his mattress because they fell out once when she changed his sheets. One cover had a girl with her naked butt in the air, looking over her shoulder and grinning. Another had a man wearing leather straps like suspenders, but no pants, holding a horsewhip. She'd stuffed the magazines away so fast she hadn't seen more than that.

It was also true that Martha had gotten only a brief glimpse of Joanne's computer screen, but she knew one thing for sure – there wasn't anything Christian about it. She'd only begun to grasp the ugly nature of its content when the gun went off. She was surprised to see the girl's head flop onto the keyboard, her mousey brown hair puffing outward before it settled. Then the screen started flashing and a noise sounded, a soft, repetitive beeping that reminded her of one of those alarms to summon the police. She was in terrible danger. She shuffled backward to the open doorway, keeping the gun aimed at the girl while she turned the doorknob lock and clicked the door shut.

Just like with Father Zeb, she remembered vaguely.

After that, she wasn't sure what happened. The next thing Martha remembered was crossing Coal Creek Bridge on the gravel road between Amity and Cynthiana. When she saw the water, she'd grabbed her Daddy's Smith & Wesson from the seat and flung it out the window, speeding off as it cleared the bridge railing. Disposing of the gun was instinctive. Even though it had discharged by itself and that wasn't her fault, she didn't want to be answering a lot of questions. If anyone came around now and asked whether she owned a gun, she could truthfully say that no, she did not.

Seeing that revolver fly was exhilarating. She never realized how all the evil in it had been weighing her down until it was gone. More importantly, it could have fired at any time and shot her in her own house! Things like that happened, and you didn't always know why. Like her Daddy disappearing. Nobody had ever found out what happened to the Reverend Gideon Brown. He was just gone. People had stopped asking about him years ago.

"It was God's will," she reminded herself.

By the time she got home, Martha also knew that God had led her to the creek to throw the gun away, something she never would have thought of without His guidance.

Like when she filled in the abandoned well at the Brown homestead. One day she up and called the concrete men, and they came and poured cement into the hole so it wouldn't be a danger to anyone. Clean and tidy, just the way she liked things.

Martha gazed at herself in the bathroom mirror, studied her pudgy mien in blackface. Before leaving home that morning, she'd rubbed Mink Brown shoe polish on her cheeks and forehead and across her nose and chin. Now she pulled off the black stocking cap her Daddy used to wear hunting and narrowed her eyes at the juxtaposition of bald, white head and smeary, brown face. With her Daddy's camouflage jacket and her dark green stretch pants, she looked like a soldier in the jungle sneaking up on the enemy.

That's what she was, she supposed, one of God's soldiers, though she hadn't thought of it like that beforehand. Mostly she'd thought about how mad Sylvia would be if she knew Martha had gone to the church office after agreeing not to. The administrator controlled access to Father, so it didn't pay to make her mad. That's why Martha had disguised herself with camouflage clothing and dark shoe polish – to prevent somebody recognizing her and telling Sylvia she was at the church.

Martha removed her Daddy's jungle jacket, revealing the black T-shirt that strained to contain her breasts and the two muffin-top bulges above the waist of her pants. The gold lettering across her chest – "Master Bait & Tackle Shop" – was backwards in the mirror, but below that a sassy cartoon fish with long eyelashes grinned out at her.

The shirt was a favorite bargain find from the local thrift store.

It took a good long time and lots of cold cream and paper towels to clean the shoe polish off her face. She'd considered leaving it on for a while, as she was feeling conspicuous after her trip to the Coal Creek Bridge. Looking feminine and pretty was important too, though, and Father was coming home.

"He might be back already!" she exclaimed in sudden realization. Time to get busy.

Martha applied her "visiting" makeup with girlish enthusiasm, then shoehorned her full figure into her red dress with the low-cut neckline. She donned her most romantic wig, the long brunette with the teased top, which she thought of as Loretta Lynn, though Dot had said was more Amy Winehouse, whoever that was.

Once attired and made up, Martha wasn't sure what to do with herself. It was barely the middle of the afternoon, and she didn't know when Father would get home. Taking matters into her own hands, she picked up the telephone and dialed the rectory number she knew by heart.

"Dang!" she cursed when that rude lady said, "Mailbox is full." Father hadn't cleared off the answering machine.

"He could *still* be home, though." Martha decided to drive to the rectory and find out, and only then did she recognize the worst mistake of her day.

"I forgot to cook something for Father's homecoming!" She threw up her hands in dismay. What with the bustle and excitement of her morning, it had slipped her mind completely. She grabbed her handbag and car keys and hustled out the door.

After a quick trip to the bakery where she grabbed the last jam cake, Martha drove to Adams Avenue, slowing as she approached the rectory. Daylight made it hard to tell if anyone was home. She pulled into the empty driveway to shorten the walk to Father's porch. She rang the doorbell several times and, when that produced no result, banged her fist on the door. She jiggled the doorknob, but it was locked.

Doggone it! She'd put on makeup and her pretty red dress, and Father wasn't even home. Martha stomped her foot. The whole day had been nothing but frustration and upset.

With a heavy sigh, she regarded the pretty pink cake box dented between her arm and hip. "Well, I can't leave it here. Someone will steal it for sure."

She made her way around the rectory to the back door.

35. Making Sense

Arthur carried his duffle, notebook, and a stack of papers up the rectory's front steps. He fished out the contents of his mailbox and added them to the pile before unlocking the door and going inside.

What a relaxing weekend. Sylvia had outdone herself. The peaceful expanse of Lake Cumberland surrounded by its thick, isolating woods proved restorative, and the Vestry had been productive. They'd planned the church calendar for the coming year, determined priorities for outreach projects, reviewed staffing needs, and made a first stab at the budget. Among other things, they'd allocated money to make Joanne's position a permanent half-time appointment. Her work as Sylvia's assistant had already become vital to church operations.

Arthur dropped his duffle in the bedroom and carried the papers to the den where he saw the number 10 flashing on the answering machine. Seemed like a lot of messages for three days. He pushed the button and tore open an envelope as the tape rewound. Though old-fashioned, the answering machine let him control access to the messages and reassure callers of confidentiality.

Beep. "Friday, 10:10 AM," said the recorded voice.

"Hi, Father, this is Martha. I'm calling to wish you a good retreat. Four days is a long time, you know. I worry so much when you're not here. I don't know what to do with myself. I guess I'll keep doing things for the church until you come back. Tomorrow I plan to – "

Arthur didn't care to listen to Martha Browne's rambling when he'd barely walked in the door. He pressed the SKIP button.

Beep. "Friday, 10:14 AM."

"Father! It's me, Martha. The machine cut me off in the middle of my story. That is so rude! Anyway, I'm going to Graham's Greenhouse to look at lilies and I – "

She was back at it. Arthur grimaced. Martha Browne had stopped her incessant calling and her intrusions at the rectory for a short time after he'd admonished her, but then she began showing up at the church every day. Sylvia was convinced the woman was infatuated with him, no matter how misguided that might be, and that if Arthur gave her no fuel for the fire, she'd eventually get past it. He'd been letting Sylvia deal with Martha since then.

He skipped to the third message.

Beep. "Friday, 12:22 PM."

"It's me," Martha said in an intimate, girlish tone. "I thought it would be nice if you had some good food to come home to, but I came over and all the doors and windows were locked, so I can't put anything in your refrigerator, but that's a good idea, I think I'll..."

Arthur hadn't noticed any casserole dishes on the front porch. He'd have to check the back porch too, sounded like. He sighed and pressed SKIP, listened, then did it again. And again. Seven more times Martha Browne's voice blared from the speaker, each with a different undertone – seductive, annoyed, impatient, wicked-witch sweet.

He flicked his fingers to shake off the woman's chaotic energy. Letting this behavior continue couldn't be good for her, and it certainly wasn't good for him. He was trained for such eventualities, female crushes on male priests being common enough, but Martha was taxing his ability to cope. Or perhaps just his will to cope.

Lord, give me strength.

He opened the machine and peered inside. The tape was thirty minutes long, and Martha had filled it. He didn't look forward to confronting her again. She had the mind of a child, easily hurt, easily provoked, and difficult to control. She was the most persistently delusional woman he'd ever dealt with. Perhaps he'd discuss the matter with Father Daniel, which made two things to bring up with his spiritual advisor.

Arthur rubbed his temples and headed to the medicine cabinet for aspirin.

Brrinng!

Her again? He considered ignoring the call. But no, someone might have been waiting for his return with a pressing need, and they couldn't leave a message with the answering machine full of Martha. He returned to the den and read "Unavailable" on the caller ID.

"Arthur Endicott."

"Arthur, it's Sylvia." He exhaled in relief. But Sylvia's voice sounded off, strained, like she was keeping some powerful emotion in check.

"Sylvia, is something wrong?"

"Yes, Arthur, it's – " Her voice cracked, and she went silent.

"Sylvia, are you okay? Where are you?" Alarm quickened his blood. Something was terribly wrong.

"Come to the church right away," she choked out.

"What's happened?" He couldn't imagine a scenario that would cause iron-spined Sylvia to break down. A car accident? A fire? He waited interminable seconds.

"It's Jo...it's Joanne. S-she's d-dead."

The blood drained from Arthur's head, and his legs collapsed, dropping him into his desk chair. He bit his tongue to keep from repeating her words in disbelief or demanding to know what was going on. She'd said exactly what she meant, and she needed help.

"You're at the church?"

"Yes."

"I'll be right there." The reflexive calm-in-a-storm demeanor that one acquired in his vocation settled over him, though his heart pounded with agitation.

Joanne is dead. That's what Sylvia had said. His mind raced with questions – *How? When? Why?* – but he forced himself to put them aside for the moment. Something terrible had happened at the church, and he must get there immediately.

Then it hit him – *suicide.*

"Oh, no," he moaned softly. "Poor Greta. Poor John."

His calm became dense and weighty, and he rose from his chair with effort, his hand reaching robotically for his car keys. After going to the church, he'd be needed at the hospital or, possibly, the morgue.

The scene outside the church was frightening but familiar, made unnaturally so by the modern glut of TV crime dramas and live news coverage of every conceivable human trauma. Three police cruisers with their lights flashing blocked most of the parking lot on the office side of the church where the activity seemed to be centered. A local fire truck was there too, but no ambulance.

Arthur parked at the edge of the lot behind the emergency vehicles. He offered a quick prayer for Joanne, for her parents, and for himself – for the strength to do whatever needed to be done.

It was nearly dark, but clusters of people had collected outside the perimeter of police vehicles. Arthur zigzagged around them, ignoring requests to know what was going on. He strode between two police cars, aiming purposefully for the church door. A sheriff's deputy stopped him.

"I'm Father Arthur Endicott, the priest here," he said. "Our office manager called me."

"Come with me, Father."

"Can you tell me what's happened? Joanne Bowman has died," he said quietly. "Is that right?"

"You'll have to talk to the sheriff."

Arthur steadied himself against the avalanche of emotions he'd have to process later. His duty was to stand strong so others might lean on him. He followed the deputy inside where yellow crime tape blocked the office. The sheriff stood on the other side of the tape, watching two non-uniformed people taking photographs and dusting surfaces for fingerprints.

"Sheriff, this is the priest."

The burly officer turned, his frame nearly filling the doorway. "Remy Boudreaux," he said.

"Arthur Endicott. What's happened?"

"Do you know a Joanne Bowman?"

"Yes, she's our office assistant."

"Arthur! Arthur!"

Sylvia hobbled toward him through the narthex, her eyes swollen and face puffy. Arthur met her with one arm outstretched, and she wrapped her arms around him and dropped her head against his sternum. She was a tiny woman, he suddenly realized, short and slight. Sylvia's take-charge attitude and absolute competence normally caused him to overlook that fact.

She released him when Sheriff Boudreaux approached.

"Miss Bowman is dead," he told Arthur. "I'm sorry for your loss." The line seemed scripted, but the man's genuine regret came through.

A stab of pain pierced Arthur's chest. "What happened?"

Sylvia started to speak but then gulped back a sob. Fresh tears spilled over and ran down her stained cheeks. Arthur settled an arm over her shoulder and pulled her to his side, letting the clean, white light collect in his solar plexus before pushing it gently toward his friend.

"Miss Bowman suffered a gunshot wound to the back of the head."

Back of the head? Arthur blinked rapidly and swallowed against the growing lump in his throat. He waited for further explanation, something that would make sense.

"She died instantly," Boudreaux added.

The truth began to filter through his shock. "Not a suicide?" Arthur locked his knees to prevent them giving way.

"Very unlikely, given the location of the wound. And no weapon was found."

"When did it happen?"

"The coroner said sometime this morning." The sheriff watched Arthur intently as he conveyed the information.

Sylvia spoke in a rush then, her body shaking. "Nobody found her until after five. When she didn't come home from work, her mom came looking for her. The office door was locked, but Greta saw her through the window and called the police."

Thoughts of Joanne's possible terror and suffering flew into Arthur's head, but he forced them away. She was safe in God's hands, and for now, he must focus on those left behind. "Where are Greta and John?"

"They left with the ambulance ten minutes ago." Sylvia sniffled, then buried her nose in a tissue. Arthur squeezed her shoulder.

"I'd like to get statements from you both," Boudreaux said. "You all worked together in this office, is that right?"

"Yes," Arthur replied.

Sylvia rested her forehead against him, and he felt energy flow out of him. He hoped it would comfort her.

"Where's Larry?" he asked, suddenly aware that she was on her own.

"Greta called me, and Larry and I rushed over. I asked him to go home and stay with the boys. I mean, if somebody k-killed Joanne – "

Arthur looked at her in surprise. Could their lives be in danger too?

≈ ≈ ≈

"You're fuckin' kidding me!" Riley exclaimed.

Larry perched on the edge of the recliner in their family room, forearms on his knees. He unclasped his hands and reclasped them the other way.

"Watch your language, son," he said, a parental reflex encouraged by his wife.

"Who was she again?" Rhett's eyebrows compressed into knots of concern.

"She was your mom's assistant and her friend."

Riley ran his fingers through his hair, then clenched a handful in his fist. "Do we know her?"

"You met her," Larry said, pressing the ends of his fingers together. "She was at Arthur's barbecue with her parents. She also helped paint the rectory."

"Oh, yeah." Rhett bit his bottom lip, and Larry saw first recognition then shock cross his son's face.

"How'd she die?" Riley asked.

Larry hated to say, but they'd find out soon enough. "She was shot."

Rhett gasped. "At the church? Jesus!"

"I know it's a shock, but you both better get the cursing under control before your mom gets home."

"Where is she?" Rhett asked, his voice rising. "Is she at the church?"

"Yes, but the area is crawling with cops, city and county. They need to question her."

"Why? Is she a suspect?" Riley asked in alarm.

"Of course not, but she might know something about Joanne's ex or somebody who had a grudge or something. You know, you watch TV."

"Mom shouldn't be alone," Rhett said. "She's probably scared."

"Father Arthur's with her. They want to question him too." Larry didn't mention that Sylvia was more scared for her boys than for herself and had insisted he come home to be with them. His job was to keep them busy. "Let's make supper so she doesn't have to worry about that when she gets here. Rhett, put a load of laundry in the washer. Your mom was sorting clothes before she left."

The boys were fed and the kitchen cleaned up before Larry heard the garage door grind open. He went to meet his wife as she climbed slowly from her car. Seeing the devastation on her face, Larry wrapped her in his arms and cocooned her against his body. She gasped and tears spilled down her face.

"Darlin'," he soothed, stroking her hair, "I'm so sorry, but to be honest, I'm also relieved as hell that you weren't there." Sylvia's body shook with bigger sobs. Larry kissed the top of her head and squeezed her into him until she quieted.

"Are the boys okay?" Sylvia rasped into his shirt.

"Yeah, they're watching the news."

"It's on the news?"

"Lexington, Cincinnati, Indianapolis, everywhere," he said. "People are scared about a church killer on the loose. That's pure evil. Do the police know anything?"

Sylvia shook her head, her nose rubbing against his chest. He was making it worse.

"Are you snotting up my shirt?" he asked in mock disapproval.

A strangled chuckle erupted, muffled in flannel. Sylvia leaned her head back and looked at him with bloodshot eyes.

"They want to question you. Your guy, Frank, was working at the church when it happened, right?"

"Nah, I sent him to clean up first thing. He was done before noon."

"It happened in the morning, they said."

Larry loosened his grip and pushed Sylvia's shoulders back. "What? Frank didn't say anything to me. Do they know what time?"

"Not exactly. The coroner thought between nine and noon."

"He must have left before it happened then," Larry concluded.

"Does he own a gun?"

"Ah, Syl, Frank didn't do this. You didn't accuse him to the cops, did you?"

"Well," she said defensively, "they asked me if I had any idea who might be responsible. I told him your crew was finishing work today, but you were at the strip mall job. Frank's name might have come up."

He clasped his wife's upper arms and stepped back. "You blamed this on Frank? Sylvia, what were you thinking? He's a veteran."

"Yes, but he's always given me the creeps, that scar on his face, and he used to sleep in the church basement. Maybe J-J-Joanne was going to tell on him." Sylvia's voice broke.

Larry grunted and pulled her close again. "Nobody kills someone in cold blood because she's getting him kicked out of the church basement. Besides, he's staying at the motel. Herb's been keeping an eye on him."

"Well, that's good, I guess. Remy will probably question him, though."

Larry stroked her hair, tamping down his irritation. "I can't believe you sic'd the cops on my worker...hell, my friend. He's been doing great."

"I'm sorry, honey." Sylvia rubbed her eyes with the heels of her palms. "I was upset and rambling. I'm not even sure what I said."

"Let's go inside. It's hot out here." Larry wrapped his arm around his wife and escorted her into the house. The twins jumped from the couch and hurried over.

"Mom, are you okay? Do they know who did it?" Rhett asked.

"I'm fine, and, no, they don't know anything yet. Have you had supper?"

"We ate," Larry said.

"What did you eat?" Sylvia asked suspiciously.

"Breakfast," Riley said. "Omelets, bacon, and toast."

"We can cook some more for you," Rhett offered.

"I got it," Larry told him. "Syl, sit down. Do you want some eggs?"

"I suppose I'd better eat something or I won't sleep tonight." She surreptitiously wiped her eyes, then said softly, "Probably won't sleep anyway."

Larry could see she was making a great effort to hold herself together in front of the boys. "Hon, why don't you go lay down?" he suggested. "I'll bring you a tray."

"Oh, I can't. I need to finish the laundry."

"We're doing it," Riley announced.

"You are? Are you folding things from the dryer?" Sylvia asked.

Riley lost his smug expression. "We'll do that now. Come on, Rhett."

Rhett gave his mother a long look before following.

Sylvia's mouth tightened, then relaxed. "I think I will lie down," she said. "Larry?"

He retrieved a bottle of Grand Marnier from the cabinet over the fridge and raised his eyebrows in question. She nodded. He poured an inch of the orange liqueur into a tumbler and handed it to her.

"Go on. I'll bring food."

"Lock the doors and windows," Sylvia mouthed after the twins were gone.

Larry nodded.

36. Reckoning

Hours later, Father still hadn't returned Martha's phone calls, not even to thank her for the cake she'd left on his back porch. She knew he'd returned because she saw his car parked in the driveway the fourth time she circled the rectory. Having missed the best parking space along Adams Avenue, she'd driven her Cadillac around the block for another shot at it and Father's car was gone.

Darn. How had she missed him in those few minutes?

Martha was still wearing her red dress, which felt confining and uncomfortable. She didn't want to remove it and peel off the Large 'n' Lovely elastic drawers she wore to consolidate her belly rolls until after Father had seen her in it. After she changed clothes, though, she was driving to the cleaners to demand they reimburse her since, obviously, they'd shrunk her dress.

Where could Father be? Though it was late for him to be working, Martha decided to check at the church.

As her car approached Trinity Episcopal, she peered through the windshield and saw a hullaballoo in the parking lot. Police cars with their lights flashing had barricaded the area, and a crowd milled around at the edges.

"Humph." Martha couldn't circle the church and park on the other side either because rubberneckers blocked the street. "How rude!" she complained, scanning the area for

Father's car. When she spotted it at the rear of the lot, she wanted to lay on her horn to disperse the nosy parkers so she could get through, but then she thought better of it. Maybe now wasn't the best time to welcome Father home.

"He's probably very busy," she noted primly with a flip of her Loretta Lynn tresses.

The following morning, Martha cruised to the rectory again. Father's car sat in the driveway, but there was no answer when she knocked on his door so she drove to the church to see if he was there. Policemen were positioned outside the door closest to Father's office. She wanted to push her way through but, on consideration, decided not to bother the good officers.

She wondered vaguely what had happened with the girl. Her Daddy's gun had discharged, sure, but that didn't tell her anything.

Was she gone?

That might be for the best. Father wouldn't have to worry about fending off the girl's sexual advances, and his reputation would remain safe and intact.

Martha resolved to stay home for a spell.

When she drove by the church two days later, Martha found to her delight that the policemen had gone and the parking lot was empty. Finally, she could visit without being accosted.

She opened the church door and trundled inside, then waited for her eyes to adjust before continuing to the office.

"Is Father here?" Martha inquired from the doorway. The woman seated at the desk jumped, then spun toward her, and she saw it was Sylvia, though looking older and more haggard than Martha remembered.

"No, he's not here," Sylvia said and returned at once to her paperwork.

How rude! She shouldn't be in the office representing the church if she couldn't be friendly and cheerful.

Martha decided to rise above it. "Can you tell me when he'll be back, please?" she inquired in her best Christian voice.

Sylvia swiveled again to face the doorway. "No, I can't."

Martha scowled. "Well, where is he?"

"Father Endicott is visiting shut-ins this afternoon."

"Oh," Martha mumbled in disappointment. "Tell him I need to speak to him, please. I've been waiting for days!"

"Okay, Martha, I'll tell him," Sylvia said, "but you have to realize this is a difficult time. We're all doing the best we can."

Martha looked around and didn't see any sign of the girl in the office. *Was she gone, then?*

"Are you here...all by yourself?" Martha queried sweetly.

"Wh-what?" Sylvia stuttered, her voice shooting up an octave. She gaped and kept gaping long after a polite person would have looked away. She shuffled her feet and rolled her desk chair backward as she stared.

Is she having a fit? Martha wondered.

Then, in a loud, unladylike voice, Sylvia said, "NO, OF COURSE NOT. CHARLIE HIGHTOWER IS HERE WITH ME!"

"Well, you don't have to shout," Martha grumbled. "I can hear perfectly well." She reached into her handbag for her keys and noticed a scuttling movement at the corner of her vision. She glanced up and saw Sylvia leap from her chair and flee – there was no other word for it – to Father's office. Martha had barely grasped what was happening before the heavy door slammed shut.

What is wrong with her? That was about the rudest thing Martha had ever witnessed. She wasn't going to stand there and be disrespected.

"Humph," she grunted, then made her way to her car.

≈ ≈ ≈

When Larry got home from work, he discovered his wife holed up in their bedroom with the door locked.

"Sylvia? Syl?" he called. They never locked their door, not since the boys had gotten old enough to know better than to walk in on them without knocking. Kids only made that mistake once.

"Larry!" Sylvia swung the door wide. "I'm so glad you're home."

His wife was a mess. Her eyes and nose were red, and her hair and makeup were in an unusual state of disarray. She'd wrapped a comforter around herself, which dropped to the floor when she dove into the shelter of his body. He closed his arms protectively around her and scanned the room.

"What's wrong?" She started crying, which she'd been doing off and on for the past two days. Larry tensed. "Where are the boys?"

Sylvia sniffled. "They said they were going to Darlene's house to play video games with Zack."

Larry relaxed slightly. "So what's wrong then?" He brushed her hair from her face.

"Oh, it's stupid." Sylvia let go of him and straightened her blouse. "Martha Browne came to the office looking for Arthur."

Larry's fists clenched. "She say something rude to you?" *That damn woman!*

"N-no, n-not really," Sylvia spluttered. She rolled the hem of her blouse between her fingers, then smoothed it back down. "When I told her Arthur was out, she asked me in a nicey-nice voice if I was there...*all by myself.*" Sylvia gave him a sheepish look. "It was just the creepy way she said it, I guess, but it made me think about Joanne being there by herself, and...well...I ran flat-out for Arthur's office, locked the door, and hid behind his desk."

Larry chuckled. "Ol' Martha Browne scared you, huh?" He pulled her in and kissed the top of her head. "Bet she didn't appreciate you hightailing it like that."

Sylvia wiped some leftover tears on Larry's work shirt. "No, she probably didn't. And I didn't come out until I saw her drive away."

A glance passed between them, then Larry raised his eyebrows and they broke into simultaneous snorts of laughter.

The following morning, Sheriff Boudreaux came to the Coal Creek jobsite to arrest Frank. *Well, no,* Larry reminded himself, Boudreaux hadn't come to arrest him, just ended up doing so when Frank lost his cool and put up a fight. Then Remy frisked him and found the knife in Frank's boot, which surprised Larry. He'd never had reason to fear Frank, and he was sure the man wouldn't kill anyone. He had a few problems was all.

After Remy hauled Frank off to the county lockup, Larry phoned his dad. Bub had an aging back, and Larry hated to ask him for help, but concrete waited for no man and this was a big commercial job.

"Can you help out at the Coal Creek Business Park?"

"When?"

"Now. I just lost a worker mid-pour."

"Twenty minutes," Bub said with his typical economy of words.

Larry hung up, then took a moment he didn't have to call Sylvia and carp at her for blabbing about Frank, even though the sheriff would have found out sooner or later that Frank was at the church around the time Joanne was killed. Boudreaux undoubtedly suspected Frank, but he couldn't charge him with murder without evidence, which didn't exist. At least Larry hoped it didn't.

After guilting his wife over Frank's arrest, Larry pressed her to ask Father Arthur to visit Frank at the jail. Larry couldn't get away from the jobsite, especially now he was one man short, but he didn't want Frank sitting behind bars thinking nobody gave a good goddam. Priests visited prisons, didn't they? Frank Crawford wasn't a churchgoer, but he'd been working at the church and that ought to count.

Larry would go himself as soon as he could, definitely before Saturday. Joanne's funeral was scheduled for Monday, and Sylvia would be a wreck all weekend.

≈ ≈ ≈

"So, now you're here." Arthur touched his fingertips together, elbows on his knees. He was seated in a wooden chair across from Frank Crawford who half-reclined on a thin mattress in a cell at the county jail. The man's otherwise unremarkable face was marred by a long, vertical scar through his eyebrow and down his cheek. His eyelid on that side sagged.

"Yeah. It's not an unfamiliar experience. At least they let me smoke here." Frank patted the Pall Malls in his pocket. "I have to ask for a light, though. It's like kindergarten."

"What are the charges?" Arthur asked.

"Concealed weapon."

"Gun?"

"No, knife, Benchmade."

"Oh? I'm afraid my knowledge of knives is limited."

"It's tactical, Army-issue," Frank said.

"So people can't carry a knife in Clarkson County?"

"Not unless they're wearing an orange vest and gutting a deer, I guess. And not in a sheath in their boot. That's the concealed part."

Arthur nodded. "But they think you shot Joanne Bowman?"

"I'm not a local yokel, and I was in the vicinity. That's probable cause in Podunk, U.S.A.," Frank said resentfully. He shifted his hip sideways, but still looked uncomfortable.

"How much is your bail?"

"Twenty-five thousand."

Arthur stiffened. "For carrying a knife?"

"And resisting arrest and threatening an officer of the law," Frank intoned.

"I see. Do you want to tell me about it? Why did you resist?"

The inmate stared at him for a moment as if the answer were obvious. Finally, he said, "You ever been in the service, Padre?"

Arthur shook his head. He was intimately familiar with the social and personal problems suffered by combat veterans, though, knowledge gained through years of ministering in hospitals, psych wards, and jails. But he wouldn't minimize this man's experience by mentioning it.

"I need a drink," Frank admitted but didn't elaborate on his military service. His leathered skin told Arthur he'd spent a lot of time in the elements, probably living on the streets.

"Are you an alcoholic?" It wasn't a judgment, merely the counselor's practice of addressing whatever issues were presented to him.

Frank's mouth tightened into a thin line. "What do you think?"

Arthur thought the man was in serious trouble and not just with the authorities, but he didn't say that out loud. "Frank, what can I do for you? Do you have family I can call? Do you need help finding a lawyer?"

"I don't suppose there's much you can do, except maybe bring me some whiskey." Frank smiled without mirth.

Arthur wasn't above giving the man a drink if it would help, but it wouldn't. Nor was it allowed. "May I pray for you?"

Frank cocked an eye at him. "You'll probably do it whether I agree or not."

Arthur smiled faintly. "I'd rather pray *with* you."

"As much as I hate to say no to a religious man, especially one who's at least pretending to give a shit, I have to decline. But thank you."

Gratitude and disdain jumbled together. Arthur didn't begrudge the man his bitterness. No doubt it was earned. "All right. I'll visit again in a day or two, but if you need anything before then, have the deputy call me."

The man was ill – extremely ill – if Arthur's intuition was correct. The moment he stepped into Frank's cell, he'd had to steady himself against the force of the man's affliction. It was like a vast low-pressure system, a vacuum almost, the way it tugged at Arthur. He'd felt less pull from people on their deathbeds, which to him meant that, though the veteran was very sick, he possessed a strong will to heal. As a priest and a human being, Arthur couldn't turn away, despite the man's dismissal of him.

He offered Frank his right hand, a gesture he'd found was rarely snubbed. Frank sat up, and after a pause, shook it. When his rough palm met Arthur's, energy gushed from the priest like water through a broken dam. The outflow was so strong that Arthur couldn't speak, couldn't even pray. It required all his concentration to draw into himself the light Frank needed, and still he couldn't keep up. His own light was draining from him faster than he could replenish it. He needed to break contact but, inexplicably, found he couldn't. Frank's pull held him immobile, while Frank himself remained rigid, seemingly in a blind stupor.

When the force between them finally waned, Arthur jerked his hand away, whispered some brief words of prayer, then called for the deputy and hastily took his leave. The cell door clanged behind him as he shuffled along the corridor to the office, keeping one hand on the cinderblock wall to steady himself. Weak, dizzy, and befuddled, feeling ninety years old, Arthur knew he was in trouble. He'd expected Frank to be feeling low but hadn't anticipated finding him so ill that he would incapacitate Arthur in his extremity.

"You all right, Mr. Endicott?" Deputy Walsh didn't wait for a response, just shoved a rolling chair behind Arthur's legs. "Sit down."

The priest collapsed, eyes shut, then dragged them open and whispered, "Is there somewhere I can get a snack, a piece of fruit, something like that?"

"You have the sugar diabetes?" The officer's hand moved to the sizeable belly hanging over his belt. "Me too. Adult onset, you know. I keep oranges in my desk in case I need something quick. Here, take one of these. Take two. They're real good."

Arthur gratefully accepted the fruit without bothering to correct the man's assumption. He peeled the first one with trembling hands and consumed it quickly before daring to rise from the chair. Then he said thank you and escaped, peeling the second orange on the way to his car. Deputy Walsh had wanted him to sit for a while, but the oranges would supply only a minimal, temporary boost when what Arthur needed was high-dosage supplementation. It was imperative that he get to his medicine cabinet while he still could.

≈ ≈ ≈

After the priest had gone, Frank collapsed onto his jail bunk and fell into an unusual, dreamless sleep. Normally, he awoke every couple hours with a start, his feet kicking, as if he were running from something, though he never knew what it was. Or he would bolt upright from sleep, distressed, with the echoes of a shout ringing in his ears. Not this time. The deputy on duty had awakened him with a clanking of keys against the bars of his cell when mealtime came around.

"Hey, there. You okay?" the deputy asked.

Frank struggled to open his eyes at the note of concern he could hear, but to which he couldn't respond. He finally pushed himself to a sitting position long enough for the deputy to accept that he was alive, then he dropped back to the mattress into another deep, blacked-out sleep. Frank was reawakened by the clang of his cage door when a different deputy collected his untouched food tray. He lay down again and didn't stir until morning.

What woke Frank this time was not a noise, but a sensation, a slow sensual gathering, collecting, and tightening, followed by a sudden explosion like an ecstatic firebomb between his legs. His eyelids snapped open, and he clutched his cock in his fist, squeezing fiercely to try to mitigate the searing pain that would follow the ejaculation. His reaction was automatic, another well-trod pathway etched in his motor neurons. If he inadvertently orgasmed in his sleep, he braced himself for the punishing aftermath, that chili-pepper burn through the core of his penis that made the pain of his crushing fingers pale to insignificance.

He waited for it, his entire body tightened against the assault that would last for twenty or thirty seconds before dulling enough that he could release his clamped jaws and pant through the several minutes of after-burn. If he was alone, he'd let himself cry out, even scream, responding in the only way he could to the flaming torture. But there he was, hunched over, squeezing, every muscle straining, his jaws clenched, waiting, waiting, and...nothing. All he felt was the steady pressure of his fingers and the pleasant afterglow of sexual release.

Unready to trust this absence of torment, Frank lay back tentatively, carefully, and waited for the ax to fall, but nothing happened – nothing, that is, but the surprise stiffening of his dick in his hand. It didn't happen often because whenever his body wandered up the road to arousal, his mind stopped it at the pass, memories of pain sidetracking any potential sexual pleasure.

It can't be. Can it? Temptation and curiosity slowly overcame his fear, and Frank reached inside his jailhouse cottons to stroke himself. He was rock hard and ready, and he rubbed tentatively, blocking his anxiety as best he could. Abandonment to pleasure came in fits and starts, but gradually he surrendered and allowed his hand to pump the length of his dick, building heat and tension, tightening his balls.

Just a few more...one...two...*ahhhh*. Frank's body stiffened and seized, and an intense gripping began at the base of his cock and exploded upward. The earth stopped turning for endless seconds while his balls emptied themselves onto his belly. He took one deep breath then reflexively grabbed the bed sheet to wipe himself clean before his skin began to burn.

But he felt nothing, not the searing pain in his urethra, not the scalding of his stomach. Nothing but pleasure persisted, plus a deep relaxation he hadn't felt in years. Without further thought, he curled onto his side and fell asleep, the remnants of a smile softening his sun-leathered face.

37. A Helping Hand

Sylvia was not looking forward to facing her husband. Every time Larry brought up Frank Crawford, she felt like a shit-heel, even though she hadn't done anything wrong. Well, not exactly. But jumping to conclusions wasn't a crime, and what if she was right?

"Did Arthur visit the jail?" Larry asked as soon as he walked in the door.

"Yes, of course he did," Sylvia replied with irritation. She pulled the dinner rolls from the oven, almost burning her finger.

She didn't begrudge Frank Crawford a little human kindness, but she also hadn't wanted Arthur to feel obligated to help someone who might take advantage. No matter what Larry said, she had a bad feeling about that man with his scar and his red nose and the spider veins crossing his cheeks. Clearly, he was alcoholic. What if he'd attacked Joanne and didn't remember? Sylvia hadn't spoken her thoughts, but her husband knew her too well not to read them on her face.

"What? What's the matter? You're not still thinking Frank's guilty are you?"

Riley joined them in the kitchen, then reached over Sylvia's arm and snatched a roll from the breadbasket. "Frank didn't do diddlysquat," he declared.

"How do you know?" Sylvia challenged.

"Because he's a good guy." Rhett answered for his brother across the breakfast bar. "He's not a killer, Mom."

Sylvia clenched her jaw. She knew she was being unfair, but Joanne was *dead* and somebody had done it. Her eyes teared up for what seemed like the hundredth time that week.

"What did Arthur say? Is Frank doing all right?" Larry asked.

"He didn't say anything." She handed the plate of sliced meatloaf to Riley and followed him to the table, carrying rolls and green beans. "I didn't see Arthur after the visit, but I assume Frank is doing as well as anyone would in that situation."

"I'm going to try and get there tomorrow." Larry pulled out his chair and sat down. "Did you hear anything from Sheriff Boudreaux? They got any leads?"

"If you want to know, ask him yourself," Sylvia snapped.

Her men stopped shoveling food onto their plates and stared at her.

"I'm sorry, hon." Larry touched her forearm. "I know this is rough on you."

Getting ticked off was more comfortable than crying all the time, but Sylvia relented at her husband's show of sympathy. "They found some fingerprints on the doorknob," she said.

"Whose?" the twins said in unison, something they did so often that their parents barely noticed it.

"They don't know," Sylvia said. "Not Frank's," she added grudgingly.

"See, I told you!"

"Dial it down, Riley." Larry grabbed another roll from the basket. "There must be all kinds of fingerprints on the doorknob, and around the office too."

"Well, that's the interesting part," Sylvia said, her emotions now under control. "There was only one set, more like a handprint, with four fingertips along one side and a thumbprint across from them like they were made by one hand holding the knob. The sheriff talked to Judy Hightower, and she said she cleaned the office first thing Monday before anyone got there.

"So the doorknob was cleaned right before the...right before...." Larry's words faltered.

"That's right. We don't touch it very often, anyway, because we leave the door open most of the time. And the door was shut and locked. So the handprint probably belongs to the perp," Sylvia said, borrowing the sheriff's word.

Riley snorted. "Did you say *perp*, Mom?"

The twins looked at each other and laughed.

"That's what they call it!" Sylvia said, her cheeks growing warm.

"Wait, what if they're – " Rhett began.

" – Joanne's prints?" Riley finished.

"They're not," Sylvia asserted. "They're not Frank's, and they're not...Joanne's." She focused on cutting her meatloaf into bite-sized pieces she couldn't eat.

"So now all they have to do is find the right hand," Larry pointed out.

"Or the left." Riley smirked, and Larry scowled at him.

"Halsey said it was a left hand." Sylvia felt a strange, sad pride knowing that secret detail, a clue to the devastating and incomprehensible situation.

"Halsey Matter? The county crime scene guy?" Larry stopped eating and put his fork down.

"Yes, they sent him down from Cynthey. This is a big deal. He said they're putting everybody they've got on it."

"Good. He say anything else?"

"He's not supposed to talk about it, but I pushed him, and he gave me that information off the record. He wanted to reassure me, I think." Sylvia was beginning to regret "blabbing," as Larry would say, but she couldn't help herself. "It was a small hand," she divulged.

"You mean like a kid?" Larry asked. "Was anything stolen?"

"No. They don't think it was a robbery attempt." Sylvia bit her lip.

"What, Mom?" Rhett pressed.

"Tell us!" Riley chimed in.

Sylvia ducked her head conspiratorially, then whispered as if doing so would keep the secret. "Halsey thinks it's a woman's hand. They sent DNA samples to Louisville. Skin cells."

"So Frank didn't do it!" Larry boomed.

"There's no proof either way. Anybody could have gone in there – for a pen, anything – and left that handprint." She stared defiantly at Larry, though he was probably right.

≈ ≈ ≈

After his volunteer coaching gig, Walker drove to the gym to burn off some excess libido, or at least tire himself out enough to sleep before his early morning shift at the factory. He stepped up to the squat rack, transferred the bar to his shoulders, and set his feet. A gym regular stepped over to spot, but Walker shrugged him off. He was taking it easy with the weight today since his concentration was in the toilet.

The previous Saturday, he'd asked Stephen to move into the guest room and start looking for somewhere else to live. Their relationship was over. Walker had known it the moment he kissed Arthur and felt the potent energy flowing between them. He couldn't stop thinking about the priest.

He hadn't seen Arthur for a week, not since their erotic tussle in the shadows had left him restless, strung piano-wire-taut by his heightened sex drive. The shooting at the church, though seemingly random, had added a layer of fear to his fixation and set him further on edge.

Arthur wasn't just a good guy with a smoking body. Walker had come to believe he was a rare breed of person, a truly righteous man. He was kind, patient, and compassionate, even with the greedy scam artists who came around inquiring about the "free grocery store" and the hopeless drunks who would trade their food for liquor as soon as they rounded the corner. He was no pushover, though. Walker sensed the steel-belted resolve behind the priest's warm demeanor. He'd like to spar with the man sometime, check out his boxing moves.

Oh, hell, might as well be honest. He'd like to wrestle him to the ground, take his cock in his hand, and get a real feel for him. Get *inside* him. An insistent erection sprang to life, distorting the front of Walker's shorts.

Shit! He'd lost focus. Time to hang it up and hit the shower. Maybe he'd find someone to trade a hand job. It wasn't uncommon at Rocco's gym, and it might help him through the drought now that he'd stopped fucking Stephen.

Walker weaved his way between the weight racks toward the locker room and noticed a man staring at his hard-on. The guy glanced up with a familiar query on his face, and Walker raised his chin but kept moving, confident he'd be followed. He didn't look at the husky, dark-haired dude but lazily undressed and wrapped a towel around his waist, in no hurry to get to the shower. He was used to attracting attention with his beefy, cut body. This guy appeared to be in his late twenties, short, hairy, and butch. Not Walker's type, especially, but he wasn't interested in a date, just a tug.

One thing Walker liked about Rocco's was the row of private showers along one wall. There was also a common shower area, so you had a choice. He hung his towel on the hook outside a private shower and stepped in, leaving the curtain partway open. He turned on the water and within a minute, the metal curtain rings jangled twice before a heavy, square palm touched his waist, then slid around to his belly.

Walker kept the water aimed at his chest and let the guy reach around. Something about having someone else's hand on you made the release more intense and the relief last longer – not like getting fully inside a man, but still good. Walker reached back to share the love, but the fellow nudged his soapy hand away and rubbed into the crack of

Walker's ass instead. That was fine. It felt good and required less effort on his part.

They both finished quickly and quietly, and the man left without a word, just how Walker preferred it. He'd long ago given up feeling guilty about such impersonal exchanges. It was safe sex, and he did it to satisfy his physical needs; that was all. He couldn't be accused of leading a guy on if he didn't engage with him.

Walker had abstained from casual encounters when he and Stephen were making a go of it, but that was over now.

"What do you want?" Stephen had sneered when Walker told him he was ready to call it quits. "You want to get married, till death do us part, forsaking all others, and all that crap?"

"That's not an option with you, is it?"

"You're serious?" Stephen had expressed shock and disbelief, which only proved how little he'd been listening for months.

Long-term monogamy wasn't in Stephen's repertoire, and he'd been dishonest about that because he wanted to have his cake and eat it too. Walker understood that now, and he didn't really blame him. Stephen had loved him in his way, probably still did, judging by the angry tears he'd shed when he realized Walker's mind was made up.

Walker considered the possibility that he was overstating Stephen's lack of commitment to justify his own fascination with another man. He shrugged off the niggling thought and left the shower, having given his spray mate plenty of time to leave. He didn't feel like making conversation. His mind was elsewhere.

He climbed into his truck and started for home but instead found himself navigating the familiar route to the priest's house. It had become a habit, driving by like an infatuated teenager – or a grownup stalker.

From a distance, Walker spied Arthur's old Chevy sitting in the driveway, and his heart leaped.

Could I stop and say hello? He could, sure, but how would the priest react?

He slowed his truck to a crawl as he approached the rectory. If he walked up and knocked, maybe Arthur would come to the door and invite him in, or at least give him a clue whether he was welcome to visit. Deciding at the last second to go for it, Walker swerved in behind Arthur's car and turned off the engine.

Wait. Someone – Arthur? – was seated behind the wheel. Maybe the priest was collecting his things to go inside. Or maybe he was leaving. Either way, he didn't turn around.

Walker climbed from his truck and approached the driver's side of the champagne-colored sedan, a nervous flutter in his stomach. Through the window, he saw Arthur's head lying cockeyed against the headrest, his eyes closed. Was he asleep?

Walker tapped two knuckles against the glass but got no response. He tapped again, a vague anxiety creeping over him. Sweat trickled behind the waistband of his jeans. Then it hit him, and his heart nearly stopped.

"Shit!" The church shooting.

Joanne Bowman's death had devastated his mother but also frightened her. As a Vestry member, Ellie was always at the church. So was Arthur. If the killer had targeted Trinity Episcopal ....

"Arthur, Arthur!" Walker knocked harder on the window.

The priest's eyelids opened and his eyes rotated slowly toward Walker, though they seemed unfocused.

"Are you okay?" Walker reached for the door handle.

Arthur's hand rose a few inches, then dropped back to his lap. Panicked now, Walker jerked the car door open and gripped Arthur's shoulder. The priest's eyes, which had closed again, reopened halfway.

"What's wrong?" Walker didn't see any blood, which was a slight relief.

"Hi," Arthur said, his voice breathy and weak. "Need to go inside." He struggled to turn his body in the seat.

"Here, let me help you." Walker maneuvered Arthur's legs from under the steering wheel and set his feet on the ground. "Are you sure you can stand?"

Arthur nodded slightly.

"On three, then. One, two, *three*," Walker said, tugging Arthur's arms.

The priest rose partway before his weight dropped him back into the seat. His head flopped backward, then popped forward, and his chin bounced off his chest.

"Arthur, are you sick? Are you hurt? Have you been drinking?"

The priest rallied enough to lift his chin. "No. Need potassium. Inside," he murmured before his head dropped again.

Walker didn't believe a mineral deficiency could account for Arthur's profound weakness, but what did he know? In high school, the football coach distributed salt tablets during practice to replace what the players lost by sweating. Extreme salt depletion could weaken, sicken, or even kill you, and potassium was a salt.

"Are you having chest pains or head pain?"

"No," Arthur whispered.

"And you're not diabetic?"

"No." The word was barely audible.

Only slightly reassured, Walker decided to help Arthur into the house, give him what he requested, then hang around to make sure he was okay, or if he wasn't okay, to call an ambulance.

"All right, then. I'm going to lift you from the car."

Walker lowered his hips, hooked his arms beneath Arthur's shoulders and, on a three-count, clean-jerked the priest to his feet. They wobbled precariously as Walker struggled to prop the taller, nearly helpless man upright. The warning *ding, ding, ding* of the keys in the ignition plucked at Walker's nerves, so he braced Arthur against the car and twisted awkwardly to yank them free.

"Ready?"

Arthur opened his eyes but didn't speak. Walker laid the priest's arm over his shoulders and gripped him around the waist, then stepped forward. With a seemingly herculean effort, Arthur shuffled his feet along the concrete drive and up the sidewalk, Walker supporting much of his weight.

"Can you climb the steps?"

Arthur's lack of response was his answer.

"I'm taking you up in a fireman's carry," Walker said, less to inform the semi-conscious man than to energize himself for the task. At 5'11", Walker was a solid 230 pounds of muscle, while the priest was taller and leaner, but still must weigh close to 190. Balance could be tricky.

Walker leaned Arthur against the brick column at the bottom of the stairs, then squatted beside him and tugged on his right arm. Arthur's upper body dropped facedown across Walker's shoulders like a semi-sentient bag of sand. Perfect. He corralled the man's right leg with his elbow, took hold of his dangling arm, and pressed their combined 420 pounds upward, grunting with the effort. Once he was upright, Walker reestablished his balance, then slowly trudged up the porch steps.

At the front door, Walker fumbled Arthur's house key into the lock and stepped over the threshold. His thigh muscles burned as they flexed continuously to balance the top-heavy weight and prevent both of them from crashing to the floor.

Walker lumbered to the living room and, in one smooth motion, bent down and deposited Arthur onto the sofa. When the priest crumpled sideways, Walker caught and rotated him onto his back, then lifted his legs onto the cushions.

"Thank you," the priest mouthed. His face was deathly pale. Drops of sweat clung to his hairline along the top of his forehead.

"What do you want me to do? Should I call an ambulance?" Walker crouched down and leaned in close, resisting the urge to cup the priest's face in his hand. Arthur's citrusy breath and the leather scent of his sweat awakened a physical memory, and Walker's cock thickened. The response was depraved with the priest in such an alarmingly helpless state, but there it was.

Arthur's eyelids rose, though his eyes remained glassy and unfocused. "Potassium, bathroom," he whispered.

Walker hurried down the hall, not at all sure he was doing the right thing, not at all sure the man was lucid. It occurred to him then that he might call his mother for nursing advice. As soon as he fetched the minerals, he would do that. Walker opened the medicine cabinet and found the bottom shelf dominated by a plastic jar labeled Potassium Chloride Powder. So Arthur wasn't entirely out of it.

The directions said to mix the powder in juice or milk. Walker dashed to the kitchen and grabbed a carton of grapefruit juice from the refrigerator. He yanked open three cabinets before locating a glass, then filled it and rustled around for a spoon. When he returned to the couch, Arthur lay motionless. His complexion, even his lips, had gone from colorless to a frightening shade of gray.

This remedy had better work and fast! Walker scanned for dosage directions, then noticed Arthur's thumb and first two fingers extend from his fist. Not a gang sign.

"Three spoonfuls?" Walker guessed.

Arthur's head bobbed minutely.

The written dosage specified one-quarter teaspoon for an adult, a fraction of that amount. Could he trust the priest's clouded mind? He wasn't sure, but potassium shouldn't hurt him. Walker dipped the spoon into the jar three times, dumping the powder into the grapefruit juice where it bubbled and fizzed like Alka-Seltzer. Walker lifted Arthur's head and tilted the glass with trembling hands.

The instant the liquid touched the priest's lips, he began to swallow convulsively. Walker poured for a few seconds, then stopped to let him breathe, but Arthur, whose eyes somehow seemed clearer, clutched the glass and tipped it himself, gulping the juice in great swallows. When the glass was nearly empty, Arthur pushed himself to a sitting position, took a few quick breaths, and poured the rest of the juice down his throat. He wiped his mouth with the back of his hand.

"Iron," he said to a startled Walker. "There's some chelated iron in the bathroom. Will you bring it? With more juice, please?"

Baffled, but fascinated, Walker complied. When he returned with the bottle of liquid and another glass of juice, he saw that Arthur's color had returned to normal.

"I'm sorry about all this," the priest said conversationally, as if he hadn't been catatonic two minutes before.

"I don't understand." Walker gaped at the man in front of him, his healthful vigor seemingly restored, all trace of his former, desperate condition gone. Irrational thoughts tumbled through Walker's mind, of magic and miracles and saintly interventions. "I thought you were dying." His voice had gone scratchy, and he cleared his throat.

Arthur regarded him for a moment before gesturing at the glass in his hand. "Let me finish this, and then I will explain as best I can."

38. Saving Grace

Walker sat motionless in the chair across from Arthur, one hand covering his mouth. He had no idea how to respond to the priest's revelation. "That's why you were so weak but now you're fine?" he said finally.

"Not quite as fine as I look, but I will be by tomorrow." Arthur rubbed the back of his neck and angled his head left, then right.

"You've had this since you were a kid?"

Arthur nodded. "It was more of a problem then. It used to get me in trouble." Amusement twitched across his lips.

"How so?" Walker inquired. He didn't think the priest would lie, but this disclosure was mindboggling at best. Walker's earlier musings on magic and miracles didn't seem so misplaced now.

"I was known for throwing things when I got angry." Arthur paused as if that might be sufficient explanation, but Walker didn't respond, and he continued. "Whenever I claimed I hadn't thrown a ball at Johnny's head or hurled an eraser at a teacher's back, I got in worse trouble, so I learned to admit to doing those things. Eventually, I figured out I *was* doing them; I just didn't have any control over it."

"Can you still do it?"

"Possibly, but I don't try. I have better ways of channeling my frustrations than I did then." Arthur smiled wryly.

"You're a healer."

"The church calls it a healing charism. It's not all that rare."

A light bulb flicked on in Walker's head. "The night I hit you – "

He stopped, embarrassed by the memory. The priest waited.

"Mom saw you afterward and said you were badly hurt, but I went to church the next day and...you looked fine. Was that...this? Can you heal yourself?" Walker leaned forward, curious and fascinated by the possibility.

"To a point, yes."

Walker paused, at a loss. "I...I don't know what to say."

"You don't have to say anything. I know it sounds preposterous."

"Are you feeling okay now? You look a lot better."

"I am," the priest said. "Or I will be after more supplements and some sleep." He clasped his hands behind his head and stretched back into the couch.

A protective impulse stiffened Walker's spine. "Who was it you helped today?"

"A jail inmate. He was seriously ill, though I'm not sure how aware of it he was." Arthur gazed at the ceiling as if thinking of the man he'd visited.

Walker clenched his teeth against an irrational jealousy. His left hand moved to crack the knuckles of his right, but he caught himself and stopped.

"Do you have any more questions for me?" Arthur lowered his arms and straightened in his seat.

Walker shook his head, diverted from the priest's strange revelation by inappropriate, but noisy, questions in his head. *Who is this man in jail? How old is he? Did you touch him? Hold him?*

"I have a question then," Arthur said, interrupting Walker's neurotic train of thought. "I'm extremely relieved that you rescued me from my car, but how did you come to be here?"

Walker almost jumped in his chair. *Shit.* "Oh...I was just driving by," he said, the words sounding false even to his ears. He rubbed the heel of his hand with a thumb, discomfort tightening his throat. "I, uh, well...to be honest, I've been thinking about you. Even before the other night when...." He looked up.

The priest caught his gaze and silently held it, waiting.

"I mean," Walker continued, one confession leading more easily to the next, "I've driven by your house...mmm...a lot in the past few weeks."

The priest's face remained an unreadable mask.

Walker crossed his legs, then uncrossed them. "So...I was driving by tonight and wanted to say hello." *Close enough.*

Arthur nodded. "Thank you. I got myself into a situation I never should have." Five seconds ticked past. "You may have saved my life." A faint tremor vibrated in his softly spoken words.

Walker's jaw dropped. "You could have died?"

"It's possible. I don't remember touching anyone as ill as this man today. The light...the energy flow...leaches potassium from my system. Today was like a hemorrhage."

The blood heating Walker's face drained away at the thought that this man – this extraordinary man – might be dead if he hadn't succumbed to his burning obsession when he did. Emotion welled and before he could think, he'd moved to the couch and wrapped his arms around Arthur, hugging him to his chest.

"I'm glad you're okay," Walker murmured into the priest's ear.

Arthur allowed the embrace but otherwise didn't react. After a few seconds, he touched the wide curve of Walker's upper arm, a request to be released. Walker let go, though he could still feel the heat of Arthur's body and smell his leathery sweet scent. Neither man moved away.

"I want you," Walker confessed, his voice dropping to a deep, quavering baritone.

Arthur pressed his hands together in a gesture of prayer, regarded them for a moment, then rotated his wrists to press his fingertips to his lips. Silence filled the room, punctuated by the swinging pendulum of a grandfather clock set against the far wall.

Handcrafted in Kentucky, Walker noted, apropos of nothing.

Then the priest reached behind his neck, and his white collar dropped free. He leaned forward to lay the solid band on the coffee table, then inhaled deliberately as if to steady himself.

"I've thought about this conversation..." – Arthur looked away before turning back to meet Walker's gaze –

"...about what I want to say versus what I ought to say. I've removed my collar because I find I can't speak to you about this as a priest."

He paused for several heartbeats, and Walker held his breath.

"I am a priest," he said slowly. "But I'm also a man, and I'm attracted to you as a man."

Sitting there, prepared for rebuke or rebuff, Walker's nervous anticipation transformed to a spine-shaking shiver.

I want you too, his fevered mind heard, and the desire that had simmered inside him for weeks instantly boiled over.

≈ ≈ ≈

"In my life, this is unprece – "

A powerful hand gripped the back of Arthur's neck, stopping his words. Insistent fingers urged him toward the lips of the potent man beside him. He resisted automatically, but Walker's intent didn't falter. It pushed, pulled, and beseeched him to surrender until – abruptly, and all at once – he did. Walker took Arthur's mouth then, nudged his lips apart and thrust his tongue inside as if it were another organ altogether.

In all his years, Arthur had felt nothing like this. The musky scent of the man, the bulk of his corded muscles, the softness of his lips, the straining erection Arthur didn't have to see to know was there, combined to turn the key in a lock he barely remembered bolting. Need as he'd never known coursed through him. He had to connect in flesh, to let the robe and collar fall, to know what it felt like to be nothing more than human, a human with appetites he didn't fully comprehend.

With a groan, Arthur simply let go, dropped his habitual restraint, his careful moral code, his compulsion to care for others first. For once, just once, he wanted something for himself, something he'd never had.

He returned Walker's kiss with an all-consuming passion. His hand found Walker's head and grabbed a fistful of hair, holding this virile man to his mouth with equal strength, equal desire. He wrapped an arm around Walker's back, the tightened mass of muscle there an aphrodisiac of its own. A moaning sound edged into his awareness, and he was unsure whether it came from him or his counterpart. Their tongues plunged and twisted, wrangled for dominance without a need to impose it. The dance developed, and Walker – being more fully in his element – gradually wrestled Arthur onto his back, but was thwarted by the hidden buttons of his clerical shirt.

"Undo it," Walker ordered in a soft, but forceful, tone as he crouched with one knee beside Arthur's hips, his opposite foot on the floor.

Arthur complied while Walker pulled his own shirt over his head, causing the priest to gape at the spread of masculinity before him. He'd seen men disrobe in locker rooms, but the one hulking over him was exceptional in form. Walker was absurdly powerful, every inch of his torso and arms curved, one muscle folding into the next with no flat planes between. He wasn't merely attractive. He was stunning in his maleness, and he manifested an intensely sexual energy that thrummed just under the surface, barely contained.

Arthur wanted him beyond reason, to feel that hard flesh in his hands, to strain against him, to push, squeeze, wrench, pound if necessary, and know that this man – this one man – would not be harmed by the force of his deferred need.

"Up," Walker directed, then pulled him to a seated position and shoved his shirt from his shoulders. He grabbed the hem of Arthur's undershirt and yanked it off, discarding it on the floor.

Walker stood and unsnapped the waistband of his jeans, then rolled down the zipper in a quick, practiced move. Arthur watched in fascination, aroused beyond control. He rose and unfastened his own trousers, and Walker moved toward him – a measured, intentional step – then leaned in and devoured Arthur's mouth.

What happened next felt like a wrestling of jungle creatures. Walker pushed his pants down his hips, then did the same to Arthur's. Arthur reached greedily for Walker's daunting erection, deep red with purple-blue veining down its length. Arthur's penis, heavy and full, rose audaciously to bump against Walker's belly, the sensation overwhelmingly intense, the furred texture there new to Arthur's deprived flesh. Grasping and stroking the man's swollen sex while Walker did the same to him seemed, not wrong, not wickedly depraved, but right – exactly right.

The men kissed and rubbed, each with his free hand exploring the backside of the other. Arthur didn't think, all possibility of that having disappeared with the smooth, steady grip of this captivating man's touch. When the sensations became too much and Arthur's hands began to falter, Walker's didn't waver.

"Let go," Walker demanded in a low, dark voice. "Give it to me."

His hand became rougher, tighter, and Arthur felt the other palm slide south to the cleft of his behind, stroking and pressing. Under the spell of this man's deep command, his insistent urging, Arthur was set free, the explosion of pleasure nearly knocking him off his feet into Walker's saving arms for the second time that day. Walker held him up as he cried out with a sound he didn't recognize.

"Come on," Walker said after Arthur's body had spent itself and slumped forward against his chest.

Mute and nearly blind, Arthur gave over and allowed himself to be led down the hall to the cocoon of his curtained bedroom.

"Off," Walker commanded, his voice strained as he pointed to Arthur's gaping trousers and briefs. Walker quickly dropped his own, then pulled Arthur onto the bed.

The two men, one older and leaner, one younger and brawnier, tangled their limbs together. Arthur reached for Walker's erection and circled it with his hand, enthralled by the power of their connection. He lost himself in Walker's response, his sharp thrusting into Arthur's fist.

"Jes – " Walker cried, then "Christ!"

Arthur might have objected to the man's choice of expletives, except that he was so far gone himself, he barely noticed.

"Un ... believable," Walker gasped. "I can feel it."

It took Arthur a moment to decipher that utterance, but when he did, he realized that light was flowing from his hands into Walker's body. Not that Walker pulled it from him, but that, in his excitement and abandon, Arthur had delivered it unconsciously.

"Jesus!" Walker shouted as a deep spasm overcame him, and he seized, his cock firing semen in long, hard spurts onto Arthur's chest and stomach. Walker collapsed with his weight across Arthur's body and his arms wrapped around Arthur's back as if afraid the priest might rise and walk away.

The thought hadn't crossed Arthur's mind.

39. Finding Father

Martha had waited long enough. She would see Father today if she had to park outside his house until he came home! She'd driven by the church several times in the late afternoon looking for his car in the parking lot. Sylvia's odd behavior the previous day had made her so uncomfortable that she didn't want to go in again unless Father was there. When six o'clock rolled around with no sign of Father's car, she gave up her church vigil and drove to Adams Avenue to see if Father had gone straight home from visiting his shut-ins, or whatever he was doing.

"Humph," she snorted in irritation. "If I was a shut-in, maybe I'd get more attention from my priest." It was something to think about.

Dusk had fallen, and Martha found it difficult to maneuver the darkening street and locate a place to park her car. But when she reached the rectory, a thrill of pleasure rushed through her. The lights were on and the driveway was full! A large black truck stuck out behind Father's car.

"He has other guests too," Martha murmured breathlessly. "He won't mind if I stop in to welcome him back. I need to know if he got my jam cake!"

She located a double-long space and ran her car onto the curb, regretting only that she hadn't re-donned her sexy red dress for their reunion. She heaved herself from the car and made her way up the walk, jubilance in her step.

Finally! She'd missed Father so much. It had been a whole week, and that freckle-face strawberry who'd tried to fill his robes on Sunday had fallen far short of what Trinity Episcopal was accustomed to. Father had set the bar too high for just anyone to take his place at the pulpit. That thick, pale hair sleeked back against his head, those deep, attentive eyes the color of sapphires, his skin tanned and smooth. She shivered in anticipation.

Martha gazed eagerly at Father's lit-up living room window as she grabbed the porch handrail to haul herself up the steps.

"Oh, oh, I see him in there!"

The additional two steps of height gave her a view of his angular face through the window sheers. She heaved herself up one more step and gazed curiously through the glass. Who was that standing behind Father? Another man, a little shorter, his face didn't look familiar.

"Wait," she murmured. "Is that...? But he's not...." She peered more closely. "His chest is bare." She climbed the last step and saw *both* men were bared to the waist.

Martha stared blankly. Before she could make sense of it, the man stepped close to Father, grasped the waist of his trousers, and tugged them down, exposing Father's naked behind! Martha slumped heavily against the porch railing and slapped both hands over her mouth to stifle a cry. Her eyes grew large as her mind struggled for an explanation. *An act of penitence? A doctor's appointment?*

"Eek!" she cried when the big man shoved down his own pants and a huge snake leaped out, red and angry, fixin' to strike. She squinted her eyes to see more clearly, and to her amazement, Father reached out and clenched it in both hands, squeezing and pulling like he meant to choke it.

"Whaaah?"

Then the snake man pulled Father toward him and pressed his mouth over Father's face. *The breath of life?* But Father was standing up. He couldn't be feeling that poorly. Martha gaped in astonishment, trying to figure. *What the heck is going on in there?* Then the duo turned and she saw Father had a snake in his pants too, and the other man was choking it while he grasped Father's butt in his hand.

"Oh, my God! Oh, my God!" Martha blubbered, grabbing the sides of her Dolly Parton wig. "The beast with two backs! With a *man!* That's his – "

She severed the thought like John the Baptist's head.

Martha remained rigidly in place, her horror morphing to fascination bit by reluctant bit. She'd never seen anything like it. It was exciting in a peculiar sort of way. Somewhere down there beneath her rolls of fat lay a dormant part of her body, except now it was beginning to tickle, and she wanted to reach down and scratch it or rub it on something. But she was too mesmerized to move.

She'd never seen a man's thingy, his peter, in real life, though she knew what one felt like. She'd been in her bed countless times sleeping when her Daddy, and later Floyd, wandered in and woke her up with a cold slick of pork grease on her backside and a forceful poke that hurt if she didn't give herself over all the way. It wasn't something she'd sought, the learnin' her Daddy had done on her after her momma died.

"A man's got rights. A woman's got duties." That's what the Reverend Gideon Brown used to say. She'd inherited her momma's duties, the cookin', the washin', the doin' for – and the learnin' in the dark. She would pretend to be asleep, and they never talked, just grunted and groaned. The first time Floyd came in she only knew it was him because his thingy was smaller and didn't hurt as much.

So that's what they look like.

Martha should have run screaming, but she didn't. She felt a queasiness in her stomach to see these two men – and especially, *Father* – wrestle with each other in a way that seemed eerily familiar, though not. What were they doing, anyway? She couldn't hear anything, and she couldn't see Father's face, but suddenly he collapsed and the man's arms circled around like he was holding him up.

What should I do? What should I do? Martha's mind raced. She thought some action was called for, but didn't know what it should be. The men seemed to be enacting a ritual that had run its course. It was intensely private. It had nothing to do with her or anyone else. The two of them were the only ones in the house, of that she was now certain.

A burning gripped her gut, a muddle of excitement, anger, and an urgent desire to disrupt their closeness. *And maybe, just maybe, take that man's place.* It wasn't really a thought, only a feeling, a feeling she wasn't even aware she had.

Then the man grabbed Father's hand and led him down the hall out of Martha's sight. She stood for a long time picturing the shape of Father's backside, the rounded, muscled flesh that attracted her to him in a new way. It was confusing and seemed bad somehow, but it gave her a secret thrill.

≈ ≈ ≈

"Walker," Arthur murmured to the man who had passed out on top of him. His dead weight compressed Arthur's chest and forced him to take shallow, panting breaths. "Walker," he repeated to no avail.

Had the light he'd unintentionally released hurt Walker? He didn't think it was possible, but he felt the need to examine the man's body for injuries, possibly burns. He tried to move, but found one of his arms pinned to his side and the other trapped between his ribcage and Walker's chest. He squeezed Walker's thigh where his free hand could reach it, trying to wake him. Then he dug in with his too-short fingernails, barely denting the man's skin. Walker was out cold.

A noise from the hall caught Arthur's attention, and he listened for several seconds, but it didn't repeat. Old houses creaked with changes in temperature and humidity. This was his first season in the rectory, so he was still getting used to its unique groans and sighs. He returned his attention to Walker, wondering whether he could execute a wrestling bridge move to dislodge him. His earlier mineral depletion had left him weakened, though. He needed more supplements.

At that moment, the ceiling light flared on directly into Arthur's eyes, and time abruptly flattened, the present fading into the past. He almost felt the scratch of tree bark against his back and the wet whisper at his groin, the warmth there turning suddenly cold when a high-powered bulb flashed and the stranger kneeling before him lurched away.

"Father! Father! Are you all right? Father!" The dreadfully familiar voice screeched from the doorway and cut through Arthur's muddled thoughts like a cleaver to the skull. He recoiled in shock, and a spasm of defensive energy whooshed from his palms. He watched, half in the present, half sunk in the past, as Walker Jones' limp body arced over the mattress and crashed headfirst into the wall beyond the foot of his bed, then collapsed to the floor with a thud.

Arthur bounded to his feet, intent on stopping the antagonist who would destroy his life. But befuddlement slowed him and, caught between remembered nightmare and present jeopardy, he froze, one hand covering his genitals, as the short, stumpy woman marched resolutely across his bedroom.

"What did you do to Father?" Martha Browne shrieked. "What did you do, you bully?"

At her approach, Walker rolled to his hands and knees, visibly dazed. Martha bent over and whaled at his head with balled-up fists. Walker tried to bat her hands away while clutching the back of his head.

"Stop!" Arthur bellowed and dashed behind Martha to grab her wrists.

She struggled momentarily before twisting to look at him. "Are you all right, Father? Did he hurt you?"

Arthur *was* hurt. Hurt, and damaged too. And in that moment of recognition, a lifetime of pain – from feelings disregarded, longings denied, unending compensations, lost opportunities, and the passing of the years – was unleashed, and fury seized him.

"Out. Get *out* of my house." He pushed the romantically misguided woman, the embodiment of all that was misshapen and warped in his life, from his bedroom and down the hall. He propelled her relentlessly to the front door, then prodded her through it.

She turned to protest, and like Adam after the fall, Arthur became aware of his nakedness. He stepped behind the door, his stomach pitching.

"Go. Please, just go."

"But Father, I was only try – "

Arthur pushed the door closed and turned the deadbolt. Martha's protests continued, but his befuddled brain blocked them as he slumped against the wood.

What had just happened? He shook his head to dispel the fog, but only slowly became aware of the cool brass doorknob against his hip, the doormat fibers tickling his toes, the fragrance of sweetspire that had floated in on the evening breeze. The temperature was mild, yet his palms felt hot.

"Let me in! Let me in!"

The sharp words were punctuated by a fist pounding at his back, and Arthur started. A feeling of hopelessness punched him in the gut.

"Father! Are you there? What's happening?"

"Martha Browne," he rasped through the door, keeping his voice as even as possible. "I've asked you to leave. If you don't, I will be forced to call the police."

"The police, yes! Let me in! I'll call the police," came the excited reply.

A restraining order. Maybe she would understand that. It seemed an unworthy thought for a priest, but it comforted him a little as he stood there filled with dread, stripped naked, vulnerable and exhausted. And right now someone else needed his attention. Arthur pushed upright and hastened down the hall.

Walker sat hunched on the floor where he'd landed, his back resting against the wall. His eyes tracked Arthur's return, but they seemed unfocused, and he didn't otherwise stir. Arthur stepped into the closet, threw on his bathrobe, and grabbed a spare quilt. He returned and draped the blanket over Walker, then perched opposite him at the foot of the bed.

"How do you feel?"

"Um...okay." Walker huddled under the quilt, pulling it over his shoulders.

"Can you tell me what day it is?" Arthur said.

Walker squinted at him. "Huh?"

"What day of the week is it?"

"Um...Friday?" Walker scowled. "No, you're here. It must be Sunday." He glanced around the room with a puzzled expression.

"Walker, do you know where you are?" Arthur kept his voice deliberately calm.

"I'm with you," Walker replied with irrefutable logic. "What happened?"

Despite his rising alarm, Arthur couldn't help trying to rationalize. "You fell into a dead sleep on top of me."

"I did?" Confusion crossed Walker's brow, then cleared. He looked at Arthur in wonder. "You touched me. I've never felt anything like that." He paused. "Wait. How did I end up down here?"

Arthur had no explanation except the obvious one. He clenched his fists. "It seems that I ... well ... I threw you."

"Threw me?"

"You collapsed on me, and I couldn't draw a full breath. Then that woman burst in and flipped on the light. She startled me."

"Are you okay? Did I hurt you?" Walker reached for Arthur's hand, but the priest pulled back and flattened both palms against the mattress.

"I hurt *you*. Your head slammed into the wall."

Walker touched the back of his skull and grimaced. "I've got a lump."

"Walker, I'm sorry, so sorry," Arthur said miserably. "I didn't mean to."

"Are you saying – "

"I don't dare touch you. Everything is so...." *Overwhelming, mixed up, frightening.* Arthur gazed into the blank distance. God seemed far away.

Walker gripped his head and moaned, and Arthur snapped to attention, shaking off his self-pity. He needed to get Walker off the floor and back into bed, and see what he could do for him. The man was injured, perhaps seriously.

Bang! Bang! Bang!

The sound from the window invaded the room like a gunshot, and both men jumped.

40. Nine-One-One

Rhett stood on the pedals of his bike and pumped hard around the corner onto Adams Avenue. He was taking the route by the church to check if his mom was still working. With any luck she would be, and he'd beat her home. Otherwise, she'd know he was coming home late, and his brother might not cover for him. Riley was getting impatient, even a little pissed off, about standing in for both of them, pretending to be him on alternate days while he pitched and batted fly balls at the Boys Club.

I'd do the same for him, though. Or maybe he wouldn't. It was hard to tell anymore what he would or wouldn't do. Sex changed everything. Rhett's dick flexed in agreement.

An angry pig – at least it sounded like – squealed, and Rhett squeezed his hand brakes, scanning for an animal to dart across the street. The noise came again from up ahead...at the rectory?

Yes. Something large lumbered through Father Arthur's front yard, a woman, and she was clearly in trouble. Without a second thought, Rhett jumped his bike over the curb and leaped off, letting it slam into the grass.

"What's wrong? Are you okay?" he called, running toward her.

"...a man in Father's house!" came her shrieking reply.

Rhett squinted into the murky dusk. The woman was short and round with big blond hair. She looked vaguely familiar. "Do you mean Father Arthur? Somebody broke into the rectory?"

She scuttled past him toward the house. "He's in the bedroom! Attacking Father!"

Adrenaline spiked through Rhett's bloodstream, and he charged in the direction of the front door before catching himself and pinwheeling back. "Shouldn't we call the police?"

"Police! Police!" the woman hollered and disappeared around the side of the house.

Rhett wasted no time digging his phone from his pocket and dialing 911.

"What is your emergency?" said a woman's voice, calm and authoritative.

"Father Arthur is being attacked. In his house," he gasped. Cold sweat broke out on his forehead and dampened his armpits.

"Does the attacker have a weapon?"

Rhett blanched. "I don't know. Please hurry."

"What is the address?"

Rhett squinted through the twilight. "It's Adams Avenue. Behind the church. The Episcopal Church." His throat tightened. He could barely breathe. "Our secretary was shot and killed." His voice squeaked on the last word.

"Officers are on their way. Please stay on the line – "

Rhett's hand shook so hard he dropped his phone. He picked it up with trembling fingers, but the call had disconnected. Should he go in and help Arthur or wait for the police? He started toward the house again, but the thought of a gun stopped him in his tracks, and he dodged behind a tree. He tapped his speed dial.

"Rhett?" At the sound of his mother's voice, tears formed in the corners of his eyes, and he wiped them away distractedly.

"Mom?" he whispered.

"Honey, what's wrong? Are you okay?"

"I'm at Father Arthur's," he whispered again. "The police are coming. Somebody's attacking him in his house."

"Oh, my gawd," his mother croaked. "Where are you?"

"In the yard." A police siren began to wail in the distance.

"Rhett, listen to me. Run to a neighbor's house. Right now. The police will take care of Arthur. Your dad and I are on our way."

His phone gave him the call-waiting signal, and he looked at the screen: *911 Dispatch.*

"Okay, Mom," he said breathlessly. "Gotta go." He tapped the screen.

"This is 9-1-1 Dispatch," said the same woman's voice as before. "Did you phone with an emergency?"

"Y-yes, I did." Rhett's throat was so dry he could barely squeeze out the words.

"Are you safe?" the dispatcher inquired.

"Yes, I'm outside."

"The officers will be there momentarily. What is your name?"

A flashing red light rounded the corner.

"They're here!" Without thinking, Rhett shoved his phone into his pocket and began waving his arms in the air.

≈ ≈ ≈

Martha charged from one window to the next at the back of the rectory, banging on them in turn, not certain which corresponded to Father's bedroom. She paused to listen at one and heard voices inside, menacing and low, but the curtains remained steadfastly closed. Father was trapped in there with that brawny man who was taking advantage of him in the worst possible way. It was lucky she'd arrived when she did.

Father had shooed her out, but sometimes during a crisis like that, you had to go along with the attacker to protect yourself. Martha understood that.

The tulip tree above her glowed crimson, faded out, then glowed crimson again – a *whoop-whoop*! She trudged across the backyard and around the corner to the front. Though her Daddy had often referred to policemen as swine, she was glad to see the two officers approaching the house with their guns drawn.

Then, *hallelujah,* Father opened the front door and stepped out, looking handsome in his priestly black. He reached up to smooth his untidy hair.

The police aimed their weapons at him. "Show us your hands," a deep voice boomed, and Father immediately raised his palms into the air.

"No, no!" yelled a boy running from the curb. "That's Father Arthur."

"Father, Father!" Martha rushed forward.

The female officer's gun re-aimed at her. *At her!*

"Stop right there!" the woman barked.

Martha stopped in confusion. "There's a dangerous man in there!" she hollered back.

The boy was talking to the policeman who glanced her way before lowering his weapon. Then Father descended the porch stairs and spoke to him, but Martha couldn't hear what they said.

The female officer eyeballed her, then finally lowered her gun too.

"Father, Father! Are you hurt?" Martha headed toward him, but the woman blocked her path.

"Stay here, please, Ma'am."

"Get out of my way. I have to talk to Father," Martha said. Clearly, the male officer was in charge. She pushed past the irritating woman who looked more like a man than she ought to.

The female grabbed her arm. Martha whirled around and slapped at the offending hand.

"Don't touch me!"

Before she knew what was happening, cold steel snapped around her left wrist. She yanked away, but then her right arm twisted behind her back and her other wrist was ensnared. Fury seized her, and she tried to strike out, but her hands had nowhere to go.

"Father!" she wailed as the woman dragged her toward the police car.

Father was still talking to the policeman and didn't look at her. She hollered as loud as she could in case he didn't realize what they were doing to her.

"Father! Father!"

Then she was being pushed into the back of the squad car. The door shut behind her. There was no handle on the inside.

"Swine!" she screamed. "Swine!"

≈ ≈ ≈

Arthur watched the policewoman – Officer Tierney, he learned later – intercept Martha Browne as she angled toward him across the lawn. He had never had a gun pointed at him, and his pulse continued to race even after both officers had lowered their weapons. One of Sylvia's sons was speaking excitedly. Arthur had no idea what he was doing there – what any of them were doing there, for that matter.

"That lady told me to call 9-1-1," the Pugh boy burst out. "She said a man broke in and attacked you in your bedroom. I thought...I thought...." He was clearly frightened, but he was over six feet tall and well-developed, and Arthur had to remind himself of his youth.

"It's okay, son," he said, placing an arm around the boy. "She was mistaken."

Officer Schmidt, according to his nametag, approached. "*Is* there a man in your house?" he asked.

Arthur's heart rate spiked. He cleared his throat. "Um...yes."

"Does he live here?"

"No, no, I live alone," Arthur answered hastily. "He's a...friend."

Officer Schmidt scrutinized him for longer than a civilian might have. "Did he attack you?"

Sylvia's son tensed beneath Arthur's arm.

"Hardly," Arthur replied dismissively before he remembered that Walker had, in fact, hit him three weeks before. "Well," he hedged, not wanting to make a false statement, "he punched me once, but it was a misunderstanding."

"He hit you today?" Schmidt probed. "Or on an earlier occasion?"

Arthur gritted his teeth and glanced away before meeting the officer's gaze. "An earlier occasion, but it was a mistake."

Schmidt eyed him for several seconds, then pulled a pen and pad from his pocket and jotted a note. The Pugh boy peeled away and began pacing through the grass.

Window curtains across the street parted to reveal a woman's face, and memories of the Illinois nightmare sprang to Arthur's mind. The officers would notice the truck in his driveway and might record its plate number as part of their report. If Martha revealed what she'd witnessed...well, it was substantiation for the bishop or anyone else who cared to investigate the matter. Arthur shuddered.

The elderly couple next door came onto their porch to watch as Officer Tierney maneuvered Martha Browne into the police cruiser. Her shrieks had become continual, like those of agitated patients in the locked wards Arthur visited. Though the noise was both nerve-wracking and exasperating, he could sense Martha's confusion and fear. He considered going over to try to calm her, but decided it could make the situation worse. Not to mention what she might blurt out in front of everyone.

"Are you arresting Martha Browne?" he asked.

Officer Schmidt glanced across the yard at his partner who signaled back.

"Looks that way. Resisting," he said, then scrawled something on his pad. "Can you explain what happened? Who is that women, and why did she tell..." – he squinted at his notes – "...Rhett here that you were being assaulted today?"

Arthur gazed into the distance and tried to collect his thoughts. He stretched his neck to one side and rubbed at the strained muscles. "She's a parishioner, and I fear she's become fixated on me. She's a bit unstable." Schmidt regarded him in silence, so Arthur went on. "She entered my house uninvited – not for the first time – and ... misinterpreted the situation. She hit my guest, my ... my friend."

A few feet away, Rhett stopped pacing and stared.

Schmidt examined Arthur's face, then pursed his lips and returned to his notepad without comment. He wrote something, then looked up again. "You're a priest?"

"Yes." Though Arthur wasn't wearing his collar, he'd pulled on his clerics before he came outside to deal with Martha and found two handguns pointed at him.

"The ladies always want what they can't have. We see it a lot," Schmidt remarked obliquely. "Do you want to press charges for trespassing?"

"No." Arthur decided not to correct the officer's assumption that he was a celibate Catholic.

Schmidt jotted another note, then coughed into his fist. "Does your ... uh ... friend want to press charges for assault?"

Or had the cop assumed something else? Arthur combed his hand nervously through his hair.

"Um ... I don't think so," he replied. "It wasn't serious." *Not as serious as being slammed headfirst into a wall.* Arthur shuffled his feet, impatient to go inside and check on Walker. He'd helped him back into bed, and Walker had passed out again instantly.

"I'd like to speak with him," said Schmidt. "Will you ask him to come out here, please?"

Arthur's stomach tightened, but he controlled his facial expression. "He's not feeling well. He's resting at the moment."

Schmidt peered at Arthur in cool appraisal. "May we go inside?"

Why did the policeman's every comment seem laden with hidden meaning and accusation, and Arthur's replies sound deceptive, at best, or, at worst, like outright lies? Where before it seemed like Schmidt thought Arthur had been attacked, possibly in a domestic dispute, now it appeared he thought Arthur might be the aggressor and was holding a debilitated Walker hostage. Or maybe the entire subtext was a figment of his imagination. Maybe he imagined the cop's knowing stare.

The wages of guilt. Arthur blew out a long breath.

"Yes, of course. He's in the back bedroom." Arthur swallowed down the bile that threatened to climb up his throat. Self-loathing had a flavor, it seemed.

Schmidt signaled something to Tierney who left her position near the patrol car and followed him into the house. In the car's back seat, a now silent Martha Browne faced belligerently forward, her face screwed into a red rosette of anger. Rhett had retrieved his bicycle from the curb and was rolling it up the driveway.

The cops returned.

"Everything appears in order," Schmidt said. "Here's my card." He extended a paper rectangle featuring the City of Amity seal. "Call if either of you change your mind about pressing charges. We'll hold Miss Browne overnight at least."

"You can't just let her go?" Arthur had asked more out of duty than compassion, and another kind of guilt pricked his conscience.

"I'm afraid not."

Arthur felt disproportionately relieved when the patrol car pulled away. Martha Browne had intruded on his privacy, summoned the law, and involved a whole host of people in his personal business. It was his worst nightmare revisited. An image of her behind bars flashed through his mind, and with it came a flare of inappropriate, retaliatory glee, which he quickly squelched. She was suffering and had likely been suffering for a long time. He derided himself for his lack of compassion. Martha had nearly depleted his supply, though.

"You'd better call your folks," Arthur said to Rhett.

"I just did," replied the youth, holding up a cell phone. "They had a flat, but they're coming."

"Let's wait inside."

Arthur ushered Rhett into his living room, then went to get him a glass of water. From the kitchen, he heard the boy's surprised query. "Walker?"

"Hey there," rumbled the reply. "Sorry, is it Riley? Or Rhett?"

"Rhett."

Arthur returned to find Walker standing at the entrance to the hallway. He'd pulled on his T-shirt and jeans, but was barefoot and looked like he'd just crawled out of bed. Which he had.

Arthur handed Rhett the glass. "Do you two know each other?"

"Yeah," Rhett replied, "from church."

Walker propped a hand against the wall. "And the Boys Club, coaching softball."

"Uh...yeah...that too." Rhett took a drink.

"How's your wrist?" Walker asked.

Arthur saw bewilderment cross Rhett's face before the young man concealed his reaction.

"It's fine, no problem." Rhett set down the glass and tucked his hands under his thighs.

Walker drooped against the wall. "Dougie hit you pretty hard on that wild swing," he said, and to Arthur added, "Then the kid freaked out and started bawling, but Rhett had him calmed down and giggling in no time." Walker returned his gaze to the teen. "How did you turn him around so fast?"

Rhett bent to tie a shoelace. "I just talked to him, you know...."

Walker stroked his chin, looking confused. Then he grimaced and cupped the back of his skull.

"How's your head?" Arthur asked.

Walker crinkled one eye closed. "Hurts." He pushed himself upright and swayed slightly on his feet.

"You should lie back down," Arthur said. "You might have a concussion."

Rhett's jaw dropped. "Did Martha Browne hit you that hard?"

"No," Walker said, "I bumped my head, but I think I will lay down just for a bit. See you Saturday, Rhett." He retreated down the hall.

Rhett's face had colored, and Arthur struggled with his own discomfort. The boy wasn't dumb. Silence loomed. In his self-consciousness, Arthur attributed the awkwardness to Walker's appearance.

Then insight struck.

He sat across from Rhett and leaned toward him. "You're not coaching softball, are you?"

Rhett's gaze darted away, and he shifted uncomfortably in his seat. "Don't tell my folks, okay?"

Arthur shook his head. "I won't, but do you want to talk about what's going on?"

Rhett cupped his knees and stared at the floor. "There's this...girl," he admitted, and then stopped.

"You're seeing a girl," Arthur said, making the slight leap.

"Riley's been helping Walker at the Boys Club for both of us."

Arthur chuckled. "That's big of him."

Rhett looked up in surprise, then grinned. "Yeah, I guess it is."

"So you like this girl enough not to be exactly truthful with your parents – or Walker, for that matter. She must be pretty special."

"She is. Very."

"Is there long-term potential, do you think?"

Rhett scowled. "That might be hard."

"How so?"

"Well, I'll be going to college next year."

"What about her? Maybe she'll go to college too," Arthur pointed out.

"She's got Za – " Rhett began. "I mean, she can't. She has to stay here."

A memory flitted at the outskirts of Arthur's mind...the rectory painting party, girls hanging on the Pugh twins, or maybe the barbecue, the boys throwing punches. He couldn't quite get ahold of it.

"So you'll have to decide how involved you want to get with this girl if you're leaving in a year. Right?"

Rhett ducked his head and nodded.

When he didn't say anything more, Arthur jumped in. "In situations like this, I find it's important to consider the longer-term consequences of my actions. Especially where intimacy is involved, the choices you make when you're young can affect your whole life."

As do the choices you don't make but just let happen because it's easier, said the quiet voice in his head. He acknowledged that truth but set it aside for the moment.

Rhett didn't look at him. Arthur would have let the matter drop but sensed the boy had something he needed to talk about, which made this a pastoral opportunity, and he was the young man's priest.

Rhett turned toward him with a look of frustration or possibly anger. He started to speak, then clamped his mouth shut.

"What is it, son?" Arthur prompted gently.

"I don't know what to do," Rhett burst out. "Riley wants – " He popped up from the couch, strode to the window and stared out, which seemed to calm him. When he turned around, he gazed deliberately down the hall and said, "What are *you* going to do?"

Out of the mouths of babes.

The doorbell chimed, and Rhett darted toward the door. Sylvia stepped inside and embraced her son.

"Sorry it took us so long. Are you okay?"

"Sure, Mom, of course."

She peered around Rhett's shoulder. "Arthur?"

"Absolutely fine, Sylvia. Hello, Larry," Arthur added when Rhett's father stepped in. "It was entirely a false alarm."

"It was? What happened?" Sylvia turned to him, but kept one arm around Rhett.

Arthur smiled wryly. "Martha Browne paid me a visit."

"You're kidding."

"Unfortunately, I'm not."

Rhett said excitedly, "She told me to call the police, that Father Arthur was being attacked." He paused, then added, "But he wasn't."

The boy glanced at Arthur who saw him decide not to say anything more, not about what had happened or about who was currently in his bedroom. And nobody mentioned the black truck parked in the driveway.

After the Pughs left, Arthur went to check on Walker and found him curled into a defensive-looking ball on the bed, his fists tucked like a child's against his sternum. A flame sparked in Arthur's chest and radiated warmth throughout his body. Already he felt a tremendous affection for this man with the generous nature and demanding, unapologetic sexuality.

Rhett's question ricocheted through his mind. What *was* he going to do? How could he possibly close the long-barred door to himself that Walker had opened?

The truth was that he didn't want to, didn't even know if he could, though the repercussions would be enormous. Across the nation, the church membership had revolted after Bishop Roberts married his same-sex partner, and separatists had formed a new church faction that excluded homosexuals. On the smaller stage of Amity, Kentucky, a similar scenario would likely consume the parish; membership and funds would dwindle; and he'd be forced out, his life and livelihood once again in tatters. He couldn't allow himself to act impulsively again with Walker or anyone else.

The thought of renewed self-denial stirred an aching in Arthur's heart and a lesser one in his groin, both of which he valiantly ignored.

He moved quietly to retrieve the supplements he required, then headed to the kitchen to dose himself. When he returned, he sat beside Walker's sleeping form and circled one of the man's enormous fists with his hand. When their skin connected, he felt the light flow from his palm and a measurable heat build there. The pull slowed within a minute, and he reached over to probe the back of Walker's head. He found no discernible swelling.

Walker slowly opened his eyes. "Guess I fell asleep," he rasped.

Arthur smiled and began to rise, but Walker seized his wrist and held it while he searched Arthur's face. Then in a move so sudden Arthur had no chance to react, Walker tugged him across his chest, grasped Arthur's head in his hands, and mashed their lips together. The man's heat, his earthy scent, and the rawness of his desire demolished Arthur's good intentions. He had no defenses against the strength of his newly awakened need.

He was only human, after all.

41. For the Record

"**I** know, honey," Ellie Jones said into her cell phone. "He's a remarkable man. So are you, you know. Love you."

She ended the call and stared out her kitchen window at her flower garden in need of weeding. According to Walker, Arthur Endicott had collapsed outside the rectory the day before, and her son had helped him inside and tended to him. Walker was still in Arthur's house – in his bedroom, if she had to guess – when Martha Browne burst in unannounced.

Ellie asked why Arthur had collapsed, but Walker remained vague. What came through clearly, though, despite being unsaid, was that her son was falling for the priest, and she had mixed feelings about that. Arthur was worthy of Walker's love, unlike a certain organist she could name, but a priest was a public figure, and any flak generated over his sexual orientation would fall equally on his partner. The Episcopal Church welcomed gay and lesbian parishioners, and even priests, but the members themselves were all over the map on the subject and feelings ran high. Homosexual priests had been targets of verbal abuse, anonymous threats, public protests, and worse.

Ellie was exhausted. It had been a long week, and she was still reeling from Joanne's shocking and senseless death. Puttering in the garden would soothe her, she decided, but the phone rang again before she could act on the plan.

"Hello?"

"Ellie, it's Arthur."

"Arthur, I was just – "

She cut off the words "talking to Walker" to avoid implying that she knew more about Arthur's private life than he might prefer. "How are you?" she said instead, which, ironically, also sounded intrusive given what Walker had just told her of Arthur's illness the previous day. She paced across the room and back to the window.

"Fine, thank you," he said, revealing nothing. "I'm calling because the police arrested Martha Browne at the rectory last night."

She considered feigning surprise, then decided that pretending ignorance was a slippery slope. "I know," she confessed, "I just spoke with Walker."

"Oh," the priest said, then went silent.

Ellie could almost feel his discomfort through the phone, which suggested that more may have happened between him and Walker than her son had admitted to.

"Listen, Arthur," she said in a rush, "he was concerned about your ... um ... spell yesterday. Are you sure you're all right?"

"I am," the priest said after a slight hesitation. "Walker found me before ...." He cleared his throat. "I owe him ... well, a lot, actually."

"I'm glad he was there." Ellie wandered into her living room to look out the window facing the street.

"Me too," Arthur said. "Anyway, they're releasing Martha this morning, and I'm picking her up. If Walker told you anything about what happened, then you'll know why she was in a position to be arrested. I feel responsible for the situation...or at least for her welfare."

"But Arthur, you have a right to your private life and not to be hounded by a lovesick woman inside your own home," Ellie protested.

"That may be true," Arthur replied, his tone thoughtful. "But on reflection, I realize that I've not been particularly forthcoming about who I am, and my reticence could be considered a form of false witness, of leading her on, if you see my point."

This man is impossibly good and decent, Ellie marveling. No ordinary human being would be self-critical where Martha Browne was concerned, but Arthur seemed intent on going the extra mile, despite the trouble it would cause him. A private joy kindled in Ellie's heart at the unquestionably premature – if not downright inappropriate – thought that Arthur might join her family one day. She tamped it down immediately. Motherly matchmaking, even in fantasy, was risky business.

"In any case," Arthur went on, "I need to talk to Martha about what happened yesterday, but I think a woman should be present. As a Vestry member, I thought you might...?"

"Chaperone? Sure. Though I'll admit it wouldn't be my first choice for an afternoon's diversion." She chuckled, but when Arthur didn't, quickly added, "Of course, I want to help."

She cringed at her own insensitivity. How could Arthur mirror her amusement when Martha had walked in on him and her son, whatever they were doing, then called the police? The experience must have been disturbing at best.

Arthur said uneasily, "You should know, Ellie, what she saw...well, I feel I need to speak frankly with her. I'm hoping she'll accept the situation...my orientation...and perhaps her fixation with me will be put into a more realistic perspective."

Ellie tried hard not to imagine what Martha might have seen, but whatever it was, it did not bode well. "I understand," she said. "It's hard to know how she might take it, though. With her limited faculties, you know."

"I have to try. She's troubled, but I'm still her priest. And I'm relatively certain her problems have little to do with me personally."

"I think you're right," Ellie said. "Between you and me, Father Zebediah struggled with Martha too. On more than one occasion, I saw him crouch behind the pulpit or duck into the sacristy when she was hunting him down. Once I found him sitting at a tiny table in the nursery, his knees up to his ears, trying to write a sermon." She paused as her mind carried this train of thought to its logical conclusion for the first time. "Arthur," she said slowly, "did you know that Father Zeb died of a heart attack in the second floor cleaning closet? Nobody found him for thirty-six hours."

"I didn't know," Arthur replied somberly.

Why was Zeb in there with the door locked anyway? Ellie wondered. The answer now seemed painfully clear.

≈ ≈ ≈

Martha perched on the edge of the jailhouse cot, her hands folded primly in her lap. The paunchy deputy had stopped by her cell and said that the charges against her were being dropped and that she would be released momentarily.

"Well, I should think so!" she barked.

She hadn't done anything wrong, so hauling her off like that had obviously been a mistake, but the experience still left her badly shaken. She didn't understand why Father had gotten so angry and kicked her out of his house when she was only trying to help. *It was all for him!*

One look had told her that he was trapped in his bedroom with that man who was abusing him. Father had thrown him off, but the bully was getting back up, probably to continue his attack. She'd *had* to do something.

Her real mistake was slapping that policewoman. Apparently, that was a no-no, but Martha didn't like being grabbed. The woman had twisted her arm and locked her wrists in handcuffs, and Father hadn't stepped in to help her.

"After I helped him," she grumbled.

But that was water under the bridge, and she'd already forgiven him for his behavior. She was still mad at him, of course, but after she explained everything the right way and he had apologized, their relationship could get back to normal. She was anxious for that.

Mr. Paunchy appeared, stuck a key in the lock, and opened her cell. "Your priest is here to take you home."

"My priest? You mean *Father*?"

"A man with a collar...Endicott. Is that all right with you? If not, we can drive you home in a cruiser."

Father had come for her! It was all Martha could do not to leap and jump her way down the corridor.

"Yes, that's fine," she said as starchily as she could manage. She *was* mad at him, after all, and this fat man in a uniform didn't need to know her business.

They reached the reception area and *there he was.* Like a young Paul Newman in his black uniform and white collar, dapper and elegant and charming and....

"Father, you came!" Martha lumbered toward him, wanting to cry and cheer at the same time. She reached out to hug him – at long last – but her arms came up empty when he stepped back and caught her hands.

"Martha, you know Ellie Jones, I believe." Father dropped her hands and gestured to the woman beside him.

"Hello, Martha," Ellie said.

Martha grunted but barely glanced over. Sure, she knew her, a Vestry fancy-pants who got to go on retreat with Father. One of those bossy church ladies always telling her what to do and when.

"They starve you in here, Father!" Martha exclaimed. "If you hadn't come, I would've shriveled away to nothing. And that thing they pass off as a mattress is more like a carpet pad. I didn't get a wink of sleep."

"You'll be glad to get home, I'm sure," Father said. "Your car is still at the rectory. I thought we'd retrieve it on our way."

Father led them through the parking lot, then opened the passenger door for her while the Vestry woman seated herself in the back where she belonged. Martha had so much to say to him but felt inhibited with that woman lurking behind them, eavesdropping on their every word.

"They've dropped the charges against you," Father said as he pulled away from the station.

"Of course they did," Martha snapped. "Assault on a police officer, my foot! That woman grabbed my arm. *She* hurt *me.*"

Nobody spoke again during the short drive to the rectory. When Father stopped the car at the curb, Martha waited politely for him to invite her in, but after a moment of silence, he said, "Martha, if you're comfortable there, why don't you let us drive your car for you. Do you have your keys?"

"Yes, Father."

She tried to hide her disappointment as she rifled through her pocketbook. No invitation then, but still, *Father driving her home.* That was almost like a date when you thought about it. But then the Vestry woman exited the back seat and Father exited the front, and the Vestry woman took the driver's seat of Father's car while Father walked across the street to Martha's Cadillac.

"But I thought – " Martha began.

" – you'll have to direct me to your home," said Ellie. They'd spoken at the same time.

"Humph," Martha grunted in irritation, then pointed. "Three blocks up Cleveland Avenue from the church. Forest Glen Condominiums," she added proudly. This woman probably didn't live in a place half as nice as hers.

Martha sniffed the interior of Father's car, which smelled spicy and dark like a man's cologne. With any luck, her car would smell like that after Father drove it.

She shut her eyes and savored the scent. He was doing all this for *her*.

"Father, will you come in for refreshments?" Martha said when they were reunited in the Forest Glen parking lot.

"Ellie and I would both like to come in," he replied, "but only to talk for a few minutes."

"Oh, all right," Martha huffed, and led them into her living room, decorated in just her style. She was especially proud of her overstuffed tangerine sofa with its throw pillows in every color of the rainbow. She'd ordered the fabrics specially. So cheerful. "Sit on the couch, Father. I'll make coffee."

"Thank you, Martha, but we don't require refreshments," he said, settling into the purple side chair. "You must be exhausted. Please sit down."

Annoyed that she couldn't sit next to Father, but gratified by his concern, Martha dropped heavily onto the couch. The woman perched beside her.

"I asked Ellie to join us while we talk about what happened at my house yesterday." Father exchanged looks with the woman, but Martha ignored her. *She* hadn't invited her in. "I know you were upset," Father went on, "and I want to make sure you're all right. I'd also like to explain myself."

"But Father," Martha objected. She held a hand to the side of her face and pointed at Ellie from behind it, meaning *how can we talk with* her *here?* Father didn't respond to that, but his next words shocked her to her orthopedic shoes.

"The man you saw in my bedroom was Ellie's son," he said.

Martha gasped, then turned toward the woman who was obviously a very bad mother.

"Did you know your son was bullying Father? I tell you, it's a good thing I got there when I did. Father had to *beat* him off. He's the one who should be in jail. I don't know why the police – "

"Now, Martha," Father interrupted, startling her into silence, "I realize this might be difficult for you to hear, but I believe you need to hear it."

Martha stared at him, bile rising in her throat.

"Walker was in my home at my invitation. He...assisted me when I was feeling unwell."

Father paused, but Martha was too stunned to speak. *Assisting* him? That's not what she would call it. Not at all.

"What you walked into was a private moment, and your intrusion was very...distressing."

"But Father," she choked out.

"There are no 'buts' about it," he said. "You invaded my privacy in a deeply disturbing fashion. I forgive you, of course, but you must understand how upsetting that was."

Martha opened her mouth and shut it again. Then in a flash of recognition, she knew why he was so upset, and she hastened to set his mind at ease. "Father, I kept my eyes to myself. I promise I didn't look at your..." She put her hand to the side of her face and mouthed *you-know-what* so Ellie Jones couldn't hear. Seeing Father's manhood through the living room window didn't count because he didn't know about that.

Father's face was rosy when he addressed her again. "This is a sensitive subject," he said, "but I feel it's important we be clear with one another so we can move past our present difficulties." He leaned toward her in a confidential manner. "Please correct me if I'm wrong, Martha, but I believe you may have certain feelings for me, feelings of a personal nature."

Martha's thoughts raced, but she couldn't think what to say. Her head felt light, and Father's deep blue eyes seemed to bore right through her.

"I need you to understand," he continued when she didn't reply, "that I'm not available for any sort of romantic involvement with a woman."

Martha scowled in confusion. "But we're Episcopalian. You can get married."

Father cleared his throat. "That's my point. I can't legally marry because I'm homosexual."

Martha cocked her head. "Whaaat?"

Father's face looked as smooth and placid as the Dead Sea – or rather, how Martha might imagine a "dead sea" since she'd never strayed beyond the confines of eastern Kentucky.

"Any partner I choose would be...male, a man," Father said.

A man.

Like tardy winter sunshine filtering into the hollers, the truth dawned on her. He meant like Mudhole Slim and One-Eyed Johnny, the hill "cousins" who were perennial targets of harassment by locals, including Floyd in his younger days. But Father wasn't like them, *couldn't* be like them. He was handsome and masculine and well-spoken, refined.

Martha knew what was going on here, where the real problem lay. She stiffened her spine and turned to address the bad, bad mother beside her. "Are you aware that your son is a *fruit*?" she said scathingly, and she didn't mean no apple or banana.

Ellie didn't react as Martha would have expected. She didn't seem surprised, but she didn't get angry or look embarrassed either. She said simply, "Walker is homosexual – or gay, as he would say."

Father looked her squarely in the face. "I'd appreciate it very much if you would respect my privacy...and Walker's as well." He held her gaze for several seconds, then stood and said, "We'll go now and leave you to recover from your ordeal. I'll see you Sunday, Martha."

He held the door for Ellie, then stepped through it and was gone. Martha remained frozen in her seat, her mouth hanging open.

"A fruit," she said in disbelief, the word echoing in the hollow cavern of her chest. Her hopes, her dreams, her *effort* ... all for nothing.

Martha's Daddy used to say that a fruit was as useless as a one-legged boar, which hadn't made much sense to her since Gideon enjoyed a nice fruit salad same as anybody else. But sometimes when he was in one of his moods, he'd beat Floyd to the ground and call him a fruit or a fairy, and Martha had gradually come to understand that he meant something else. A thought tickled in a corner of her mind, then faded before it was fully formed.

Disappointment, then anger, roiled in her stomach as the full extent of Father's betrayal started to become clear. How dare he dress in priest's robes and pretend to be a man?

How *dare* he?

42. Balancing Books

Sylvia set the bucket of chicken Larry had brought home on the dining room table along with the smaller containers of mashed potatoes, gravy, and biscuits. Thank goodness for takeout. This had been one of the worst weeks of her life, and she was dropping balls right and left, including basic tasks like grocery shopping. She dumped reheated green beans into a serving bowl and poked in a spoon.

"Come and get it," she called, and Larry rose from his easy chair in the family room.

The twins bounded up the basement steps, banging against the walls as they jostled each other along the way. At the top, Riley checked Rhett with his forearms, then beat his brother to the table and snatched his choice from the chicken bucket.

"Boys, settle down," Larry chided so Sylvia wouldn't have to. He'd been her rock all week.

"So what did old lady what's-her-name get arrested for?" Riley asked with his mouth full.

"Martha Browne," Sylvia said. "They took her in for attacking a police officer, but they let her go today." Ellie had dropped by the church that afternoon and shared the details.

"About time," Riley said after swallowing. "Dad practically had to tear her off me when she got upset by my snake rattles that day."

"If nobody broke into the rectory, why were the police there in the first place?" Larry wiped his mouth with a takeout napkin. "I never understood that part."

Sylvia looked to Rhett to explain since he'd been involved, but he kept gnawing on his chicken leg. He'd been oddly quiet about the incident, considering how worked up he was when he called Sylvia from the scene. The shooting had everyone's nerves on edge, though.

"Martha trespassed again," Sylvia said. "She marched into Arthur's house like she owned the place and then claimed there was an intruder. I encouraged Arthur to press charges, but he decided not to."

She didn't want to say more in front of the boys. Ellie had revealed that Walker was the so-called intruder and had witnessed the incident. Sylvia didn't ask what Walker was doing at the rectory because she had a pretty good idea, and if she was right, the proverbial crap would hit the fan when that information got around town. The knowledge triggered her protective instincts.

Then her chest constricted, and she had to gulp for breath. Joanne wouldn't be there to form a united front at the church office. Her friend was gone. It seemed impossible. She had to drag her mind back to the ongoing dinner conversation.

"She likes to walk in on people," Riley was saying. "Especially at the rectory. Didn't she walk in on you and Da – ?"

Crack!

Sylvia flinched. Rhett had accidentally upturned a large glass of tea into his brother's plate, which overflowed and drained into Riley's lap.

"Mother humper!" Riley hollered and punched Rhett's arm.

"Settle down, boys," Larry said. "Rhett, get some paper towels and clean that up."

Sylvia shot her husband a look of appreciation. She could not deal right now.

Larry took the opportunity to press his earlier question. "So was there an intruder in the rectory then? Besides Martha Browne?"

Sylvia wanted to give him the "zip-your-lip" signal, but the twins were too observant not to notice. Rhett hadn't mentioned seeing Walker there so he must not know, and she didn't want to be the one to let that cat out of the bag. After talking to Ellie, Sylvia had remembered a black truck parked in the rectory driveway, but nobody else seemed to have noticed it.

She tried staring Larry down as she offered another abbreviated explanation. "No, Martha surprised Arthur and he kicked her out, but then she went around knocking on the windows. When Rhett rode by, Martha screamed for him to call 9-1-1."

Larry swallowed his mouthful of potatoes. "She got the police involved, but then they arrested her?"

"The police tried to talk to her, and she hit one of them," Sylvia explained.

Larry hooted a laugh. "Well, there's some instant karma for you." He reached for a third biscuit and dragged it through the gravy on his plate. "Martha Browne makes a lot of noise, but she's pretty harmless if you ask me."

"You might not think so if she charged into our bedroom." *Especially if we were having sex.* But Sylvia didn't say the last part aloud. She didn't know that anything had been going on between Arthur and Walker. Probably not, in fact.

Rhett returned from the kitchen and lobbed a roll of paper towels at his brother, who caught it cleanly above his head.

Larry scowled at them. "What did you two do today? You get jobs yet?"

"They've been volunteering at the Boys Club with Walker Jones," Sylvia answered for them. She was sure she'd mentioned it. Larry's memory must be going.

"Doing what?"

"Coaching softball," the twins replied, and Riley whacked Rhett on the head with the roll of towels for no apparent reason.

"Well, that's something, anyway," Larry said. "I could use you both on a driveway pour next week. We're shorthanded with Frank out of commission."

The boys glanced at each other, silently conferring, then said, "Sure, Dad."

Sylvia looked up, her mom's radar going on high alert. Their response, so quick and in unison, meant they were probably up to something. At the moment, though, she couldn't come up with the right question to ferret out what it might be nor did she have the energy to try. She tucked the knowledge into her mental to-do file for later.

≈ ≈ ≈

Riley woke up Saturday morning with a giant boner, probably in anticipation of the activities he had planned for the day.

Heh, heh.

He'd been so patient about Darlene, letting his brother visit her twice that week while he'd served as their placeholder at the Boys Club, tossing pitches and batting fly balls. He'd waited for Rhett to invite him along or to offer to trade places, but his brother had put him off both times. It was unusual for Rhett to be so cagey, and that's how Riley knew that Darlene was becoming important to him. Nothing good could come of that, so he'd decided to stage an intervention.

No one had ever come between them, especially not a girl. They were a team, a unit, one for all and all that crap. It frosted his 'nads that his brother didn't want to share. Darlene was the gold standard of sex – built, experienced, and hot for it – and if her hand jobs were any indication, she'd know how to suck a dick. But he'd take whatever she wanted to give. He'd rather do it with Rhett's go-ahead, but if his brother didn't want to play fair, so be it.

Walker Jones was expecting Rhett to field softballs that afternoon, and Riley had told his brother he couldn't substitute for him because he had plans to practice gadget plays with Darius. Though he'd possibly forgotten to mention that to Darius himself.

After Rhett left, Riley made his preparations, then gave himself the once over. Hair? *Check.* Shoes? *Check.* A splash of Rhett's new Fierce cologne? *Check.* Ready.

He hopped on his bike and jammed it to Darlene's house, keeping his fingers crossed that she'd be home.

Zack would return from church camp in a couple of days, so it was now or never. He had to strike while the fire was hot. Or whatever.

Darlene didn't answer the door, so Riley dropped onto the porch swing to wait for a while and consider his options. If the neighbors saw him, they'd figure he was visiting Zack, though Riley didn't really care what they thought.

"Rhett! What're you doin' here? Ah wasn't expectin' you!"

Riley snapped awake, shut his gaping mouth, and rubbed his kinked neck. "Uh, they didn't need me at the Boys Club," he said, which was true, more or less.

Darlene ushered him into the house and didn't object when he grabbed her butt and pulled her against him, a move that instantly made his dick hard. He was kissing her and backing her down the hall before she could work up any resistance.

"Wait...ah gotta make a phone call," Darlene gasped when Riley gave her a second to breathe. He followed her back to the living room, one hand cupping her butt cheek.

Darlene dug her cell phone from her purse and called about a delivery while Riley smooched the back of her neck. When she hung up, he nabbed her phone, turned it off, and tossed it onto the couch. Then he spun her around and sealed his mouth over hers, plunging his tongue inside with possibly more enthusiasm than finesse. Darlene responded, though, and Riley silently commended his twin. Rhett must be doing something right for her to be so willing.

Riley's dick ached with impatience. He'd already waited a week longer than he'd wanted to get naked with Darlene. He decided to pull a Tarzan and wordlessly scooped her up and hauled her to the bedroom. He laid her on the mattress, then toed off his sneakers and bounced down beside her.

It took some fumbling before Riley got the tiny buttons on Darlene's blouse unfastened, but none at all to unhook the front clasp of her bra and release those gorgeous breasts. He massaged them roughly in his excitement, captivated by their soft fullness and the rosy pink nipples the size of poker chips tightening at his touch. His cock twitched in response to Darlene's feminine moans, and he had to unzip his jeans to give the monster some breathing room.

She sat up to slide her blouse and bra off her shoulders, then lay back and lowered her white cropped pants over her hips. Riley's gaze homed in on the dark blond triangle of hair peeking through her sexy lace panties. *Scorching!*

He scooted off the bed and shed the rest of his clothes. His cock was so swollen and achy that he unconsciously squeezed it while he stared at Darlene's lush, womanly form. When she pushed off her panties and dropped them to the floor, his cock grew even harder in his hand.

"Come 'ere," she beckoned, and Riley wasted no time getting on top of her. He rubbed his tight, purplish cockhead against her smooth skin, leaking fluid onto her belly.

"Oh, Rhett," murmured Darlene, taking his hard flesh in her hand.

"*Fuck*," Riley groaned and pushed himself onto his arms while she stroked him with one hand and then the other.

"Shall ah make you come?" she whispered.

He was so primed and ready that the question didn't bear answering. He clenched his jaw and scrunched his face to resist the stimulation but lost the struggle on Darlene's eighth or ninth stroke. His balls spasmed so hard that semen arced over her and splashed onto her forehead before running into her bleached blond hair.

"Fuck!" he cried. Each subsequent spasm was less forceful, leaving a stripe of cum on her neck, tits, and stomach, the last bit draining into a small pool on her abdomen. Riley's arms gave way and his torso fell against hers, slipping and sliding. Darlene caressed his back with sticky fingers while he nestled into her hair and inhaled her sweet scent. He rocked his hips, and his cock stiffened between them.

≈ ≈ ≈

"Can I get inside you now?" Darlene's young stud asked, his handsome face flushed, eyes bright.

"You bring condoms?" She reached for a box of tissues on the bedside table.

"Yeah."

Darlene watched him move nimbly from the bed, then bend over to dig in the pocket of his jeans. She gazed at the smooth skin of his side ribs until something caught her eye, a dark birthmark in the shape of Australia under his left armpit.

Her jaw dropped in recognition. "Oh, my wor – "

Bang! The startling sound came from the living room, the front door slamming shut.

"You bastard! If you're – " A clothed version of the young man in Darlene's bedroom burst in and charged the naked one. "Mother*fucker*!"

"No, Rhett, no!" Darlene shrieked, too late.

Riley grunted hard as his brother's forearms connected with his diaphragm. He fell backward onto the bed, landing on her in a tangle of arms and legs, then curled in on himself and gasped for air like a beached fish. Rhett came at him again as Darlene struggled to free herself. Rhett aimed a punch at his brother's jaw, but Riley managed to roll to the side and take the blow on his shoulder. Rhett landed two more on Riley's back before Darlene could intervene.

"Rhett, stop! Please, stop!" She scrambled to her knees and raised her palms toward Rhett's upraised fists. His face was blotchy red, and Darlene sensed the testosterone pumping through his veins, ramping up his aggression. "Rhett, Rhett, it's okay. Please. *Please.*"

He started toward Riley again but, with Darlene in the way, abruptly turned and smacked the wall with his fist, half-yelling, half-growling in fury. Darlene grabbed Rhett's wrists and looked into his eyes.

"It's okay. It's okay," she soothed as she slid her fingers up to wrap around his biceps. He stomped his feet in agitation, his body shaking. She touched his cheek to calm him, then angled her body back toward his twin who was still gasping and writhing on the mattress.

"Riley, shame on you!" Darlene pointed to his birthmark and said to Rhett, "Ah just now noticed this."

"The mark of the beast," Rhett snarled. He paced several times, then turned and half-lunged at his twin.

Riley scrambled backward before drawing himself up to lean against the headboard, still sucking in hard breaths.

"Come 'ere," Darlene urged Rhett, who allowed her to take his hands and pull him toward the bed. She settled his arms around her neck, and Rhett's gaze dropped to her breasts.

Male pheromones thickened the air. Darlene, who was more sensitive to male scent than she'd been in years, unfastened Rhett's jeans and pushed them down his hips. She helped him remove his T-shirt, then balanced him as he kicked off his shoes and stepped out of his pants and boxers. She raised up on her knees and pressed her naked body against his and felt his anger transform to arousal.

He stared pointedly over her shoulder with a grim expression and jerked his chin sharply to the side. Darlene felt Riley move from the bed, and Rhett returned his attention to her. He pulled her to her feet, then gripped the back of her head and drew her lips to his in an intense, focused kiss, traces of anger heightening his passion. Darlene yielded to it body and soul. She had no desire to arbitrate the twins' dispute, especially with Rhett touching her like they were already alone. His rigid penis nudged her mound, and the scent of her arousal wafted up.

Without warning, a swath of warm skin covered Darlene's back from shoulders to hips, and she started in surprise. When a stiff cock nestled between her butt cheeks, she twisted around, but Rhett caught her chin and pulled it back toward him.

"Ignore him," he mumbled and pressed his hardness more firmly against her front.

Darlene wasn't sure what was happening, but she must have fallen asleep, for she'd had this dream before.

≈ ≈ ≈

Rhett still wanted to pound his twin for tricking him, but it was hard to stay focused after Darlene unfastened his jeans and pushed them down. He'd given Riley the "take off" signal, but instead of following through, his douchebag brother had slimed up behind her and joined in. Rhett was faced with a choice: he could either keep rubbing his bare dick against Darlene's silky smooth skin, or he could break away and smack Riley down. It was no contest really. After getting this far, Ry wouldn't forfeit easily and, well, for the moment at least, Darlene didn't seem to mind him being there.

She moaned against Rhett's lips, and he glanced down to see his brother playing tiddlywinks with her nipples and massaging her butt crack with his hard-on or, more accurately, massaging his hard-on with her butt crack. Either way, she was so turned on that when Rhett bent his knees and swiped his dick between her thighs, it came away wet. Her arousal set his balls throbbing, and he slid through her slickness from root to tip and back, but it wasn't enough. Not nearly enough.

Darlene wrapped her fingers around his crazy-hard dick, and after a few scintillating strokes, he looked down and found himself weirdly turned on to see the wet head of Riley's cock push between Darlene's thighs from behind. His natural sensory connection to his twin kicked in full force, mingling Riley's excitement with his own. It was thrilling beyond words, and Rhett surrendered to the pleasure, letting Darlene and his brother ease away his vexation of moments before.

Darlene moaned again, and Rhett saw her press Riley's cock against her pussy as his brother pumped high between her thighs. She was doing them both. So fucking *hot*! Rhett crushed Darlene's lips and sucked her tongue greedily into his mouth. Then suddenly, he couldn't take anymore.

"I'm gonna come!" he croaked, stretching his head back and closing his eyes.

Darlene stroked up his length and passed her thumb over his cock head. Rhett froze on the brink for several endless seconds until a slither of wetness slapped the underside of his balls and threw him over the top.

"Auuuugh," he groaned and heard the sound echoed by his twin.

Without thinking, he reached for Riley's arm and felt the comforting grip of his twin's palm clutching his opposite biceps. They steadied each other in their post-orgasmic haze, leaning into Darlene sandwiched between them.

After a few moments, Darlene grasped an arm in each hand and pulled them both toward the bed. "Come over here," she said. "It's my turn."

The twins glanced at each other, silently sharing their surprise and delight. *How lucky could you get?*

Rhett pulled away to retrieve three condoms he'd stashed in his wallet, and when he turned around, Riley had Darlene cradled against him on the bed, her back to his front with his hand nestled over her pussy. Looking at them, Rhett could feel her springy pubic hair tickling his own palm and the soft flesh of her butt enveloping his cock, which stood to attention at the thought.

Riley lifted Darlene's thigh over his own, giving Rhett an eyeful of wet pink. His heart skipped a beat and his cock tightened to his belly. He tapped his thumb to his chest, and his brother nodded to the implied *me first*, though Riley – the devil's seed – took the opportunity to plunge two fingers into Darlene's pussy.

"*Oooooh*," she moaned, sweeping away any lingering irritation on Rhett's part. This loving and fun woman – who qualified as a centerfold model, no mistake about it – lay spread out in front of him, practically begging for sex. How she'd gotten there no longer mattered.

"Come join us, sugar," she purred.

Rhett perched on the bed, his fingers trembling, and rolled on another condom lifted from his dad's stash. He wondered briefly whether he should top up the supply to avoid any awkward questions at home. Then Riley tweaked one of Darlene's nipples, making her whimper, and Rhett couldn't wait any longer. His brother scooted to the side and propped his head in his hand, and Rhett rolled over Darlene, going breathless when she took him in her hand.

He eased in with shallow, probing strokes the way she'd encouraged him before, and he felt her gradually stretch. When he finally sank to the hilt, his balls against her butt, they groaned in unison. Nothing on earth could be more pleasurable than that soft suck on his excited flesh. He wallowed in it to the tune of Darlene's moans.

When a hand snaked down toward his cock, Rhett slit his eyes to see Darlene pushing Riley's fingers between their joined bodies. The hand probed lower.

"Right there. *Mmmm*," Darlene intoned, all breathy and erotic.

Rhett groaned. Though his experience was admittedly limited, he liked how sex let him revel in sensation without having to contemplate whatever weird-ass shit was getting him off. His brother's fingers brushing against his dick, for instance. At that moment, it was surprisingly untroubling. Good, even.

"Gawd," Rhett groaned, unable to contain himself. He began pumping hard and fast, feeling Riley's fingers bump him with each stroke.

"Yes, *yes*," Darlene murmured, raw desire threaded through her voice. How a sound could command his body, Rhett didn't know, but her utterance released the tightly wound spring at the base of his cock and sent him flying into the hardest orgasm he could remember. Through his ecstatic fog, he heard a keening wail and felt Darlene's internal muscles squeeze down rhythmically, a pleasure so singular it stole his breath. Riley withdrew his hand and transferred it to his own dick, and Rhett dropped heavily onto Darlene, inhaling her scent, now diluted by cum and latex and male sweat. He rested there until Darlene pushed at his chest.

"You better pull out, darlin'."

Rhett gripped the condom and eased himself away, then sat up to toss it in the trash.

"You poor thing," Darlene said behind him, and Rhett swiveled to see her grip his brother's stiffy in her fist. She caught Rhett's eye deliberately, as if seeking his assent.

Being asked made all the difference, and Rhett nodded benevolently. He watched her press the heel of her palm into his twin's hard flesh, and when Riley groaned, Rhett's groin muscles clenched. He could feel his brother's desperate, screaming need, so he tossed him a condom. Darlene rolled onto her hands and knees, then pulled Rhett's chin toward her, and he kissed her fervently while Riley kneeled up behind her.

Sweat moistened Darlene's face and her eyes shone. Rhett wanted her again, but he made do with stroking her soft skin, her cheeks and arms, breasts and stomach. He gasped along with his brother when she reached between her legs and guided Riley's shaft into her slick channel. His twin began plunging like he'd never been inside a woman, which technically he hadn't, only girls. It was totally different.

Darlene directed Rhett's hand lower. After his short apprenticeship, he knew where she liked to be touched and also that it might be a buzzkill for his brother. Oh well, served him right if it was. Rhett's fingers met latex, but Riley only pumped faster until he lost it a few strokes later.

"Jesus, *fuck!*" he cried and wrapped himself around Darlene's back while Rhett finished her with his fingers.

"Whoa," Riley murmured when Darlene came, then pulled her down to the mattress, her back to his front.

Darlene reached up and palmed Riley's cheek. Riley leaned over to kiss her, and Rhett found, surprisingly, that he didn't mind.

43. Naked

Organ music played softly as Martha entered the church on Monday afternoon. People spilled from the sanctuary and milled around the narthex and vestibule. She would have enjoyed watching Father lead a service in his funeral getup, but funerals themselves could be depressing so she'd timed things so she could join the crowd after the service.

Where *was* he? Maybe funerals were different from regular services because he wasn't standing in the archway between the narthex and vestibule like he did on Sundays to greet people. She had to see him. She'd planned to join the receiving line and shake his hand, to act like nothing had happened, like he'd never said those awful things to her at her condo.

A fruit? Ridiculous! Father was no more a fruit than she was. So why had he told her that? It made no sense except that anyone might be confused after what had happened between him and that man at his house. You could get confused when somebody put their will on you. She knew that. She'd stayed in Hickory Switch Holler for years – decades – because her Daddy had told her no man would want her. She'd begun to suspect over the years that he might be telling a falsehood, though, because if she left, who would do the woman's work at the homestead?

Women had come and gone after her momma died, but none stuck around for long.

It was up to her to set Father Arthur straight, to make him see it wasn't his fault he was confused. After all he'd done for her – coming to the jail, driving her home, sitting with her in her living room – it was the least she could do. And maybe he would come to see her as more than a parishioner, maybe see her as a friend, someone he could rely on and talk to. From there, who knew where things might lead? All she had to do was stick with him, let him know she understood.

But she had to find him first. "Humph."

She ambled to the information table in the vestibule. It had been cleared of the usual donation cards, pencils, and church information and held a vase of white roses and a stack of bulletin-like cards. She picked one up. The dead girl's picture dominated the page. It was the same picture Martha had seen in the church staff brochure but fancied up with an oval frame of stylized roses.

In Remembrance, Joanne Allison Bowman, it said, with dates below the picture.

"Huh, thirty-two years old. I guess she liked older men." Martha sniffed. It really was too bad that the girl had died so young. Coincidentally, she was the same age as Martha's momma when she passed.

Voices rose behind her, and Martha spun around, abandoning the card.

Father? But it was a man and woman leaving the narthex with their arms linked. A large group followed them, and the room began to empty.

A lady in a showy hat with an old-fashioned veil walked by, and Martha grabbed her elbow. The woman flinched and backed away.

"Where's everybody going?" Martha demanded. She couldn't see the lady's eyes. Wasn't it rude to hide your face in public like that?

The woman dabbed at her nose with a handkerchief before answering. "There's a graveside service, then Greta and John are opening their home to anyone who wants to pay their respects."

"Where's that?"

≈ ≈ ≈

The service had been beautiful, and Sylvia cried, though she'd kept it to a minimum, thankfully. Arthur was magnificent at the pulpit, sharing in a non-priestly way his personal connection to Joanne, how she'd come to their church in need and found the love and support of the people in the congregation, and how she'd blossomed in the weeks he'd known her. It was a message about hope and the power of love, every word of it relevant and true.

After the service, Sylvia had sought him out at the sacristy exit, catching him as he left to arrange the funeral procession. When she gripped his hand, he'd pulled her in and wrapped an arm around her shoulders, and while the whole day had been painful in the extreme, his love fortified her enough to get through it. He was an extraordinary person, and she was so grateful – *thank you, Lord!* – that Trinity Episcopal had been lucky enough to land him.

At Greta and John's house, Sylvia selected a canapé from the overloaded table in the dining room. She took a bite, then froze in disbelief. She recognized that voice.

Martha Browne is here? How did she know about the reception?

In the turmoil of the week's events, Sylvia hadn't considered the possibility that Martha would show up at Joanne's funeral. Why would she when she hadn't even liked her? *Oh.* She must be there looking for Arthur. No one in her right mind would stalk a priest at a funeral gathering, but then Martha wasn't exactly "right."

Sylvia had just decided to evict her from the premises when she felt a familiar arm wrap around her back. Larry took the plate of food from her hand and guided her outside to the porch.

"Martha Browne is in there," Sylvia protested.

"I know." Larry stuffed a deviled egg in his mouth and licked his fingers.

"We have to get her out of here. I don't want her upsetting Greta and John."

"That's why we're on the porch," Larry said around the egg in his mouth, "to avoid upset. They're doing fine with Martha." He might as well have said he hoped the Louisville Cardinals would win the Governor's Cup.

Sylvia scowled. "What? What do you mean?"

"She showed up with a pie, and last I saw, she was chatting with them nice as you please."

"You're kidding me."

"Nope. I was right there keeping an eye on her." Larry dipped a hushpuppy in hot mustard and took a bite.

"That's just...wrong," Sylvia said. "Martha was no friend. She harassed Joanne every chance she got."

"I know, but I wasn't going to bring that up, especially not today. Better to let sleeping dogs lie, let Greta handle it however she can. Martha wandered off to find the food right after that. I think she'll leave quietly if we let her be."

"But what about Arthur? Where is he?" Sylvia wiped some mustard off her husband's bottom lip.

"Haven't seen him yet."

"Larry, promise me you'll get Martha out of here before Arthur arrives. He seemed okay after the service, but he shouldn't have to deal with her today." Sylvia plopped onto one of the porch rockers as tears welled up again.

"Okay, darlin', I'll do my best," Larry said, stroking her neck.

≈ ≈ ≈

Arthur was the last to leave the cemetery, not unusual since it was his duty to shepherd the mourners through the rituals of grief, and several had sought words with him after the interment. Funerals were among the most demanding of his responsibilities. The collective emotional pain of mourners pulled at him, but the light was only minimally effective in easing such loss. The effort could sap his strength as much as healing himself but without the striking results.

Arthur's thoughts veered to the last time he'd healed himself and the man who had necessitated it. He sighed. Even in sorrowful moments, he couldn't stop thinking about Walker. Arthur hadn't seen him at Sunday service and hadn't talked to Stephen either, so he had no idea how things stood between them.

Can't be all that good if Walker's been chasing me.

He grimaced at the unworthy thought and silently prayed for pardon. It had been wrong – very wrong – to let himself get between the two men, but he vowed to do whatever was necessary to set things right. Father Daniel would be gravely disappointed if he knew what Arthur had done. The bishop would go apoplectic.

As Arthur climbed from his car outside Greta and John's, a familiar, high-pitched screech rent the air. He cringed, his entire body recoiling, and he dropped back into the driver's seat. Irrationally, he pulled his legs inside and shut the door, then hunched down and peered through the window for any sign of Martha Browne. There she was.

God bless Larry Pugh was Arthur's only thought. Sylvia's brawny husband held the woman firmly in his grip and was escorting her, though by all appearances in a gentlemanly, formal way, along the sidewalk to her vehicle.

Nausea struck, and Arthur clutched the steering wheel and shuddered as memories of Martha's ghastly bedroom intrusion gripped him. With his eyes squeezed shut, Arthur tried to slow his breath while the entire incident rolled through his mind, outrageous and horrifying at first, then gradually progressing to life-affirming and wondrous. He exhaled and smiled sadly.

When he opened his eyes, Larry was striding toward him alone.

"Hello," he said jovially as Arthur emerged from his car.

"Thank you. Thank you so much," Arthur replied, holding out his hand.

Larry winked. "You're welcome. I told her you had an emergency call at the hospital, and she bought it. I don't think she'll be back. It seemed like a little white lie might be in order today."

"It's certainly a difficult day, and I can't say I'm sorry to avoid Martha Browne right now."

"What are you going to do about her?" Larry asked as the two men proceeded toward the house. "Maybe trespassing charges wouldn't be a bad idea."

"I met with her, and I'm hoping our conversation will curb her behavior," Arthur said. "If things don't improve, I understand the county provides mental health support for senior citizens. The police located a brother up in the hills, but he has no registered phone number."

"Well, Syl and me want to help in any way we can."

"I really appreciate that. But for today...." Arthur gestured toward the Bowmans' house.

"Let's go in," Larry said, clapping him on the back.

Arthur moved through the small crowd shaking hands, offering condolences, and introducing himself to conservatively attired people he'd never seen at the Episcopal services. Some of the ladies wore bonnets and dresses with built-in modesty shawls. The men wore shirts and trousers without visible fasteners.

"They call us Whiskey Piskies," Greta confided when they got a moment alone. "John's side of the family is Mennonite. They don't drink, but they assume all Episcopalians are lushes." She crumpled a tissue in her hand. "Thank you for the wonderful service. I'm so grateful you're here."

He settled a hand on her shoulder and felt only a slight pull on his energy despite Greta's terrible grief. Intuition and experience told him that those with a strong personal faith derived their healing directly from the source.

"Joanne loved you, Arthur," Greta said, surprising him. "She talked about your aura, you know. Said you had light around you. Kind of like a halo, I guess." She squinted at him. "I don't see it myself, but you *are* an angel to me."

She raised her arms, and Arthur hugged her wholeheartedly, his breath catching in his throat.

"You made our daughter's life better these last few weeks," Greta said close to Arthur's ear, "and I thank you from the bottom of my heart."

Arthur looked into Greta's brimming eyes and said, "Joanne was a fine person, a friend as well as a coworker. We're going to miss her terribly."

Greta's husband approached, and Arthur took his outstretched hand.

"Episcopal services are fancier than the Mennonite," John said, "but our Jojo would have liked what you did for her today."

Poignancy stabbed Arthur's chest, but before he could respond, the intimacy of the moment was shattered by a shrill cry.

"Father!"

Arthur scanned the room, first for the source of the familiar noise, then for an avenue of escape before he gained control of his panic.

"Sorry, Arthur," Larry Pugh said behind him. "I was

sure I'd sent her on her way."

"Father!" Martha trudged across the room with Arthur in her sights.

"Lordy, lordy," John Bowman murmured. He ushered Greta to a nearby settee and draped a protective arm around her.

"Excuse me, everyone," Arthur said, then moved to intercept Martha.

"Let me know if you need help," Larry muttered under his breath.

"Hello, Martha." Arthur's voice projected a calm he didn't feel.

She clutched his forearm. "I looked for you after the funeral, but you weren't anywhere."

"Is there something you need?"

"Yes, Father, I need to talk to you about...you know...the stuff you said on Friday." She screened her mouth with her palm and stage-whispered, "About that *man*."

Dread gripped Arthur's chest, and he tried to shake it off. "Martha, this isn't the time or the place. Greta and John have lost their daughter, and I'm here to provide them whatever comfort I can."

Martha stamped her foot. "I don't see why everything always has to be about her. She's *dead*."

Audible gasps exploded like miniature bombs around the room. Arthur clenched his fists to shore up his self-control. He couldn't recall ever wanting to shake someone with the intensity he did at that moment. The woman's narcissism was beyond sufferance.

"It would be best if you left now," he said tightly. "I'll

escort you to your car." He gripped Martha's upper arm and pulled her briskly toward the front door.

"No!" She dragged her feet and yanked away. "I came to see you. You *have* to talk to me."

"Not here and not now I don't, especially when you're behaving so inappropriately."

"Inappropriate? *Me?*" she shrieked. "What about you with that naked man in your bed? What about you and him with your pants down in your living room? I saw that, yes I did. How about you making the beast with two backs with a man? How about you being a *fruit*?"

Her piercing tone had halted all other conversation, and the final word pealed like a church bell in the stillness. Arthur froze in mortification.

"Fruit!" Martha screeched into the now complete, almost eerie, silence.

Endless moments ticked past before Arthur pivoted to face twenty people staring at him, mouths agape. He barely noticed Larry hustling Martha outside.

"I apologize for the disturbance," he managed to say before following them out, his face blazing and his back dripping with sweat.

"It was you!" Martha's accusation fired in a different direction now, at Sylvia and Darlene Rohrbach who sat together on the Bowmans' front porch. Arthur shut the door to give the mourners inside some peace.

"She was naked at the rectory," Martha ranted, pointing at Darlene. "I saw them in the bedroom." When no one responded, Martha repeated, "It was *her!*"

Darlene looked distinctly uncomfortable, but Sylvia arched an eyebrow at Arthur. Was that amusement twitching at the corners of her mouth? He shook his head and resisted rolling his eyes. The absurdity of being outed as gay one minute and accused of entertaining a naked woman in his bedroom the next would almost be funny, but he had no mirth in him today. Larry seized one of Martha's arms, and Arthur reached for the other.

"Don't touch me," she barked, and Arthur backed away. Given his agitation, he didn't trust his hands anyway.

"She was naked with him on the floor," Martha squealed, her sexually tinged allegations becoming a sorry litany.

"And I was naked with a goat on my ATV," Larry said drolly. "Come on."

44. Outings

*S*hit, shit, shit!

Darlene's mind raced. Her nightmare was coming true, that Sylvia should discover her involvement with her friend's teenaged son – no, *both* sons. Darlene cringed. The plural sounded so much worse.

Sylvia could hardly ignore the accusations made by Miss Browne, who might sound crazy but wasn't, at least not in this case. Darlene lowered her head and squeezed her hands between her thighs as she struggled to keep down the two mini-quiches warring in her stomach. More than anything she wanted to flee, but running like a street-corner pickpocket would only confirm her guilt.

Except for the voice, Darlene wouldn't have recognized this woman as the one she'd mistaken for a hired clown at the rectory painting party or who'd walked in on her and Rhett messing around there a few days later. Today Miss Browne wore a strawberry-blond wig with Ann-Margret-style bangs and a blue, Hawaiian-print muumuu. She seemed a master of disguises.

A muffled sob startled Darlene, and she twisted sideways.

Crying? She'd have expected her friend to yell or threaten, maybe even slap Darlene's face, but seeing Sylvia break down was far worse.

"Oh nooo ... are you all right?" *Good one, Darlene.*

Sylvia's drooping head wagged slowly side-to-side.

"Ah'm sorry...ah'm just *so sorry* ... ah never ..." Darlene stammered before shutting her mouth. Words couldn't fix this. Trembling, she scooted her rocking chair closer to her soon-to-be-former friend and patted her impotently on the back.

"We're going to lose Arthur," Sylvia choked out.

Wait. What did that have to do with Miss Browne's revelation? Darlene's panic and remorse gave way to confusion. "Um ... what do you mean?"

"What Martha just announced in there. Didn't you hear her? That Arthur's a ..." – Sylvia made finger quotes in the air – "... fruit."

"A 'fruit'? You mean like...homosexual? Is Arthur gay?"

Sylvia nodded.

"Oh." Had Sylvia not heard the other part? Had she not put two and two together? Did she not understand that Darlene was, if not a child molester, then at least a dirty skank corrupting high school boys? *Sylvia's* boys?

"It's not a secret." Sylvia wiped her nose with a handkerchief and stared at her lap for a moment. "Not exactly, but he hasn't come right out – no pun intended – and said so except to a few close friends. The Vestry can probably handle it, but I don't see the right-wingers in the congregation taking this quietly. There'll be chin wagging and secret meetings, maybe petitions, maybe boycotts, possibly vandalism at the rectory or the church – who knows what all? – and why would Arthur stick around to be harassed like that? We just got him, and he's so wonderful, really, you have no idea, I couldn't stand to lose him, and if he leaves, what priest in his right mind would come to Amity where the previous rector died under suspicious circumstances and his replacement was hounded out of the community?" Sylvia paused to take a breath.

Her upset has nothing to do with me, Darlene finally realized. Nobody knew about her affair with the Pugh twins, and nobody ever had to know. She could keep them in her life, which had felt new and exhilarating and loaded with possibilities since they entered it. Her relief morphed into giddiness, and giddiness begat confidence, perhaps even overconfidence.

"Maybe you're gettin' ahead of yourself," she said. "Ah mean, that woman is spoutin' a lot of crazy stuff, right?"

Sylvia turned and fixed her bloodshot gaze on Darlene. "She pointed at you. Are you saying you *weren't* naked at the rectory?"

Darlene's self-assurance evaporated instantly and defensiveness took its place. "Ah certainly wasn't! You said yourself Arthur is gay." Not that Martha Browne was even talking about Arthur. Not that Martha Browne wasn't speaking the God's honest truth. Darlene hadn't been bare-assed naked, but that was splitting hairs.

Sylvia looked stricken. "No...hey, I know. That was a joke." She touched Darlene's hand. "Not a very good one. Sorry." Sylvia offered an apologetic smile.

"Oh, right. Of course." Darlene's return smile felt tight and unnatural on her face.

≈ ≈ ≈

"Fruit, fruit, fruit!" the congregation chanted as he ran naked down the center aisle of the sanctuary. A

camera flashed, blinding him, and he stumbled on, groping for the exit.

Arthur awoke in a cold sweat, shivering and disoriented. He pushed himself upright and rubbed his eyes before scraping his sodden undershirt up his back and off. He rose to retrieve his bathrobe, then pulled it on over his flannel pajama pants. Despite the drama generated by his subconscious mind, he almost smiled. Being called a fruit by a fruitcake in a room full of churchgoers wasn't the worst thing that could happen to a person. And the "beast with two backs" reference was amusing in a way, though not to Martha. She'd been traumatized.

After Larry Pugh had steered Martha from the Bowmans' property and convinced her to leave, Arthur had set the incident aside as best he could and tried to resume his duties, mingling with Joanne's grief-stricken loved ones and making himself available for those who sought comfort or counsel. It probably wasn't his imagination that some in the gathering looked askance at him and others avoided him. Ellie, who arrived late but apparently had been told of the uproar, approached him privately.

"If you want someone to stand with you to address the Vestry, I'd be proud to do that," she said and touched his hand before walking away.

Her kindness had warmed his heart at the same time her words alarmed him. She was right, though. There could be no more waffling on the matter. Charlie Hightower, Dean Werner, and at least two other Vestry members had been in the Bowmans' living room during the incident.

In his bathroom, Arthur dunked his head in cold water to shake off the nightmare, then let his hair drip as he padded to the kitchen for coffee. The Vestry met tomorrow, and he could postpone his disclosure no longer. He had to talk to Father Daniel too – today.

Walker had left several messages on the rectory answering machine, but Martha Browne's release from jail and Joanne's funeral had given Arthur legitimate excuses for putting off returning the calls. The truth was that he didn't know what to say. He clearly had no self-control where Walker Jones was concerned, and yet a man of the cloth didn't just wander into a sexual liaison with a parishioner. It was wrong to yield to lust without purpose or meaning, wrong to devalue another's humanity by using him as a sexual outlet, wrong to endanger someone's spiritual well-being for self-gratification. It went against all Arthur's beliefs, his moral code, and his commitment to thoughtful living and careful action. He couldn't allow the affair to continue, no matter how physically drawn he was to the man. Even if Walker were free, it wouldn't be fair to him either since Arthur couldn't give himself wholeheartedly knowing it would likely prompt a scandal that would destroy his already tenuous career.

Bang, bang, bang!

Arthur flinched at the sound. *Martha Browne?* Notwithstanding her recent incursions into his life, such desperate knocking at that hour of the morning usually signaled an emergency, and he hurried to respond despite his state of undress.

He swung open the front door, then stood transfixed by the disheveled wall of masculinity filling the doorway and blocking the morning light.

"Walker?"

"Thank God, you're all right," Walker said inexplicably before bursting into the foyer.

Arthur backed up with one hand raised.

Walker stopped short and shifted his weight from foot to foot while he clenched and unclenched his fists. He looked slightly crazed, and his restless energy created an uncomfortable vibration in the air.

"Yes, I'm all right," Arthur reassured him. "Why would you think otherwise?"

Walker cracked three knuckles on his right hand with his thumb. His eyes were wild. "You haven't answered my calls, and you had that funeral yesterday, and...."

"What is it?" Arthur asked softly.

Walker's gaze darted around the room before returning to Arthur. "I keep seeing you slumped over in your car, and I can't stop thinking how easily you might have...died." The last word sounded like the stifled rasp of a debarked dog.

Arthur lowered his hand. "Ah, I see. But I'm fi – "

In a flash, Walker had stepped forward and gripped Arthur's shoulders, leaned in, and pressed their mouths together. Naked, unfiltered emotion – fear, relief, *something more?* – streamed through that point of contact. It felt like water in a desert, a sunbeam cutting through fog, manna from Heaven, life-giving sustenance.

But still....

Arthur pushed against Walker's chest, but the man didn't release him outright. Instead, he gentled the kiss, let it fade from desperation to supplication as he slid his palms up Arthur's neck to his face. Arthur took a moment – a mere instant in a lifetime of missed opportunities – to savor this loving touch. Never before Walker had a kiss stirred his heart and body equally, unified his entire being, made him feel ... whole. It was impossible to resist, though he couldn't let it continue. Arthur nudged him again.

Walker disengaged his lips but rested his forehead against Arthur's for five or six heartbeats before he stepped back and turned away, his eyes lowered. He pulled the door closed as he left, and Arthur stared blindly at the carved wood panels, too stunned to move, until a ringing phone jolted him to awareness. He staggered down the hall to answer it.

Ah. "Daniel."

"Arthur, are you all right?"

Trust the all-knowing Father Daniel to call at the precise moment when Arthur was distinctly not all right, hadn't been so for some time, and possibly never would be again. Tears pricked at the corners of his eyes.

"What's going on?" Daniel pressed.

Arthur inhaled slowly, then released the breath in a whoosh. "Well, Father...there's a man...." He was unable to continue.

Daniel waited several moments before coming to his rescue. "Okay, Arthur. Are we talking love here or strictly temptation?"

Arthur squeezed his eyes closed and forced out the words. "Both, I'm afraid."

45. Concrete

"The DNA is female," Sylvia told Larry over the phone on Wednesday morning.

"Female? Well, dammit! They got no cause to keep Frank in jail. I'm calling Boudreaux. They have to let him go or at least give him a reasonable bail. Hell! I'll pay it myself."

"You're right that they have no evidence," Sylvia agreed, "but shouldn't the public defender take care of this?"

"I'm calling him." *Damn yahoo cops.*

Frank was out that afternoon, released on his own recognizance with the understanding that he'd stay in town and work at Pugh's Concrete until his hearing date. Larry had visited him in jail, but he was still shocked by the change in Frank. The veteran looked like a different person. His face was smooth and relaxed; he showed no evidence of the shakes; and he seemed to be moving around better too. A break from the booze and time to rest must account for it.

"I 'spect the D.A. will drop the charges," Larry said as he drove them to the jobsite where his sons were already at work. "The arrest was bogus, and you spent almost a week in jail."

"Six long days."

"That should be plenty for carrying a knife. Stupid charge, anyway. Lots of people carry knives."

"It was the hidden-in-my-boot aspect they took exception to," Frank said. "Bootlegging it."

Frank settled safety goggles on his nose and switched on the grinder. He cut a piece of rebar to length and delivered it to Rhett to be laid into the grid. The twins were slow with the wiring, so Larry high-stepped his way over to help, cutting short lengths of wire and twisting them around each intersection of rebar with a flick of his wrist.

Frank measured a corner of the two-by-four frame for length, then abruptly straightened and raised his goggles. "I've got it! I knew I'd seen her before."

"What? Saw who before?" Larry asked.

"They brought a woman to the jail last week. It's been bugging me. I thought I recognized her." Frank cocked his head. "Ohhh."

"What?" Larry abandoned the grid to give Frank his full attention.

Frank tapped his index finger against his lips. "I think I know where that snake came from."

"The one at the church?"

"The diamondback, yeah," Frank replied, his tone dropping.

The twins looked up.

"Keep working," Larry ordered. "Grandpa's on his way with the mix."

Rhett and Riley grumbled but returned to wiring.

"I was at a nip joint awhile back when this hillbilly delivered a load of bootleg whiskey. A fat old lady – his sister, I think – asked him to bring her a pet snake. He called it 'Mabel' or something. Anyway, I'm pretty sure she's the gal they brought in. She was yapping about her father, best I could make out. She looked different, but that voice was memorable."

"Martha," Larry muttered, "Martha Browne." Arthur had said Martha's brother lived in the hills. It made sense.

"You know her?"

"Yes, she goes to our church. She got arrested stalking Arthur, the priest. He's single, and all the ladies like him, but Martha went overboard, kept breaking into his house." Larry shook his head. "She's old enough to be his mother."

"You think she might have left her snake at the church?" Frank said.

"Anything's possible with Martha. Was that her brother's moonshine you gave me? Sylvia thought it was vodka. It knocked her on her butt." Larry laughed.

"Yeah, that was his. His name's Lloyd...no, Floyd. He wears overalls without a shirt and transports homemade whiskey to town in an ancient Ford pickup. The real McCoy." Frank grinned. "Keeps snakes too, I guess."

"Probably a snake handler," Larry said.

"Huh?"

"They call 'em snake handlers, people in the hills who fool around with venomous snakes as part of their church service. Kentucky is known for its snake handlers."

"You're kidding me."

"Nope."

"Why would they do that?"

Larry flipped off his feed cap, scratched his scalp, and pulled it back on. "It's in the Bible, something Jesus said. 'Ye all shall take up serpents.'"

"Must have been out of his mind," Frank muttered.

≈ ≈ ≈

Rhett raked wet concrete into the corner of the frame, then stepped away to stretch his back.

"Is that good enough?" he yelled to his dad.

"I don't know. Did you push out all the air bubbles?"

Rhett sighed. Concrete sucked. It didn't seem like it should be that big of a deal to dump some cement into a wooden form, but there were rules to it, steps, refinements of a million sorts, and everything had to be perfect or the concrete would crack as it dried. They'd been shoving the heavy glop around for two hours, seemed like, but it still had to be leveled, edged, and floated before they could go home. He and Riley had started the day all double entendres and sexy blonde jokes, but their exuberance didn't last because wet concrete will suck the slaphappy right out of you. At least the afternoon wasn't too hot.

Rhett raked some more, his back aching, and let his mind drift to the previous Saturday, his favorite day in recent memory – *hell*, one of the top three days of his life. Given how things turned out, he hadn't been able to stay mad at Riley, though he still planned to pay him back for his dirty trick.

Rhett had never wanted to share Darlene, in all honesty, but he especially didn't want her to dump him in reaction to Riley's antics. Amazingly, though, she'd liked being with both of them, and even more amazingly, Rhett discovered he liked it too. It was like playing offense with his brother, taking a handoff and running hard, then recovering while Riley took the next one. And while Rhett was "on the bench," he lived through Riley's skin, could feel what his twin felt secondhand.

"Hey, dreamer, get with the program! The mix is getting stiff," Larry yelled.

Stiff...yeah.

Rhett glanced over his shoulder and saw his dad waving for his attention. "On it," he hollered back. He'd been shoving the rake into the same corner repeatedly for he didn't know how long. He backed up and raked, then backed up again and raked again.

The important thing about last Saturday, though, was that Darlene had kissed both him and Riley when they left, but she'd lingered over him, which was only right.

She'd put her lips to his ear and murmured, "Thank you, Rhett," in her low, sexy twang.

Hell, *whatever* she wanted was cool with him.

"Damn, I'm still sore," Riley complained from his bed three days later.

Rhett plopped onto his own bed and stretched his ribs sideways. "Me too. Fuckin' concrete."

"Fuckin' *fuckin'*," his brother quipped.

Rhett smirked. It had been a week since their afternoon with Darlene, so he was itchy, obsessed, and hyped for a repeat performance, but the concrete alone was to blame for his sore muscles.

"Boys! Lunch is ready," their mom called.

The brothers rose and bounded up the stairs for a barbecue lunch to celebrate Frank Crawford's release from jail earlier in the week. In the backyard, Rhett filled his plate, then popped open the ice chest to find only one Coke. He grabbed two Mountain Dews and tossed one to Riley.

"So you think it was Martha Browne's snake at the church?" Sylvia said.

"Yeah, don't you?" Larry replied. "How many people keep rattlesnakes?"

Frank nodded in agreement.

"What're you talking about?" Riley asked with his mouth full of ribs and barbecue sauce smeared on his chin. Sylvia scowled at him, and Rhett balled up a napkin and tossed it at his head.

"Frank heard Martha Browne ask her brother to bring her a pet rattlesnake," Larry explained.

Sylvia began passing around dishes of food for second helpings. "But why would she bring her snake to the church?" She froze then, and the color drained from her face. The breadbasket in her hand drooped, and butter rolls slipped from their cloth one by one to plunk onto the table. She covered her mouth with her free hand. "Oh, my gawd!"

"Mom?" Rhett took the basket from her while Riley and Frank collected the wayward rolls and tucked them back under the cloth.

"What is it, hon?"

Sylvia's gaze landed on Larry. "Joanne."

"What about her?" he asked gently.

"Martha hated Joanne. She was jealous of her for being close to Arthur."

Larry looked puzzled for a second, then realization dawned. "You think Martha left the rattlesnake in the church on purpose."

"Yes, in the office." Sylvia whispered the words as if speaking softly could negate them. "She knew Arthur and I were gone and Joanne would be the only one there on Friday."

"But the snake was in the vestibule," Riley pointed out.

"It would have crawled toward the sunlight in there," Frank said like some weird-ass snake whisperer.

"Planting the snake didn't work," Sylvia went on, "so maybe she asked her brother for a gun next." Pain tightened her face, and tears welled in her eyes.

"You said the handprint on the office doorknob was a woman's," Rhett said. "Right, Mom?" He hated seeing her cry, something she'd been doing a lot lately.

"And the DNA was female," Larry added.

"Are you saying the old lady was the shooter?" Frank's eyes widened.

Everyone looked at Sylvia, and she nodded, slowly at first, then definitively.

"Since Martha was arrested," Larry said, "they'll have her fingerprints at the police station for comparison." He remained motionless for a second, then rose and extracted his legs from behind the bench. "I'm calling the sheriff."

46. Physics

"**L**et me out! You did something." Riley banged the inside of Darlene's bathroom door. "Fucker! What did you do?"

"He'll never get out of there," Rhett whispered to Zack while they tiptoed to the living room.

"Really?"

"Yeah, it's physics," Rhett said.

Zack looked at him skeptically.

"Well, maybe not physics. But geometry or something." Rhett winked and Zack giggled.

"Come on. You're pissing me off!" came Riley's voice from down the hall.

Zack giggled again. "Shouldn't we let him out, though?"

"We'll let him chill for a while first. Believe me, he deserves it." Rhett ruffled Zack's hair. "You want to play vids?"

"Yeah!" Zack enthused. "Mom got me the LEGO game."

"Awesome. Let's play," Rhett said, ignoring his brother's bellowing as they plopped onto Darlene's leather couch.

Zack dug between the cushions for a controller. "I can't believe we could trap him in the bathroom with pennies."

"Cool, huh? It only takes three if the door opens in the right direction. You shove the pennies between the door and the frame and the person inside can't escape." Rhett laughed. Even if Riley's con job had paid off in the end, you couldn't let something like that go unanswered. "When's Dar – your mom getting back?"

"Six o'clock. But we're going to a cheap Monday movie, right?"

"Ah, sorry Zack, no. I've got a...thing tonight," Rhett said, "but Riley's free. Well, if we set him free, I mean." Rhett snorted and held up his fist.

Zack bumped knuckles. "Maybe we should let him out, or he'll be mad and won't want to go with me."

"He won't blame you," Rhett said. He might have to make a deal giving his brother alone time with Darlene later, but it was still worth it.

"It seems like I never get to do stuff with both of you at the same time," Zack complained. "And you're gonna miss out."

I don't think so. Rhett smiled.

Riley pounded on the door. "Damn it! Let me out!"

A few minutes passed, then Rhett heard cupboard doors slam in the bathroom, followed by some sharp knocks and a long *creeeak,* the sound of a stuck window sash being pried open.

≈ ≈ ≈

Three weeks had passed since Arthur's first phone call with Father Daniel, that breakthrough moment when the warring factions in his head stared each other down and began to hammer out a compromise path. Speaking to the Vestry was the first step.

After extensive prayer, Arthur had approached the group with an unexpected calm. Ironically, he owed Martha Browne a measure of gratitude for her outburst at the funeral reception. Mentioning the "fruit" incident broke the ice, and when Arthur said, "The truth is that I am homosexual," no one seemed shocked. Charlie Hightower and Dean Werner, who'd witnessed Martha's exhibition, nodded in apparent sympathy at Arthur's humiliation, though expressions had hardened on the faces of the more traditional Vestry members, causing Arthur some momentary regret.

After he returned to his seat, feeling intolerably exposed – but also relieved – Ellie asked to speak. In a highly controlled, yet heartfelt, way, she shared the fact that the fatal pneumonia which took her husband of thirteen years had been caused by the AIDS virus.

"I believe it was fear that killed my Geary, fear that stole my sons' father from them. But times have changed, and I'd like to think that any gay or lesbian person among us could feel free to live openly, knowing they would remain a welcome and beloved member of our church community," Ellie said.

Arthur didn't know how many Vestry members had known Geary Jones, but Sylvia's eyes weren't the only ones that misted over, and throat clearings punctuated the ensuing silence. No one spoke until Dean Werner stood and requested that everyone join him in asking the Lord's guidance moving forward. When the prayer ended and the meeting adjourned, all but one person approached Arthur. Some expressed their appreciation for his bravery, and several mentioned having gay or lesbian family members.

Their kindness eased, but didn't eliminate, his prickling self-consciousness.

Word spread to the congregation over the next couple of weeks, and Arthur became aware of a disgruntled faction among the flock. Though attendance didn't decline noticeably, a few parishioners seemed to avoid shaking his hand – whether as stinging reproof or from fear or revulsion, he couldn't tell – and angry-sounding whispers followed him once or twice through the Fellowship Hall. One woman privately encouraged him to "pray the gay away." It was not an uncommon sentiment among religious conservatives who considered themselves open-minded, and he accepted that the advice came from a loving, if misguided, place.

On the positive side, new faces appeared in the congregation, and several same-sex couples presented themselves to Arthur as such, including Kendra Washington and Geneva Goldman. Two other parishioners opened their hearts and admitted to living secret lives they desired to change. Redemption – for them and for him – seemed possible.

The longer-term consequences of Arthur's announcement remained to play out. Father Daniel had said the bishop was "monitoring the situation." Anxiety dogged Arthur in weaker moments, but prayer, physical exertion, and a renewed dedication to his healing ministry kept him moving forward one day at a time.

The second step in putting his life in order was to face the man haunting his dreams. Walker hadn't returned to the rectory after his early morning visit. He'd stepped back in accession to Arthur's wishes, but he hadn't walked away. Shaking Walker's hand after Sunday services – alone, since Stephen and Walker had separated, according to Sylvia – had increasingly become an exercise in restraint. The warmth of the man's smile never concealed the smoldering desire in his eyes, and all the thinking and praying in the world didn't lessen his sheer physical magnetism. Walker was loving and lovable, beyond desirable, and had lived openly gay for years, something Arthur both respected and envied.

On the twentieth day, he finally picked up the phone. "Can you come to dinner? It's time we talked."

Walker had arrived at the rectory with a bottle of French burgundy, and they'd eaten and they'd talked. Then they'd touched, and Arthur embraced what, in the afterglow of the encounter, seemed always to have been inevitable. And right. Absolutely right.

"I can't go back, but I don't know how to go forward either," he admitted to the man lying next to him, their bare hips touching.

"Maybe we can do it together," Walker said, then kissed him slow and deep, coaxing him to respond.

Arthur wasn't used to this desiring of the one who desired him, and inhibitions he'd fostered over many years rose up anew each time Walker drew close. He broke the kiss, then asked, "How are things between you and Stephen?" The question was a deflection, and he immediately regretted voicing it, despite needing an answer.

Walker sighed and rolled onto his back. "He moved into his mom's place last month, but he's still not speaking to me. He'll soon find someone new, knowing him."

Walker went still for a few seconds, then propped himself on his forearm and fixed Arthur with his gaze. "I realized that he's not who I want."

Walker intertwined their legs and pressed his imposing erection against Arthur's side. Arthur's breath hitched. Walker was more man than most, a powerful enticement to a gay priest who'd made do with a feminine embrace his entire life.

When Arthur failed to reply, Walker leaned over and mouthed his neck, kissing and nipping none too gently. He continued downward, sucked Arthur's nipple, bit down, then licked the stinging flesh, a dichotomy of pain and pleasure shocking in its effect. Sensation echoed between Arthur's legs, and his penis swelled and lengthened.

"Oww, ahh ..." he moaned, half in protest, half in encouragement.

Letting go with his teeth, Walker moved lower, sucking and biting his way down Arthur's ribs and belly while his hand found and fondled the priest's scrotum. A pinch came from where Arthur's appendix scar used to be, followed by a gentle lapping, and the proximity of Walker's mouth to his straining erection drove Arthur mad with want. He grabbed desperately at the man's skull, and then soft lips caressed him where he craved. Walker sucked him into his mouth, letting him sink deep, then deeper, until Arthur gasped at the pleasure of it.

How does he do that? he wondered vaguely when the head of his penis met the back of Walker's throat. The man didn't gag or choke, just took him relentlessly in, out, then in again, squeezing his throat muscles at the bottom of the stroke. Sex had never been like this, so all-encompassing, so unsparing, immobilizing in its intensity.

A hand moved past his balls to the most forbidden part of a man's body, or so Arthur had believed since his youth. A finger, dampened somehow, circled that tender, untouched flesh, and he was both agitated and thrilled by the flouting of taboo. Half-formed objections died on his lips as the finger stroked and pressed, the illicit attention nothing close to medical, the only experience he had to compare it to.

"Walker...." The barely expressed objection changed to grasping dismay when the man pulled his mouth away.

"First time?" Walker raised his eyes to meet Arthur's, but his finger did not cease stroking.

"I'm not sure that's – "

Arthur's protest vanished into some void when Walker pushed through the tight ring of muscle and simultaneously sucked down his penis in a long, wet gulp. Arthur couldn't reconcile the extreme pleasure of the latter with the odd discomfort of the former.

"Relax and let me in," Walker instructed, then lowered his mouth again.

Arthur abandoned his protests in the rush of stimulation. The intruding digit sank inward and twisted left and right, inducing darkly pleasurable sensations. When it was withdrawn, Arthur gasped at the sudden absence.

"More?"

He nodded in spite of himself, jaw sagging, eyelids drooping. Walker's finger probed deeper this time, then stroked a spot so intensely pleasurable that Arthur lost himself to the rhythm of it, his every breath dependent on the repetition. Time veered sideways, warped, then lost all meaning in the narrowing grip of expectation.

His orgasm took him without warning, and he ejaculated into his lover's mouth in time to the squeezing of his anal muscles. This sex was raw and dirty and forbidden – and absolutely electrifying. Arthur drifted in a post-orgasmic haze until Walker withdrew his mouth and pulled his finger away.

"That's not something I thought I'd want," Arthur murmured after Walker slid up beside him. "Being penetrated."

"Everyone says that," Walker responded with a chuckle, "until they try it."

"I thought it would hurt."

"It can if it's not done right. It can anyway at the beginning, but it changes."

This kind of intimacy required a great deal of trust, and Arthur found, surprisingly, that he trusted this man who'd just planted a trail of mouth-shaped bruises down his torso – or what would become bruises if Arthur didn't intervene, which he wouldn't. Letting go was the only path by which he could realign who he was with how he lived.

Could a Christian priest allow himself such a union? Many believed the Bible forbade it, but Bishop Roberts had responded to the controversy of his same-sex marriage in a way that Arthur, at least, could not refute. His exact words were "God believes in love."

Is this love?

"How do you feel?" Walker asked.

Arthur drew in a breath and released it slowly. "Amazed...moved...changed," he said, choosing each word carefully.

"Changed?"

"I can no longer be the person I thought I was before I met you."

"I like that," Walker said in a low rumble. "I want to change you more."

Arthur turned his head, pondering what that meant, but knowing too.

"I want that," he said. "I want it all."

47. Cows Come Home

Larry sat in the office at Pugh Concrete on a Saturday, his official day of the week to shuffle paperwork around his desk for an hour before throwing up his hands and leaving the piles for Sylvia to sort out. Across from him, his father lounged on the bench seat of an old Ford truck that served as guest furniture. The aging Pugh patriarch had been helping out more since Frank Crawford left to reconnect with his family in New Mexico, but today Bub just sucked his pipe and periodically cleared his throat in an annoying old man way.

"Dad, if you're gonna hang around, you might as well pick up a broom," Larry said.

"You know, I was thinkin' about that old gal, Martha Browne," came Bub's laconic reply.

"It's damned awful," Larry said. "I can't believe they let her go after her fingerprints matched the ones from the crime scene. She had to be the shooter. Sylvia is sick about it."

"They had to. Circumstantial evidence. The D.A. don't think he can get a conviction without a weapon." Bub sucked on his pipe, then added, "But that's not what I meant."

"What did you mean then?" Larry asked irritably.

"I mean there's more to her past than people realize. Did you know her momma died of a snake bite?" Bub tapped his pipe into the filched motel ashtray next to him, then pulled his tobacco pouch from his pocket.

"I saw that in the paper. That was a long time ago."

"Some people think it weren't no accident. Her brother got hisself bit too, real bad, I understand, but that were his own fault, supposedly."

"What're you sayin'? Martha Browne attacked her mother with a snake?" Sometimes getting a straight answer out of the man was like catching minnows with your bare hands.

"Oh, I doubt it," Bub said, scratching his jowls. "She was just a girl back then, but she's the one what found her momma's body. Sheriff looked into it. No suspicion fell on the girl, but everybody knew Gideon was a drinker. Talk was he beat his wife and kids."

"Oh, I've heard of him. He was a preacher, right?"

"Yup, a snake handler, but that don't mean he were a nice man." Bub pushed loose tobacco into the bowl of his pipe, then checked it for draw. "Your granny and pappy followed the whole business. He was brought in for murder, but there weren't no evidence. Just the little girl is all, and she wouldn't say nothin' against him."

"Why would he kill his wife?"

"Rumor was she was fixin' to leave him," Bub said.

"So Martha Browne lost her mother to a snake bite, and her father might have had a hand in causing it."

"Yup. She stayed home, lookin' after Gideon and her brother most of her life. Only been in town here ten or fifteen years."

Larry stared at Bub. "How do you know so much about it? You never mentioned her to me."

516

"Were a long time ago. Took me awhile to realize it were the same family my folks used to go on about."

"Humph." Larry rifled through his catch-all drawer and pulled out a jumble of receipts. Sylvia had been asking for them for days so she could finish their third-quarter estimated taxes.

Bub lit his pipe and sucked on it, then blew aromatic smoke into the air. Silence settled over them as Larry sorted the pile of receipts into irregular groupings based mostly on size and shape.

"Her daddy disappeared some years ago," Bub said five minutes later. He touched another match to his pipe and pulled air through the stem.

"Huh? Who?" Larry said absentmindedly.

"The snake handler's daughter. Who else we talkin' about?"

"I thought we'd stopped talking. But what do you mean 'disappeared'?"

"He was living on their homestead up in the hills. Took off one day and never was heard of again." Bub probed between the buttons of his flannel work shirt and lazily scratched his chest.

"When was that?" Larry's interest was piqued despite his father's irritating habit of dragging out a story till the cows came home.

"Not too long before she moved to town, I s'pose."

"When did you get to be such an expert on Martha Browne's comings and goings?" Larry gave up organizing the receipts and leaned back to put his feet on the desk.

"Well, that's interestin'," Bub replied. "I'd forgot all about it, it's been so long. But after this business with her gettin' arrested and all, Marty reminded me she called us around that time, ten, twelve years ago."

"I don't remember that," Larry said.

"Maybe I never told you. I dunno."

"What did she want?"

"She had an old well on her property she wanted filled. Said an animal fell in there and was stinkin' to high Heaven."

"Did you fill it?"

"Nope. I didn't know who she was. She must've got our name from the tri-county business directory. I told her it was too far for us to take a mixer, and we gave her Delaney's name in Cynthey. She might not have gone through with it, come to think of it. I dunno."

Larry dropped his feet to the floor and leaned forward. Seemed he'd have to extract this story tooth by tooth.

"What are you saying, Dad? There's a connection between Martha Browne wanting to plug the well and her father's disappearance?" Goose bumps formed on Larry's forearms, and he rubbed his palms over them.

"I wasn't thinkin' that exactly, but now you mention it...and now they suspect her of killing this gal at the church. Makes you wonder, don't it?"

Larry whistled through his teeth. "Holy shit! Do you think that old lady killed her daddy?"

"I dunno, but they never found him, far as I know. People from his church made a stink, but townsfolk here didn't get too excited. Nobody stipulated, but it was implied he might've run off with a woman."

Bub was getting loquacious now, both to Larry's relief and his growing consternation.

"Or he drank too much of his own liquor and got lost in the hollers, maybe fell into a mine shaft. I understand he had quite a moonshine operation. A hillbilly from a long line of 'em, and a hell-and-damnation preacher to boot. Crazy snake handler."

"Jiminy Christmas, Dad!" Larry stood abruptly, bumping his chair backward. "Did anybody ever check that well?"

"I don't know that anybody knows about it, 'cept me and Marty. And Preston Delaney, if she called him for the work. I don't know that she did."

"Well, that might be something we should mention to Sheriff Boudreaux, don't you think?" Larry said, dripping sarcasm.

"I reckon."

≈ ≈ ≈

Rhett vaulted the porch steps and snatched up his parents' newspaper before going inside. He noticed the photograph on the front page and hurriedly unrolled it.

"Un-fucking-believable," he said and whistled a down-sliding glissando.

"What?" Riley slammed their dad's favorite recliner to its upright position and ambled over.

"They found a skeleton in a well at that crazy old lady's farm. Grandpa put the cops onto it last month, remember?"

Riley plucked the paper from Rhett's hands, scanned, then mumbled aloud:

DNA extracted from a rear molar of the male victim indicated a familial relationship to Martha

Mae Brown, 66, of Amity who recently was held for questioning in the shooting death of Joanne Bowman, secretary at Trinity Episcopal Church. Martha Brown was arrested and charged with the murder of her father, Reverend Gideon Gabriel Brown, who went missing fifteen years ago. Miss Brown is also expected to be charged in the capital murder of Joanne Bowman. When asked whether the death penalty might be reduced to life-without-parole in exchange for a guilty plea, the prosecutor said, "No comment."

Just then, the kitchen door opened and Sylvia and Larry shuffled in, weighed down by grocery bags.

Rhett rushed over. "They got her! Martha Browne killed her father *and* Joanne."

"Are you serious?" Larry set his bags on the breakfast bar.

"Yeah, it's in today's paper." Riley ambled over, still reading.

Larry whistled. "So Dad was right. What else does it say?"

"Some kid fished up an old pistol in Coal Creek that belonged to the dead preacher." Riley ran his finger along the newsprint, then quoted:

Ballistics on the bullets found in the skeletal remains match those of the one that killed Miss Bowman, according to an anonymous source close to the case.

Sylvia sank into a dining chair and dropped her head into her hands. Larry moved close and wrapped his arms around her from behind. "It's all over, hon," he said softly. "They got her."

Rhett jerked his chin at his brother, and Riley followed him back to the couch where they made half-hearted moves toward the game controllers and TV remote. Rhett peeked back at his mom who was sniffling and rubbing her eyes.

"You think it'll stick this time?" she asked.

"No doubt in my mind," Larry said and massaged her shoulders. "They've got her for two deaths now. She'll never get out of prison."

"If Bub had remembered Martha's phone call earlier, Joanne might still be alive," Sylvia said miserably.

Riley caught Rhett's eye and twisted his mouth in an *uh oh* way. Rhett scowled.

"You can't think that way, Syl," their dad replied. "There's no telling what would've happened. Besides, it was Martha getting arrested that jogged Dad's memory."

"I know." Sylvia sighed and rose. "I can't dwell on this right now. We've got dinner guests in..." – she looked at her watch – "...forty-five minutes."

When the doorbell rang, Rhett muscled Riley out of the way to answer it, and a tension-relieving scuffle ensued.

"Boys, *behave*," Sylvia hollered from the kitchen, and the twins swapped grins. The world was right-side-up again.

"Hi, Mrs. Jones. Come in," Rhett said.

"I brought dessert." Ellie stepped inside and lifted the lid of a shallow pink box to reveal a chocolate sheet cake nestled inside.

Rhett relieved her of it, and Riley came over to inspect. "Looks good, Mrs. Jones."

"It should be, the way I slaved over it. Tough choice at the bakery." Ellie smiled, and the boys laughed.

"Can I take your coat?" Larry offered.

"Yes, thanks."

The doorbell rang again, and Riley opened it this time. Rhett turned to see Father Arthur, who was still a Father, Sylvia had assured everyone, despite recently taking a leave of absence from his position at Trinity Episcopal. Tonight he looked ten years younger than normal in his black jeans and blue crewneck sweater, without his priest's collar.

"Arthur, it's so good to see you," Sylvia said, rushing toward him.

"Likewise. Thank you for inviting me." He bent to receive her spirited hug. "I've missed seeing you every day at the church."

"We're not taking down your nameplate. Everybody wants you back in your office as soon as possible," she replied.

"Well, perhaps not everybody." Father Arthur smiled wryly. "At least one bishop has expressed serious misgivings."

Ellie clasped Arthur's hand. "Our diocesan bishop is the only one who matters, and he'll come around, I'm sure," she said. "The Vestry wants you back. By unanimous vote."

"And the congregation," Sylvia added.

Riley started to close the door when the screen swung wide and a set of broad shoulders spanned the doorframe.

"Look who's here," Ellie said.

Well, well, well...Walker Jones. Rhett grinned.

"Dude!" Riley raised his hand toward Walker to initiate a multi-phased fist bump, knuckle grip, two-beat shake, ending with flyaway fingers. It came off perfect like the two had practiced the sequence, which maybe they had.

Walker laughed, then turned toward Rhett. He turned back to Riley, studied him for a second, looked at Rhett again, then back at Riley. "Wow, I've never seen you two together in one place. You do look alike."

Oh, shit. Rhett glanced surreptitiously over his shoulder and noticed Riley do the same. Fortunately, their dad was futzing in the kitchen, and their mom was too busy gabbing with Arthur and Ellie to have heard the remark.

"Oops, sorry," Walker muttered, recognizing his gaffe.

"No prob." Rhett stepped closer and said just loud enough for Walker and Riley to hear, "I told Ry he ought to get 'Peckerwood' tattooed on his forehead so people could tell us apart."

"I'm thinking I'll shorten it to 'Wood', though," Riley said, "and ink it under my bellybutton. Or maybe just 'Pecker'. Haven't decided."

"Classy," Walker deadpanned, and the brothers cracked up.

"Better tattoo it upside-down so you can read the label," Rhett said.

"No tattoos!" Sylvia interjected from across the room.

Rhett almost jumped. How the hell had she heard that? Their mom had eyes in the back of her head, for sure, but did she have microphones planted around the house?

Walker strode further into the room and stopped behind Father Arthur, so close that their bodies almost touched. Walker's hand settled at the base of the priest's neck – and stayed there. Not a "bro" sort of gesture, Rhett noted.

"Dad, you're spilling it," Riley called.

Rhett glanced over to see his dad in the dining room doorway, standing stiff as a wooden Indian, staring blankly at Walker and Arthur. The pitcher of tea in his hand had sagged and was dribbling liquid onto the floor.

Rhett snorted. Dudes were together. *Duh.*

Larry jerked the pitcher level and about-faced to the kitchen before returning with paper towels. He crouched to wipe up the mess – and probably to hide his flaming cheeks.

Ever since Rhett had witnessed Walker coming out of Arthur's back hallway with bare feet and bed-head, the twins had been making veiled references to the men's relationship and waiting for their parents to catch on. Their mom hadn't reacted to the hints, but she must have figured it out since she'd invited Arthur and Walker to dinner, more or less like a couple. Obviously, their dad had remained clueless until now.

Father Arthur was forever golden in Rhett's eyes. The priest had never hassled him about scamming the Boys Club gig to hook up with his girl. That the girl in question was thirty-something and that he was more or less sharing her with his brother weren't things Rhett felt it necessary to divulge. Arthur might know now, though, because Riley had let both facts slip out, along with Darlene's *actual name*, while tossing softballs with Walker.

"You mean Darlene, as in Zack's mom, Darlene?" Walker had asked.

Like a dumbass, Riley thought Walker wouldn't know her, but Walker did volunteer work with kids, and Amity was a freakin' small town. Good thing Rhett hadn't been there, 'cause he'd have punched his brother's lights out for that blunder.

It was cool, though. According to Riley, Walker had stared him down until his lack of an answer became the answer, then Walker said, "Whoa! Way to go."

He might be a gay dude, but he was still a dude, yo.

Larry finished mopping up the spilled tea, then discarded the paper towels and moseyed across the living room. He held out his big paw to Father Arthur first, shook his hand, then did the same to Walker.

"Welcome," he said, cool as a cucumber. "Glad you two could make it."

Epilogue

Six Months Later

Martha hunched on her narrow bunk, fiddling with the big turquoise bow on top of her head. She couldn't get it right no matter how many times she re-tied it. If only they'd allow her a selection of wigs, she could decorate them on their stands, then shift one wig off her head and another on, neat as you please. Even in prison, she liked to look her best, and being bald and all...well, it just wasn't *feminine*. They only let her have the one wig, though, her Dorothy Hamill, the one she happened to be wearing when they came for her.

That had been a sad day, all in all, but when the policeman knocked on the door of her condo and asked to come in, of course she'd said yes. Her momma had raised a Southern lady and hospitality was important, not that you could count on that with young people these days. The policeman didn't look like an officer of the law, more like a gentleman caller, since he was an investigator, he'd said, Detective Northup, he'd said. He was polite and well-kept, as a gentleman should be, but he showed her his badge, and Martha saw the gun he carried in a shoulder holster under his jacket.

Then he'd asked about that girl at the church.

"The one that died?" She handed him a glass of sweet tea he'd said he didn't want. It pleased her that he sipped it anyway, though he didn't eat any of her special lemon bars she brought in on a decorative plate.

"She was shot in the head, you may recall," Detective Northup said, and Martha allowed as she might have heard something about that.

"Do you own a gun, Mrs. Browne?"

"That's *Miss* Browne, Miss Martha Mae Browne, but you can call me Martha."

"Do you own a gun, Miss Browne?"

"No, I do not," she answered truthfully.

"Have you ever owned a gun?"

"No. My Daddy had guns when I was growing up."

"Have you ever shot any of those guns, Miss Browne?"

Then it came out after a lot of back and forth that some kid had found her Daddy's pistol in the creek. Seems he'd dredged it up with some pondweed that got tangled in his fishing line.

"I believe you fired your father's gun at Joanne Bowman in the office of your church," Northup said. "Then you threw the gun in the creek to conceal your crime. Why did you do it, Martha? You must have had a very good reason. Did she threaten your life? Did she steal from you? Did she hurt someone you love?"

Martha's fear and confusion from that day had rolled over her like an avalanche, burying her under its weight, squeezing the life out of her. She gasped for breath, then sputtered, "You don't know what you're talking about! I did no such thing. That gun isn't mine, and anyway, it went off by itself. I had nothing to do with it. But that girl was evil, I tell you. Evil and perverted. You ask Father Arthur. He knows what she did. It wasn't my fault!"

Detective Northup – the turncoat – calmly stood up, instructed her to stand, and snapped handcuffs on her wrists. Then he put her in the back of his car in a repeat of the incident at Father Arthur's house the previous summer.

Martha screwed up her face at the memory of Father Arthur. He'd been such a disappointment when all was said and done.

She flattened the loops of her hair bow and pulled them upward to draw attention away from her ugly prison garb. She'd lost her taste for orange since it was the only color she got to wear anymore. That was just one of the many trials she now had to bear. This was God's plan, she supposed, that she should be a witness unto Him in prison. She did her best too, every day witnessing for Jesus to the inmates, the guards, and any prison volunteers who crossed her path.

Detective Northup already knew when he came to interview her that the bullet that killed the girl was fired from Gideon's gun. So he'd tricked her, Martha realized later. And the police completely ignored that it was an *accident*, a misfire, more or less. They wouldn't listen to her explanation that the gun was defective. They especially wouldn't listen after Floyd let them dig up the abandoned well on the Brown homestead.

Martha didn't like to think of what they'd found, a bullet lodged in some old bones in the hole. Turned out they could tell it was her Daddy in the concrete down there and also that the bullet matched the one from the dead girl. Martha tried to explain how Gideon had fallen into the well, it wasn't her fault, but they kept harping about that bullet in his collarbone. Or three bullets, actually. Not all in the collarbone.

God must have a reason for sending her to prison, though. Martha had come to terms with that and humbly accepted her fate. Her faith paid off five months into her incarceration when Father Marcus Washington joined the rotation of ministers who held Sunday services at the penitentiary. His Wednesday Bible study group started today.

Father Marcus was stocky and masculine-looking in his black clerical outfit and white priest's collar, and rumor had it that he'd once been married, so he obviously liked girls. A real man, in other words, unlike some other priest Martha could mention. Father Marcus was dark in his coloring – a welcome change, really – with deep brown, teddy-bear eyes, and curly black hair liberally frosted with silver. Martha would guess him to be in his early fifties.

Not that much younger than her when you thought about it.

Acknowledgements

I'm grateful to all those who supported and cheered me on in this endeavor, including critique partners, friends, and the loyal and enthusiastic readership at my fan fiction website palassiter.wordpress.com. You gave me the support and confidence to create this world of my own. My heartfelt thanks go out to RJ Conn, Emilya Naymark, Jean Carper, Heidi Ritter, Ellen McRae, J. A. Canter, Ron Burk, Nancy Bilyeau, Amber Tosto, Susan S., Mimi McDonald, and Rebecca Tomlinson.

Thank you for reading.
Please review this book. Reviews help others find
Absolutely Amazing eBooks and inspire us to keep
providing these marvelous tales.

If you would like to be put on our email list to receive
updates on new releases, contests, and promotions, please
go to AbsolutelyAmazingEbooks.com and sign up.

About the Author

P. A. Lassiter grew up on a cattle and wheat farm in the Midwest and now divides her time between Seattle, Washington, and Key West, Florida. She holds degrees in English Literature, Psychology, and Computer Science, and her alter ego wrote two best-selling computer books that have been translated into a dozen languages and used as university texts. She returns to her first love – fiction – by penning a series of humorous novels set in small-town Kentucky.

The New
Atlantian Library

NewAtlantianLibrary.com or
AbsolutelyAmazingEbooks.com or
AA-eBooks.com